I0601283

Escape from Andromeda

'It's a ship! A spaceship! Don't ask me how, I just know!'
He walked towards the third marking and placed his right hand over that area. He positioned his fingers directly above the lines with palm touching the inner circle.
As if by magic a silvery shimmering glow appeared towards the ship's centre and that part simply melted into an entrance and stairway, throwing him to one side.
A voice thundered in an ancient tongue.

'Please enter, Son of Goh!'

He called out to Merol who hesitantly followed from behind, eager to retreat well away from the strange alien craft than enter.
'Merol! Please hurry!' Jon insisted, fearing the worst to body and soul but with little intention of running away and lose the adventure of a lifetime.
They were both completely shaken by the experience but bravely scaled the glittering stairway into the bowels of the strange ship.

First Edition

CHRONICLES OF OSMARON

ESCAPE FROM ANDROMEDA

Galactic turmoil - They must save their people before it's too late

By

Adrian Graye

Nutralian Publishing
http://nutralianpublishing.com

Nutralian
An imprint of Nutralian Publishing
5 Brayford Square, London E1 0SG
http://nutralianpublishing.com

This paperback edition 2007
B00005555

First published in Great Britain by
Amazon KDP 2024

Copyright © Adrian Graye 2007

The Author Adrian Graye asserts the moral right to
be identified as the author of this Work in accordance
with the Copyright, Design and Patents Act 1988.

ISBN 978-1-0687902-2-5

Printed and bound in Great Britain by Amazon KDP Publishing.

A CIP catalogue record for this title
is available from the British Library.

All rights reserved. No part of this publication may be reproduced, stored
in a retrieval system, or transmitted, in any form or by any means,
electronic, mechanical, photocopying, recording or otherwise, without the
prior permission of the publishers.

This book is distributed subject to the conditions that it will not, by way of
trade or otherwise, be lent, resold, hired out, or otherwise circulated
without the publisher's prior consent in any form of binding or cover other
than that in which it is published and without similar conditions, including
these conditions being imposed on any subsequent purchaser.

All characters in this publication are fictitious and any
resemblance to real persons, living or dead is purely coincidental.

This book is dedicated to my family and friends for
their frequent encouragement,

&

To all those who believe in universal existence and
appreciate the lowliest of life, for like babes, they are
the beginning.

TABLE OF CONTENTS

Part III
In our times

ON PLANETS WE LIVE

We occupy organisms to live and breathe as one,
To observe light in all its wondrous colours and enjoy symphonic
sounds of music alone.
We sense feelings and emotions with conviction and
conscience,
To think, create and invent, in art and in science.

All this from an aggregate of microcosmic cells to form a
macrocosmic being?
Because of an urge to survive from some strange primordial
beginning?
A union of conscious spirit, mind and cell,
And in death, where will my Identity spirit dwell?

Within a Cosmos of infinite proportions,
For how long will I remain devoid of senses and emotions?
Will I once again be conceived to another race?
Into a different land of time and space?

For what is reality or even solid mass.
Is a ghost within its own universe as real as shining glass?
Perhaps within a Greater Computer Mind,
We are all just players of a different kind.

Appearances can be deceptive; for mass reduces to nothing,
And only when matter with matter touch we think there is
something.
A form of Causal Order imposed upon a sea of chaos prime.
A self sustaining battle till the very end of time.

For time itself, whether forward or backwards be, is just another
player,
And our laws of science here may not relate within another
cosmic layer.
But I am sure that any death to me will not be long,
For within a Cosmos of Infinity a space time traveller I belong.

Victor E. Roche

Prologue

Earth-times...

3005 BCE... Seno initiates the repairs of his dying world.

1172 BCE... The deadly Javols are created by Micol's descendants. During the following period of about 3000 years, the Javols consume almost all life within the galaxy of Andromeda.

2041 CE... Lumak arrives on Earth from his home world of Kanaefon, within the globular cluster of Kalboron..

2043 CE... The young six Andromedans escape to Osmaron.

THE ANDROMEDAN ANCIENTS

Very much like Earth, the human population on their world Caefon had undergone many phases of human survival. During the first phase they almost lost the struggle due to over-population, unrestricted industrial growth, capitalism and self-indulgence. Planetary neglect led to atmospheric pollution and global warming, with disastrous consequences. Luckily they were rescued from certain extinction by a race of very advanced aliens called Octans.

During the second phase of their existence they became a stellar force to be reckoned with and expanded their empire to engulf Sector 15 within Precinct Seven of the Andromeda galaxy. However their expansion was soon halted by a most deadly foe. One that would eventually destroy all important life within that galaxy and attempt to remove all primal life from our universe. That was the end of the second phase of their existence. During that time they missed extinction by the skin of their teeth.

Will they resume a third phase of survival and to where will they go next for assistance?

After the appearance of the deadly Nano-bot blood sucking Javols in Galaxy Andromeda - due to a failed experiment by the Ancients , most of the primal life in that galaxy was made extinct. The Javols saw all such naturally occurring organisms as ready food and did not hesitate in removing those civilizations they considered a threat.

The seven Gohran Grand Lords of our plane of universes or multiverse discussed the dire problem and place its solution in the hands of Grand Lord Gerra, the Seventh Grand Lord of all Seven Universes. He soon put his complex plan in operation for the survival of all primal life. He is to send his trained Shadites to locate suitable intelligent worlds. Those chosen worlds are to be converted to higher technological levels and given the necessary abilities to fight the unrelenting and rapacious Javols.

Using his Shadites, who are his special priests, many suitable life-forms are being recruited and new worlds probed for acceptance within the Greater Purpose for their mutual survival.

While probing, the Shadite Lumak discovers a Class 1 civilization in a hitherto uncharted part of Galaxy Osmaron (our Milky Way Galaxy) and despatches interstellar probes to investigate. Lumak, previously a sexless Semonite (a giant bee-like creature), is subsequently transformed into a male human and transposed to the world they call Pleron. That previously unknown world is called Earth by its human inhabitants.

Lumak is to advance Earth's technologies to Class 5, from its present, Class 1. This classification represents advancement on a scale to the power of 10. By this method Class 5 may be taken to be about 100,000 years more advanced than Class 1. A Class 1 civilization would have discovered, understood and developed nuclear devices.

During Lumak's visit to Earth he lands in the hills of Turkey and meets the hillbilly shepherdess Sarah and her father Bengizara

Khan. Sarah later becomes his wife.

Lumak soon finds a general cure for cancer, introduces Micro-Robotics, Stellar Drives and a Longevity Serum.

However the almost indestructible Javols are presently on their way to our Milky Way galaxy and will arrive in under 200 years.

The few Andromedan survivors numbering about 10 million, still remaining on their world Caefon within Andromeda must be evacuated within a period of two years. A suitable world must be found in time for them within our galaxy of Osmaron. But that world cannot be Earth.

Part I

Before The Ancients

CHAPTER 1

The Plains of Herron

Earth Time... 3180 BCE. The beginning of decline.

Place... Planet Caefon in Andromeda.

The Plains of War, later to be called The Plains of Death were once the most beautiful meadows on Caefon. At that time the world was one of violet, blue and green. That was before the lovers of industry and capitalism ruled the roost and greedy men and women immersed themselves in self-indulgence and licentious activities at the expense of others.

At that time they paid little notice to their population growth and even less on the final effects of pollution and global warming.

It was then that Mother Nature sensed the true nature of mankind and with vehemence began to react most negatively and with extreme prejudice. It was then that global temperatures began to soar, causing polar ice to melt. As the seas and oceans rose, populations became displaced and the ever changing conditions led to further survival crises.

Within a century the global temperature had increased by another six degrees centigrade, making intolerable human existence within tropical regions. The plants shrivelled and died and those areas soon became sandy deserts driven by furious storms, hurricanes and tornadoes. With a soaring human population of over 12 billion, quick solutions had to be found to reverse the convulsive processes of a dying world.

Their many capitalistic politicians considered the task too costly for their generation. They declined any financial assistance thinking those problems would go away by themselves or solved by future generations. With such little enthusiasm, incentive or political will, many clever minds tried and failed.

Despite their lack of enthusiasm to grasp the larger picture, a few city elders realized the most possible tragic outcome and prepared several biblical volumes, including an Oracle for the guidance of the few survivors that were expected to exist sometime in the bleak future. It was housed in a sacred building that could only be entered with a special key. Within its structure were hidden all their advanced knowledge and weaponry.

The Oracle was an intelligent quantum computer that would scan their world through satellites and keep the chosen survivors up-to-date on life-threatening changes. It could also communicate beyond their solar system to aid the chosen few. In such ways it would assist their survival until the time was right for planetary recovery.

Despite all its powers the Oracle could not affect planetary decline. That most difficult and hazardous future was already written in the wind by past generations and had to run its course to an ultimate conclusion.

With desertification came a reduction in essential food resources and as it did, farming and industry declined. Their main producers that once existed on their continent of Feltwol reduced supplies when large areas within that continent became barren and unproductive. At that time it was quite natural for complete families to commit mass suicide. Their lands shrivelled, they starved and could see no future ahead.

It was at that time that the seeds of discontent were sown by many in the name of religion. It was about the same time that the rioting and demonstrations took precedence, until all their marketplaces and utilities were systematically looted and burnt to the ground. The rampaging fury of the mobs continued unabated until even the displaced began fighting among themselves for dominance.

To add even more salt to their wounds, as the sea levels rose, their cities and coastal regions became submerged, leading to more refugees. Those that survived the first hundred years of such turbulence and turmoil became hardened veterans and wandered to and fro searching for a paradise on which to settle, but no such places could be found.

The last remaining area on their world that was less affected by those problems was the smallest continent of Nimia. It was situated in the northern latitudes and many left for that place. Then mankind separated into several warring factions and tribes to fight for the few remaining fertile areas. During that time many factions were formed and alliances made.

Their wise leaders realizing the problems ahead, settled on a set of rules for the battlefield. It was then that the noble land-wars began. They were not wars in the truest sense but more like ordered challenges, whereby one group would fight another of the same number in a planned way in fields and arenas. By that time the survivors had separated into two opposing factions that constantly challenged each other to extend their territories.

In order to survive everyone had to partake or their possessions forfeited and families condemned to the unrelenting deserts. Along with those planned battles were the trained gladiators for the numerous spectators in their large arenas. All wanting the same thing, namely; the possessions and lands of others on which to spread their families' tents. Only by winning could the survivors gain the lands of their vanquished opponents. So it went on, challenge upon challenge, until even the winners lost to their opponents.

The process of warfare soon became a spectator sport where bets were laid and the more skilled played in large arenas for trophy and fame. Those could also be chosen to represent others for a share of their lands. Soon, even those playful sessions ceased. The food stopped coming and it was then that men began to fight for the bodies of the vanquished; their nutritious flesh being the only remaining sustenance left. They would simply hack off an arm or leg for their troubles; for land was no more of importance and could not compete with an empty belly.

In such situations the dishonourable rule-breakers and cannibals remained the fattest and strongest. Those were always the last to die. During that time of retribution the skies were blood red, waters were polluted and it was difficult for women to bear children.

At that period of utter dread only one people remained singled out among all the others for greatness. They remained the defenders of the ancient laws and suffered dearly because of it; for cannibalism was disallowed among the remaining faithful. Because of those reasons many were mal-nourished. The extreme survival stresses of that time made their women almost barren. In such a manner did both chosen tribes barely survive while on the brink of extinction.

Despite their Oracle and its many powers, their enemies on the plains had isolated them and were eager to plunder their uniquely guarded hill town and all their possessions. They were saved from starvation only because of their unique piracy and scavenging skills.

They had no reason to expect favours from anyone and when it came, it was unexpected and beyond their wildest comprehension.

CHAPTER 2

The ancient oracle

(About 185 years after the creation of the Oracle.)

Earth Time... 3005 BCE

Today the waters near the bank was calm and mucky. The food scavengers had arrived early and salvaged more thoroughly closer to shore than before. They would have recovered very few ancient food containers from that part of the submerged city..

Deep water salvaging had presently become unproductive from submerged levels of the lost city. Our Ancients lost city of Nim. A complete past civilization that had been lost to Global Warming. The easier upper floors of this once great city had been cleared time and time again until not even a pin remained.

The ancient food markets were closer to the centre of this dead submerged city and much lower in the water then before. It was fortuitous for Seno's tribes that canned foods still remained pure after the passing of over two centuries. Those recovery attempts required trained divers in protective suits. They always tried their hardest at risk of life and limb for the survival of their tribes. Too much was at stake. There were so many water bourne diseases and traps, making such ventures the most dangerous to all concerned.

Presently that was one of the few ways remaining for Seno's tribes to survive, but even that source of the Ancient's food was running low, and there were fewer cities to plunder. With over 10 thousand mouths to feed, more fertile land was needed in a hurry if they were to survive the coming harsh wintry months.

Seno pondered those thoughts while carefully making his way across murky waters rowing quietly. Not wanting to disturb anyone except still waters. Least of all his envious enemies. In the distance he could observe rolling clouds approaching and relished some clean rain water falling from the sky. He soon realized those were stormy clouds that most likely carried painful and acrid acid rain. His skin was always sensitive to those droplets and usually came out in rashes and boils, even from the smallest spray. His thick woolen tunic only assisted in retaining and spreading the contaminants with more associated discomfort.

His king had always chosen his clothes for him from salvaged bounty, and always selected the long priestly garments that made him stand out among his people. Those robes were not fashionable; not even in the days of his ancient ancestors, and were never the most comfortable during his travels.

While wandering his duties were varied. On The Hill they included full-time occupation as doctor, priest and councillor to both his tribes. Since deaths were more frequent than illness he considered himself a priest.

Seno had always been curious of the ancient technologies, particularly those in the field of medicine. He wanted to create his own portions to heal the sick and wounded but was not sure where to begin. So many souls were lost to his tribes on a daily basis from battle, starvation, suicide and illness. He felt helpless.

'We suffer, because it's the will of Kanac.' Veruna would say. Yet he was not convinced it was the will of any god. After all, it was mankind who started the problems of global warming and left them for future generations to solve, so why blame those detrimental conditions on any God.

He must hurry if he is to miss the downpour. Seno knew well about his ancestral past before the dire changes took over his world. That disastrous process started about 300 years ago. He had seen what they called photos of its people and their technologies within the many unsubmerged floors of the taller buildings. All scattered in dusty piles of innocent faces, with happily smiling children casting their eyes in each and every direction when he stood in different places. At that time people were always happy and smiling, with many incredible appliances and vehicles at their disposal. There were powerful weapons that could destroy a complete city.

They had taken too much of their existence for granted. They had used up and abused all his planet's resources in the process, with no consideration for future generations, leaving very little for him and his kind. Now they have all gone to dust like beautiful Photos... covered with dust.

'Oh! What a sinful waste!' he sighed aloud, while regurgitating those hateful thoughts. Then he realized what little knowledge his tribes had gained from that enlightened past. Although quite insignificant by the standards of the ancient ones, it was probably the main reason why they had survived those painful decades.

'Anyway, we learnt the technology to distill water years ago from the great book. Processing drinking water from acid rain is no longer a problem for our water-venders, thanks to Mohria. Despite the pollution it contained, rain water was always free of the deadly bacteria and disease that infested the surface waters. Thanks to our holy books and my helpful Oracle. God save Mohria!' he shouted, now in a happier mood. Then he realized he could be overheard by someone and shut up.

He observed the glittering, almost still water, with a thin film of oil that highlighted reflections. Seno took an extended stroke with his oar on the right, then another on the left, to adjust the small boat within a narrow passage between two large buildings. In the distance he could observe a large pirate ship on fire.

'What a waste of good firewood,' he murmured to himself.

Resources like wood was expensive and almost non-existent. Fires were used for cooking only when it was absolutely necessary. Large uncontrollable fires had destroyed most of the forests over the decades.

He also realized the dense dark clouds approaching signalled the coming of tornadoes and terrible storms. Such destructive turbulence could last for days, while taking their ferocious fury out on land and water. He must hurry if he is to miss such deadly ferocity.

The place he visited was unknown to others. Only he, the chosen, knew the route. He checked several times to see that he was not followed.

The special map and key of knowledge was handed down to him by his priestly father, Jess.

'My Son, this is now your responsibility. Guard it with your life and train a well chosen apprentice when the time is right.' He left for battle without even a proper goodbye.

'That was the last time I set eyes on you, my dear father. I have not been able to train anyone since. What if something untoward happened to me or I met with one of those unfortunate accidents... all that knowledge would be lost to humanity forever. Choosing a suitable person from tribes of warriors was no easy task. Out of all the people I know, only three could be fully trusted and they were not of my priestly line or bearing,' Seno thought.

He realized he was resigned to a sedentary life of loneliness, without a female companion. He accepted that freedom. The freedom to do as he pleased and wander about his tribal territories. What little of it was left; to assist mankind and in the process discover the ancient cultures and philosophies. Anyway, productive women were very hard to find. The chance of a son to carry on his line was virtually nil.

'My dear father...it's only two years since. Just before you left for battle... to the Plains of Death. You eagerly left to face your challenger and did not expect to be hoodwinked or cheated that way to your death. In the name of Mohria and everything sacred, that vile Salmon will pay dearly for his crimes against our tribes.' He took another narrow entrance but continued thinking about his father.

'That was the last time I would see you... wearing your crimson priestly tunic above your light armour. Even now, that image is as clear in my mind as the day you left your only son.' Seno contemplated his past with a few tears running down his cheeks, but continued his journey with that last image of his father indelibly engraved on his mind.

The existence of the Oracle was probably the only reason why his Safa and Medoin tribes had survived the dreaded centuries of death, until now. His once great people of tens of million had diminished so much over the decades. Presently only about ten thousand was left. With most of the women becoming barren as the result of contaminants, constant battles and other day-to-day worries, stresses and struggles for survival. This placed his tribes' death rate on a permanent downward slope to extinction.

During the previous century the waters throughout his world had risen by more than 50 metres. All coastal cities with their tall sky-scrapers had been submerged. In most cases only the highest tops and spires remained as a pertinent reminder of their once prominent position in the service of a more advanced human civilization.

Seno progressed slowly, not knowing what he would meet around the next bend. He took a path through a large broken window frame of a partly submerged building. That pane had escaped the frame decades before. That passage was conveniently placed to mask his progress through the building. Over the years salvaged glass was commonly used to cover green houses for the growing of vegetable crops. It was ideal for isolating them from the harsh weather, acid rain and persistent pests. Presently such enclosures had become too hot for growing crops. Neither could acid rain nor the contaminated surface waters be used for irrigating such life-sustaining crops.

With greater sense of safety, Seno rowed hard with both oars through that building then another and another, until he came upon the one with the strange spiky spire. At its very top was a crucifix or sword. That object was made of solid gold, a now almost valueless metal. It shown brightly onto the waters below. Its radiant reflection seemingly inviting with a promise of better times to come. He tied his boat to a large metallic hook stuck in the stone wall in better times and followed towards the top of a spiral staircase. His progress was soon blocked by a thick metallic door with a strange symbol engraved dead centre.

He retrieved a small container from his inner coat pocket. It was of a shiny metal that never faded. He retrieved a black key from the box and said a prayer before inserting it into the door's orifice. There was a clunk, then a click and the heavy door slid open. On the floor within the centre of that room were many strange markings. He took position just before the largest ring. While in that room he always showed the greatest reverence. It was the only tangible connection between him and his distant past and its powers were awe-inspiring. He had always admired the technological greatness of his ancient forefathers.

'May the god of Istara and Icura come to our assistance in our time of need,' he chanted calmly, with his palms held together. Then he began a louder chant in the strange language of the ancient priests.

'Ana at cro, Kanac Ali oh AK..oh Ana....' He repeated the ancient text time and time again. This time with both palms facing the central circle. A glow appeared in the middle of the ring and a female figure of light slowly grew into view. She was dressed in a red tunic with golden armour and held a golden sword in her right hand. It was identical to the larger one on the spire. The Oracle Mohria represented the god of war.

'*Place your key within the chamber so that you may be identified!*' the figure said while pointing her sword. He followed her every command. The object was scanned by bluish light and a container opened. He went forward to retrieve the key.

'*You are Seno, son of Jess and others of the Medoin line... Wait and be counselled.*' He stood at attention and listened.

'*This day marks the 147th year from when I was created. I have assessed the climate of our world and condition of your body. Both require immediate repair. The waters have stopped rising. Therefore this day marks the beginning of the end of your struggles. As specified by our ancient Code... from this day on our tribes are unbound from all our ancient laws and rules. Therefore let no one bind you to any such rules; for you have been specially chosen for a more important task. Nevertheless, I can still see serious problems ahead for our people and our world. Because of those reasons you and your people must continue the struggle to save our tribes from the persistent barbarians.*

'*In future our tribal colours will change to blue. Therefore you must hold and protect our people and their lands from the savages, even with these weapons.*' As he watched the colours of her tunic changed to a radiant blue while her sword changed to a silver crucifix. Mohria was no longer a god of war, but of creation.

A large part of the floor lifted to expose many books, weapons and ammunition. Yet he remained transfixed on the glowing figure.

She continued her lesson:

'Those barbaric savages have little respect for anyone or anything and will exterminate your people at the least opportunity. This is the only self-sustaining way for you to survive; and survive you must; for the survival of our world and its other few remaining life depend on it.

'For many years now I have sent signals beyond this world for assistance and have finally received a message.' He was astonished by that knowledge.

'From where, my Siend?' he inquired, respectfully.

'From outside our stellar system. They are on their way to assist and will follow my instructions. Listen to their words and we shall survive this mess. However, I must relay an important warning... Your enemies are jealous and are even more treacherous now than before. They wish to exterminate all our tribes. Therefore you must train our faithful in the ways of the new weapons. Be always careful and ready to retreat at the first sign of danger.' A strange bluish glow went from her eyes and made contact with his and information of all kinds flowed between them, until his mind was overwhelmed by knowledge from his ancient ancestors.

'Take the weapons! Go now! Go quickly, and inform your leaders of those dangers and of the visitor's arrival!' She dissolved and faded back into the system. Seno had a splitting headache with a most confused mind, but was able to regain his composure just enough to make his way back to the boat. He had become a changed person, with an overwhelming desire to complete an important mission. But he knew not the purpose for which he strode so eagerly.

After resting from his ordeal he made several trips to collect the weapons, along with numerous instruction manuals, until his boat was full.

He rowed the boat towards the more hidden side of a bank. Then moored it between the top of a submerged building and thick walled ramparts to shelter it from the storm. Then he removed the weapons and ammunition. One by one he stored them in a secured place. He took two items including one of the smaller weapons and subconsciously loaded, but did not fire. Finally he placed them within his large pouch. Carefully he scaled the old metallic spikes along the high wall. That part of The Hill was always guarded and well shielded from view.

Seno entered the western side of the ancient city close to that side of the high wall. He climbed along the steep hill and progressed towards the old buildings at its summit. In the easterly direction was the more secured land wall that protected his hill town from enemy troupes attempting to gain entry from the direction of the plains. That thick metallic gate led towards the main land routes. The Hill was almost unapproachable from the northern sea, which was the most likely path for their more sneakier enemies. That small unsubmerged area of The Hill within the once great city of Nim was presently their home and prison. Since all other tribes wanted to take what they had, they could never leave. It was built like a fortress in earlier times and had remained that way until now.

Everyone within its walls were trained warriors since childhood. Beyond that small area of land were their enemies territory in virtually all directions.

Proudly he strode up the narrow path towards the small citadel at the very top. In the distance he could observe the giant Clovis practising his moves. He was over 8 ft tall and attained the strength of 8 men. He always wielded the double head axe as his first choice, but was equally accomplished with the long sword. The sound of each encounter with the dummy pole carried well into the distance. Despite his many scars, Clovis had seen over 50 challenges for the good name of his people. He was kept in reserve and always guaranteed a good meal. After all, he had earned it many times over.

The Citadel was also the residence of his leader, King Melor.

Seno, priest, holy man, healer and doctor, as he was usually known by his people, resided at its very top.

On either side of the broad path were the training fields, with numerous warriors practising their combat skills and tactics. They had not fought since one long moon cycle, well rested and eager for combat.

As he approached the sirens sounded so everyone disappeared indoors to shelter from approaching stormy clouds. Their buildings were thickly walled with small observation windows that protected well from the constant fury of mother nature.

CHAPTER 3

A free meal

The ancient citadel was chosen because of its strategic position at the summit. From there the areas around could always be in full view. Most of the other occupied buildings on The Hill were contaminated with all forms of vermin and insects that carried disease. Those few remaining creatures could only survive by feeding off the scraps of humanity.

In any event, the citadel was considered the safest place for their leader who occupied the lower levels. Seno had always accepted his royal company and leadership. His single room was close to the spire and only accessible by an expanding metallic ladder. That ancient mechanism could be hidden or retrieved from two levels at a moments notice with his small key. That way, he could pray and meditate peaceably in a spiritual place while shut off from the noisy world outside. The only problem he faced, although infrequent, was the occasional whine of the wind-driven warning sirens. One had been fitted to the spire to warn the area of approaching dangers.

'My lord, I have important news for you! I've met with the Oracle and she... she changed all our plans!' Seno was gasping, almost out of breath.

His king, Melor, observed his pallid features and realized he was not eating well. Seno was in his mid twenties , about 5 feet 9 inches tall and slim to skeletal. His face included a goatee beard that gave him dignity.

King Melor was two years older and about two inches taller. Unlike Seno, who was his closest friend and counsellor, Melor was a skilled warrior through and through and spent all his days practising and challenging. Nevertheless Seno was also a skilful swordsman and knew well the arts and techniques of all types of hand to hand combat. Both men had numerous scars on their bodies. It was a natural hazzard in their warring occupation. Melor scanned his friend's puny form with his eyes ending on Seno's feet.

Despite the many waterborne diseases Seno always wore the more comfortable sandals and that attitude worried Melor. What if he was to cut one of his feet while in mucky waters. The ensuing infection would in all probability have deprived him of his only good doctor and counsellor. Seno returned his gaze, but was slightly embarrassed, so Melor changed the topic out of mutual respect.

'My Friend, please join us for dinner today. It's Yale's birthday.'

'Are you sure, Sire?'

'I am and must insist! We have enough today for you, Yale and Kant. Then you can tell us all about the sacred words of our esteemed oracle,' Melor said enthusiastically with a broad smile. Then they walked towards the citadel.

At 5 feet 11 inches King Melor stood tall in new attire and was always clean shaven. His padded titanium armour, leg and arm shields, and weapons were boldly displayed on racks close by the main entrance. They were his tools of battle, blood-stained, battered and worn from many challenges. They were his lifesavers and always kept at arms length.

His queen Veruna was also an adept warrior and good cook. She could turn most items into a delicious dish. Seno always bowed his head to her. Women always held special significance among priests in his Medoin tribe.

As king and leader, Melor always had first choice in the loot and bounty returned by his scavenging pirates. There were many submerged cities so their large wind-powered ships with their deep-sea divers went on weekly expeditions to collect from those free-for-all places. However not all ships returned, because pirating, looting and deceit were rife among the tribes.

Being king, Melor could choose from such bounty for seven people including himself. Therefore he used that choice to collect for Seno and a few close friends and family members. These were difficult times and he never liked any of his people to go without, so he always gave his used clothes to those in need and sometimes declined his position of choice to their captains.

Veruna showed surprised when Seno mentioned the word, Oracle. She realized he was pale and malnourished, so she made sure he had a full plate.

'You must be very brave to have followed the dangerous water routes through the old city,' she cautioned.

'I took my own path... which is less dangerous at dusk... after everyone left the area. There was also a storm on the way. Most pirates and scavengers tend to avoid such bad weather and leave those areas well before dusk. Anyway, our old city of Nim has very little in salvage left, so they visit Mond and others instead.' Seno took a chair by the oval table.

Nim was once the main city of that part of the great continent of Nimia and had served the people of the Safa tribe in days gone bye. Mond was the city of the Medoin tribe towards the north west. Both had always been allies and survived together as one since their cities were flooded. Seno was born in Mond and his family were originally from that city. Melor, Hale, Kant and Veruna were from the Safa tribe and always remained close to their original city of Nim.

'If what you say is true... I mean, about the pirates and scavengers leaving the submerged parts of our city... it will become much safer for us to exist in this area from now. That place across the sea-wall has always been a worrying kink in our security. Nevertheless only a single line of troops can scale the walls from that direction while Hale and his eager troupes are always ready and waiting. They will quickly challenge anyone visiting us from there,' Melor said with a broad smile.

'Except, of course, present company,' Hale said and they laughed, realizing Seno was always the wanderer to traverse those walls.

'For the life of me, I could never understand the reasons for our famed Oracle. Her advice is always wide off the mark and most of the time she speaks in riddles,' Veruna said and Seno felt challenged and upset.

'Our esteemed Oracle was engineered by the city fathers before the upheaval. They knew what was coming, saw the dangers and tried their best to assist their future generations during our time of need... but she can never be too specific. However this time she was and I was utterly surprised,' he said and they remained silent.

'What do you mean exactly?' Melor interjected.

'I am very happy today and bring hope and good news for all our tribes.' They waited patiently for more.

'The waters have stopped rising throughout our world and we should expect to receive help soon.'

'What do you mean? Where from?' Melor inquired.

'In ancient times our ancestors were very advanced. So advanced, they had the technology to travel to distant stars... even to other galaxies. All that technology was built into the Oracle for us to use sometime in the future... when the time was right. She has been... over the years... trying to contact other civilizations beyond our own stellar system and have been successful. A friendly one is coming to assist us during this major moon cycle. However, there is one problem... she sense treachery in our enemies... so we must keep our senses alert and eyes peeled during our future encounters. We should retreat at the least sign of any treachery.'

'Retreat! We never retreat from anyone!' Hale interjected.

'Really?' Melor was curious.

'Times are worsening for them and they are after our place here for its location and security. One more thing, from this day our battle colours must be changed to light blue. That colour will identify us from all others. It will be the chosen colour of change to better times. From now we must prepare ourselves and have hope for a better future,' he said and they were astounded. As he spoke they could see the Oracle in him. His words were profound and clear.

'Are you sure she said all that? We can't just retreat while in combat. Such an act would break the laws of war. Many tribes would come after us. Even our trade with the friendlier tribes will stop when word of our cowardice gets around. And it will!' Melor stressed.

'Since we are the specially chosen, these rules no longer apply, and in answer to your first question:

'Yes friends, I am sure as I am alive, that she said those words., Since these laws and rules are no more, we may do as we please. From this day our weapons will escalate until we are able to vanquish all remaining tribes. But we must not take life for its own sake.'

'The colour blue is for cowards and wimps. If we wear that colour we will be defeated for sure,' Hale warned.

'Perhaps, but it might get them annoyed and aggravated enough to loose concentration during battle. Also, I think Mohria sees it as a form of identification... so we should wear blue from now,' Seno replied.

'I see your point. That might give us the edge we've been looking for. We really do need an edge more than those on the carefully sharpened blades of our swords,' Kant said.

'I shall have to give instructions to our scavengers. We can get word to the people for whatever little blue clothes they have remaining. If not, we shall have to dye our existing ones,' Melor said, still not relishing the change.

As always Melor listened patiently to his family and friends. His main concern was in saving his people and the Oracle was not always right in her predictions. Nevertheless he had never seen Seno in such a strange and excitable state before. It was as if he was possessed by another. He realized they could not survive for long on their meagre resources so if deliverance was on its way, it couldn't be sooner. He also realized the Ancients were very advanced and had put in place several orbiting stations to observe the world during its period of change, so Seno could be right at this time. The time of their deliverance could well be when he and his tribes faced the greatest perils and harshest period of their existence.

'Please follow me towards the field,' Seno said and the six left their cold meals and followed patiently.

They walked towards a practising totem. It was a large metallic pole covered in thick layers of straw and rope for sword training and practising other skills. He moved forward and fired a single blast of the weapon and the pole simply vaporized.

Then he removed a small item and clipped it around his waist. He pressed a button and there was a low humming sound. His body glistened as he moved through air. He handed the weapon to Melor.

'Now I shall take the place of the totem. You may fire at will. Kill me if you can,' Seno said, tauntingly.

'Don't worry, I am immune from all projectiles. So please prove my point and fire.' Melor hesitated.

'I cannot take the chance to lose my counsel and only true healer. Nor shall I have your innocent death on my conscience.' Melor handed the weapon to Hale. Without any hesitation Hale fired, but shimmering fields enveloped Seno and he was untouched by the enormous energies at play.

A once sceptical Veruna couldn't believe her eyes.

'With such weapons we shall have little need of the other tribes in future. We can simply go and take back our lands from the filthy vermin!' she exclaimed.

Many warriors came forward to observe the strange weapons and were astonished by what they saw. Then they bowed toward their king and his priest and left.

Melor had recently lost all their fertile tribal lands and enclosures to the Shofta and Goel tribes. Now he would do almost anything, short of cannibalism, to regain his people's territories, and here was a way. Both of those enemy tribes dominated the plains and were the most dishonest and warlike. They hated the Safa and Medoin tribes and would go out of their way to destroy them, even to the point of extinction. However their hatred was mutual.

Melor's people were in desperate need for more fresh food, while the enemy tribes grew strong and fat from the lands they stole and the bodies they collected from the fields of battle for meat. Presently Melor's tribes only survived from scavenging and whatever little they could barter with friendly tribes, but that method of existence could only last so long.

Despite the new powerful weapons, Melor would honour every challenge as he had always done. He would follow the ancient rules until there was evidence his enemy tribes were in contravention of the ancient rules of war. He also realized that despite the odds in their enemies favour, the only way he could ever hope to win the next battle with normal weapons was to give it his very best.

For that purpose he would meditate and place himself in the land of Hellios, where every possible foe would be unleashed against him. Then take position with his back to the high wall and begin his program of mass slaughter, killing each opponent with a different thrust or swipe of his sword. That process required utmost skill and precision.

To get the most from his sword arm and feel the hatred flowing, all he would do was imagine the ugly face of Salmon the Goel with his filthy yellow teeth. It was a method Jess thought him since childhood that always aroused his keener senses before battle.

Nevertheless the very survival of his two tribes depended on his victory. He would keep the giant, Clovis, and some of his best warriors back to defend their hill. Hale could take control in his absence. This was in case the enemies succeeded in their diabolical plans. Assuming they had made such plans in the first place.

The next time they faced a challenge even the women would be involved in battle. He hoped there was enough time to train for their next tournament to the death. The way things had turned out, a swift death on the battlefield could be better than the alternative of slow starvation on the hill. In such a case he hoped his Veruna would die quickly and not suffer endlessly from a low body wound or from the painful knives of greedy cannibals while still alive.

'My lord, a messenger approaches baring a flag of truce! It must be a challenge!' Kant shouted from the high wall. He was presently on duty in an observation tower and could view the area for miles around. He used a small rusty telescope mounted on a creaky swivel arm to observe the man's approach. The messenger rode a brown pedris and was unarmed. Kant's companion, Notwin, aimed his crossbow at the animal's front thigh. It was the most vulnerable part and presented a larger target.

'Let him through!' Melor yelled. The large retaining bolts were released as the thick metallic gate creaked open under powerful hydraulic rams.

'My Lord, I am from the Sittin tribe and neutral in this matter,' he said and handed him the sealed scroll. Melor unrolled the document quickly, while scanning the challenger's name as he slowly read its contents.

"We fight in three days within the fields of Seven. It will be mixed and must be one trintec (1024) strong, of each mature sex to the death, until one side is vanquished. All combatants that can no longer compete for any reason may be considered spoils of war. Any approved weapon may be used. Standard rules of combat must be obeyed.

This duel will be for your remaining lands and homes. If we lose, you will regain the lands you lost to us during our previous engagement. This will settle most of our accounts for now.

You still have your ships and can always move to another land.

Salmon of Goel."

Melor carefully read the document again while searching for discrepancies, but it was fair. Anyway he desperately wanted the chance to regain his lost territories, even though the price was high.

'I wonder what games are afoot this time,' he thought and handed the document to Veruna.

'They are not a bit worried. They realize we are thin and weak, while they grow fat and strong from our losses. They must also think that even the worst of theirs can defeat the best of ours, one to one. If they defeat us this time it will be the end of us and they will gain a great prize. Therefore we must train hard and eat well... but there is little time,' Veruna said, sadly.

'But my love, they do not realize we have enough food for our immediate needs. So there is a major flaw in their thinking, if they consider us in that light,' Melor replied, smiling.

'Darling, thank goodness you were so clever in showing our sick and dying on the high walls. Now they are convinced we are in dire straights and are already defeated.'

'We must keep up the pretense for a bit longer. Even so, we're running low on essentials and I'm sure they will have several tricks up their sleeves, if they are not winning as intended.'

This time, Hale, his second in command and brother would take control of those left behind on The Hill. He had orders to defend their hill fortress against any assaults from land or sea and would only surrender with direct orders from his king.

Seno had collected the Ancient's weapons and spent two days training the few chosen soldiers in their use. They were to defend the fortress at all cost.

In such life and death situations Seno always remained close to his king as aid and council. He preferred a quick death on the battlefield while fighting on the side of his king, to alternatives if they lost. Also as a doctor he could be useful in administering drugs and bandages to the wounded during battle.

This in all probability was going to be their last battle so any help would be welcomed. The severely wounded tended to die quickly, when they lost strength and couldn't put up any defence. Nevertheless on that faithful day every living man and woman would fight until their last breath; for everything depended on their vigour and determination.

Taking the warnings of the Oracle, Melor got all his remaining people together. He was to warn them of their enemies and point a practical way forward.

'My dear people of Nimia, this time our enemies are stronger and will play many dirty tricks and devious games to defeat us. Come what may, it is your duty to survive, even without your king. Therefore, following the commands of our ancient Oracle, I have decided to revoke the rules of war in our favour. That simply means the rules of war on the Fields of Battle no longer apply to us, the specially chosen. From this moment on we may follow whatever course necessary for our guaranteed survival. Henceforth we shall not under any circumstances give up our place here to anyone, least of all to our enemies.'

'But my lord, we shall have all the tribes up in arms against us for breaking the ancient rules,' someone shouted from the rear.

'You will mount the ancient weapons on the walls and around our city to keep our enemies at bay. As pirates we stand a much better chance of survival. We can dominate the sea-ways and take from our enemies by force. That way we may replenish our stocks and grow strong. Therefore if my warriors are defeated, this is the path you must follow in order to survive. We have tried to play fair in all things, but sadly, our enemies are treacherous and constantly bend the rules to their satisfaction. To those of you with me, we fight like devils from hell!'

'Devils from hell!' they yelled.

Melor realized he drank a sour chalice, making the chance of his survival in this next battle to be very slim.

It had taken them two days by land and sea to get to the fields of battle or Plains of Death. Melor chose his best trained for his first encounter with the enemy. Seno made sure he took along a full bag of medicine and bandages, but also wore his best armour. He realized this was going to be his hardest fight yet. Even so, he had faith in the future and did not pass any of his priestly knowledge or keys over to anyone for safe keeping. If they failed everything was lost anyway.

The women had also been well chosen and led by Veruna. Their tournament was held in a more distant part of the fields that were remote from the men. Women always fought out of sight and sound of their men.

With the exception of Melor they carried little food in their pouches and planned to starve for the duration until the battle was won.

Melor and his people had been handed down the art of shipbuilding by their noble ancestors but were also the best at salvaging and refurbishing. Thus, they excelled in the re-use of reclaimed materials like glass, cutlery, utensils and other more practical items that others could use. Those could be recycled and traded with the other tribes for food and clothes. All those trades would be redundant if they decided to go it alone.

Melor didn't realize at the time that Seno held the key to their long term survival. With the reversing of the waters the time of change had come and their survival rules of past were no longer relevant. For some reason he had realized the change. It was because of the greater unrest among his worried people and the desperate nature of the tribes on the plains. They were all in dire straights being finally in a critical struggle for survival. It was as if the final test had come that would make or break everyone.

They were the only tribes that held the holy volumes or bibles for human survival. Those books contained most of the technologies of their past and could be used to construct advanced weapons and machines. Since the human population on their world had become virtually illiterate, having dropped to insignificant levels, the possibility of any escalation of warfare to an advanced level was non-existent. Further, there wasn't much of a world or wildlife left to protect from such dangerous warfare if it occurred.

Notwithstanding the Oracle had filled Seno's mind with numerous amounts of knowledge that he could use to educate his people in more advanced ways at the appropriate time. All that knowledge would be triggered and released by the occurrence of certain events in his future.

CHAPTER 4

Melor's last battle

On the crucial day of battle Melor and his warriors arrived in eight of his best ships. Many tribal seniors rode high on saddled pedris. Those animals were mild-tempered quadruped similar to a cross between a horse and camel, but without the hump. The animals were well armoured and carried the colourful banners and flags of the tribes they represented. Their riders were not combatants and did not partake in the fighting, but acted as observers. From their lofty position they could carefully over-view the proceedings and complain to the referees if there was cheating.

When Melor and his group approached the main entrance they were greeted by jeers and curses from the other tribes. It was probably because they wore blue, which was not a battlefield colour and singled them out as different. Within the culture of warrior tribes the colour blue had always been considered disdainful on the battlefield and represented defeat and weakness.

'Everyone... lift your swords to the once great ruler... now in coward's blue... King Melor Safa of Nim! Soon to be defeated by the mighty Salmon of Goel! Then we shall hang his head on a pointed pole while I enjoy his cold blue heart with mother's hottest and most delicious gravy!' Salmon jeered while his followers lifted their swords and axes in agreement.

'Yum, yum!' they chanted while mouthing the words as of eating a tasty meal, but Melor retained his dignity and honour.

'I hope you are as brave a warrior as you are big-mouthed,' Melor replied and spat at his feet. They had always hated each other and it had presently reached the boil.

As Melor rode through the ancient broken down pavilion he could observe no other fighters throughout the extensive fields with its many fences. He realized some other plan was amiss.

Usually on such days, battles could be observed as far as the eye could see, each in their specific field and fighting for their piece of his continent. Either that or to regain their losses from previous unsuccessful encounters. Neither was there the usual gambling vendors or cheering spectators in their multitudes within the walled pavilions.

'There could have been some underhanded agreements with the other tribes?' he thought.

The tribes on the plains had always seen Melor and his kind as arrogant, stuck-up and different. After all, they were of fairer complexion and had once ruled the whole continent of Nimia. Furthermore their ancestors were mainly responsible for most of the technologies that caused the destruction of their world. Even so, the other tribes were equally neglectful by partaking in those changes and in using the technologies of his ancestors. So everyone was of equal guilt in the demise of their world.

Many realized Melor and his people, with their well defended position on the hill and other technological abilities to be a major threat. Therefore they wanted to see the back of him and his kind. They also knew his people were supposed to be the chosen ones and educated in the strict cultural ways of their ancestors. Being highly technological they would be the first to make more deadlier weapons once they were no more in keeping with the ancient rules of battle.

The remaining tribes had only followed the ancient rules because it had become imbedded in their culture and religious beliefs over the decades. The noble tribes wanted it that way because it prevented escalation of weaponry and was also a form of entertainment for the masses.

The neutral tribes used it for entertainment and would cast bets for land and food among their own during such life and death gladiatorial tournaments.

The power-hungry Salmon of Goel and his tribes were keen on taking the lot and in subjugating the weak as their slaves. Therefore they would have gone to any lengths to fulfil those aims. The main obstacle in their way was Melor and his tribe, with their almost impenetrable fortress on the hill and their pirating ships. Once Melor was removed from the equation they could plunder the remaining tribes and quickly take control of all their resources. Further, since Melor's hill was virtually impregnable, it would make a permanent camp from which they could strike out at the other tribes in the more fertile plains. Therefore it was essential that they took the hill by fair or foul means.

'They could have convinced the other tribes of such gains and made them false promises? Anyway, with our numbers diminishing because of fewer births, more deaths from fights, disease and natural causes, many may have realized the time for drastic change had finally arrived.' Melor whispered while preparing himself for battle aided by Seno.

'Yes, my lord. Something serious is afoot. We must be ready when the time comes,' Seno whispered back.

'Presently they must consider the whole concept of hand-to-hand combat to be out of date and want a quicker and more final solution to all problems. So this time the Oracle was right. Since both enemy tribes on the plains were considered the strongest, why not join with them. That way many could also revenge their enemies of past,' Melor thought.

In the circumstance Melor could not even be sure of the so-called neutral referees. Even they could have been bought for a basket of groceries.

As he watched he could observe his men outnumbered two to one, with the strongest of the enemy standing by to observe the weakest in combat and waiting to take over the fight after Melor's men were sufficiently reduced and weakened. This was not as agreed.

He had already planned for such treachery by ensuring most of his best warriors rode high on pedris. They were encased in the toughest titanium alloy and could at a moment's notice take on the others. However Melor didn't take along any of the special weapons of the Ancients. He considered that option unfair and too far beyond the accepted rules of war.

If things went seriously wrong he and his men had to find a suitable escape route. From their present position the only choice was down the steep banks into the cursed River of Souls. So named because it was where the remains of dead warriors were cast. Since it appeared to be their only means of escape, they could quickly mount the wall on foot and disappear down the steep muddy bank while their enemies were distracted by those on pedris. That way Melor and his remaining combatants could escape the field into the river bed.

Although filled with dead bodies and bones of previous warriors, it was the only way to retreat before the other tribes surrounded them for the kill. He just hoped his pedris riders were able to kill the few remaining enemy warriors with hidden crossbow and board ship before the other enemy tribes arrived en masse. Many of the other tribes were hidden nearby and hopefully, not in the trench of the dead (River of Souls) or their retreat would certainly fail. The only ones he worried about were his wife, Veruna, and her women warriors. They were the beloved wives of his men and were protected in similar manner by many of his best female warriors on pedris while ships were standing by. But that would not be enough if they were surrounded en masse.

The pedris were adorned in the most beautiful colours to mask their hidden weapons. Their riders highlighted their blue with gold and purple braid. Melor's group in all blue, made them stand out among their enemies. Both groups jeered at each other on either side of the line of combat. Then warriors spaced themselves and took their positions on either side of the long battle ramp. This was just an elevated wall about four metres wide on top. It stood about three metres tall and tapered, with parallel stairs on either side.

The engagement would begin the moment they were signalled by the raising of two flag poles in front of each line of combatants. The ramp extended to a distance of several hundred metres . It was usually draped in the dried blood of previous victims. Not to mention pests and roving swarms of blood-sucking insects.

Two referees stood at either end in cages. They could observe the many warriors along that line. However cheating could not always be observed from their positions and many took advantage of those blind spots. On that day over 3000 warriors were involved so they could not concern themselves with the individual, only in the overall conduct of battle.

Before battle there were 1024 of Melor's male combatants vs over 2000 of Goel's with their respective assistants and medical teams sited high on pedris to observe.

Those totalled over 5000 on the battlefield, including a few spectators.

The high pedris and their riders were positioned at the rear of their fighters and could closely observe the battle from that position. Those would signal the referees on any illegal activities.

The gladiatorial battle began at noon and was stopped three hours later. The referees always allowed an hour's break after every three hours battle. At that time their wounds could be attended. During the first bout Melor and his troupes had held their ground and inflicted more wounds on the enemy than they had received. There were just 82 dead of his, with 405 on his enemy's side.

Salmon of Goel was unhappy with the way the battle went and began to jeer the other side hoping to distract them, but by so doing he distracted his own warriors. During such battles a warrior could take on more than a single combatant at any time by signalling the referee with extended fingers and Melor excelled in such combat.

Having had their break and wounds cleaned and bandaged, the remaining warriors continued the fight. Unluckily Melor took a slight wound on his risk but it was at the back of the left hand and did not bleed too profusely. The pain made him cry out and Salmon yelled and jeered so that his warrior could take advantage, but instead Melor thrust his opponent between the ribs. He fell limp unto the pile of bodies at the bottom of the ramp. Beneath the ramp where Melor stood were an ever ascending mound of bloody dead bodies.

Soon Salmon decided to take on Melor by himself. He always wanted to be the one, and realized killing Melor would bring him fame among the tribes. He assumed his men had weakened and worn him down enough making him ready for the kill, but he was sadly mistaken. Melor was a trained warrior, with the ability to play his enemies and make them think whatever he wanted. He had been specially trained since childhood and spent most of his time practising his strategies and skills on the battlefield. He had honed his skills until achieving virtual perfection in power and accuracy.

Seno was almost as good as Melor and was usually one of Melor's most vicious opponents during training. Both always stood side by side in battle.

Seno seeing his king wounded wanted to assist but could do nothing until that bout was ended. Only at that time was he allowed to dress the wound and prevent infection.

'Now let's see how well your sword arm works above you mouth,' Melor said and Salmon was furious and sneered.

'I said I was going to kill you and I will!' Salmon snarled and trusted his blade towards Melor's chest, but it simply slid harmlessly across the titanium breastplate and ended between his left arm. Like lightning, Melor returned a blow that severed his sword-arm. It fell with a mighty clamour unto the ramp. The twitching fingers still clutching the handle of his sword. Then Melor simply beheaded his enemy with a single swipe of his jewelled sword, to be drenched by a gushing fountain of blood.

Then Seno came forward to thrust his own sword through one eye of Salmon's head.

'This is for my father, you pitiful vermin!' he cried. Then he stuck the head on a spear and planted it in the ground. There Salmon's head remained on the makeshift pole for everyone to see.

'Stolah! Stolah! Stolah!' Seno yelled. Realizing many of Salmon-'s people were about to rush them.

No one other than Melor knew the meaning of those words. He realized it was the sign to retreat so he gave a signal to those riding on pedris.

'Fight your way and return to the ships! We shall take another route out of this mess!'

The few remaining enemy, also mounted on pedris, decided to send signal by mirror to the hidden tribes. They approached from almost every direction. They had remained hidden in trenches throughout the fields and could not be visible from their position. Before long the fields were swarming with his enemies. Each wanting to eliminate Melor and his warriors. Despite their sordid intentions, Melor's people escaped in the nick of time, leaving behind their frustrated enemies with an even greater desire to revenge Salmon's death.

Melor and his remaining troupes followed the narrow pass between two high mountains. They presumed they were safe from their immediate enemies but were not prepared for what was to follow.

This time the enemy tribes were disappointed with the outcome, but were still on a path for revenge. They killed the referees, who were the only neutral witnesses, and decided to lay blame at Melor's door.

CHAPTER 5

Two little angels

Due to the more severe and life-threatening changes to their world, the more extreme conditions had triggered many mutations. During that experimental process of adaptation, Mother Nature had selected a brand new human species. It would be one infinitely more suited to survival within the extremely harsh environments of planet Caefon. She had inevitably discarded the old and uncaring type in favour of the newer and more intelligent, hoping her next choice for humanity would be better suited than her last as caretakers to her dying world.

There were just two of those children on Caefon. They were born to an enemy tribe on the plains, but by different parents. At that time most of the surviving humans had a pale yellowish complexion with greenish eyes. Those two children had a pinkish complexion with piercing sea-blue eyes. Due to their peculiar appearance and other differences, they were considered children of the Evil One and scorned by their families and tribes.

Their families had to obey certain religious rules, which forbade the killing of such children. Once they were able to fend for themselves, they were discarded by their tribe and placed in the wilderness as food for the wild beast. Being highly intelligent and tough they survived for a while by hunting and scavenging.

Because of those reasons the feral children hated the tribes of the plains, who had refused to help and always chased them away.

As always, mankind would destroy whatever he considered different and couldn't understand. He always endeavoured to exterminate the competition if they were not of his kind and would naturally have considered all such life a threat. Soon after the two feral children took to the safety of the dangerous swamps where remaining prey was still plentiful. Despite the overwhelming stench of that place, they could exist freely and well away from the more savage humans. Because of certain ferocious predators of past, the swamp was a place scorned by everyone, so no one entered that place except the cursed and accused.

'Follow me now! For safety!' a childish voice screamed and in the spur of the moment Melor and his remaining troops followed his path. It took them under a high fence and over the high wall. Then they slid down the steep embankment among the bones and decaying bodies of previous combatants, into the almost dried river bed.

He had a lucky escape with his remaining warriors and followed a southward path across a deep trench towards the west. Those that were left behind on pedris galloped as fast as they could towards their ships in the northern port.

Melor and his troupe's progress was slow and tedious across the swamps, amidst more rotting corpses and skeletons of the previously vanquished. The stench was overpowering.

He still worried for his Veruna and her women warriors. They were in a more distant part of the field and well away from his other warriors. However as instructed by the Oracle, they had worn the colour blue on that day, while their enemies always wore red, violet and black. Their protectors on pedris were the best at their tasks and in all probability would have heard the commotion with the signalling mirrors and taken their own escape routes out of danger. If not, their deaths would be swift as revenge for Salmon's death.

While Melor and his troupes retreated they were astounded by what they could observe in the distance approaching their position. It was a most fearful giant obstacle of blackness that persistently followed from the sky. That knowledge speeded their progress through unknown territory.

Amidst thunder, lightning and a great fire in the sky above Melor's retreating position, a massive black ship appeared. It came over the mountain and hovered above his troops while shadowing as if to protect them.

Melor couldn't help but observe his two young feral guides who so carefully and patiently manoeuvred his troupes over boulders and rocks., Across sand pits they progressed towards the edge of the treacherous swamp with swarms of predatory insects playing catchup. The larger predators had since died of starvation.

The two smelly children were skinny while dressed in decaying rags. Yet, they would have given their last breath to save him and his men. He had never set eyes on them before and wondered who they were. As he approached the two children he realized they were completely different to anyone he had set eyes on before. The strangest thing of all were their penetrating sea-blue eyes. It was as if they could see deeply into his very soul.

'My lord! This place is safe! It leads to a narrow pass just yonder, which is clear this time of year!' the boy said. His female companion remained shy and silent. That part of the swamp was once the home of the infamous Seko Dragons - a type of carnivorous giant lizard - that species had since been extinct. In ancient times that place was used for sacrifices and most severe punishments.

Melor removed his small pouch and retrieved several pieces of bread and fish which he handed to the children. They took the food and began to devour ravenously. Seno and the other warriors could hardly bear the stench of that place and constantly placed part of their tunic over their faces, but it did not help.

'That hungry eh!' Melor exclaimed with a smile, but they continued devouring his rations until every bit was gone.

'Thank you, my Lord!' the boy said, wiped his lips with his dirty fingers and bowed. In all probability he hadn't had a meal like that since his existence in the swamps.

'What is your name?' Melor asked. The boy stuttered a little. Then he looked King Melor straight in the eye. For some reason Melor was transformed by the goodness in those children and was humbled. It was as if his day of judgement had arrived and was now to atone for all his sins of past.

'Me...ko! My Lord. I am Meko and she is Sefran. She is not able to speak yet.'

'Meko is a name for clowns. It is no name for a prince. From this day let it be known to all that you are Micol. Yes, from now on you shall take my middle name. Both of you will become my children!' Melor yelled with sword at hand so everyone would hear and they were awed. Both children went up to him and knelt before him with the sole intention of kissing his armoured boots.

'Come on! On your feet! Never again must you kneel before anyone. You are now royalty of my own tribe, so from this day, be honourable in all your undertakings,' he commanded with sword in hand and they bowed again before him.

They followed a narrow path between two mountains and waited to renew their homeward plans. They had to find a safe route to The Hill. Then Seno came forward to advise his king. Everyone was eager to leave that place as soon as they could.

The great black ship's shadow was soon cast upon their position. Powerful plasma beams were ejected from the sides of the monstrous blackness. With one massive explosion both ends of the narrow pass were sealed. Suddenly their relentless progress was halted by landslides and falling rock. They considered themselves doomed.

They were caught in the narrow pass between two vertical cliffs and there they remained with shields held high to save themselves from whatever dangers approached. Even now, they were determined to fight to the last man. With the consolation that not even their enemies' foot soldiers could enter the area of their confinement to take revenge.

'What is this great demon of the Ancients' technology that follow after us and curse the very ground upon which we walk? What diabolical trick is this?' an irritated Melor exclaimed.

'My lord I'm not sure from whence it came, but we are now in serious trouble. Our warriors are locked between these mountains with no way out but vertical,' his close advisor Seno stressed, somewhat disturbed.

Despite their present situation, they had been through many dangers together and were brave in that knowledge. That was providing their physical strength would carry. They hadn't eaten for more than a day and water was scarce.

'Who do you think is responsible for this atrocious deed? To imprison us here with the sole intention of mass murder without honour?' a furious Melor exclaimed, realising the great power of the ship's weaponry.

'I don't know my lord. This flying monster is beyond description. Any tribe that can build such flying machines and venture so low in stature, will soon have everyone in our main dynasties against them. They must indeed be either very brave or exceedingly foolish, to have broken the rules of council... But no one hereabouts will have such devastating technologies, or they would have conquered us years ago,' Seno replied.

'My dear princely friend and noble counsel, our main dynasties are no more. They were dissolved decades ago and now all that's left is a few poor warriors like us, still trying to defend their homes, good name and honour from barbarians,' Melor rebuked.

Seno soon realized the truth of the situation, but had to hold on to something tangible and sacred... even that faintest thread of truth or else their many generations of sacrifices on the battlefield would have been for nothing and they would have lost all hope for the future.

Seno had always represented the old ways and yearned for the good old days, when advanced technology was rife and people were free within a system of democracy. On the other hand, Melor was practical and more concerned with the safety of his tribes at the present time.

Even so, their threat was ever present and overwhelming. Whoever or whatever it was had won and it was 'check mate' for Melor and his troupes. Therefore they resolved themselves to a quick and painless death and there waited for the crucial blast to follow. Instead the whole area lit up brightly.

CHAPTER 6

Their ultimate rescue

'Let us form circles to defend ourselves from this giant nemesis!' King Melor yelled. They followed their leader's commands and placed their small shields above their heads. Deep in his mind he realized something was seriously amiss and regurgitated a thought. It was something his father made him read time and time again when he was a boy. That passage was from the first holy book, "the use of explosives and missiles on the battlefield against the less prepared must always be deemed dishonourable. It will doubtlessly cause an escalation in warfare. All such callous actions can eventually create disastrous consequences to all planetary life". At that time he knew not the true meaning of those holy words.

He had read them so many time and did not realize their true significance, until now. It was probably the reason why they had survived the struggle for this long. Then Melor knew the course of their survival had been intricately planned by the Ancients and guided by their great books and the Oracle for planetary survival.

Despite those honourable principles, at present time there wasn't much life left on his world to make a difference one way or the other. Yet he realized if there was escalation and advanced technology used in their wars, although the damage would have been greater, the wars would have been shorter with lesser suffering to all. Then Global Warming might not have stripped his world bare. Then he thought again about honour, respect and love.

'One should always meet violence with an equivalent force, so thank God we had always followed those honourable principles.' Then he paused to consider their present dilemma.

'If indeed such powerful weapons and giant flying ships still remained in tact? And If they do not, from where would this one have come?'

'That's a very big question, My Lord!'

'Who would have the knowledge and skills of the Ancients to

create massive flying machines, with such powerful weapons of mass destruction?' Melor reasoned, not even considering for a brief moment what Seno had said about the Oracle's prophesy. Then he began to question his own actions.

'This was a war of survival between humans; for it was through their greed and selfishness that such hostilities begun in the first place. The Gondrils and others of lesser intelligence were innocent bystanders and could not be directly involved, other than to carry water and such like. The use of weapons of mass destruction had been declared banned by the Grand Councils of Tribes over one hundred years ago. That ban included all technological weapons. For reasons of planetary survival only melee weapons like blades and spears had been allowed on the battlefield, not even ranged weapons... now I'm not sure what should be allowed and whether any of it made a difference anymore.'

'My Lord, the ship approaches!' Seno cried fearfully. Melor cast his eyes on the massive obstacle as it descended to engulf them.

'Seno and his Oracle was right about the old rules being rescinded, but sadly, not in our tribes' favour.'

The massive ship adjusted its position above its quarry. In a vane effort their shields were turned upwards to protect their bodies from whatever weapon would be discharged from its underbelly.

A focussed beam soon appeared. It expanded and lit the troupes brightly. Then a bluish cone of energy descended to engulf them. In an instant they were transferred within the bowels of the black monster.

The environment within the ship was pleasant. The air cool and refreshing. It was less pungent than the air they breathe on Caefon's surface and completely free of dust. Neither was the temperature as extreme. The stench of death had almost disappeared from their clothes and bodies.

As they viewed towards the distant bay they could observe their loyal wives and concubines, all dressed in blue with splashes of blood. They had also escaped the perils of battle. The men ran forward to embrace their women and King Melor, to embrace his loyal princess Veruna.

'My beloved wife! I thought you women were lost to our savage enemies for ever?' he cried and they embraced tightly.

'I thought the same for you...I lost my friend Ana. She was my truest friend! My best friend! They took her away like she was a lump of meat for their pots. Anyway, she died quickly.

'I took on her challenge and cut her head off. It was done in pure rage and I felt much better for it!' She began to sob.

'I also lost many good men today. However, I took the same pleasure when I removed Salmons head and felt my father's death revenged. Pity I hadn't time to stick his ugly mush on a pointed pole. Seno had that pleasure as I watched.' She suddenly felt better. Seno was also pleased, for Salmon had cheated his father in like manner.

'Where do you think we are?' Veruna asked in a more sombre mood.

'I don't know, but they should show themselves soon,' Melor replied.

It was then that a strange alien creature appeared. It was quite large with many seething tentacles that balanced its progress through the air with no audible means of propulsion. It included a central beaklike mouth from where it would communicate its thoughts. It floated in the air as if gravity did not exist and could change colour like an overactive chameleon. They soon learned that method to be another form of personal communication.

The troupes remained transfixed as if hypnotised by the colourful alien monster.

'I am Kronus... a friendly visitor from a distant world in another galaxy. I have been sent by Grand Lord Gerron. Lord of this part of our universe to assist in your time of need.

'I'm afraid your world is almost lost to all life. Many have died, including numerous innocent species. This is because your previous generations overpopulated and over-polluted your planet's environment. Now only drastic measures can take your world back from the brink. That can only be done after the human population have reduced below 400 million, which is presently the case.

'Your planetary population is presently well below 400 million. Therefore it is time for you to implement the necessary changes and repairs. With the present crises faced, this will take about ten more years of your time. Since your species are responsible for this problem, by Universal Law you must make it right again.

'In the mean time you are to visit our world at the farthest reaches of space, where you will learn new technologies and efficient ways to revive your world at the appropriate time.' Melor was stunned by that knowledge.

'Are we your prisoners?' he inquired.

'I suppose the answer is yes; since we are under orders and unable to return you from whence you came. This is also because the loss of a living world and all its species is much more important to us than your personal comforts and survival... furthermore you are the only ones and chosen few that can save your world.'

'Well, at least you've given us an honest answer?' Melor replied.

'Darling, I'm scared of what they will do to us when we visit their world,' brave, weak and wounded Veruna complained. She knelt before him with tears running down her pallid cheeks.

'They will do nothing to you, my love! Not while you are with me!' Melor stressed and she was comforted. She was still suffering from the loss of her friends and needed more comforting.

'In that case please visit the room next door. You may collect a small communicator as you enter. When asked, you may give your names to the device. Each of you must be thoroughly checked for wounds and illness so that you may be healed. '

'We shall!' Melor replied.

'All your weapons and shields must be left in this area. You will not require them. They will be returned to you when we leave again for your home world.'

'Ok, warriors, drop all weapons, armour and shields!' Melor commanded, but many also dropped their filthy garments on the pile.

'You should not be worried, we are all creatures of peace; for it is only through kind deeds that we may attain respect, honour and glory within The Greater Purpose.' Kronus said.

'I trust, we shall be treated kindly by your people?'

'We are here only to assist you. There are many bunks where you may rest during our brief voyage. It will take us only two days to make the trip to Balion, our home galaxy, which is at the borders of Osmaron. Food is also available in the area of your bunks, so please be relaxed during our journey,' Kronus added. A door slid open while they entered.

KIND SURRENDER

With utter disgust Melor removed his bloodstained sword from its jewelled scabbard and kissed it for luck. Then he undid his shield straps, then armbands where he kept his dagger. They had been his loyal companions that had saved his life through many battles. He placed them at his feet where he stood. Then his soldiers did the same. They placed their shields, knives, swords and axes above his as if to protect those of their leader. The women did likewise on Princess Veruna's shield and sword.

While holding the hands of Veruna, Melor guided his 1314 remaining troupes, 605 male and 709 female, to their new area of residence. He realized he could do little to escape while on route to another galaxy. Nevertheless he was determined to continue his fight for the good name of his dynasty. He was not the type to be enslaved by anyone and would eventually find a way to escape, or so he thought.

'Darling, I am so hungry! We haven't eaten a thing since morning,' Veruna said. She was grossly mal-nourished and on the verge of fainting. She was the type to always sacrifice herself for others.

'And we, for well over a day. This time I had a premonition that we were going to die on the battlefield for sure. I even considered that idea better than the alternative. Then I thought of you and my loyal friends. If you died this time I'm sure I would have given up the fight the next time I faced our enemies.... that is if we were not rescued first by these alien monsters,' he replied.

'Yes, my darling, sometimes I felt the same about death as an alternative. All our enemies fight well and grow fat on the flesh of our brave while we starve. We see cannibalism as dishonourable and will always lose because of that,' she said.

'Yes, I am afraid we must always follow the rules and laws of our forefathers. Their world was kind, pleasant and fair for all,' he said with disappointment in his voice.

'Until they screwed it all up with their adventures in industry and commerce. During that time of capitalistic self-indulgence they showed little concern for their future generations. They never once considered their overpopulation and environmental abuse! Never once, during their moments of licentious fun and pleasure for its own sake! Therefore I dam them all to hell for what they have done to us! Never again will I ever consider them as my ancestors! Nor shall I ever consider a single chapter of our past history or dammed holy books again!' she screamed with rage and Melor felt sad for her. He hugged and comforted her as best he could.

She had suddenly changed from a loving wife to one seeking revenge and retribution for past sins against their families and world. Since the real enemies were no longer alive, it was better hitting one's head against a hard wall, and so he thought.

During this time Melor was nervous and thought the only logical way out of their present dilemma was to be a good listener and remain reticent for the sake of his crippled troops. Therefore he listened carefully to the strange alien and nodded his head in response to its words.

Soon after their names were called. Then each went through for a thorough medical check. During those scans, by the greatest miracle all their physical wounds were repaired. Their psychological ones took a little longer.

The two ferrel children, Micol and Sefran, were the last to be taken and returned like little angels, dressed in radiant white. The Octans realized they were different from the others and scanned their genes to assess to what extent and were surprised by what they found.

Melor and his group of warriors were quite young for Ancients. Everyone was less than thirty in years. All their parents and other relatives had been sacrificed on the battlefield years before so they were the last remnants of his dynasty. Their noble Safa and Medoin tribes numbered just under 10,000 and now even less. From all those only 98 babies were born in the previous year.

Their losses were always considerably more than their natural ability to compensate by migration and childbearing. Therefore if nothing was done to assist the process, they faced extinction well within 10 years. Their planetary wars had taken its toll in more than 100 years and with the exception of scavenging, they had known no other skills other than those required for the battlefield.

Any form of advanced technologies could not be used in their battles of honour during hand-to-hand combat, where one could only survive because of their fitness and skills in the art of warfare. That method of culling was selected because it was fairer, did not use too many planetary resources and tended to select the fittest. It also did not involve the lower species and had less impact on the environment.

For the first time in their lives they were relaxed and properly fed. It was not the ancient canned food discovered from the submerged buildings, shrivelled roots, starving wild animals or poisoned fish, to which they had grown accustomed. They soon got used to the colourful protein jelly-like materials and strange food from the alien machines and were healthy again.

A smile soon returned to Veruna's cheeks as they considered themselves in paradise compared to where they had been since birth.

'My lord, our gracious Oracle was right and we were well received. Despite their differences, we should trust them; for they have good in their hearts,' Seno said and Melor nodded in agreement.

'We shall see... and must repay all good deeds in like manner and make the same sacrifices for others, even to the suffering of our enemies on our world,' Melor replied. He was now a changed man and realized there was a greater purpose in his ancestor's long term plans for planetary survival.

'My lord, is everything all right?' a caring Seno inquired, for he had never seen Melor in such an accommodating mood before. 'Better than I've ever been, dearest Seno,' Melor replied.

CHAPTER 7

A different world

Place... Planet Orban, within the small colliding galaxy of Balion, was slowly merging with the larger Galaxy of Osmaron. Both colliding galaxies were filled with numerous life. Nevertheless the chance of stellar collisions were remote. Balion was the original home galaxy of the Plorans. Unlike the Octans, they were an ancient race of humans who had since evolved beyond their physical bodies.

Osmaron was known to Earth's humans as the Milky-Way galaxy.

The world they visited was not like anywhere they had been before. It was blue, violet and green, with the most pleasant temperature that one could only experience on a paradise world. The Octans took life at their own pace and lived in the most beautiful structures close to the clear blue seas and oceans of their world.

They were very advanced and so highly technological that virtually anything was possible for them. With such knowledge they were able to convert matter directly into energy at the sub-atomic level. Most of their equipment was self-repairing and self-perpetuating. Further, they were able to take forms of energy from the raw quantum world and from those create artificial forms of matter and energy not natural to our universe. Those they would design to spec and blend in predictable ways with those of our own universe for whatever force or field they required.

In fact, they could be measured as Class 6 on the technological ladder of advancement. That made them about a million years more advanced than modern day Earth humans. Over the years they had worked hard to preserve the natural order of their beautiful world. As a result, their technologies and production facilities were sited on moons and dead planets; well away from their home world.

As a matter of fact, they could never pollute the environment of any living or habitable world. Their colourful societies were not based on money. Every individual of Octan society was chosen since birth for a particular task and so trained to their optimum. Nevertheless they relished freedom and were always involved in their different creative activities and hobbies. By so doing, everyone in their complex societies were equally appreciated and shared equally in their common wealth.

Melor and his warriors were pleasantly surprised when they found they were in Osmaron and many millions of light-years away from their homes in the galaxy of Andromeda. Although that fact worried him, he decided to take the Octan's advice and learn as much as he could to assist his people and save his world. Anyway, he was presently weary of warfare and relished the break for freedom from their past misery. That was providing he and his troops did not become the prisoners or slaves of another. He soon realized the Octans cared too much for other creatures to do him and his people any harm.

With the help of the Octans, within a single week Melor and his previously hapless and starving warriors soon recovered from the trauma of their past brutish existence and decided to take a well deserved break. During that time they contemplated their past existence on their world, Caefon, while comparing it with their new existence and found their previous lives infinitely lacking. Nevertheless Melor's main concern was in keeping his people together for a single cause and purpose. He called them together in the place that was to be their residence for the duration of their stay.

The two young feral children they met in the swamp were still with the Octans and he wondered why. They soon appeared at the doorway and walked towards him and his troupes. When they entered all the soldiers including Seno bowed to show homage to their new royalty. Veruna was surprised by the situation; for they were so young, looked quite human, but not like anyone she had ever seen before.

'Who are these young ones, my husband?' she inquired of Melor.

'Why, my dear, they are ours. They rescued me and my warriors from a faith worse than death... so I decided to adopt them as my own. I trust you don't mind... so please meet your new children!' he said and she couldn't hold back a surprised smile. They had tried for many years for a family and had not been successful. Children were the rarest commodity within their tribes and had always given them a sense of renewal with celebrations. Yet, these children were so different, with a pinkish complexion and piercing sea-blue eyes.

'Enuma nacta ehito, Veruna,' the little girl said, and Melor was surprised; for she was once a mute and could not speak a word to save her life.

Veruna looked dismayed, for she could not understand a word of that language, although familiar with most of the languages of her people.

'She now speaks the holy words of the Ancients?' a surprised Melor exclaimed. That particular language had only been spoken by the Oracle in recent times and only to Seno.

'Yes, indeed, my lord! And speaks it more eloquently than I!' Seno interrupted and began to laugh. Soon the whole room resounded in laughter as the others caught on. At that moment laughter had become contagious. It was probably the first time they had seen the need to laugh in years. The two children stood smiling.

'She thanks Veruna for taking the place of her mother,' Seno added, still laughing, and went forward to embrace both children. At that time the warriors knew of the true purpose in their lives and what they were fighting for... it was for a brand new world like Orban with its young humans like the children Micol and his female companion, Sefran.

Just beyond them a female warrior was having problems with one of the food dispensing machines and the boy, Micol, went through the crowd to assist. As he approached the women moved away and kept their distance, fearing his kind.

'What was your order?' he asked the woman and she told him. He simply touched the machine and the container of food suddenly appeared as if by magic. They were amazed and began to call them the Children of God.

ON REFLECTION

Melor considered the plight of his ravaged world. Realizing that during the past few centuries the larger tribes and dynasties had been decimated through self-imposed warfare. They fought each other for whatever wealth they possessed, until there was nothing left other than their few possessions and the ground they stood upon to defend.

That process of human culling was devised to further reduce human population to a more tolerable level, without destroying the planet or affecting its lower life-forms. However they did not take into consideration other pressures due to extreme climate change.

During that period of overwhelming change, his once beautiful world with its many great cities, including a population of over 12 billion, had shrunk to under 400 million. While its magnificent structures had turned to ruins and rubble in but a few centuries. Presently all that remained were the few hundred million humans with some remaining animals, birds and insects. All that destruction and extinctions had been caused by human overpopulation, leading to Global Warming in under 200 years of planetary abuse. Mother Nature could become a formidable foe when she felt threatened.

'Of all those, the remnants were but a small fraction by comparison. Most of the once great cities with their populations bustling with every form of diverse activity were partially submerged by the rising oceans and seas. Thank goodness the waters had stopped rising or The Hill and all the local plains would also be submerged with more loss of life,' he thought, realizing how mammoth the task was in bringing his world back from the brink of death.

Most of the larger life-forms had become extinct in under 100 years. What a very sad loss it was to their world. The Pedris, Malaks and Gondrils remained only because of their overwhelming use to humanity. They were mainly herbivores that could be happy with just dried moss and water. The Gondrils could scavenge and were pleased with their masters scraps and leftovers.

Other than his loyal friend Seno, with his links to the Oracle, there was not a single person with enough knowledge to take Caefon back from the brink. A large part of his world had become desert while other parts had disappeared under the polluted waters. They had become ignorant and mal-nourished due to the progress of the deserts and the overwhelming greed for what others possessed. That savage attitude had progressed to the exclusion of all other necessary means for a civilized existence. This was further exemplified by a lack of farming for food and schools to educate the young.

In the past they had to focus all their efforts on their mere day to day survival at the exclusion of all others. Food had become so rear that many relied on the bodies of the dead on battlefields for sustenance. Such were the hard and difficult ways of a remnant warrior.

Any existence on this world, Orban, was a million times better than his own. It also reminded him of the way his world could have been before greed, capitalism, industry and self-indulgence polluted and destroyed it. He regurgitated those thoughts time and time again; for the plight of his people and their world worried him to almost bursting point. Therefore, come what may, he would learn the wise and noble ways of the Octans, who appeared to be successful in such methods and had excluded all self-indulgent ways from their world.

When he returned to Caefon all that would change. Given those abilities and knowledge, he would make it his duty to bring Caefon back to where she was over 200 years before but without its selfish capitalism.

'My lord, we are required in their main hall to meet one of their leaders,' Seno advised.

'Warriors of Nim! You are to follow us to the main hall, and please be on your best behaviour,' a more subdued Melor commanded and everyone followed Seno to the place. The many Octans were excited, showing it in their numerous changing colours. They gave the impression that a very important leader was to visit from another world, but no great ships were apparent anywhere in their blue skies.

Melor and his people were told to assemble in one of their largest buildings. Then one dressed in a black cloak suddenly materialized in front of them from nowhere. His hood slid back to reveal a figure with human likeness.

'I am Siit, the Shadite, and represent The Greater Purpose in all things. I have adopted this form in order to be more acceptable to you. I am to personally take care of your training and assist when we return to your world,' he said. They remained quietly at attention while Melor nodded his head in appreciation. Such technologies were far beyond their senses of reasoning to have even contemplated their realization.

'Please wait here for a short while, the overlord of this galaxy will soon be with us,' he said and took a stance at attention to one side. Just in front of them was what appeared to be a golden throne. It was soon enveloped in a greenish light. Then as if from nowhere a large sphere of black materialized and hovered above that area. It displayed a green insignia but every other part was jet black and did not reflect any light. Although extremely fearful of what they saw, they kept their nerve and would remain obedient to their leader, Melor, unto death.

'I am the Ploran, Faemon... I am responsible for all life within this sector of Osmaron... including all within my home galaxy, Balion. Because of the urgency of your situation I felt compelled to assist. This explains the reasons for your speedy transfer to this world.

'I trust you are pleased with your present accommodation and supplies? Anyway, during your stay on this world you may consider yourselves free individuals... and also feel free to ask Siit if you have any worries or problems. He has been assigned to you for the duration,' the spherical form said, as if eating its words. It

spoke in a powerful male voice and they assumed it was of that sex.

'Oh! Melor! You and your people have been through so much suffering together. Sadly, many worlds like yours are sometimes lost to us. We cannot be everywhere, you know... in these expansive galaxies, with numerous evolving species. However, we received your signal and caught yours just in the nick of time. Regrettably, many advancing species follow the same path as yours and get hypnotised by technological progress, greed and the desires of the flesh, to the exclusion of all others.

'You must not blame your ancestors for the damage they have unintentionally inflicted on your world. They were infected by that particular disease of the soul and could not have avoided those particular currents of change. It is also a universal test that not many advancing civilizations may pass.

'Nevertheless, with your assistance we shall try our best to repair your world and take it back from the brink of death.

'No more should you and your proud people wage war on others of your kind; for you have been chosen to collect all tribes and bring them together for the common good.

'After you leave here, your main concerns should be to improve your world and its people, through a program of assistance and education. With the good counsel of my Shadite, Siit, you may face and win those challenges. Then one day in the not too distant future you will become the most powerful leader on your world.

'Certain changes have been made whereby your people have been chosen by Grand Lord Gerron, Lord of this part of our universe for a special purpose. That special purpose will be revealed in the fullness of time.

'It is prophesied that your two fair children will one day form the foundation of your race. It is their seed that will remain and prosper after you are gone from this existence.

'For that great purpose I have decided to expand the lifespan of the chosen and their seed to over ten times your present natural age limit. This increase will also apply to all here standing, but not to their future offspring. In so doing, your bodies will be thoroughly repaired and renewed genetically, enabling all your

women to procure offspring. Further, each of you will be given implants which will contain all information you will require to repair your world and reestablish your societies in a more caring manner. Regarding your implants, you will each be given a choice in selecting a suitable profession.

'I shall visit you again before you return to your world. Presently I shall leave you in the competent hands of Shadite, Siit,' Lord Faemon said, then he faded into nothing.

Lord Faemon, the Ploran, was billions of years old and had existed since the early stages of the Balion galaxy. His once humanlike race was so ancient that they had evolved beyond their material bodies aeons ago. The Octans, on the other hand, were a much younger race that had originally evolved like octopuses in the seas and oceans of their world and were over a million years advanced, technologically.

They had all the technologies needed to create a complete human body from scratch in minutes with large machines. Such machines could record every atom in the human body and every bit of data in the human brain that could be stored in small blinking blocks. They also possessed massive machines that could repair dying worlds.

Soon Siit, the Shadite, called Melor and his seniors together, including the two children to inform them of a possible course of action.

'What I am to tell you may sound incredible, but it is necessary if you are to extend your minds and successfully complete your mission.'

'We shall do whatever is necessary, if it's imperative to our mission!' Melor replied.

'Yes, this program is imperative, if you are to improve the course of your people and repair your world in the short time remaining.'

'Whatever is necessary for that purpose will be acceptable to my lord and his people,' Seno said.

'In that case, you will each be given brain implants. They will extend your minds tenfold and include all the information necessary for fulfilling those plans. The method used is completely safe and painless. By so doing each of you will become brilliant scientists in the knowledge of the most advanced sciences.'

'Brain im...plants?' Veruna stuttered. She was not agreeable.

'You must follow the broader plan and encourage your women warriors to do what's necessary for our long-term survival!' Melor whispered in her ear. She relented and decided to follow his lead. Yet Siit continued his briefing.

'The process of education and training will take just two weeks. After that time you may return to your world to commence the necessary changes.' Melor opened his mouth to object but Seno nudged him on the shoulder. His main problem was how to explain such bizarre actions to his people. Later he decided not to mention a word to them about brain implants. Instead he made a list of likely professions for each of his warriors and handed it to Siit.

Within two weeks their bodies and minds had recovered from the traumas of the past and with their new brain implants were soon trained in the ways of the Octans. Once their minds had expanded with those implants they were able to visualize a broader cosmic picture and that picture included the survival of all living worlds. They were each made clever scientists in many fields and were finally ready to take on and terra-form even the worst of dying worlds.

Melor couldn't believe the changes that were possible with their sciences. To him they were like gods, even with the powers to replenish bodies and revive the dead. Nevertheless he realized it was all founded on universal knowledge, in the form of clever minds moulding their technologies for any purpose that could be conceived through thought.

CHAPTER 8

Plans laid

During their brief stay on Orban they were thought many things, including new languages like Sunolingua. This was a unique conceptual language almost galactic in scope and used by the most advanced civilizations in Osmaron. Being highly logical it blended seamlessly with the use of implants and interpreted thoughts directly. It also enabled translation and interpretation to be precise and unambiguous through other brain implants. It was a unique interface between any two minds including those of lower life. With that type of language interpretation, communication between different species became irrelevant since thought and feelings were transferred.

The minds of the two children, Micol and Sefran, expanded exponentially, until they knew virtually all that was needed for the task ahead. Seno found the whole situation of using brain implants, with its many menus and functions to be a dream.

The only real problem he encountered was in not being able to observe their bizarre technologies in detail. Since the Octans had evolved in a more telepathic manner than humans, who were more visual, all their controls and displays were never visible or real. Instead they existed within Virtual Worlds in their minds, where they could directly interface to control their equipment. It was indeed a strange concept Melor and his people found great difficulty in grasping. Nevertheless such systems were infinitely efficient, since they were just 3D constructs in some Master Computer's mind. Anyway why build structures and equipment in the real world, with the added dangers and costs when virtually identical ones could be virtualized in better and more efficient ways. As a matter of fact, although they were quite advanced and powerful, their technological equipment on the physical plane were few and far. Thus, they were able to complete tasks in their

Virtual Worlds hundreds of times faster than was possible in the Real World and be years ahead in solving most problems.

Seno was so impressed with the ways of the Octans that he wanted to remain on their world for a longer period to study and record their culture and technologies. However he also realized he was the only one with a direct link to the Oracle, and was probably the one that possessed the key to its knowledge. Little did he know all that knowledge had already been downloaded into his brain and were awaiting the right time and trigger for implementation.

Seno had gotten quite close to the children, Micol and Sefran, and continued writing down his experiences and poems of life and love. At other times he would counsel them in the noble and princely ways of the royal families of old.

During that time Melor and his warriors were busier than ever, learning to use their new brain implants within their strange Virtual Worlds that mimicked reality in every detail. They could by suggestion enter tunnels in their minds to practise their relevant new professions virtually. That way if an experiment failed no one was hurt and they could practise as many times as they liked with simulacra until they got that experiment right. Then those learned experiences would become an integral part of their brain as if learned by experience in the Real World.

The whole process was truly incredible. In a short time they were like gods, with the ability to process thought and manouevre objects many times faster than they could with their original selves. By so doing they became formidable fighters and brilliant scientists. The once bedraggled group of savage barbarians had been transformed into a most cultured group that could make a future for themselves on almost any barren world. Even Grand Lord Gerron; lord of that part of the seventh universe was pleased with the outcome.

They now followed the ways of the Octans and even adopted the Grand Lord as their true god; for he was the one who had come to their rescue in their hour of need. They accepted everything he represented in what he called The Greater Purpose.

More than anyone, Seno was always involved advising his people. He wrote down everything of importance in his little book. It was all to be included in his new bible for the benefit of their future generations. That was the one he was going to complete after his return to Caefon.

That book he would call, "Chronicles of a dying world".

'My lord, young Micol would like to say a few words to the people,' Seno advised.

'In that case, let my son speak to all of our people if it concerns them,' Melor replied.

It was then that Veruna went up to Seno to speak her mind.

'I am very sorry for the bad things I said about our ancestors of past. Not all were evil, wasteful and self-indulgent. And the Oracle has always been a shining beacon of light in our darkest hour. It is because of her that we are here today.'

I see!'

'I wonder if you can ever forgive me for my ridiculous outburst on that day?' She apologized with tears running down her cheeks.

'I knew exactly how you felt and it was a good thing you aired those thoughts and got those pent-up feelings out of your system. Now, you must feel much better for it... and there is nothing to forgive. You thought aloud on that day what many of us thought in silence, so in that way we are all sinners. Please, say not another word on the subject,' Seno said and Veruna was at that time one of the happiest people.

Since their arrival on Orban all her wounds had been miraculously healed. Even the scars from the long gash on her right cheek, which constantly embarrassed her had disappeared. Presently she was a perfect and most beautiful woman and a lot fitter than she had ever been.

They gathered in the main hall as both children dressed in radiant white ascended the large stage to speak to their people. They were fearless and instilled hope and inspiration in the troops. Young Micol was the first to speak. This time he spoke to them in their dialect and not in the strange language of the Ancient priests.

'My dear people of Nimia, I would like to say a few words about our plans and their implementation when we return to Caefon. I am also to inform you of an important fact that might assist us in repairing our dying world.

'Some of our noble ancestors left behind many satellites that contained stores of genetic material of most of the past flora and fauna of our world. Therefore, with little effort we should be able to repopulate Caefon with almost all of the more recently extinct life-forms,' he said and they cheered, but he silenced them.

'There is a lot more. The large satellites contain many inflatable balloons and chemicals. Once released into the atmosphere, those balloons will follow the trade winds above our world and spread harmless bacteria. They will neutralize most of the atmospheric pollution and induce clouds to give heavier rainfall. Some of the chemicals will spread throughout the ionosphere and neutralize harmful chemicals within the upper layers. On these stations also exists many robots, including a few ancestors currently in hibernation. They have been patiently awaiting the time of awakening to assist us during this period of change. Therefore, the process of planetary conversion should be initiated immediately on our return.

'The Shadite Siit has informed me, that he will assist us during the processes involved, thanks to our Octan friends. We shall therefore always be indebted to them for their kind assistance to our cause. They have also allowed us one ship for our journey home and four Tetrions to shield our world during the process of planetary conversion. Tetrions are enormous ships also called maulers. They can weave a mesh of reflective material close to our star. Like ginormous spiders they will weave a web many thousands of miles across space. By so doing the output of our star in the direction of our world can be reduce by about 30 percent, thus accelerating the formation of our polar ice caps by cooling our world.

'This process will make our world, Caefon, a much more pleasant environment for its remaining inhabitants during this period of change.

'Once more, most of our submerged coastal cities may be

reclaimed and reused for our future generations. Then our once beautiful city of Nim will rise again from the waves to be habitable once more and bustling with commerce as before. However, this time we must be more careful in the type of society we wish to build. We should follow the Octans as a model for all our societies. In future we must always consider the needs of our world, including its other life-forms and eco-systems, in our planning before we make our own choices. Incidently, this process also includes our methods of energy conservation and anti-pollution.

'In future, all our production, with the exclusion of agricultural farming and packaging, will be cited on local moons and uninhabitable worlds within our system. Never again should we make the same mistakes as our forefathers.

'We are now on an exciting course, with renewed vigour and faith in our future. With this enthusiasm, let us go forth and build a new future for our world, its people and all its varied life. We know what is expected from each of us, so let us exert ourselves in the knowledge that we shall soon reclaim our once beautiful world from death's door... and let us build a fair and honest future with no recriminations to others, even our supposed enemies.

'A future built on solid foundations for all the surviving families, including all our future generations.' The crowd roared and cheered. Even his adopted parents, Melor and Veruna cheered with pride at his brilliance.

With the intervention of the Octans, the children's minds had been extended while becoming like super geniuses, with an intricate knowledge of most things. Seno had also educated them well in the ways of the Ancients.

Then the girl decided to say a few words of her own.

'My good people of Nimia, when we return home, one of our first tasks will be to stop the fighting and bring the tribes together to assist in our program. This also includes those still remaining on isolated islands and continents. We must also educate them in our ways if they are to survive. By now many will be in dire straights so in setting a good example they will not fear us for what we have

become.

'In future, we should show all our people love and charity, but without risking our lives and livelihood in the process. With the help of robots, we shall build large environmental domes, even in the harshest deserts where we shall live and grow our crops well away from our persistent enemies.

'Once we have become established, we can begin to assist everyone on our world to attain our goals. Such great domes will also be ideal for isolating the endangered species and in introducing new ones. They can also be places of refuge during the process of change. Once large areas of our world become fertile again, and the ground waters become pure, there will be no need for anyone to fight for the possessions of others. This process of normalization will take about 100 years. However, over 75 percent of the damage will be repaired during the first 10 years.

'All relevant knowledge must be imparted to the tribes, so that the friendly ones may come over to our side and partake in those changes for the common good.

'As the Oracle, Mohria, has decreed, from this day let each of us, the chosen few, wear a small sword as our crucifix. It will represent the souls of our people who died honourably and sacrificed themselves on the Fields of Battle for the survival of our world. Let that symbol also remind us of our duties. One of which is, never again to take arms against our people unless in the case of self-defence. Those are the wishes of our faithful Oracle. So shall it be written and so shall it be enacted,' Sefran said and everyone cheered. Then Seno took the stage.

'My dear people and friends, we have had a most pleasant stay on Orban. Therefore I would like us to build a beautiful monument in this place as thanks to a great people who went out of their way to assist us in our hour of need. I know we only have a short time remaining, but with your assistance I'm sure together we can cut a beautiful statue out of the local rocks. As for the figure we carve... we shall take a vote.' The audience began to converse among themselves. Then they decided on a large sphere, surrounded by the most important Octans. Their Grand Lord, Gerron, would be represented by a bright star, with the Shadite Siit as his angel or messenger.

CHAPTER 9

Lord of lords

On the day of their departure they were made to stand in the large hall in front of the golden throne. Everyone, including the Octans were excited. This behaviour was evident from their motion and ever changing colours. Melor and his people assumed another visit from Lord Faemon, the Ploran, was expected.

The black sphere of Lord Faemon suddenly appeared and took its place on the throne while most of the senior Octans took position close by, with the Shadite, Siit, on the other side close to Melor and his group. There they remained in expectation of some even greater occurrence. Suddenly everyone froze in their places.

There was much tension building in the air, to be followed by thunder and lightning. The lightning was extremely intense everywhere and arced from pillar to post. They became fearful for their very lives. Melor and his group's hair stood on end. Although scared out of their wits end they bravely stood their ground.

A bright point of light suddenly appeared in front of Melor's group. It's brilliance was so intense that many of the humans placed their hands in front of their faces to shield their pupils. In a flash the intense brilliance had transformed into the figure of a powerful human being. It was in the express image of Melor's father, Stefan, before he went to battle.

Although he was one of the greatest and bravest warriors in battle, he was another that was tricked by the Goel, Salmon. Presently there he stood in all his glory and Melor couldn't believe his eyes.

The human figure stood about 20 feet tall and overwhelmed everyone with its radiance. Then the Grand Lord of the Seventh part of The Seventh Universe began to speak to them with the same voice as Melor's father. At times his words could enter their minds directly without his lips moving. While he spoke every creature could understand his every word, and a single word could carry a thousand stories. Even the small rodents that lived in the rocks remained obedient and at attention.

'Melor, you and your people may call me Gerron. Over the aeons I have been called by many names. However, you and your people may call me by that name to posterity.

'I have appeared here because it signifies a very important turning point in the future of our universe. I shall also take this opportunity to place your minds at ease regarding certain notions you may harbour about your future... which incidentally will be a great one. However problems will occur in your distant future. At that time many decisions will be taken to maintain the survival of your people. During that time... many of my own servants will intervene. When that period has passed, your people will visit this galaxy again and make it their permanent home. Those events will occur many thousands of years hence and may not concern you at this time. However, let it be known that you are now my concern, therefore I shall always be there for you in the future. So do not worry unduly on that score.

'Now, let me change the topic and educate you on a few pertinent facts...

'All naturally evolving lives within the Cosmos are unique but predatory. In other words, the only way Primal Life can exist is by taking nutrients from others. This tends to separate life into two kinds, prey and predator. Nevertheless even vegetarians and herbivores may be considered predators, since they take nutrients from others within their food chain including the soil. By so doing some may evolve into natural prey and predator, while others improve their survival instincts and armour themselves against their predatory foe. So it has always been and so it will always be.., if such a natural order or system of Primal Life is to exist to perpetuity.

'Despite this Nature of evolution called the Natural Order, the more intelligent species have always been able to create their own nutrients from raw materials and natural chemicals within their environment. Thus removing their societies from the natural food chain. By so doing many have become less predatory on the

naturally evolving systems. We find such unique capabilities in the more advanced civilizations above Class 3.

'Further, only a few at lower technological levels are able to plan their existence in the long term. The majority may survive natural catastrophes, before they in turn become extinct and relinquish their position to others.

'Therefore, it might be said that the Cosmos places us under several survival tests during our evolution and only a few species may survive to a high level of technological advancement.

'The Natural Order is cruel and unforgiving. Therefore, we in The Greater Purpose have decided to change that order into a fairer one. By so doing, we can only intervene if the seriously threatened have attained a high level of advancement, technologically, and your forefathers had increased beyond Class 3.

'Even so, the Natural Order must prevail at the lower levels; for it is because of it that important life like yourselves have been able to evolve your various attributes, abilities and senses.

'When promising species face extinction through no fault of their own, it is our duty and responsibility to save them. If we cannot at the appropriate time, we should store their genes until suitable conditions prevail for the re-establishment of such life.

'We are now the keepers of all life within the Cosmos, therefore it is our duty to take stock and ensure that a Greater Order prevails through the Greater Purpose, so that all intelligent life may be unified under a single banner of survival.

'However alien we may appear to each other, we are all important children of the Cosmos by virtue of our existence. Therefore, please bear those important thoughts in mind when you return to your home world.

'You would have learnt many lessons from your forefathers, both good and bad. Carry those thoughts with you during your many endeavours, so that never again will those same mistakes be repeated.

'I shall leave you now, my beautiful children, but will return one day in your distant future, when your people have settled within this galaxy.' Grand Lord Gerron's figure simply faded into thin

air. However the intense arcing and lightning continued for a while.

Seno, Melor and his people knelt for a while in appreciation of a visit from their incredible Grand Lord. Someone they thought had never existed. Nevertheless there he stood in the image of his own father, and showed significant respect for him and his people. He had also sent his ship to save them in their hour of need.

Finally, after all the suffering, their race had finally come of age and had been given the key to the door. Melor was aghast by it all. Mere words were beyond the description of such events. On the other hand, Seno was in his world of intrigue. He had always believed in the supreme being, albeit in his own religious ways. Nevertheless Grand Lord Gerron had proved one of his own ideas... that his god was one of many names and faces, and of all things he was proven right.

CHAPTER 10

Problems back home

With the keen assistance of the Octans, Melor and his people built a most stunning monument in the local square. It contained several incredible symbolic figurines. The images were carved from a greenish marble and illuminated in such a manner that its glow was quite soothing to the minds of its observers.

The main statue itself composed the spherical figure of Lord Faemon, with his obedient senior Octans. They orbited about him like planetary satellites. Their extended tentacles resembling antennae in some bizarre motion. On top of the primary statue were suspended their powerful being, Grand Lord Gerron. He was portrayed in the form of their most brilliant star that continually showered them with light and blessings from on high. Siit, the Shadite, was also included. His attire more priestly while acting as their god's chosen messenger.

All around the great monument were planted the most beautiful flowers. Many specially selected from remote areas of the world for that purpose. That type of art was unknown to the Octan's. They couldn't stop admiring the concepts and simplicity in its design.

On the day of their departure they were guided to a special area and from that platform were transferred unto the decks of the great black ship for their voyage home. They were sad in leaving and constantly waved the senior Octans, who changed colours and moved their tentacles to impart the same emotions. That day only Siit, the Shadite, followed them on board.

With the exception of their living quarters, the ship was void of any other life except the ship itself, which could be considered a super intelligent being in its own right. Being mainly composed of nano-bots, it was a non biological living organism, with the ability to defend and repair itself. However like all other types of intelligence, it could communicate with its specially chosen human crew and they could relay important information via their brain implants. Nevertheless that process could only be done telepathically through those implants.

Their world Caefon was just over 2.5 million light years away in Androme da and it would have taken them just two of Caefon's days to complete the journey within their own time and space. During the period of their return voyage they were more relaxed and trained themselves in the new ways they had learnt from the Octans.

On the day of arrival to their world, Caefon, they viewed their hot dying planet on the main screen. Instead of large blue and green patches as on Orban, most of it was brown. Even so, despite the larger areas of brown with violent weather patterns, there were small patches of green in remote places inaccessible to most humans. Those were areas to which many species had migrated for mutual survival. Seno and Micol realized the wonders of Mother Nature in trying to save her children during such times of extreme crises and took note of those areas.

Most of the equatorial regions of the planet was void of life, except for the numerous skeletons bleaching in the desert's sands. Many had migrated to the more northern latitudes decades before, thinking those areas more suited to long term survival.

Throughout those desert regions the scavenging vultures and giant bats were many and competed as aggressively as did the remaining humans in the north for their sparsely populated territories.

When they moved the viewer towards their Sun, they could observe four gigantic Tetrions or Maulers. Like super-giant spiders they continued weaving a gigantic web several thousand miles across in space between the world and its parent star. The ginormous mesh would hold its position in space while orbiting the star to maintain its semi-eclipsing position towards their world Caefon. When completed the reflective mesh would follow its programmed orbit, while reducing solar radiation towards that world by about 30 percent for many years to come. Those changes would be maintained until the mesh dissolved away naturally from the bombardment of solar radiation and energetic particle flux that were constantly emitted from the star.

The task ahead was truly enormous. Seno and the others didn't know where to begin so Siit realized the situation and decided to stir them into action.

'The main satellite station must be visited in order to initiate the process of planetary convergence. Hopefully, that one will trigger the other thirteen into a wake-up scenario. Then the robots and operators can be revived to initiate the process. The stations contain large amounts of frozen embryos and other DNA materials necessary for the completion of this process. However, to enter the main station we require the key!' Siit advised.

'The key?' Seno inquired.

'Yes! For security reasons... that will be the only way to initiate the process.'

'But, who will possess such an important key?' Seno replied. He looked quite worried and harboured a disappointing frown.

'Uncle Seno... it is you! You must be the chosen one. You will have the codes. It could have been written into your mind by the Oracle during your last meeting. Therefore, you must be the key for initiating the process of planetary conversion,' Sefran said and he was utterly surprised by that knowledge. Micol and Sefran had been given all kinds of information by the clever Octans. Therefore Seno always heeded their advice.

'Are you sure? Of all the things I know and can recollect, that key is not one of them... other than the ones I use for doors,' he replied, and they giggled.

'It is not a physical key that can be stolen from you. That particular one can only be used by your subconscious mind when you are at the point of arrival, and not before,' an astute Micol replied.

'In that case we must visit the station together and locate the point of entry for the key,' Seno advised, but both children quickly shied away. Visiting an ancient space station was not on their list of favourite games and hobbies.

'It's good that you have found the location of the key. However, it's in a place where no one can go, except of course, you and Sentral. If you are unable to find it by yourself, I'm sure she will enjoy sifting through your mind to locate it for you. Don't worry, the process is quite painless and not in the least dangerous,' Siit said and they became seriously worried for Seno.

'Who is this demon that takes the souls of men and women,' Seno exclaimed naively. He knew the incredible technologies of Octans and Shadites, and was suddenly worried for more meddling in his mind.

'I can assure you she is no demon. After all, she saved your people once before and have taken you back to your home world in one piece,' Siit said in jest.

'He means the ship... that must be her name. Now we know how to call her!' Micol interrupted.

'You must have always known, Micol. After all, you have all her specifications and codes in your head. While Sefran has all her stellar maps and navigation controls. However, there was no need to use them, until now,' Siit replied. The children were happy again and soon disappeared in the direction of the upper deck, towards the control room where two chairs and helmets were available for them to use. That method was more personal than interfacing through implants.

'Don't worry about the children. I shall accompany you to the station, myself. Your environmental suit has already been synthesized for a close fit. However, we must be careful during this delicate operation. Security sentinels could be waiting for us to make a false move and can react in many violent ways. Therefore you must follow your most innermost thoughts and see where they lead,' Shadite Siit further advised.

They had been away from their world for just three weeks. During that time their Safa and Medoin tribes on the hill had been under constant siege from their enemies in the plains. All the tribes in the plains had come together and the situation had escalated to all out war. Everyone that could fight were involved. During that time their tribes were unable to scavenge or hunt for food. Neither could they barter with the friendlier tribes. Once word had got around that they were betrayers, their names suddenly became taboo. Everyone was required to hunt them down until every member was obliterated.

Out of curiosity Stefan pointed the ship's telescopic array towards that part of their world and she became concerned for their safety.

'Father, our people on the hill are in serious trouble. Everyone are up in arms against them!' Then he brought his warriors together.

'I thought it was going to happen eventually, but not so soon. Our people are under constant siege by all the enemy tribes. During this time they must be starving. Therefore we should visit them immediately to assist, if it means postponing our other important plans for a day or so.

'This must be settled by our ways and by our existing laws that are the same for all. I want no advanced technologies involved, other than the few defensive weapons located on the walls... placed there by Seno and our own warriors to warn them off and defend our territories,' Melor said. He was insistent in his attitude and did not wish to further escalate the problem.

'Father, why don't we evacuate our tribes to the continent I showed you earlier, where green belts exist within the high mountains. We can use those unpopulated areas to build our first city and establish ourselves well away from these tribal problems. We can take everyone with us and build temporary shelters close by the hills near the desert. Building materials can be recovered from the ruins of the ancient city close by,' Micol said.

'You know... your mother, Veruna, and I have always wanted children of our own, and we can still have them, but of all the sons a leader may have, you will always be the one chosen to lead. Therefore I shall pass those decisions over to you. Do as you see fit my loyal son, and ask if you should ever need my advise,' Melor said and calmly walked away.

Micol soon communicated to Seno and the others through his

brain implants. Telepathic thought via brain implants took some time in getting trained and they had not gotten that far in their knowledge of such technologies. That form of communication could take place anywhere on board ship, but had an external range of about 200 metres without the usual boosters and networks.

'Uncle Seno, I'm afraid we shall have to visit the Space Station on another day. Our tribes are in grave danger from those on the plains. Therefore we are to evacuate them with all their belongings, immediately.'

'Oh my god! What's happening to my brain. Now I hear voices in my head,' Seno complained.

'Uncle Seno, don't be silly. I am using the implants to communicate to you. I shall teach you how to respond in due course,' Micol said and disconnected.

Micol realized that violence could not be used, but knew the effects the monstrous ship would have if it suddenly appeared over the area. Therefore he planned that operation well, with the aid of the ship.

Suddenly the giant black monster of a ship appeared overhead. Everyone in the vicinity of the fortified hill scrambled for cover as quickly as they could. The opposing enemy troupes scattered in every direction, leaving behind their heavier weapons and ramparts.

They had seen the powers of the devil's ship before. That was when it levelled the mountains to destroy their enemy including Melor and his troops; never to be seen again or so they thought.

In a flash, Melor, Seno and a few of his troupes appeared near the citadel and began to shout.

'My people, where are you! Where is my brother, Hale? I give you all 10 seconds more to show yourselves, then the ship will blast this village to smithereens!' he yelled. Hale was soon out with the remainder of his people.

'I thought you were dead, my brother!' he cried out and they embraced.

'I am not that easy to kill, Brother!' He glanced at the mighty black ship that silently hovered above them. It remained in that position as if anchored to that spot in the sky. It cast a deep foreboding shadow above the area that instilled fear even in the minds of the local rodents.

'Get your things together. We are leaving this place permanently. Everyone will be moving out of this area right now. We found a better place many thousands of miles away from this continent. We shall build a great city and rear our families there. So get all your belongings together now and be ready to leave. We shall take the people today and return for their other possessions later!' Melor ordered.

'You heard our leader. Pack some of your important belongings and get ready to leave. Our scavenging vessels can remain docked for now. I don't think our enemies will ever return to these gates again. Not while we have this hell's monster looking over us,' Hale said.

While on board they were healed and nourished. They found an ancient city close to the area they chose. From that place they recovered all the building materials necessary and began to construct their temporary shelters. Since no humans existed on that continent, they had no problems using the lands and could concentrate on their important tasks ahead.

They soon established farming in the areas of the hills. That part of the valley was very fertile and rainfall almost free of acidic content. It was probably because the warm air and rising air currents initiated the process locally, causing a type of micro climate in that area.

Once the people were settled Seno decided it was time to begin the process of planetary conversion.

CHAPTER 11

The system awakens

Except for the heavy breathing of brave Seno in his synthesized spacesuit, the main space station was as still and peaceful as the grave. He felt awkward in the bloated suit and was unprepared for that type of operation. It was one for which he had not been trained, prepared or briefed, with several possible worst case scenarios. None of which appeared beneficial to both his short and long term health. Nevertheless he found a little courage in the company of Siit and hoped Sefran was right about the key that would suddenly pop out of his mind at the appropriate time. Even so, however hard he tried to locate that mind key nothing happened.

He bravely strode across the bleak metallic platform while Siit followed from a safe distance. To add even more suspense to the mix, certain objects cast deep shadows. While at other times he was bathed in pure stellar radiation that was deadly to any living organism without protection. He just prayed his cumbersome suit had been designed to absorb those invisible rays.

Suddenly he came upon a large red lever and couldn't resist the temptation to pull it down with both hands. Close by was an inscription in ancient hieroglyphs. It read, 'Main Power Control'.

He found the going difficult in low gravity with magnetic boots. Since the Octans' ship was not very familiar with the operation of the human form, his suit's specification was less than perfect, being fabricated for a task that was intended to be a simple one-off job.

To further add to his stresses, large screens began to expand outward from the sides of the great station amidst a symphony of vibrations and sparkles. He nearly tripped over himself when a large parabolic dish surfaced from the centre of the platform to transmit its ancient message. Within seconds the darkest corners of the station were artificially lit by its own secondary power generators.

'This is only the first step. We must follow the arrows until we arrive at the special panel. Only then are we able to initiate the process,' Siit advised through their implants and Seno was even more nervous. He realized if he followed an incorrect path he might initiate the station's own defences. In all probability it would react vehemently against them and might even shut itself down and go to sleep for another two hundred years or so. Then it would probably reset its codes to different values. All those ideas passed through Seno's mind.

They soon came upon a large door. Close by was a thick pillar about one metre tall. At the very top of the pillar were a bluish panel with an array of buttons. Each engraved with the strange hieroglyphs of the Ancients. He went towards the panel and appeared hypnotised by its rays. He began entering several codes on the pad. Suddenly the panel's colours turned to green.

A large door lifted and gasses were expelled. They entered a cylindrical area with other panels. There were three such areas of air-locks. This time the codes were the same. When they left the final air-lock they entered into the innermost parts of the massive station.

Both went for a stroll and could observe thousands of containers, each holding thousands of vials with frozen samples. There were just three incubation chambers with their near frozen human occupants. They were heavily drugged and would require certain antidotes and rejuvenators to take them out of their near 200 years sleep. That would be done automatically by their equipment. The robots were in another area, all linked to an umbilical cord for power. Once awakened, their batteries would be charged by primary power.

'We have done our job here. We must leave this place and return to the ship. Soon the fusion generators will power up and the programmed sequence will be initiated. When that happens we should be well away from this place,' Siit said and Seno agreed. Nevertheless Seno's curiosity had been aroused. He wanted to learn more about the Ancient's technologies.

Melor and his chosen group remained on board ship to observe the great spectacle and were please when Seno and Siit returned with success written across their faces.

They tuned their implants with the ship's computer to acquire a closer look at the processes involved. From there they could observe all the intricate changes on the station below while at a safe distance.

When they glanced in the direction of their Sun, the great Maulers had completed their weaving and moved on, leaving behind four orbiting terminals. Those had been placed in synchronous orbit and acted as gravitation anchors for the weblike mesh. The great mesh, many thousands of miles across deep space, glowed in many colours like a most spectacular prismatic rainbow in space, as if signalling the birth of a new world. It would reduce solar radiation by about 30 percent, initially.

The powerful fusion generators were brought on line throughout all the other thirteen stations. Large containers were ejected only to explode at fixed distances from each other within the planet's atmosphere. The display and pyrotechnics were truly spectacular as the whole atmosphere of the world began to change from blood red to a beautiful blue.

Another set of large containers were fired from the stations. They were filled with stabilizing ozone molecules. Those exploded at predetermined positions above the world. They would absorb all harmful solar radiation for years to come, until the planet was able to supply her own ozone.

Finally, large containers of balloons were ejected. Those would slowly fall until driven by the trade winds. They would disperse certain strains of engineered bacteria in the lower atmosphere to initiate more frequent and heavier rainfall and prevent acid rain. They would also enter into the surface waters and purify them. This last part of the process would continue for several decades, until the bacteria had remove all contaminants which was their natural food. Then they in turn would die from lack of nutrients.

'Seno's eyes were filled with tears while King Melor embraced Veruna and the two children. It was the saddest and perhaps happiest moments of their lives. They were sad that their past was gone for good. The next time they landed on Caefon they would be visiting a brand new world. Although its landmarks would be the same, its skies and weather patterns would be completely different, as it was in the days of the Ancients.

They were happy because they could now build cities and grow crops under a milder climate. Soon, even the deserts would change to forests as the patches of green began to spread and take control under the guiding hands of Mother Nature. Yet, their task had only just begun. They had to replace all those extinct animals and plants. Even with the assistance of the revived Ancients that task was going to be truly enormous and take many decades to complete.

'Father, I am so happy for us and our people. We must create a great city and place a monument at its very centre to commemorate this day. That most spectacular monument can also be used as a temple for worshipping our glorious lord,' Micol said.

'It's all in your most capable hands, my son. Do what you think is right,' Melor said and Veruna smiled. Realizing she and Melor could never compete with the young and their incredible ideas for change.

Soon after, the three revived ancient scientists went to work in the large laboratory onboard the main station. Since they were the chosen ones with intricate knowledge of the organisms and genetic materials involved, they had a precise knowledge of the processes to be initiated for the re-establishment of such life on the world below.

Those three had made a great sacrifice when they left their families and friends behind two hundred years ago. Now they had to start all over on a near desolate world and bring it back to life.

Since the station was completely isolated from planetary contaminants, it was the right place for such intricate operations. During that time they remained isolated from all other human contact, except for the occasional visits by Sefran and her chosen few to collect samples. As the samples were made ready, they were passed on to Sefran and her group for re-introduction into local habitats.

Micol had decided to begin the building of his great city in the desert plains. It was called Cantor, meaning "A New Beginning". Its centre being about five miles from the nearest sea. At its very centre was placed the great monument. From that spot four main avenues radiated outwards in the direction of the four main planetary axes, North, South, East and West. From space they represented a great cross with the monument at their very centre.

The great monument Micol decided on was none other than the ancient building in Nim that housed the Oracle. It was taken apart and assembled in Cantor several thousand kilometres away. During that great feat many ships were used. It took their best workmen over a year to dismantle the structure, including the Oracle itself and transfer the separate parts to its new location. Then it was re-assembled in the centre of their great city. Strangely enough, since that time the Oracle never came to life again. It was as if Mohria had completed her scheduled tasks and had shut down. That most important survival program she had achieved well for her chosen people. Nevertheless Mohria would always be there in silence, listening to their prayers in the holy place of worship. She would remind their future generations of the sacrifices made by so many to save a dying world.

On the top of their holy monument was the golden sword or was it a crucifix. Soon, everyone of the Safa and Medoin tribes would wear a crucifix about their necks in memory of the sacrifices made for their survival. The incredible planning of the Ancients had spanned a period of almost two hundred years. Those clever elders realized too little could be done during the short time available to save their world and had postponed their great handiwork for when the time was right and the whole world was ready for that type of medicine.

CHAPTER 12

New world, new life
(In the final analysis)

Melor had tried on several occasions to bring the tribes together, but generations of violence had become ingrained in their nature. Despite everything that could be done to show them a better way to coexist, the fighting between the tribes continued and escalated. Once locked in the spiral of vendettas, there was too much hatred and vengeance-seeking among them for any reconciliation on their part. Within 50 years most of the larger tribes had decimated each other to such an extent that their remnants became vagrant wanderers. Without proper medical assistance and lack of nutrients, those in turn died soon after.

During that period of irreversible change the more advanced Safa and Medoin tribes continued to build their society on the distant continent of Akadia; far away from the human turmoil in Nimia and elsewhere.

Their new city of Cantor was beautifully arranged on the principles of the Octans and did not contain any capitalizing industries. All such polluting industries were initially placed on the 13 large space stations that were originally used for planetary conversion. Their main plans however, were to site such industries on uninhabited planets and moons, which they would do at the appropriate time.

Under their new leader, Micol, with the guidance of Siit, the Shadite, the young were well trained in the arts and sciences. Everything in their society were shared almost equally, with strong incentives for those that gave more of themselves to society. They had modelled almost every aspects of their communities along the principles of the Octan's.

Everything from atmospheric constituents to pollution was closely monitored and swiftly repaired with their new brand of

Class 3 technologies. During that phase many citadels were built at key positions throughout the planet's jungles. Their purpose being to observe and assist wild life in those areas.

The continent of Feltwol was the only part of their world that was reserved for farming and packaging of food products for human consumption. That way, the human population was restricted from advancing towards the major rain forests.

They soon realized that their world was equally owned by all its diverse species, who also had legal rights by virtue of their existence, so they limited human encroachment only within a few chosen areas. However, people were free to visit those areas at their own risks.

Natural paper was originally process from trees and used for books and poetry. They soon realized however that such materials destroyed the natural forests and important habitats. That process was soon discontinued in favour of renewable plants that could be specially grown on Feltwol for that purpose. Soon, even that method was discontinued when new synthetic materials were discovered for that purpose.

The new Ancients, with their mainly sea blue eyes and light complexion followed the footsteps of their great writer and poet Siend Seno of Mond. Because of King Micol, Seno's name had become great among their society. Despite their advanced culture, with its many forms of technologies, including super intelligent computers; they found poetry, song and writing to be their main hobbies. Those and other forms of art were soon accepted and ingrained in their culture.

The orbiting stations had also been updated to assist in planetary repair, but they had built many powerful ground stations for carbon dioxide extraction and ozone generation. Those were only used initially during the period of planetary recovery. Once the rain forests had expanded throughout most of the world, natures own natural repairing cycles had taken over all such controls.

With the assistant of the three young Ancients that were revived on the space station, they were able to bring their world back from the brink in just 100 years. During that time most of Caefon became violet and green again, with the exception of the Craile Desert towards the north west of their city of Cantor.

At that time the submerged cities slowly became unsubmerged, but were soon overgrown with vine and weed. They became natural habitats for all kinds of wild life. The Cantonians seldom ventured into those places and use them as monumental reminders to what could happen when greed and self-indulgence predominates any human society.

It so happened that in a relatively short time their world had become as pleasant as the Octans own world of Orban. At that time Mother Nature had spread her wings to fill in almost every blind spot. It was then that a multitude of new species abounded and diversified in every possible colour, shape and size. With mankind removed from most of the planet, life had time to spout and explode, and naturally expanded to fill every conceivable nook and cranny.

KING MELOR & VERUNA

Melor had observed the abilities and handiwork of Micol, his adopted son, and realized his people were in safe hands with Micol at the helm. During one of their accession ceremonies Micol was given Melor's special sword with the jewelled scabbard. He was then made Chief Lord and Chancellor, and became their leader. Micol never accepted the title of king. After that time Melor resigned himself to more religious and diplomatic matters.

Their Grand Governing Council was formed soon after. It had democratic powers to pass laws and procure judgement.

Melor continued aiding his enemies while trying his utmost to bring those remnant tribes together for the common good. However he failed on every attempt. They had become too ingrained in violence. Many carried extreme prejudice and hatred in their hearts for others not of their tribes.

It was during one of those meetings that he was betrayed and killed. It was his brother Hale who broke the bad news to Micol.

He quickly summoned his best warriors together and hurried to the place where his father's body lay. For that urgent task the great ship was utilized. However nothing could be done to revive Melor.

'What have these wicked people done to my dear father! They have butcher such an innocent man, who only tried to bring them out of their savagery!' Micol bawled loudly and couldn't stop the tears from flowing or his frantic and uncontrollable movements before his father's body.

'I will never forgive them for their cruelty to us and my father. As the day is long, they shall pay for this crime!'

Sefran placed Melor's still head on her lap with the neck wound quite visible and showing where his throat was slit. She embraced and lifted it up several times, as if to summon a miracle to bring him back to life.

'My dear father, I've always loved you and always will!' she said, with tears flowing uncontrollably.

Veruna was late on arrival, but ran to Melor's body when she observed the distraught bewilderment of Sefran and Micol.

Seno went forward to console them, but found even he could not hold back the welling torment within his brain and he also bursted out in sorrowful tears.

'I don't quite know what I shall do now, without my best and honoured friend always there to assist and listen to my bellyaching,' he said and embraced the women. Then he lifted his hand to signal the warriors to prepare Melor's body for the trip home. Micol was in no fit state for any planning at that time.

Once Micol realized a Goel was responsible for his father's death, which was most likely revenge for Salmon's death, that tribe was marked for obliteration. Although he could have destroyed them with a powerful plasma weapon that could easily be used to vaporize a complete city, he respected his fathers wishes and decided not to use his advanced weapons against them. He also realized they had all suffered long enough. It was not their fault for the savage attitude imposed upon them by the recent harsh history of their dying world. Anyway, during the following months the cannibalistic Goel were one of the first tribes to disappear from the planes. They were wiped out by a stronger tribe.

Veruna mourned Melor's death. Living was never the same for her again. At that time the changes in society were too extreme for her generation and others from the old world to absorb. Only the young had the knowledge and impetus to absorb the new society with its more modern brand of technologies. After Melor's death she never remarried. Most of her remaining life was spent with her children and grandchildren.

Despite those troubles she remained a model for others to follow. Most of all, she became a good councillor and advisor to others.

During one of their national ceremonies Melor's body was subsequently placed within one of the vaults in their great monument. Micol mourned his death for weeks after, but did not carry vengeance in his heart. Nevertheless he followed in his father's footsteps and tried to assist the few remaining starving tribes.

SIEND SENO of MOND

Seno wrote his holy bible of many volumes, which included some of the older volumes that were handed down by the Ancients. His curiosity in science waned however, but he continued his main interests as writer, poet and counsellor. As his world changed for the better, he like many others of his generation felt misplaced. Further, many had become infertile and realized the new world order was not for them. They had been contaminated by their brutal past and that particular disease was partly genetic. He always advised Micol and Sefran on matters of the heart. He was always uncle to them and remained that way with their children. During his final years he concentrated on writing books containing the history of his world from the time of Global Warming and the dispersion of humanity. Those records he named, "Chronicles of a dying world" and "Salvation".

Seno lived for another 600 years and left no children behind to take his place. The young considered Seno their greatest mentor and profit. They revered the very ground on which he walked and founded their new religion in his name. It was also called Seno and they were called Senots..

He was the last of his line of ancient priests until his new type was founded by the new societies. Although the Senots were a type of priesthood they soon became the spiritual caretakers of their world.

MICOL, THE GREAT

At the age of 18, Micol married a local girl of his own age and began to establish their family. She was a rear born from the Safa tribe and bore him many children. Since he was born to a tribe on the plains, he was never sure of his real tribal roots. Because of that reason he tended to consider himself in more planetary terms. Nevertheless he accepted the Safa and Medoin tribes as his own with no bias one way or the other.

He was a brilliant leader and genius, and contrary to his father, Melor, soon realized it was pointless bringing the old tribes together. Such a union could create serious problems for his own people, with little or no rewards in return for either. He also realized the time had come for their extinction and could not stand in the way of Mother Nature and her most unforgiving angels of death.

Anyway, he had always hated them for what they had done to Melor, Sefran and himself and would never forgive them for those painful years in the wilderness, when he was cast out because of his difference as a child. All those races had become infertile and were quickly fading from view. It was as if the world no longer wanted them around. However most of their problems were due to certain bacterial strains that had contaminated everything in their part of the planet. That problem of infertility tended to affect the men more than the women. Even so, such environments were not suitable for rearing children and also inhibited the women.

Micol continued to advance the sciences, until they were able to build their own space ships and visit distant worlds for trade. Their technologies were even more advanced than their ancient ancestors of the previous epoch that had preceded them.

They soon began trade with others in their part of the galaxy. On several occasions they visited Orban, the Octans home world, to trade and pay homage to their god at the monument they had built there.

Micol lived for over 1200 years. It was said that his god, Grand Lord Gerron took him away to his own heaven. The place they called Gohenna or Goh. From there he could be born again and brought back into corporeal existence to further assist his people when the time was right.

SEFRAN

Sefran married one of the Ancient's young men that had been revived on the main space station. His name was Landus. He was the main contributor to the proliferation of new life on Caefon.

She was the one who proposed the use of Citadels for housing her special caretakers and animal doctors. They were more like holy men that were educated in the use of medicine and healing. They were all Senots and followed in the footsteps of Seno. They were also used as guides and trackers through the jungles. Their main purpose however was in caring for the local wild life. Those Senots respected all life. It is said that no one could truly love life and the Cosmos like a Senot.

Strangely enough, although Micol had always loved Sefran, they had always considered each more like brother and sister.

She also bore many children and was treated like a royal princess by her people.

SHADITE SIIT and THE BLACK SHIP

Siit and the Octans ship assisted Micol and his people during the first hundred years of planetary conversion. One day, Siit, the

Shadite, brought them together to say his goodbyes. His task on Caefon was finally at an end. Anyway, the great black ship was due for a needed overhaul and refit after 100 years of wear and tear, despite its self-repairing technologies.

THE NEW ANCIENTS

Despite their genetic mix, they also contained the genes of the previous ancients and local tribes. Although both of their world's previous occupants were now virtually extinct, the young, despite their sea blue eyes and light complexion, carried all the genes of their previous races. Therefore nothing was lost.

Micol and Sefran's children intermarried to form the new Ancients. Within 2000 years they had multiplied to several billion and spread throughout their world and several local stellar systems.

They soon became one of the most powerful empires in Andromeda. But sadly, their success was not to last. Their advanced sciences led them on the wrong path to create an almost indestructible monster that now threatens the whole universe. One that would eventually destroy all major life within the Andromedan galaxy and then their home world, Caefon.

That new human society continued unabated for almost 2000 years.
(From 3005 BCE to 1172 BCE...Earth time)

UNTIL NEAR EXTINCTION

The rapacious and unrelenting nano-bot Javols are presently on their way to our own galaxy, Osmaron and will eventually destroy all life within those regions, including our own humanity on Earth, unless we stop their progress.

Part II

The Javols' creation

CHAPTER 13

Another new world

(2000 years had passed since Seno visited the station to initiate repairs to the dying world of Caefon.)

Ancients... *The real Ancients were the direct descendants of Micol and Sefran. Unlike their previous ancestors and warring tribes, they were very tall and had a pinkish complexion with sea blue eyes. They were known as the true Ancients by succeeding generations.*

Planet Silo... *That new world was almost half the size of planet Caefon and formed part of the Tregulan System within the Galaxy of Andromeda . It lay within. sector fifteen of the Andromedan Precinct Seven as listed by those Ancients. Later to be occupied by the bird people or Colmi and subsequently renamed Coln.*

Earth time... *1172 BCE*

ON PLANET SILO

Ranul stood on the high balcony while gazing in silence at the distant city of Chaum. Its multi-storey blocks reaching dauntlessly into the evening sky. A spectre of charcoal grey impeding the orange-red from yet another serenely beautiful sunset. On that part of the Heaver mountains he could get a panoramic view for many miles around. That view extended flawlessly in every direction. He couldn't stop admiring the beautiful sights he beheld.

Ranul remembered his first visit to Silo, as if a thousand years ago. At that time its population of settlers were just two point five million and rising steeply, limited only by imported food supplies and immigration control. Presently it was over eleven million, excluding its numerous tourists, and that population was still rising beyond normal growth.

The slow process of land reclamation from the deserts and seas of that small exo-planet had only recently begun, while its domed cities gradually expanded to cope with those new pressures. Its raw surface was not yet suitable for human habitation. They found its thin atmosphere just bearable for short periods without an oxygen mask.

In earlier times the mining planet was much more inhospitable to outsiders. At that time Chaum was a mere pressurize environmental dome with a population of fifty thousand. Now and with all its internal buildings, it had become a most prominent city, servicing the largest of space ports in the Tregulan System. With all its massive cargo docks, industrial, scientific and military bases.

To all intents and purpose the planet Silo was sterile, but for a few primitive strains of protozoa type life. Those had multiplied in previous years to enhance the original oxygen levels by another 6 percent. Despite those environmental factors, that most beautiful and dormant world was almost dead until mankind arrived with his many advanced technologies. Those they would use to reform uninhabited but habitable worlds. So that even Silo would one day be like planet Caefon, with its own beautiful parks, vineyards, fruit orchards and wild life.

It had taken close to a 100 years for the oxygen levels to reach its present 16 percent. A little below normality for their type of Andromedan humans, but just enough to maintain plant life in a consistent and sustainable manner. Further increases would be forthcoming with the introduction of special crops, until a natural balance was reached. The temperature range being made moderate by a thicker carbon dioxide layer in the upper strata of its atmosphere. Terra-forming was always at its best on such world-types that didn't need too much technology to change them into habitable ones and Ranul was a genius in such creative methods.

'How fortunate for me, being given control of the largest project on Silo. A terra-forming project that would have taken several normal lifetimes to completion. I, Ranul, was the one lucky enough to be left at the tail-end of its completion. Now and finally, we have a world that can function normally for most living organisms and without the use of environmental suits or oxygen masks'.

Ranul pondered those thoughts of success with fervour but in silence as he watched the terminator progress through yet another momentous and colourful sunset.

Silo's present climate was controlled by several orbiting magnetron satellites, filter-separators, pacifiers and ion generators. They were strategically placed throughout the planet for optimum results. Ranul had also added several strains of a special type of bio-engineered algae to her oceans. They would form the basis of all life within the food chain. Then he would introduce a variety of marine life, to be added much later. That particular tiny organism was good at producing oxygen in vast quantities that would soon optimize planetary levels.

Most of Silo's food and raw materials, with the exception of certain minerals were still imported from other planets within the empire. Caefon supplied 70 percent of her foodstuffs. The other 30 percent were grown locally within the smaller agricultural domes at much higher cost.

Since earlier times Silo had been a major mining colony, for gold, platinum, copper, iron and rear-earths, which had made her one of the wealthiest worlds in the federation.

As Ranul viewed the magical sunset, he reflected on family and friends that he had left behind on his home world, Caefon.

YEARS BEFORE ON PLANET CAEFON

Now and at long last they had begun the program of reclamation on planet Silo and wanted someone to initiate the propagation of natural, self-sustaining indigenous agriculture on its still intolerant surface areas. Because of its ever increasing populations biological farming was in great demand, so the Ministry needed a senior for that unique project. Someone with a desire for adventure and one who didn't mind the rougher edges of Silo.

'Professor Ranul, please be seated,' Director Hermyon snapped, with an air of genuine satisfaction in her manner and voice.

'Your report makes exciting reading. Two postings on Volva III, three on Solman and two on Trint. All within a period of twenty years and with an 80 percent success rate. This successful trend makes you one of our best operatives in the field and your advice has always brought reward.'

'Thanks, Mam!'

'How would you consider controlling your own project for a change? Answerable only to me, with ministerial promotion after five years. If you achieve our targets, of course!'

'I would jump to it, Mam!'

'I hope you are not too disappointed, but it's on Silo. You will be away from Caefon for many years, with just the occasional biannual visits. However, you will be given a free diplomatic pass.' He gazed at his senior somewhat disappointingly.

'I trust you will give me time to consider and discuss this matter with my wife and children?' Suddenly his cavalier attitude had changed as his interest waned.

'Will two weeks be enough?' she inquired, firmly.

'Yes, Director. That should be sufficient.'

When he mentioned his intentions to his wife Merian that evening she was furious.

'I thought your wandering days were over!' she bellowed at him with anger and despair.

'After all the heated discussions we had... You promised me you would remain here with me and the children, and it's not even on Caefon. Despite everything we decided, you intend to wander off to yet another barren world on yet another of your lengthy projects for God knows how long!'

'Sorry! Sorry! Sorry! But it's my chance of a lifetime. If I don't take it now, I might never see another!' he shouted back.

'What am I to do in the mean time? Wait for your occasional

communication and annual visits?'

'I'm sure we can work something out!'

'Work things out! Thank goodness the children are now inde-pendents, so that leaves just me, our home and my work!' She was in tears but he couldn't console her, knowing his mind was already made up.

He was an adventurer by nature and nine months within a sterilized ministerial office on Caefon, despite its pleasant surroundings, was too much for any seasoned adventurer to suffer. He needed a challenge and that was not possible on beautiful Caefon, where everything was perfect and tailor-made for human consumption.

Ranul had spent most of his life since graduation with the Ministry of Agriculture and assisted on many projects, both local and distant. Finally he had been offered this incredible opportunity to run his own project. It had always been his lifelong ambition to transform a completely barren world into a beautiful green and violet paradise. An opportunity to create his own brand of clean agriculture from scratch using the latest technologies, with little restraint on funding, so how could he give up this opportunity of a lifetime.

'Now I can truly build something with my own hands from the raw dust of an uncontaminated world. No more the use of unnatural and poisonous fertilizers. No more the use of genetically assisted strains. Badly considered methods and actions bred bad farming habits, with the resultant negative after-effects.' He pondered a few disasters of past, when he had to help clean up the mess. Despite extensive mopping up they still had dire effects on life within the environment.

'Theories that had worked perfectly well in the past for thou-sands seldom benefited millions in like manner. Like some bio-fertilizers for instance, that had polluted the rivers and water tables for generations. All such ill considered short-term actions always left a mess behind and the fallout was usually extensive and long-term.' He muttered those words to himself, having observed such disasters in the past with many of his capitalist peers wanting quick results. He had enough of those problems during his troubleshooting years for the Empire. Anyway, he was Senot and could never break the code of his beliefs, life was much too important for that.

His mind was made up, so after explaining the situation to his married children and their families, he contacted the director and told her he had accepted the post.

PLANET SILO AT PRESENT TIME

'Darling, dreaming again?' Sura asked sympathetically, while placing both her hands around his waist and squeezing him gently from behind. She was Safa from one of the oldest and most respected mining families on Silo. She had been his personal secretary since his arrival and now his concubine.

'This place can be truly beautiful, and I guarantee, will become a lot more natural with some mauve and green vegetation along the local valleys.' Both admired the beautiful prismatic sunset in silence, as the blue star dipped behind the horizon.

'Yes. I can imagine it,' she replied.

'I don't know what I would have done without you, my dearest.'

'And your wife? What would she say if she could see us here together like this?'

'How should I know? I have been away for over two long years. That last time we had an almighty burst-up, but thank God the kids understood. Anyway, she has become a very responsible politician these days and is quite absorbed by her political responsibilities.'

'But you have made up since?'

'Yes, we have! Being a senior councillor, she is always involved with some scientific project or another. When she is not in the Pericedium she is lecturing to students at some ancient university on Caefon's history. Anyway, I do write the occasional letter and send her the rear pieces to add to our collection of artifacts.'

'You still care a lot for her? I can see it!'

'My dearest, it's you I really love and you know I am not due to return to Caefon for another year. When I do, you are welcomed to join me. But I can't divorce my wife. Not yet, anyway. It would affect her too much,' he said, somewhat disappointingly.

Ranul turned his attention to Vista Dome just beyond the local valley. The multiple orange reflections of the distant horizon lighting it up like an incandescent fireball. It was one of the largest habitable domes on Silo, with a population in excess of fifty thousand. Vista contained some of the best hotels for out-worlders. While he watched, the solar reflections slowly died away until internal lights automatically switched on. It was once again ablaze but this time with bluish light that transformed it into a most beautiful diamond. He knew that its night life was just beginning to stir and wondered whether some of his old friends would be partaking in those festivities that evening.

Ranul's department and project was sited in the Southern Agricultural District and built around three of the largest agricultural environmental domes. Within their sealed environments almost any range of climatic conditions could be simulated.

They were situated a few kilometres south of Vista Dome, further along the valley's floor and just about a mile from the Sea of Jem and its desalination plants.

There were several canals of water leading from the desalination plants to Vista that bypassed the newly prepared fields for irrigation. Later for human consumption after further filtration and purification. A similar method was used for supplying water to Chaum city and its surroundings towards the west.

The processed human and animal waste would be used for topsoil while the first hardy Acarria seedlings planted for the purpose of recycling. Those, it was hoped, would transform the sand by adding a layer of thick topsoil to encourage the recently introduced earthworms to do their mulching jobs more efficiently.

At current planetary oxygen levels, the time was ripe for the growing of its first natural exposed food crops, so the necessary preparations had begun.

Soon that area was filled with the correct balance of nutrients for sustainable plant growth. Then it was finally made ready for planting the first arable crops.

With a population of just under twelve million there was always a surplus of natural fertilizer. More when the few Malaks and Pedris were considered. They were the most recently introduced grazing animals that supplied most of the colonies' milk. However at present they were confined to the few controlled agricultural domes.

Ranul and his team had just sown the first experimental crops and were quite pleased with the results. The seedlings were thriving in what was considered summertime on Silo throughout its erratic weather changes. So Ranul was encouraged in his efforts.

All such unwanted variations were due to a faster spin of nineteen hours, which maintained a more pronounced Coriolis effect that fed storms in equatorial regions. There were also the many unnatural climatic aids that attempted to control an atmosphere still in its infancy, with a tendency to overshoot and overcorrect. Nevertheless, more stability had arrived with the introduction of solar reflecting satellites and powerful magnatrons. Those large machines tended to focus deadly solar radiation towards its weaker poles.

However, most experimental farms were still grown under movable transparent shelters that could be easily adjusted to varying weather conditions by computers. Thus eliminating most of the local unpredictable weather problems.

'Darling, a call for you,' Sura shouted. He ran to the Vidicom in lurid anticipation.

'Yes, Director. That will be fine. I am looking forward to his visit,' Ranul said and the communication terminated.

'It's my director, Dear. The call was from Caefon via the special H-wave link. We are to expect an urgent visit from a senior councillor. Have you heard of Councillor Hamil?'

'No!'

'Well, he is expected here in two days. I said he could stay with us for the duration. It's his first visit, you know. I hope you don't mind the extra work?' He was apologetic.

'His company can be a pleasant change for us both and I would like to know more about beautiful Caefon.'

'I think he is coming to do a little snooping around. He is to assess who deserves funding for the next financial year.'

'You should be ok, then!'

'Perhaps! But I don't think he will be too impressed with Andra and his Microid Robots, do you?' he jested, knowing she would retaliate fervently on her cousin's behalf.

'Why did you say that?' she inquired with astonishment.

'You know how I feel about small bugs, and more so, microid bugs made by man. It's so unnatural. They are so tiny, you cant even see them with the naked eye. What if they were used by some criminal mind to control us?'

'I know how you feel, but Andra is very conscientious and doing his best for the empire,' she replied.

'Since Lord Meron took away that prototype ship they have not been able to build another, have they?' he pointed out sarcastically.

'Don't think ill of Andra and his hard working colleagues. I have been told they are on the threshold of a new discovery, but he didn't want to tell me too much about it, despite his excitement. He became very quiet when I asked what it was about and abruptly changed the topic. Whatever little he said was because he thought I was just a trainee agri-farmer who was little concerned about robots the size of body cells. I am also one who take a very dim view of such things roaming about inside one's body while being remotely controlled by some half-witted operator,' she said.

'But progress must go on!' he replied, sarcastically.

'Yes, to our ultimate destruction!' she warned.

'I just hope he knows what he is doing,'

'I also dread the thought of what might happen if things went wrong and the operator lost control,' she said with utter disgust in her manner.

'They can't multiply on their own, Dear. After all, they are not like bacteria, with genetic coding. The worst that can result is a loss of their own natural protection barrier. When that happens they will simply dissolve away naturally or be consumed by our body's own natural defences.'

'Yes, but that depends on technology!'

'Anyway, those used by the medics have been around for decades and have been improved within that field for a specific and simple purpose. Namely, to enter our bodies, which is fully mapped, and complete a specific programmed task.'

'Even so, just thinking about those tiny metallic bugs make my blood crawl, so please change the topic and wish him success!' She continued busily laying the table for their evening meal.

CHAPTER 14

Andra's Microids

Andra Safarar was born on Silo within its largest city dome called Chaum and now in his early thirties. He was Sura's first cousin on their mother's side. Both grew up together and went to the same primary school within the old central dome. They were closest friends and of similar age.

The main city had been built around that dome, which remained a symbolic reminder of bygone times to its ever mobile mining inhabitants. Many of the recreation and educational facilities were supplied free to its population, so they grew up like normal people within that relatively free but enclosed environment.

At the age of seventeen Andra won a science scholarship and left for Caefon's famous Institute of Science and Technology. There he remained for ten years before returning to his home-world a changed and wiser man. While away he had lost both his parents in a mining accident. Presently his only remaining family was his dear cousin, Sura. She had also lost her family in a similar accident decades before and was also alone in the world, except for her living companion Ranul.

Presently professor Andra Safarar was chief science officer for project MIMMIC. That name was the acronym for Microid Induction and Motivation by Microwave and Intercellular Communications. He was a brilliant scientist in charge of all such projects on planet Silo. Being fully absorbed by work in his chosen branch of Nano-technology, he had no time for more personal relationships and led a simple bachelor existence.

Specialist Microids had existed in the medical field for several decades before. During that time many different types of active molecules had been synthesized with a tendency towards further miniaturization. During that period many had been used to repair brains and other internal organs. Presently they were being used to form flexible structures and containers because of their strange and varied attributes.

On one hand they could behave like a block of solid metal with the ability to change shape to virtually any form and on the other, become a shiny metallic liquid that could be absorbed or become impervious to any known substance. With such varied qualities and attributes they made the perfect semi-solid. However as yet no suitable communication media had been found to control a mass of billions at any given time and that limitation further hindered development.

It was one thing creating a small block of microids, but quite another making that block alter its shape and motion by a single remote instruction, from say, a stationery cube to a rolling sphere. The processing power and phase modulation required to control that number of microids were well beyond present day means of storage, translation, modulation and transmission.

Most of the few microids used by the medical profession were usually in dust form and in an appropriate medium for injecting into an artery or inhalation by the patient. The doctors were specially trained and numbers were seldom in excess of a few thousand. Nevertheless a block ten inches or so across required hundreds of billions of individual instructions, each minutely phased to the appropriate individual microid. Larger masses required proportionate measures to scale by volume. That task was an incredibly difficult one and pressure were in finding a solution to those particular problems.

The Director of Finance, Hamil, needed something substantial to take back with him to his committee. Then decisions would be made before any more resources were poured into the project in the year that followed. There was now serious financial consider-ations at every level of government. That situation resulted in cutbacks during a period of recession and the hammer fell indiscriminately.

Sura knew very little about that particular branch of science. The more she pleaded ignorance, the more he tried to explain the intricacies and peculiarities of the microscopic bugs to her. That was how she thought of them, with disdain and dread. During that time knowledge of new discoveries and inventions were restricted by law until released by subcommittee and tagged suitable for public knowledge. That process took several years and depended to a great extent on military usage.

'You look worried?' she probed, with curiosity, while sipping a sweet alcoholic drink. She enjoyed Taki. It had grown on her over the years and was now her favourite drink. Certain additives heightened her senses and the balanced nutrition tended to energize her. It was specially imported from Caefon and not the most common drink on Silo.

'Just a little,' Andra replied, with a despondent frown. He had a sip of something stronger. Sala was similar to Vodka, but well diluted with a neutral additive. There were several of such nutritional sweeteners and additives that were colour-dyed differently for identification. Caefonites tended to colour-code their food and drink for easy identification. That way many could appreciate the more subtler flavours and changes in the recipe by observation.

'What is it about?' she inquired.

'We have the financial committee breathing down our necks and I am worried that our latest development will not prove worthy enough. There are too many variables and unknowns. But if we are successful it could save our necks for another year or so.'

She thought of Hamil's visit but changed the topic.

'I heard a rumour regarding the authorities changing our planetary status from a free-tech zone to full-ecological. If it went through they could expel and ban all research, development, large-scale engineering and manufacture from our world, including your project.'

'Nonsense!' he stressed.

'I can't imagine all our industries being re-sited on moons like Zorus and Tabia, or gas giant Promas in the neighbouring systems. They are moons with little atmosphere, with very extreme conditions and many are less than half our gravity with almost no water, while Promas is too massive for any colonization.' she said.

'That should not be too great a problem. I've seen them terraform and convert hundreds of square kilometres within days. All they would do is seal off a suitable large area of the planet with a large sealed transparent dome. After the initial installation was completed by robots, the correct mix of gases would either be extracted or imported from a nearby uninhabited world. Then suitable bio-engineered micro organisms would be introduced to begin the process of oxygen and carbon dioxide creation and the ball is rolling. Most of the required gasses can be extracted from Promas and toured across space by massive robot ships.' He replied.

'Wow! Sounds incredible!'

'Once the blueprints are done the complete process should require a couple of years for the system to stabilize. But it wouldn't prevent the immediate mass transfer of industry from Silo once such a decision was made. But Silo is not at that stage yet. Not for another 50 years or so,' he said, proudly.

'But that depends on the success of outdoor farming, doesn't it? Which in turn depends on soil creation and such like,' she replied.

'I have been hearing those particular rumours since my return from Caefon. I can assure you they are completely unfounded, with not a single shred of truth. Those rumours are propagated by a few discontented settlers and extreme Senots that would like to stir the population against all forms of scientific development in favour of more tourism and terra-forming. Anyway, our projects are more than ninety-nine percent clean, and the population of Silo is far too small to warrant such drastic measures.'

'I hope you are right!' she said.

'Presently, the Empire has little choice in the matter, because such changes require much funding and we have now reached a period of minimum growth. Sort of catching up on our gains of previous years. Cutbacks are now quite prevalent. Despite those economical factors, our project is still considered a very important one that could lead us into another period of high growth.'

'You think?'

'Well, we have Chief Councillor Meron to argue our claims in Council. He is one of the most senior politicians. When we become successful our concept will revolutionize every aspect of industry and transport. The military also realises its potential and implications for the future. Many heads will role before they place the final seal on our project,' Andra said, affirmatively.

'I just hope you are correct for your own sake. Anyway, Ranul is quite determined and from current progress, will change most of the surface of this world into a paradise like Caefon. If that happened, wouldn't it be wonderful? I have always dreamt of visiting Caefon. Perhaps I wouldn't need if our world became as beautiful,' Sura replied, and glanced through the transparent dome at her home in the distant hills. That part of the restaurant was her favourite spot, where she could get a clearer view of the wild and rugged landscape all the way up to her and Ranul's home.

There it stood like a small castle perched on the very top of the Heaver mountain.

She took her turn to pay for lunch in their favourite restaurant within Vista Dome and parted company.

CHAPTER 15

Hamil's visit

Hamil arrived on Silo the following day and was met by Ranul at the space-port.

'I am very pleased to meet you, Director!' Ranul said.

'And you, also!' He greeted with a handshake, then helped with the cases.

'Please follow!'

'Your director told me about you and your enthusiasm for your work. I trust you don't mind this imposition, but I had to get this job finished quickly, and yours happens to be the best option.'

'No, Sir. We shall be delighted to accommodate you for the duration.'

Ranul assisted him and his belongings into the LPD hopper and their local flight took barely five minutes to Ranul's Heaver Mountain residential retreat.

'This is truly a beautiful world, despite its lower gravity and lack of green and violet. Yet, I find its untamed terrain has a type of poetic beauty of its own,' Hamil was overwhelmed by the undulating twist and turns of the passing landscape.

'Yes. I know what you mean. This place becomes enchanting to most Caefonites and has a tendency to grow on one almost to a point of addiction. I think it's to do with the sharp contrasts between both worlds. However, it does tend to keep one on their toes, with its utter extremes; from mountains jutting into its orange-blue sky to deepest valleys and craters, sometimes several thousand feet below sea level. Then you have its most frequent harsh weather conditions, with raging seas and storm driven deserts.'

'Yes, so I was informed!'

'Many of the original miners and settlers lost their lives in the process, but as you see, this once hash world is now being tamed by man's ingenuity.'

'You mean, by your ingenuity!' Hamil replied, giving Ranul full credit.

'Very soon there will be green and violet patches, even within the remotest desert regions and it will happen within our lifetime.' Ranul showed pride and certainty in his manner.

'Your wife Merian told me a lot about your enthusiasm for your work and your collecting hobbies.'

'Oh! I hope everything is ok with family back home?'

'They are ok! By the way, she sends her love and gave me a small parcel for you.'

They soon landed on the pad and Sura went out to assist.

'This is my close friend, Sura. We are living together, and if you don't mind, I would rather my wife didn't know of our close relationship.' Ranul showed slight guilt in his manner.

'Your secret is quite safe with me. I myself have several.' Hamil appeared unconcerned and they went into the house. It was quite common on Caefon for the wealthy men to have several concubines plus their wife. However that aspect varied with culture and those on Silo were mainly from Senot stock and more old-fashioned in those choices.

'I was hoping you would accompany me to the microid base tomorrow and perhaps take me around yours the following day. Just a formality of course. Your project has already been accepted for funding. But regrettably, at last year's level. I trust it will be sufficient?'

'Thank you, Sir! That amount will have to do,' Ranul replied with extreme gratitude. Nevertheless his agricultural projects were just beginning to break even and that much funding was more than enough for his current needs.

'I shall be happy to accompany you to the base tomorrow, Director. But I have to inform Doctor Stark of my absence and give him a number to call, in case of any unforseen problems.'

That evening they took Hamil to Vista Dome where they partied with several friends.

Vista Dome was almost half a kilometre high and close to three kilometres in diameter. There were numerous levels and each one was self-contained. It was almost transparent, sealed environ mentally and designed to mimic Caefon's atmosphere and pressure. However Silo's gravity was about one half that of Caefon's and that was the only major difference felt by its many newcomers.

Within Vista Dome were the most expensive and luxurious hotels. Many were used by newly weds on their honeymoons. Others were attracted by its gambling and entertainment venues. Even so, they never took things to the extreme and were always conscious of their place within society and the dangers to their almost perfect environments should they divert from the normal course. Those attitudes had been handed down by Seno, Micol and Sefran to their future generations and still remained ingrained in their culture, despite the passing of several thousand years.

CHAPTER 16

The first Microid demonstration

There was a tap on the door and in walked Doctor Luman. He had only recently passed middle-age, with bronze-like hair intermingled with dull golden instead of the usual shiny gold. He boasted a well-trimmed moustache and beard to match. He was Caefonian and a modest 450 years old.

'Professor Andra,' he said in a low clear voice. 'The experiment is ready.'

'Please give me a couple of minutes?' Andra replied and buzzed his secretary.

'Kaileen, please take along your recorder, and ask reception to use secured auto-answer. They can store all important calls for later.' Then Andra took Hamil, Ranul and others in the ground-car to a local laboratory. Because of the sensitivity of that project the building involved was doubly secured and externally reenforced.

The experiment was to demonstrate a brand new concept in microid communication and much depended on its success.

Hamil was nervous but followed Doctor Luman into the observation booth in one of the many secured rooms of the laboratories. They were each given environmental suits as a further precaution and made to sit behind a sealed transparent screen to observe the proceedings.

Several scientists could be seen sat behind displays with multicolored blinking crystal blocks. They were for initiating and analysing the several phases of the experiment.

'This is all so fantastic! I want to see some positive results today.' Hamil was excited and in anticipation of an incredible experience.

'The only serious problems we had in past was with contamination. Even the smallest quantities of unwanted materials during the initial phase can lead to molecular dissociations and failure. We have since changed our methods of production,' Andra explained, while an enthusiastic Doctor Luman patiently waited for the experiment to begin.

'Unlike previous experiments, with ten times more apparatus and equipment, here we use a single microwave transceiver to link with corresponding sensitive connectives within the target sample. To each connective has been added a sub molecular helix to initiate multiple bonding along specific predetermined bipolar nodes.'

'Oh?' Ranul responded, not quite knowing what the doctor was yapping on about, but allowed him his moment.

'During the second phase of this demonstration, it will initiate the formation of microid neurons with corresponding synapsis. If all goes to plan, it should grow a small microid brain which will make redundant many of the multiple memory modules, transmitters and correspondingly, the lengthy computer processing time required for an equivalent microid size and mass. This process is more akin to natural evolution, but accelerated a billion times. We are also able to trigger diversions or create new nodes with the aid of specially induced templates at certain critical stages during transformation.' Doctor Luman was absorbed in his work and tried his best to impress his important visitors.

'How soon for a fully working prototype?' Hamil inquired.

'At a guess I would say within two years, but don't quote me on that figure. We might have some tweaking to do before the system functions reliably enough within our safety criteria,' Andra replied, reservedly. Then he entered a code within the master computer and amazingly the seemingly solid metallic cube melted into a heap and began to reform into a little man about twenty centimetres tall. It was the exact copy, in miniature, of Doctor Luman.

After several more minutes and further changes, the figure stabilised and began to slowly walk across the platform, jerkily at first, but forming several hand tools in the process, which were extensions of its own arms. The transmitter was then switched off and although the figure remained still for several seconds, it again began to change. This time into a more appropriate structure that optimised its own independent survival causation.

The new form was egg-like. It slowly crawled along the table like a semi solid blob.

'You see! It now moves on its own volition without any external assistance, yet without eyes and other external senses. It will struggle in this manner for a while until certain specialised groupings are stimulated and trigger relevant cells into formation to benefit its present motion. By so doing, any necessary organs will grow as and when required to enhance its survival causation. During this phase a small central brain will also be formed to further coordinate its many senses and functions,' Andra said with excitement in his voice.

The blob soon developed a single eye in its forward direction with the ability to move about the surface of its body as it changed direction. It had no front or rear and could willingly change its motion in any given direction by reforming and crawling like a slug or snail. Any chosen direction of motion being its front. Soon there was another eye and elongations that formed into legs for more efficient movement and better visual perception.

The blob continued to change its shape, getting into more bizarre forms as it did, even growing what appeared to be veins and arteries, including a crude heart to move materials about. A transmitter was switched on and the blob collapsed into a pile of grey dust.

'As you have seen, we can terminate the experiment at any time. Nevertheless this small demonstration shows the principle of self-creation.' Andra said.

'I am truly impressed,' Hamil replied with equal enthusiasm. 'What are the real dangers, if any?'

'With every experiment there is always an element of danger, but as you have seen, we have taken every necessary precaution,' Andra replied.

'It will be an incredible device, if you can use a self-induced brain instead of the bulky transmitters and memory blocks. Then we can use them as independent individuals, even as imperial soldiers with the ability to function independently and in any environment,' A happy Hamil said while congratulating Andra.

Despite the success of that demonstration Hamil was somewhat disturbed by the strange and lifelike exhibit, but was convinced by the experiment and Andra's determination. He allowed the experiments to continue for two more years, pending progressive annual reports and reviews.

CHAPTER 17

The Second Microid demonstration

Two years had passed since Hamil's visit and many large areas of Silo had been transformed from arid desert to lush fertile green and violet. The terrain within the large valley where Vista Dome stood had been converted to recreation and botanical parks.

Despite restrictions in previous years regarding the thinner atmosphere, the new flora combined with a thicker carbon dioxide layer had improved planetary conditions significantly. It was now possible to live outside the environmental domes without any oxygen assistance.

Vista Dome could no longer cope with the increased numbers of visitors from Caefon and elsewhere, so several adjoining hotels had been built externally to absorb the surplus. In any event small oxygen masks were always available to those with more labour intensive activities.

Since Hamil's visit the terrain had changed significantly. It had slowly transformed from the near dormant moss covering, more suited to the lower oxygen levels, to proper crop-bearing vegetation. Many of the imported plants from Caefon had been genetically hardened for life on Silo.

At the furthest end close to the sea were fields of golden rye. Like waves they shifted to and fro in the bright sunlight. Those had been the first food bearing crops to be tested for normal yields in an exposed environment. All those changes made the world enticing to its many visitors. Further, most supplies could finally be made and processed indigenously. Those were at a fraction of the cost of their imported equivalents from elsewhere in the empire. Nevertheless, Silo still retained its planetary status as free-tech, for all forms of industry. Anyway, it was thought that environmental pollution was beneficial and assisted the desired atmospheric changes during the process of planetary conversion.

More of those greenhouse gasses would increase surface temperatures and enhance protection from stellar radiation.

While the planet steadily became more tolerant to its humans, so did the Caefonians flock in their greater numbers for settlement, recreation and adventure. The attraction was mainly due to its harsher and more natural environments that had seldom been explored during its mining past. Silo was quickly becoming one of the best holiday resorts of the federation, with many visiting industrialists, explorers and students. Wild-life parks were being introduced, with their usual venues of excitement. Despite all those improvements, as yet there was no change in the planet's status regarding its undesirability for manufacture and scientific experiments.

Soon there were several daily passenger shuttles from Caefon; a journey of barely eight days with the latest improved LPD Drives.

Ranul had since revisited Caefon and did not take Sura with him on that occasion. Neither did he tell his wife Merian of his extra marital affair with Sura. He was to attend a special conference for the Ministry of Agriculture and publish a paper on his successful methods, as used on Silo. During that time he received several commendations for his many agricultural successes and duly admired by his peers. He celebrated just two weeks on Caefon, during which time he gave several lectures to members of his fraternity and students.

He renewed his relationship with his wife Merian, who was very proud of her husband for his many accomplishments. He told her of his intentions to return to Silo for another two years and she sadly nodded, but knew he had more important things to do on that world. At that time she was a senior councillor with many responsibilities of her own and preferred her independence.

Andra had acquired many successes since. He had increased the microids' sample mass from that original small size to one approaching a fully grown human. As his team approached the day of the final experiment they became critical of all equipment and personnel. They selected a more secured building for that purpose. Scientists were everywhere setting up their tests and measuring equipment for the forthcoming demonstration.

The many different batches of microid material had been processed in several independent laboratories to prevent cross-contamination and despite a few unexpected minor setbacks, the experiment was on schedule. This time Hamil could not attend and asked Ranul to be his deputy on that occasion.

Since his return from Caefon, Ranul had become a celebrity on Silo and was selected as their first governor. His new post did not prevent him from continuing his agricultural projects. Nevertheless Ranul's presence at Andra's demonstration was equivalent to dignitary from Caefon and Andra looked forward to his visit. Sura still didn't like the concept of the nano-bot microids and thought the whole process to be quite risky and extremely dangerous. Andra had tried to convinced her otherwise, so she remained unconcerned but still sceptical.

On the day of the experiment Sura accompanied Ranul as his confidant. They were taken to the demonstration building to be introduced to the many rows of scientists and engineers. Afterwards Doctor Luman guided them to a high balcony. That one was secured behind a special transparent metallic alloy for overseeing the proceedings. That area was further sealed from all operations and enclosed by thick metallic doors. Once locked, the only exit was through a concealed trapdoor hidden under the flooring. It led by elevator to a parked underground streetcar.

The many scientists controlling the project were themselves hidden behind protective screens, but on the same level as the microid samples.

The samples were delivered to the site by special trucks. This time over 100 kilograms of the grey microid dust was used. The different batches of microid powder were guided through shoots and sequentially added and mixed by ultrasonics in a transparent biodegradable container.

Several parabolic reflectors were subsequently positioned on the far side of the sample and many small blocks placed on marked squares. They were the LPD modules that the mass would use to facilitate vertical motion.

When the scientists were finished, they thoroughly inspected the site and returned to a nearby observation control room. A buzzer sounded on the high observation balcony and Andra took the Vidicom.

'Good! In that case we shall commence!' he hailed and turned his attention to Ranul.

'The sample is ready. If you don't mind, perhaps Sura could do us the honour and initiate the program.' Sura gazed at both men in astonishment and hesitated. An excited Doctor Luman patiently awaited her response.

'Are you sure?' She was now a worried woman and did not wish to be responsible for initiating a process that could be detrimental to others.

'Yes! Just press the blue button and the computer will start the process. From then on it's fully automated,' Andra oozed confidence.

She pressed the button and the Microid mass began to move. Like one enormous living blob it protruded vertically from the cylindrical container. The large container slowly disintegrated as the sample began to form into the figure of a man. This time it was identical to Doctor Luman's form, but more similar to the one on their first public demonstration over two years before. Although now more like his true size and therefore much more massive. The newly formed figure towered over two metres tall.

The metallic human figure walked across the large platform without a hitch. It collected several of the small LPD blocks which it positioned about its person. Then it lifted itself bodily from the platform and remained stationary in mid air while observing everything in its vicinity. During that period it continued showing prowess using its many modes of movement. Then it landed softly on its feet and began to grow tools as an extension of its arms. It was then given several commands through the computer and successfully relayed its responses.

'Its observation is precise!' shouted an excited Doctor Luman, who seemed to be enjoying the fruits of his several years intense research and development.

'It can utilize the LPD's precisely without any additional controls.'

'Is the mass now under its own control?' Ranul inquired.

'No, not fully. We are now testing its repetitive functions. We have programmed those into some of its specialized microid cells. Those basic changes have significantly reduced the external computer overhead. So that the computer is able to concentrate more intensely on structural integration and microid metabolic functions.

'A blueprint is constantly being transmitted to the sample. However each time less information is sent as the sample learns and realigns to that particular order. When the transmitted information reduces below 1 percent of the original, it will be time to switch off the transmitter. After that point is reached, hopefully, the sample will be its own living entity, but functioning to the original blueprint. Well, that's the theory and so far, so good,' Andra said.

'Now for Camouflage!' Doctor Luman said.

The sample quickly transformed into a range of different civilians, then military human forms. Afterwards it transformed into a dead tree. Then a large boulder and other unsuspicious objects.

'The perfect universal soldier on the field of battle,' Ranul said.

'Can it reproduce? I mean, with another of its own kind?' Sura inquired in ignorance.

'Yes! The final unit will be able to separate into two smaller masses with identical knowledge, experiences and functions. However that process can only occur at very high energy thresholds when seriously threatened. It is sexless and cannot mate with another as we do. I mean as with most biological systems, because it is non biological. It can also synthesize, copy and fabricate almost everything it observes, while utilizing certain raw materials like iron and phosphorus for food as and when required. However those functions will be strictly controlled and can only be initiated by an external command. It can also absorb nutrients from the environment by a type of osmosis. Any surface area can be used for that purpose,' Andra replied.

'The most perfect and almost indestructible soldier, that doesn't even require military rations! That can also duplicate itself on the battlefield!' an astonished Ranul exclaimed and Andra interjected.

'It can camouflage itself in many different ways, is very difficult to kill and can utilize most forms of energy to enhance its own functions,' Doctor Lumen replied.

'What would happen if there was the tiniest flaw in the original program. That original blueprint?' Sura asked.

'If it became dangerous during the experimental phase we could simply transmit a disruptive blueprint. One not too dissimilar from the original. Like a poison it would move through the sample causing multiple dissociations in its cellular structure, and the sample would simply fall apart under its own weight,' Andra replied.

'What's happening now? Part of the sample has disappeared!' inquired Ranul, nervously.

'The sample is able to align its molecules to reflect or absorb electromagnetic radiation, including light, in a manner to make it invisible. This function is essential for some military operations where that type of camouflage is essential. That particular function is now being tested. However, it can be detected at higher wavelengths as we are now able to observe on the monitor. That parameter can be programmed within the sample. That way it can still be observed by us, but not by the enemy or visibly,' Andra said.

The sample became visible once more and the tests changed to that of dexterity and strength. Finally it transformed away from its original format to other more alien life-forms to frighten the enemy. The thing was comprised of numerous nano-bots that could change into almost any form of an equivalent mass. They could also be individually programmed at a later date for more specific operations.

After all preliminary tests had been carried out successfully, it was hoped that all acquired data would be stored within the sample's own neurons, ready for linking into a new and more adaptable life-form. One with its own brain and nervous system.

That new independent Microid organism would be created during the final phase of the experiment, when it would evolve into a stable life-form but with the learned data.. If all went successfully the sample could be induced, to partially collapse without the erasure of any previous memory or synapsis.

The order was given and a nervous Sura hesitantly pressed the orange button to initiate the final phase of the experiment.

CHAPTER 18

Microid cancer

The large human-like object collapsed into a black powdery heap with two almost separate peaks. The smallest one grew into an egg-like shape and began to slowly absorb the second, growing larger as it did. After the conversion was complete, as if by magic the new form suddenly disappeared from view. As it did, so did the local parabolic reflectors and other metallic devices and equipment, including LPD modules.

Ranul and Sura became alarmed by what they observed.

'Oh my God! Is that normal?' Sura exclaimed, thinking of a worst possible scenario should the sample decide to leave its present location.

'What is happening?' Ranul inquired, as Andra quickly took the communicator to call the senior scientist at the lower level. From his replies what had occurred was not part of the tests.

'Take all necessary security precautions and transmit the Destructor signal, now!' Andra commanded.

He had become quite irritable and wanted quick results, so he gave particular instructions to all his supervisors at the lower levels.

'You know the evacuation and safety procedures. Follow them to the book. I want to see that sample terminated, forthwith!' Everyone went into acute activity at the lower levels.

The Destructor signal was transmitted but no visible change had occurred in the sample. Although the object had become visible again, it remained motionless for a while and slowly changed into a most bizarre and unknown form. It was a type more suited to its own survival causation. The Destructor signal was transmitted numerous times but had no effect and perhaps aided the sample in its new transformation. Soon, all the remaining metallic dishes and other equipment in that area went the same way as the previous apparatus, to satisfy the thing's hunger. Since all the local transmitters had been destroyed by the sample, they had to quickly rig a new system for the same purpose. Without the parabolic dishes no destructor signal could be transmitted to destroy the sample.

It was now hovering above the large platform and growing many new embellishments. They included semi-spherical knobs on either side of its now flattened egg-like protrusions. There it remained, making a strange buzzing sound while what appeared to be throbbing metallic arteries continuing to form and expand all over its body. Its semi-spherical protrusions continued to enlarge and diversify.

'It's changing into a different form with its own innate intelligence and metabolic structure. One not true to our original blueprint specifications and instructions. However, it appears to be using our original survival template to accomplish that goal. We are observing natural evolution speeded up a billion times. I am afraid of what I see. We shall not be able to control such an intelligence by any external means. We must find a method to destroy it before it gets too powerful and begins to...,' Andra paused, disappointingly. Then turning to Doctor Luman, he spoke more sternly.

'I want you to seal off this entire base completely from the outside world and see to the sample's immediate destruction by whatever means. Call the military immediately if our isolation methods fail. Use our intense lasers to cut the target in small sections. Store the separate parts in thick concrete blocks if necessary. When you are finished I want a detailed report on events!' Then he ushered Ranul and Sura through the central trapdoor for the lift. It took them to a lower level towards a waiting underground car.

For Andra it was the greatest disappointment of his entire life.

'The sample had functioned so precisely at the beginning, just before the final phase of the experiment. What could have gone so dreadfully wrong? Could it have been due to sample contamination? Was it due to a microid defect during sample production? A few defective cancerous cells could have imposed certain restrictions on the natural bonding process. Like a virus it could have duplicated itself to infect the larger mass before anyone had time to react and correct those deficiencies. A one in a million chance but it happened all the same.' Andra considered worst case scenarios as they entered the car and took the shortest route home to Heaver Mountain.

'May I apologize on behalf of my colleagues and myself for a most disappointing result? I suppose we were overconfident of success, not realising there was a remote chance of contamination,' Andra said.

'I believe the demonstration itself was not a complete failure, in the context of your primary objective, namely: the creation of a sustainable microid life-form. However, it is obviously not what the ministry of defence wishes. If the present form could be reprogrammed and controlled by our military? Is that possible?' Ranul asked, sympathetically.

'No! Not possible I am afraid. The will to survive in such self-aware independents will be far too strong for us to overcome. When it learns its true potentials and capabilities it might wish to control us instead.'

'Can you really destroy this thing before it can do any damage?' Sura asked, showing concern.

'Yes. We have been able in the past with destructors and lasers. However, that new one has been specifically designed to avoid and deflect such weapons. It is highly absorbent and can become reflective and invisible. It is also much larger and will require a lot more focussed energy. Then there is its behaviour and evasiveness due to its adopted intelligence,' Andra replied, with failure written all over his features.

Andra had taken Ranul and Sura to their home in Heaver Mountain. It had recently been redecorated with a new wing added. The view was even more spectacular from the high balcony than before. There they remained for a while discussing those issues. At that time mass evacuation was the least thing on their minds.

It was not long before the Vidicom buzzed and Andra was called to the set. That call was soon terminated.

'I am very sorry, but I have to return to base urgently!' He was now quite pale. A small shuttle car soon arrived and he boarded with two military crew members.

'I wonder what has happened?' Sura asked, looking more worried than ever.

'Perhaps they have been unable to destroy the monster,' Ranul intimated, with a sordid smile.

'Don't you jest at a time like this?' She was seemingly annoyed by his uncaring demeanor and remarks.

'I don't think you truly appreciate what we are dealing with here. That thing could be very dangerous if it was allowed to reproduce its own kind. For all we know it could even destroy this world if there were enough of them.'

'But we don't know if it's capable of reproduction. Do we?' Ranul replied, now more concerned.

'Didn't Andra mention about certain reproducible factors, like if they were threatened and given high energies, including separating into two independent forms and feeding on chemicals like phosphates and raw metals like iron? Don't you realise that we also use phosphorus and metals in our bodies, including iron to transport oxygen? We could become a natural food for those things if they were able to reproduce.' She uttered those words with strong foreboding. Sura was always highly intuitive and tended to be correct in her assessments, but that one was the worst case scenario and much too horrible to even contemplate.

Ranul remained silent and pondered her last remarks with strong foreboding. They had struck a very sensitive nerve.

'Good God! If what you say is true we have to warn Caefon immediately! What an idiot, to have created such a monster without realising the implications should things go wrong?' He went forward to hug her but she drew away and remained still and in deep contemplation for a moment.

'We can't just contact Caefon. We have to arrange such calls several days in advance through channels. What do you think would happen if the operator got wind of our current dilemma? There would be panic on a major scale. Let's wait for a while and see how things pan out. If the situation gets out of hand the military will become involved. But I think Andra will find a way to destroy this thing first and when he does he'll call us,' she advised, confidently.

'And what if he is unable to destroy it?' Ranul asked, even more concerned.

'Then he will immediately inform the military and a plan of evacuation will be considered. We must allow him a little time and latitude to find his own solution. After all, it's his project!'

'What a bloody mess! I should have received my own dedicated H-Wave link to Caefon months ago. Always so many damn delays due to inappropriate funding. If only we had it now we wouldn't be worried about making a simple call and idle operators eaves-dropping on our conversations!' Ranul felt utterly frustrated by his inability to act in such an emergency.

'It's not that, Darling,' she replied. 'All transmissions in and out of Silo are monitored for security reasons because of our many sensitive and important scientific projects.'

After an hour had passed they could observe major activity about the distant base, but as yet there was no public announcement. An exhausted Andra soon called and Sura answered the Vidicom.

'I am very sorry, Sura, but we have not been able to destroy the sample. All scientific personnel have been evacuated to a local underground shelter. The military are actively involved and others are standing by. Large weapons have been installed locally, but we are still waiting for some response from the sample. If it remains in its present position without nutrients it should die within a few hours. If we use high energy weapons it could become more energetic and be forced to move away from the base to populate some other area. We are not sure what might happen if it survives our lasers and other beam weapons... it could even duplicate its kind. A catch twenty two situation, so we have decided to be cautious and wait.

'You and Ranul should start making plans to leave Silo. Pack a few items in case of an urgent evacuation. I have already arranged a star ship through the military. It's waiting in readiness. You should take the underground car directly to the space port. It will be safer that way.'

'I am so worried for you. Could you not come with us?' Sura

begged, but they both knew he had to remain and see it through to the bitter end.

CHAPTER 19

Evacuation plans

Both did as Andra had suggested. They packed two hand-cases with essentials for a speedy evacuation. To avoid further unforeseen problems, the few helpers were given time off their domestic duties. Then both waited patiently at home for another hopeful call from Andra. That call never came and they became more worried for the future survival of the inhabitants of planet Silo. Although ready for a quick retreat they would not leave until receiving further instructions from Andra.

They constantly viewed the Vidicom for the local news but there was no mention of any military operations within the areas involved. Since that project was at the highest security levels, all such operations would have been kept top secret and unknown to the public and its reporters.

That evening the sunset was out-staged by a conflagration of pyrotechnics across the lower valley. That location was in the general area of the laboratories. It went on well into the evening and slowly died away. Then they thought they heard distant screams and minor explosions on the wind coming from the direction of Vista Dome. That dome was five kilometres away. From there it was just another five kilometres to the microid laboratories.

The City of Chaum was sixteen kilometres towards the west of Vista Dome and still remained as serenely as ever in the distant haze until engulfed by nightfall.

The Vidicom buzzed and Sura answered. This time it was an unhappy and frustrated Andra on the line.

'The sample... it was fired on and... and it transformed into two, then four... multiplying exponentially whenever it absorbed nutrients and energy. They have either destroyed or absorbed all local weapons including the human crew... They have ingested every human in the vicinity of the base. Several of its identical offspring have departed towards Vista Dome. They adapt and learn very quickly, and can sense and discriminate between animal sounds and smells! God, help us all!'

'My God!' Sura exclaimed.

'Several of my personnel, including myself, have sealed ourselves for now in one of the underground tunnels beneath the laboratories. We shall be waiting here until they leave this area. In the mean time I shall try to rig a long-range transmitter to warn local space-shipping and hopefully relay our disaster to Caefon. However, I have little hope of success. This is why I would like you and Ranul to get on that special flight to Caefon. You might be the only means left to warn them, so you must take that flight!'

'I just hope we can make it in time!'

'You must! Give my regards to Ranul and remember me, my beloved cousin, because I don't think I shall make it through this mess. Conceal yourselves as best you can and do not attract the creatures by excessive noise or bright lights. They can also sense our body warmth.'

Oh... My God! What have you done?' Sura yelled

'Yes! I know! I have become the destroyer of worlds! I must go now, in case they are able to tap the line or detect our sound vibrations,' Andra said and terminated the call. Sura grew even more bewildered and was soon overwhelmed by worries for their future survival. Tears of sadness ran down her pallid cheeks as she went to assist a very tired Ranul out of bed.

'Oh, my God! What are we to do? Darling, it's a lot worst than we had anticipated. The thing has reproduced its own kind in number and are multiplying exponentially. All the base weapons and soldiers have been either destroyed or consumed.' She was most irritable and sobbing. Ranul was startled by her manner and immediatcly jumped out of bed to get dressed.

'As governor of Silo it's my duty to warn the controlling council. I can't just leave them to fend for themselves in a critical time like this? This is going to be a major disaster! A bloody nightmare!' he replied, nervously.

'It is now too late to save our world and its people. If the military couldn't stop them with all their fire power, how can we do any better. All you can do is advisc them to join us, and if so, the special ship won't have any spare seats to take them all. Some of the senior military will also decide likewise. In the mean time there will be riots and god knows what else if everyone knows. The less people know about this looming disaster, the better.

'We are to move now and inform Caefon of the disaster on this world or suffer the severest consequences later. Because very soon the things will be hovering above our heads. I am afraid our beautiful world and its people are lost forever,' she chuckled fearfully and another tear rolled down her cheek. He saw her expressions of foreboding and knew that she was correct in her assessment of the dangers. Even so, he would still have to inform city security and the local council. That was assuming they hadn't already been told.

His attitude changed to one of stoicism and resilience in the face of pending disaster. He blamed no one for the present crisis but calmly dialled a few numbers to explained the almost unbelievable situation as best he could. That local call was soon made to a few important colleagues and friends based in Chaum City, their capital. Then he hugged Sura and both departed towards the sealed elevator on the cliff near their house. They decided against taking the hopper or shuttle car, as those options could have drawn the attention of the things.

That elevator led to an underground complex of ground-car tube tunnels. The route from their house led directly to Vista Dome which was to be avoided. From the main hub at that point they usually changed tubes for other destinations. However they could also change course in mid-tunnel during an emergency. It could take them to Chaum City by entering an emergency code into their car console. That more recent addition had been carried out since Ranul became governor and was mainly for security reasons.

Hopefully on arrival they would get connected to the space-port from Chaum's main station.

Not knowing what had occurred in Vista Dome the previous evening, they decided to take the second more direct route to Chaum City. That journey avoided most of the traffic and interchanges during travel.

Sura couldn't contain her nervousness and had difficulty in pressing the necessary emergency codes to alter the car's direction. The switching of lights to red at the interchange made her see blood and she fumbled, so Ranul embraced her for a while. Then he sat her down and took over the controls.

'Darling, I have to call my dear friend Anna in Vista. I don't care. I have to warn them!' She nervously dialled the codes several times but the line was dead and once again she began to cry. Ranul wanted to stop her but hesitated. From what Andra had said, he realized the monsters could be listening to such calls.

'Those bloody monsters... they have already killed my friends!' she cried.

'My dear, please calm yourself. We have work to do, you know!' Ranul subdued her in a mild and peaceful voice and she became calm once more and wiped her tearful eyes.

As far as they could see the main line to Vista Dome was clear of all transport. They wondered whether the things had already destroyed the dome and was on their way to Chaum. If that was the case they would have little chance reaching the space-port alive. Many depended on their survival so they persevered.

When they arrived at Chaum's central station there were soldiers everywhere. Most unusually no one asked for their identification so they boarded a larger car on route to the space-port. That passenger car followed the sealed ancient underground route that was built more than a thousand years before by the first settlers. At that time the City of Chaum was a small environmental dome. During that period Silo's atmosphere was quite thin and could not have directly sustained human or normal plant life. At that time accommodation and such transport was sealed from the rarefied air and the finer desert's dust.

On arrival they visited the military section of the space-port and Governor Ranul handed them his special pass.

'Please follow me, Mister Governor,' said a young female officer, while taking them into a small reception area.

As yet there were no visible signs or indeed any talk of impending disaster and Ranul began to doubt his own sanity. After all, if

Vista had been taken why was there no mention of that fact on the Vidicom. Was it all just a strange dream? Then he realised the stressful disposition of the young officer who had not ask him a single question, despite his senior position. Neither did anyone show a simple smile. He realised she was holding back something and so did all the other military officers they had encountered on route. They were following strict orders, even at the jeopardy of their own families and friends.

Suddenly overwhelming guilt absorbed him as he realised only a few, if any of those people, would survive the onslaught of a failed experiment. In any event not many could have been evacuated in the short time allotted.

Suddenly there was turmoil throughout the base as a large group of swarming microid forms appeared in the air above. They were on their way to the western part of Chaum City. An elderly female officer shouted uncontrollably.

'My children! Oh God, my dear children!' She fainted and was immediately taken out by stretcher.

It was now early morning and those waiting were immediately escorted to the small ship within the sealed base. The young female officer never uttered a word during their short journey to the ship, but while they climbed the stairs she turned to Ranul.

'Good luck Mister Governor. Please have a successful trip and pray for us here. Please try and get us some urgent help as soon as you can!' She stressed the point sorrowfully before closing the door behind them. It was then that Ranul realised he was Silo's only hope and the one expected to warn Caefon and others of their dire circumstance.

At that time normal communications, although much faster than electromagnetic, took longer than LPD travel. Only H-wave could have made such calls almost instantaneously and that facility had already been destroyed by the monstrous things.

If everything went to plan, the faster than light star-ship could have arrived on Caefon almost a few days before any transmission reached that world from Silo. Therefore that single factor made his trip a most vital one.

Their estimated time of arrival on Caefon by the super-fast frigate was about six hours. Once there he could explain the situation to Hamil and Meron. Soon after, they would despatch their most powerful destroyers, or so he thought. Even so, by that time most of Silo would have been obliterated and the things would have adapted and become too numerous and widespread to be destroyed by such methods.

The ship was class four, quite small by interstellar standards but obviously built for speed. It included larger than normal LPDs, but with no mounted pods or weapons that would increase its mass to slow its progress.

With the exception of the captain and his navigator, who were within their small secured cabins, there were twelve passenger seats fitted towards the rear. Those reclined into beds. There was also one small cabin for the preparation of food, and a single small toilet.

That ship was obviously used for urgent local interstellar flights by dignitaries and designed for speed and comfort during such flights.

'This is your captain. We leave in one click (about one hour) and expect to receive two more passengers before our departure,' the intercom snapped.

Sura was still sad and fearful but in anticipation of her first trip to Caefon. For her it was a completely unknown world, but that was not the main reason for her fears. She was now locked inside a confined space and realized she had become a sitting duck should the things ever decide to move in their direction during their waiting moments. To her, an hour in such confinement could well become an eternity when faced with such uncertainties. It was like sitting on a time-bomb that was ticking to go off.

Although she never accepted microids, she never in her wildest dream could have imagined that she would one day be experiencing her worst case scenario. In her distressed mind it was almost as if she had seen the whole sordid episode before, except of course, the end part which included their possible survival on the thinnest hair string.

She realised they could have been much more secure in one of the underground tunnels. Assuming it was suitably prepared and stocked with enough rations for a month or so. The things would have had to leave that area eventually when their food supplies became exhausted. However that process could equally have taken well over a month. During that time all incoming flights would have been a continual source of nutrients to the things, if their crews were not forewarned well in advance. Anyway, since that was the only populated part of the planet, the things would have remained in that area until it was time to leave Silo for another world. In any event, it was by far too late to save the population of Silo. Too much initial planning, taking many days to complete, would have been required at this late minute to save the day. It seemed to her there was no way out of their present dilemma.

'My dearest, don't look so gloomy. Everything will be all right when we arrive on Caefon. You'll see!' Ranul said, putting on a brave face. However she was not convinced.

'I hope you are right for everyone's sake!' She replied.

'Those things cannot stand up against the military might of our empire.' He touched her affectionately on her shoulder. Then took her hand and squeezed her fingers while trying to cheer her up. But those words did little to abate her tumultuous feelings of despair.

'Darling, do you really think we will get to Caefon in time to warn them?' she replied with uncertainty written all over her nervous features. Although equally troubled, he maintained his brave stance.

'Of course, we shall!'

Deep within his mind he had a nagging sense of a major disaster pending that was well beyond anyone's control. Knowing they faced such crucial unknowns made him strong. He put on his bravest face and decided to follow established protocols on this one, wherever it led.

CHAPTER 20

Their rescue flight

A senior officer came forward to greet the couple. He was dressed in a white uniform with gold buttons and golden shoulder braid.

'Mister Governor. Our captain would like a private word in your ear. Could you please follow me?'

'I would like my lady to join us, if you don't mind,' Ranul insisted.

'That will be all right, Sir!' Then Sura followed.

'My name is Captain Sulman and this is my Navigator, Lieutenant Mullen. I am to take this flight to Caefon. By now you should have realised our position here to be untenable. Unless we depart this place immediately there will be little chance of us ever leaving Silo. Our scanners have detected large swarms of the creatures over Chaum City and most of our main installations are already down. At this time any form of interstellar communication is not possible.'

'I didn't realize the situation was as bad as this!' Ranul replied.

'From current reports, these things have already destroyed half the human population within the city while theirs have duplicated and increased a thousand fold. It had taken them under five hours to destroy the complete population of Vista Dome last night. Because of their significantly increased numbers, they should do the same to Chaum City in less than half that time.'

'My God!' Ranul exclaimed.

'Going on their present growth rate we shall have them in this area within the hour. Smaller communities in the islands are presently under attack. All major communication facilities including the main transmitters to Caefon have been disabled. I am afraid, Sire, there is now little hope for this world.'

'They must be very clever to have figured all that out so quickly-?'

'They are super intelligent and are constantly evolving and

learning. By now their mental capacities will be more than a thousand times greater than ours.'

'Of all monsters, what have we created?'

'At the nano-bot levels matter is much smaller, so one of our brains with all its billions of neurons will only occupy a space comparable to a large cell. That's the scale we are dealing with here. Further, at those atomic levels matter is much more difficult to affect or damage.'

'Atomic?' Ranul inquired.

'Yes, Sire! I'm afraid we have created the worst monster in the universe. When we begin our take off, I am sure they will follow us into deep space and might even attack us before we are able to gain hyper-speed. I am also afraid of leading them to Caefon. Because if they are clever enough to calculate and anticipate our flight vectors they can also follow us there and I think they are quite capable. So you see, I am at an impasse and cannot make a decision either way should I endanger more lives in the process,' Captain Sulman kept his calm well in the situation.

'I understand your problem. Can they really follow us into deep space without oxygen?' Ranul asked, surprised.

'Yes. I am sure they can and they are not oxygen breathers. They synthesize chemicals and utilise heat energy directly to survive and reproduce. They can also hibernate in deep space for long periods of time. Well in excess of a thousand years. A lack of either bio-nutrients or radiant energy will simply put them into a state of hibernation or trigger in reverse their joining together as one, in order to conserve and share what little reserves and energies they have. Whatever happens to be the most tolerant mode of survival at the time. Some surpluses they can store for later use.'

'What have you done, Andra?' Ranul thought.

'They are supreme copiers and can adapt well to any situation, even fabricate the most intricate of designs to their immediate needs. They have also been able to adopt our stores of LPD's to their design and will no doubt begin to produce their own types in due course. That is, when our supplies run out. They are also able to transform parts of their bodies into wings for flying and gliding through the atmosphere.'

'How bloody adaptable!' Ranul exclaimed, disappointingly.

'Yes, they can easily adapt to new situations almost immediately, and will change their form to improve their survival. Even linking together to form giant monsters to destroy a small city after its occupants had been absorbed. They may continue like this for a while until they have learnt enough, then they will adopt more efficient survival forms, cultures and scenarios. Instead of creating the perfect soldier, we have succeeded in creating the perfect predator. May God help us all!'

'How do you know so much about these things?' Sura asked while wiping her tearful eyes.

'I am also a scientist and was assigned to this task by Professor Andra. He asked me to look after you both in case he couldn't make it.'

'Who are the two passengers you are waiting for?' Sura again inquired.

'The Professor and Doctor Luman. But I don't think they will be able to get here now. Transportation through the city is presently non-operational and they will not attempt the trip by air,' the captain replied.

'In that case, may I suggest we leave this place immediately. If we are followed we can take a slightly longer zigzag route to lose them. But if we remain here we shall have little chance to warn Caefon. I suppose you have a self-destruct device on board in case of emergencies?' Ranul inquired, sadly.

'I don't know if you realize, Sire, but these aliens are super intelligent and will predict our every move well before we make them. If we are not followed, it would simply mean that we are being used by them to locate Caefon,' the pilot interjected while turning his head towards his captain for information about the self-destruct device.

'Yes, Sire. All our military vessels are fitted with such devices, but I have not anticipated using one,' the captain replied, nervously.

'Andra and his colleagues are better off for now in one of their hidden underground tunnels. I am sure they have taken enough reserves for a prolonged period of hiding. So, let's get away from this place!' Ranul insisted.

'Yes, Sire! Nevertheless it will be a very rough ride if we are to shake them off. They will quickly realize our mode of departure and begin to follow,' the captain said while taking the intercom from its holder.

'Attention! Everyone! This is your captain speaking! You are to secure yourselves for a speedy departure and please ensure all loose items are contained!'

Ranul and Sura made their way back to their seats and adjusted their harnesses as tightly as they could bear. They held hands and prayed for a future that would lead them away from the nightmare and its alien monsters.

The ship lifted off and climbed as quickly as it could in Silo's thin atmosphere. They arrived close to one of the main weather control satellites for a final bearing to Caefon. Not too distant and blocking the intense satellite's rays was a large dark segmented globe. There it remained, suspended in space until it sensed their presence. Luckily the passengers hadn't an external view of the ship and outer-space. The navigator was alarmed by what he saw and nervously shuffled his keys in an attempt to program the computer for the first linear acceleration phase.

'What is it?' the captain asked, nervously.

'I simply do not know? That structure was not there on our arrival!' replied the pilot, with utter dread and dismay.

To their utter surprise the globe broke apart into hundreds of the monstrous things which were now in pursuit. The things had anticipated their flight to Caefon and were determined to curtail their actions. Almost as quickly as lightning, several attached themselves to the underside of the ship in an attempt to remove the LPD drive modules. They had realized the implications should the ship warn others and were attempting to remove its means of travel. Soon, more arrived to take up positions on the other side of the ship. The captain tried desperately but could not gain the required acceleration due to the extra clinging masses. Those creatures could create virtually any tools to order for any task and were over ten times faster than any human in performing those tasks.

Within the ship the passengers could clearly hear the things hammering and cutting away at the hull.

'We are all going to die!' Sura cried out in panic.

They were conscious of the most dreadful possibility of death and were numbed by that realization. The only thing left to do was ready themselves for that most final of experiences. Such could only be accomplished through meditation and prayer, so they began to say a prayer. Ranul still held on firmly to her hand. Then he embraced her tightly.

'Yes, Dear. It happens sooner or later, you know. But thank God, it will not be by their hands.'

'Please, Darling! Let it be quick and painless!'

'If he sets the timer for two minutes that should give us enough time to say a short prayer for civilization and our selves before we meet our maker, and we can go together in each other's arms. If you agree, that is?' Ranul said, being gentlemanly to the very end. But her mind was made up.

'Darling, you must go now and see the captain,' a brave Sura insisted. He released his harness and staggered towards the front cabin. During that time the motion of the space ship was like a rocking boat on rough seas and it took Ranul much effort to keep his balance.

'Captain. Our situation here is hopeless. I would rather die with a little dignity while holding the one I love in my arms, than like fodder for some failed laboratory experiment.'

'It appears so, Sire! What shall we do?'

'Please set the destruct timer for two minutes and join us at the rear to pray: for ourselves, for the poor souls left on this world, for Caefon and for all other populated systems within our empire. Our task here is done. Let us hope that we are able to take a few with us in the process, and Caefon finds a quick solution to these monsters before it's too late for all within our galaxy,' Ranul said.

The captain and his co-pilot could not disobey a direct order from their governor and would have made a similar decision, had he not been aboard. He nervously entered the destruct code, set the timer and both joined the group of passengers. The captain and his pilot now sat in the two vacant seats reserved for the two missing passengers. There they prayed together amidst the constant screaming of the other passengers as if destiny had decreed it that way.

The timer was already counting down to zero.

'May our forgiving lord, Grand Lord Gerron, accept us all into his loving arms,' Ranul said. Then he removed his harness and hugged Sura tightly while awaiting their predetermined faith.

CHAPTER 21

Andra's last words

Andra realised the importance of warning Caefon, but the main interstellar transmitter had been destroyed. His only hope was in contacting a local ship within a seven light year range. He and his scientists quickly assembled a semi-mobile medium-range transmitter with several meshes. They were aligned to point in different directions away from Silo. The H-Wave device would pan out to cover a large overlapping area of sky, but it could also attract the things. H-Wave was not electro-magnetic, but a more advanced form of communication.

Nevertheless that was a chance worth taking. Any warning message had to be prerecorded in such a manner as to instill fear in any would-be listener. The recorder was connected and backup power enabled via concealed cables to drive the surface transmitter. The power device would enable such transmissions for just over a week. That was due to limitations of the power source. They hoped someone would receive the message in that time and warn the authorities of the disaster.

Most modern cruisers, freighters and military vessels had sensitive H-wave transceivers so it was hoped their message would be intercepted sooner rather than later. The message itself was designed to keep all ships away from Silo and relay the warning to Caefon as soon as possible.

Andra and his colleagues had detected the small nuclear explosion many miles above and knew it was the star-ship using her self-destruct. He suddenly realised he had lost everything dear to him in that single explosion. His only remaining family and trusted friend had been transformed into interstellar dust.

He also realized he was the only person to blame for the complete destruction of his world. Not to mention so many million lives. The guilt from those thoughts were too much for him to carry. Since their food supplies were limited to less than a week, his people had only one option if they were to die in dignity. What a bomb did for Sura and Ranul, poisonous gas pellets would do for his crew and their families in the sealed underground tunnels. At least that method was a lot better than being located and summarily dissected and eaten by those monsters.

He knew their situation was hopeless, but many lives were involved so a vote was necessary in the circumstances.

He called the senior members together and explained his intentions. Tears of sadness filled their eyes while they listened, but it was better that their families, most of all the children, knew little of their faith. No one could have seen a better way out of their dilemma. At the very least such a death would be quick and painless.

Doctor Lumen had recorded the special message and worked extremely hard in maintaining the transmitter. He had even extended its range and power. Even so, he realized any rescue in the foreseeable future would be fraught with too many dangers and uncertainties before anyone could reach their hideout. By that time the ever hungry and ravenous predators would have detected them by infrared or some other means. Knowing the resourcefulness of the monsters they had created, they realized it was just a matter of time before their location was detected.

A vote was subsequently taken and the system of tunnels fitted with relevant devices that were connected to timers. The timers were set. The transmitter was running and the count down had begun.

They sat quietly together in the underground tunnel and said a silent prayer to their Grand Lord before the curtain descended.

THE END OF AN EMPIRE

As predicted by their Grand Lord Gerron, The Ancients, their interstellar empire and Caefon's extinction would follow a short time after. Then the complete galaxy of Andromeda would be overrun and harvested for food by those nano-bot monsters.

During that time almost all significant civilizations would be considered a threat and made extinct in the process. The microid monsters would dominate that galaxy for several millennia and later be called the Javols.

In the following 3000 years the rapacious nano-bot Javols had exterminated virtually all life in Andromeda, including those on the surface of planet Caefon (the Ancients home world) and were presently on their way back from the galactic centre. Their purpose were to harvest the few remaining life that had time to multiply since they left those outermost galactic regions.

Many were on their way to the local galaxies, including our own, Osmaron (The Milky-Way), to do the same to all our civilizations and primal life.

A NEW WORLD ENDS

Part III

In Our Times

CHAPTER 22

Five Javols are sighted

**(A long 3000 years had passed since the
creation of the most deadly Javols on planet Silo.
Our time 2043 CE (2043 AD) is approximately 5000 years
from when Seno initiated the repairs to his world, Caefon .)**

Galaxy Andromeda... known to the past Ancients as Hyparon.

*Planet Caefon ...3015 years after the Ancients extinction by the
Javols. That time is about 3280 years after the creation of
the Javols on the planet Silo.*

*This planet is within sector fifteen of the Andromedan
Precinct Seven and is known to its present and past
inhabitants as Caefon.*

*Planet Silo... presently called Coln. It has only recently been
occupied by the bird people. They are refugees from
another stellar system..*

*The Ancients... Micol's descendants, with Sea-blue eyes and
pinkish complexion. The Javols made all those Ancients on the
surface of Caefon extinct about 3000 years before.*

Present Earth time... 2043 CE (2043 AD).

THE SIGHTINGS

The bleeper sounded as the viewing screen displayed the
important information.

*'ENCRYPTED DATA FOR CONTROLLER ASSESSMENT
AND DISPOSAL THROUGH SECURITY HELMET.....DATA*

CONTENT TO BE TRANSLATED THROUGH SECURED CHANNELS....'

Jon placed the large helmet over his head and in his usual attentive manner began to assimilate the secured information. He was well versed in the language of the Osmaronites and considered such efforts a challenge. Usually he would give that particular task to one of his more junior interpreters, but this time the order was unscheduled and somewhat different from the norm. He sensed an urgency within his present situation. Something he hadn't felt before.

'FIVE CIRCULAR OBJECTS HAVE BEEN SIGHTED WITHIN OUR SECOND STELLAR QUADRANT... TWO LIGHT YEARS DISTANT... BY REMOTE ALPHA SURVEILLANCE PROBES.
THE INTRUDERS FAIL TO SUPPLY THE NECESSARY SECURITY CODES AND HAVE VENTURED WITHIN OUR OUTER PERIMETER.
FROM CLOSE OBSERVATION AND ANALYSIS THESE FORMS DO NOT SEEM FRIENDLY BY INTENTION. THEY APPEAR TO BE SOME TYPE OF AUTOMATED SCOUT BY DESIGN AND MOTION.

INSTRUCTIONS AND WARNINGS HAVE BEEN BROADCASTED IN ALL RELEVANT SPECTRA, BUT THEY FAIL TO RESPOND EITHER BY INTENTION OR IGNORANCE.

MILITARY SYSTEMS HAVE BEEN PLACED ON FULL ALERT. FRIGATES ARE BEING PREPARED TO INTERCEPT FROM OUTER SPACE STATION PRON 7...

WARNING: THEY MAY WELL PRELUDE A LARGE OCCUPATION FORCE.

END OF SECURED MESSAGE.'

Jon watched his stereo screens intensely, wondering whether the five objects sighted were the head of a stray meteoric cluster. Although extremely rear, such occurrences were expected on occasion. But they should have been observed by the outer scanners well before entering his planet's orbit. How strange they had not been detected by the outer orbiting stations, and... their velocities were not constant as would be expected for natural objects like meteors and comets....

He thought again, realizing the likelihood of such an occurrence to be less than billions to one in that part of the galaxy. He just couldn't believe that report and murmured his doubts audibly.

'The robots and surveillance satellites manning the outer stations have always been so reliable in their past analysis of intruding bodies... They were always so accurate with their acquired data. How could these objects have evaded them?'

He was bemused by the information displayed. 'Anyway, why are all circular if they are meteors?'

Since the arrival of the Osmaronites, for some strange reason the whole system had been mined with probes and placed on alert.

Why were they so scared? What were they expecting from beyond deep space? Whatever it was, it couldn't be from any of the local systems.

'Since the one and only war between our world and the neighbouring Coln System, some twelve light years away, both have been trading peacefully together under treaty. Both worlds have since become fully self-reliant on their own. Anyway, that war occurred over one hundred and fifty years ago... when the Colmi arrived from some other part of the galaxy to avoid a hostile enemy.

'After their settlement on almost desolate Coln, they attacked us out of share desperation. Mainly due to a misunderstanding and diminished resources after their long space voyage... They were then a very frightened people who had little trust in other intelligent species... Least of all humans, who may have appeared quite alien to them... and perhaps not the best of neighbours to ask for immediate assistance.

'At that time they were ignorant of our language and peaceful *culture... and for reasons, including their own security, shied away from negotiating with yet another possible hostile enemy.*

'They lost that war in space and after many negotiations were allowed to remain in that system under treaty. At that time and despite many misunderstandings, we always preferred intelligent company in our sparsely populated region of space. Also, they had much to offer us technologically.

'We have always mutually assisted each other, with diplomats and families now settled in both systems... not to mention the several joint projects on planet Meron and elsewhere... It could not be them!'

Jon pondered those thoughts while staring at the screen while punching a few buttons on the small keyboard.

'The Colmi... a race of bird-like beings had over a relatively short period of time converted an almost barren and desolate world into a paradise. They were well respected by all for those great achievements. Why would they risk it all and start a war?

'Present observations, using the latest deep space probes, had indicated the absence of any superior intelligence beyond Class 2 - our current levels of technologies - up to a distance of eighty light years and possibly beyond.

'All biological life probed in those regions of our galaxy hadn't any advanced technologies, so if it isn't the Colmi, who could those intruders be? With technology advanced enough to travel over eighty light years of sparsely populated space. After travelling those great distances they are able to conserve enough energy to probe our outer observation stations and now inner planets and installations?

'Perhaps the Ancients would have known, if they were alive today? They had a unique knowledge of our galaxy and beyond.

'It had to be misinterpretation of data by the observation posts, but the Headrons... they would not screen any data unless it was thoroughly checked. After all, they were the most advanced minds from Osmaron and like the Ancients, almost knew all.'

Having completed his current task, Jon removed the security helmet from his head. Taking a small container of soft drink from a refrigerated metal container, he casually drank its contents all at once. Then he entered several code numbers into the computer and proceeded to contact his friend Merol, now excavating in the Craile Desert. It was just outside their main city of Cantor on planet Caefon.

Although Jon included archaeology as one of his main hobbies, he could only become seriously involved during his biannual holiday breaks. However he was always keen to receive news about new finds from his old college friend, Merol, since taking it up as his life's ambition.

'Hi Mere!' Jon greeted, with keen anticipation.'

'Hi, Jon!'

'How is the new excavation coming along?' Jon inquired.

'Jon, we have completely unearthed a large object. It appears to be constructed from solid metal and displays a few geometric patterns, including symbols of the Ancients. But... the thing is seamless with no doors or anything... it's perfectly smooth and brand spanking new... like it was manufactured yesterday in one of our robotic production plants. We have stopped all excavation on that part of the ancient city until we can find out more about the artifact. For all we know it could be a doomsday bomb.'

'That's incredible news!'

'The project leader reckons it's a hoax, but how could that be and who would go to such lengths and bury this large structure way out here in the middle of nowhere?'

'I agree! Now two ominous strangers in a single day.'

Jon whispered those words to himself in surprise and wonderment.

'What did you say, Jon?'

'Sorry, just thinking aloud to myself.'

'The object is being secretly transported to Cantor in the morning, so perhaps you could view it there. I have Grade One clearance so it shouldn't be a problem for us.'

'I would like that!' Jon replied.

'I don't think you'll need Grade One if you accompany me. After all, if it's supposed to be a hoax, it can't be considered a very sensitive matter. I need your opinion on the shape and composition of this thing, you being the scientist.'

'I will do my best!'

'Please try and make it as soon as possible,' Merol said.

'And please try to keep me informed of any new developments,' Jon replied, not quite knowing what to make of the strange discovery.

Jon broke off the communication, still in deep thought and looking even more apprehensive than before.

He was once again muttering to himself.

'For more than a hundred years, not one real problem and in a single week two bizarre occurrences.

'Were both matters in some way related?

'The object found in the Craile Desert, now part of the Ancients' city, if made by the Ancients, could be over three thousand years old. It had no doors, but from Merol's description was the size of a class five frigate...not like any bomb he knew. That size was the smallest and most manoeuvrable of ancient spaceships. Could it really be some form of spaceship and if so, how could such a craft fly without the necessary trust propulsion modules? Without doors or entrances, who could get in to fly that ship; an invisible phantom pilot?

'Ancient historical records and archaeological findings had indicated the Ancients to be very advanced technologically... So advanced they even traded with the Osmaron Galaxy... That was before they were wiped out by some unknown disaster or plague.

'No one knows how or why...

'From those early records we have since learned that a few ancestors working in deep mines and underground shelters managed to survive... and now we are all that's left of those few survivors.

'All animals gone, except for a few small reptiles and a limited variety of sea life... All others completely wiped out. The later pets having been introduced from Coln Major... The planet once called Silo by the Ancients.

'Although we have regained some of the Ancients' technologies, we might never again return to the former glory and higher levels

of science attained by them over three thousand years ago.'

And so Jon reasoned, never realising for a moment he was observing the return of the terrible Javols. The microid species that had decimated almost all primal life within the galaxy of Andromeda during the past three thousand years since the demise of planet Silo. Their spectre had already been and gone and once again were on their way back for the final harvesting of his and other local worlds. The secrets of the Javols, their most insatiable appetites and horrible ways, had died with the Ancients over three thousand years before. Those relevant facts were unknown to the later inhabitants of the once beautiful but now almost desolate planet called Caefon in Andromeda.

During the following two days Jon was quite busy analysing technical data as it was received in and out of the stereo helmet. He was still looking for clues towards the identification of the strange sightings. This also meant following their complex trajectories and analysing through his computers to find some pattern in their motion and deduce their modus operandi.

He was in the process of carrying out yet another analysis on the objects when to his amazement they suddenly vanished from the plasma screen and even stranger was the abrupt change in the information displayed:

'ALL OBJECTS HAVE NOW FADED FROM VIEW. OBSERVATION WILL BE RESUMED WHEN THEY REAPPEAR, WHICH WE HAVE DEDUCED TO BE IN THE NOT TOO DISTANT FUTURE.

ALL FURTHER DATA WILL HENCEFORTH BE ANALYSED AND SCREENED BY H-CONTROL FOR OPTIMUM SPEED AND SECURITY.

YOU MAY FEEL FREE TO PURSUE YOUR OTHER COMMITMENTS.

END OF SECURED MESSAGE.'

Jon reacted vehemently.

'What other commitments, indeed? I have not been given new

orders, neither have I been advised of any change in my work schedule! Has everyone gone stack raving mad?' he shouted disappointingly, at the risk of being overheard by his subordinates. In the process throwing a disposable cup at the trash bin and missing his intended target by several feet.

Feeling confused and in many ways dejected by the system he handed over to his next in line for promotion and called Merol. They arranged a time to meet and discuss the strange occurrences.

CHAPTER 23

The Ancients' ship

Having discussed most of his recent findings with Merol, they decided to evade local security and entered the secured enclosure where the strange artifact was held. There it stood firmly on its 3 powerful telescopic legs, fenced off on all sides.

The large metallic object was about twenty metres long and appeared about nine metres across its widest cross section. It was almost elliptical about its longest axis, with rippling ridges running along its length on both sides of its topmost parts. Those ran horizontally and were of the same material as on the main body. The three telescopic legs extended to three equally firm gripping feet.

There were no doors, protrusions or depressions that anyone could observe. It was marked with three symbols.

They included a seven-pronged star on top. That one was positioned centrally on the object's front. Then there was the Ancient Crucifix, or was it a sword? The Ancient Senots used that symbol on most of their important possessions.

Finally was the symbol with the three short lines or bars. They pointed towards a lower circle positioned on the starboard side between middle and tail where a door should be.

Those symbols were not drawings or engravings, but seemed instead to be formed by the contrasting effects of different metallic alloys.

Jon glanced towards Merol with overwhelming curiosity.

'It's a ship! A spaceship! Don't ask me why, I just know!' Merol was intrigued in anticipation, but also extremely cautious.

Suddenly Jon went towards the third marking and placed his right hand; with three fingers positioned exactly above the lines with his palm touching the central circle.

A silvery shimmering glow appeared towards the ship's centre and that part of the ship simply melted into an entrance and stairway, throwing him to one side.

A voice thundered in an ancient tongue.

'Please enter, Sons of Goh!'

He called out to Merol who hesitantly followed from behind. Merol was more eager to retreat well away from the strange alien craft as soon as he could than enter.

'Merol! Please hurry, I need you here!' Jon called, with little intention to run away and ruin the adventure of a lifetime.

Both brave men were initially shaken by the experience but nervously scaled the glittering stairway into the bowels of the strange ship.

Jon first wandered through what appeared to be a narrow passage. It allowed access to just one person at a time. The place was illuminated by a bluish light that highlighted all edges and made relevant parts stand out in a strange manner. It was a type of technology they had never seen before..

The five-metre long passage led into a small cabin with three large helmets suspended from the ceiling by telescopic poles.

The three pilots' seats were of black leathery material, somewhat different to the metal the ship was made from, or so it appeared. But there were no instrument panels or indeed any visual indicators within that cabin.

The voice remained silent. They soon realised it could have been a verbal annunciator linked to a hidden computer.

After a short time and having observed as much as they dared, they did not wish to explore the ship's interior any further and left. They nervously treaded the glittering, but seemingly firm stairway and were relieved when their feet felt terra firma again.

As they departed the stairs were miraculously absorbed by the ship as if composed of some form of metallic liquid and the entrance sealed itself in a strange reddish glow.

The situation was too incredible for both brave men to have accepted unquestionably.

'Oh my God, Jon! What have we done? This is definitely not a hoax. There is something very strange going on here!' Merol whispered, while still shivering from fear.

'Pal, we've got to keep all this a secret for now, until we can acquire more information. I am quite shaken by all this, but it's too interesting and important to let go,' Jon replied, with little thought of impending dangers.

They shook hands and parted company to ponder the implications of their exceedingly strange discovery.

CHAPTER 24

The Ancients' underground city

The following morning Jon was eagerly escorted by two senior guards from his surveillance building towards H-Control. It was the tallest building in that area and contained a large revolving sphere at its topmost spire. The sphere was suspended between three long rods which held its motion in place. Many thought it was used to relay interstellar communications to distant systems.

Nobody he knew were ever allowed within the vicinity of that building, not even senior security personnel. Yet, on this occasion and for some unknown reason, he was the specially chosen. He wondered whether it was anything to do with his clandestine observation of the strange ship with Merol.

'Where are you taking me?' he inquired of his military escort, but they remained serious and silent.

'I knew there was something wrong about that ship. Pity I couldn't get more information about it from the historical archives. Merol may have got his facts wrong about its importance to H.Q ... No way could this thing be a hoax or bomb,' he thought, while anticipating the worse punishment to follow for their indiscretion.

After passing several corridors he and his military escort entered an elevator, codes were selected and it descended for about five minutes into the bowels of the planet. He felt the most extreme acceleration. It was faster than any speed he had ever experienced in any vehicle.

When they emerged from the elevator he couldn't believe his own eyes; for he gazed in awe at an expansive underground city. It was spread out in all directions, as far as the eye could see. He marvelled at the incredible powers and technologies behind its creation and maintenance. There was activity everywhere and the place was brilliantly lit as if from surface daylight.

The underworld included an artificial sky with several suns and stars, moving clouds, a distant sea in the horizon, small lakes and a forest towards the left.

His present position appeared to be elevated by about a mile above the main lower city.

'What an incredible feat of engineering! What a fantastic place!' he shouted, but his military escort took little notice of his youthful exuberance.

An officer nudged him gently unto a moving walkway and within another five minutes or so he arrived at his scheduled destination. He was still at the same level above the main city.

They escorted him towards a bizarre looking black octagonal building within the centre of a small square. A part of the apparently solid wall parted as they approached and the entrance sealed behind them.

'What incredible technology!' he uttered, but followed.

Group Captain Mortima stood at attention to greet him and he saluted. Captain Mortima was then his senior officer at the work station.

'At ease!' the captain ordered and the two guards saluted and left.

'Hello, Captain, what's going on?' Jon greeted nervously in a quiet voice while awaiting his punishment, but the captain ignored his last words.

'Please follow me!' the captain replied in a rather stern manner. They both followed into another room through a second sliding door.

As he entered he could observe five others in the brilliantly lit room. They included three young women and two men. They stood firmly at attention and to his further surprise Merol was among them.

'I must be in real big trouble!' Jon muttered to himself, thinking of worst case scenarios, including serious demotion and loss of privileges. He assumed he had been brought before a panel of judges for all his past misdemeanours, which in his opinion were many.

To his further surprise and dismay, the young group were standing in front of what appeared to be a large circular desk. To his utter amazement a spherical object floated soundlessly in mid air above the desk.

The object displayed a bluish winged insignia and was about a metre in diameter. It appeared to be perfectly spherical and would have been completely black except for the winged insignia. There it remained suspended silently in mid air as if gravity did not exist.

'Please remain here!' the captain advised while placing Jon close to the other five. He bowed to the spherical object and swiftly departed. All six were now standing in a straight line, nervously facing the spherical object. It slowly bumped along the air while getting ever closer to them, as if to carefully observe each in turn. With little warning it suddenly went into an excited phase. Then it moved backwards, away from them, and began to speak in a powerful voice as if eating its own words.

'Grand Lord Gerra will be pleased!... I am Vektron, Intergalactic Coordinator to the Greater Purpose and you have been chosen for a special mission!

'I am sure you will accept your roles unquestionably when you learn of the implications and you Jon have been chosen as Chief Coordinator among your group of six.

'Your individual records show you to possess an innate competence in the pursuance of a given purpose.

'As predicted by our Grand Lord Gerron several millennia ago, this mission will take you to my home galaxy, Osmaron, where you will meet your destiny.'

He spoke again, this time in a more sombre mood,

'A truly great adventure in space and in time. You should be proud that you have been so chosen!

'It will change you all into Great Masters of the Sword of Goh.'

He bobbed up and down until he went back to his original position, this time talking quietly.

'You may now leave to get acquainted with your temporary

quarters and please retire early; you have a very busy schedule of tests to complete tomorrow.'

  A soldier soon appeared to escort them to an adjacent building for more counselling.

CHAPTER 25

The chosen six

Later that day the six young were escorted to the accommodation compound. It was one of the largest complexes within that part of the underground city which included the recreation-facilities block. It was situated about two hundred metres from the main control building that they had attended earlier that day.

After the guards had shown them around their living quarters and local amenities, Jon and Merol formally introduced themselves to the other four.

'So you are their favourite boy in all this? They can't just hold us in this place against our will, you know! Kidnapping was banned since the days of Seno!' Lira yelled, showing extreme annoyance for her present situation.

'I am sorry for any misunderstandings, but I am as much in the dark as all of you. I didn't know anything about this place before my virtual arrest and military escort,' Jon was at his most defensive.

'Me to!' Merol interjected.

'Judging from the security about, I think we are here for the duration. So we should make ourselves comfortable for now and act as a single group. That way, if the situation here becomes unbearable we can act together to find a way out of this place. However, all discussions about such matters should be held in a more public place. This is just in case our departments have been wired. Places such as these can have eyes and ears everywhere,' Jon said.

'You think?' Lira replied, sarcastically. Jon ignored her bellyaching.

'In the mean time, why don't we introduce ourselves to each other like friends?' Soon the others began to respect Jon for his calm, simple logics and candour.

'You guys can do what you want! When my parents find out they won't take it so bloody lightly! Anyway, for want of a better choice, I will accept this situation for now. But may I stress... only under strong protest!' Lira yelled again and in no uncertain terms. Others of the young group soon realized she was another natural leader that stood up for her rights.

Their quarters were separated into two main areas for each of the sexes. Containers and cupboards were stocked with clothes and other essentials for their brief stay. Although everything was basic, some planning was obvious in their acquisition. The garments and shoes fitted precisely and yet were practical in any environment. Even so, not all of the six considered their choices of fashion in the same vane.

'They call these rags clothes. I wouldn't give these to an extinct Gondril to wear. What happened to fashion in this place, anyway!' Petra commented, while sorting through a pile of rather bland clothes.

'I am sure they were specially designed for our spherical friends from Osmaron!' Julia replied and the girls began to giggle together. It was one way of getting rid of their pent up feelings while confined.

They soon learnt that their companions were also in their early twenties. Each a qualified scientist in a different profession, but had no idea of the nature of their future mission.

Jon realised the most important part of his tasks was in keeping his group calm and together. That attitude was paramount if they were to face their present ordeal, whatever it was.

At that time the human population of planet Caefon was about twelve million. It was the only populated human world in that galactic region of space, with the exception of planet Coln, previously known as Silo. Coln contained just over 8 hundred thousand bird people. The bird people, also known as Colmi and other aliens totalled just over one million on Coln. That population excluded the few lower life-forms and pets. Those figures only represented the surface populations of both worlds. Knowledge of an underground city was yet unknown to all but the six young adventurers. Most of the wildlife on Coln (originally Silo) had somehow survived the Javols first onslaught.

The surface population of Caefon had been rigidly maintained at under twelve million by its well-chosen leaders, councilors and controllers, until a balance was met between birth and death rates. Their superiors followed an ancient code of rules that was written in one of their ancient books which they adhered to religiously for the benefit of the people.

Every successive leader would take a special oath of office during their inauguration, as laid down in their constitution. The name of that ancient book was the Anacromecron. Within its pages were instructions of law, farming methods, mathematics and the sciences. There were also many drawings and descriptions of technologies used in ancient times. Although not religious, that book was their bible in matters of knowledge for their survival.

It had taken just under three thousand years for the human population of Caefon to have grown from its first six introduced human couples to present levels, now in the year 3015 since the Ancients extinction. Presently six million of the inhabitants remained within the capital and most ancient city of Cantor, which had since been rebuilt further to the south. Three million remained on Feltwol, their largest and most fertile continent and the remainder on many of the smaller islands.

For reasons unknown to Caefon's society it's population was closely controlled. Every member filled a niche for the common good and rebels were virtually unknown. That type of control was not manifested by lower levels of freedom, with cruel punishment for lawbreakers. Many were free enough to take undue advantage if they so desired.

Their system remained simple and functional because that way was most practical and benefited everyone equally. In so doing, whatever wealth remained on the now harsher world was more or less evenly distributed among its fellow citizens. Their day to day survival relied on such political controls, if extreme poverty was to be averted. In many respects it was a well balanced society of the more technocratic type.

Because of those reasons they learnt to be highly responsible and practical from a young age, but had no specific religion to follow. All concepts of the supernatural and other religious beliefs were discouraged. However they had historical knowledge of the Senots that preceded them, but all such beliefs were considered folklore. Those ideas had been instilled in them since the cradle with many incentives to reenforce those attitudes for their mutual survival.

Over the years their leaders had put forward many excuses for their sometimes tough measures. They even gave reasons for the restrictions in population growth to food shortages. Many knew that there were no food shortages. Strangely enough, many of those restrictions had been more strongly enforced since the last decade. That was soon after the arrival of the strange visitors from Osmaron (our Milky Way galaxy).

Human nature being what it was, many of the more despondent were quite willing to sit back and observe where things led before making their move. Yet, any misplaced rebellion could have destabilized their lives and spoilt it for everyone, including those of the perpetrators. Therefore they accepted the present version of stability, even with its rougher edges and retained their dislike of the authorities.

Since the last decade there had been several demonstrations by families and newlyweds. Those few frequently aired their desire for a reduction in the pregnancy time limit restrictions, which was 10 years minimum from the age of consent to the birth of the first offspring. To prevent further problems in the community, that group of female agitators were quickly silenced with generous incentives and given a 5 year minimum instead of the usual 10. Then they in turn was made to carry the stick and ensure the 10 year minimum were upheld, but with a few more family incentives. The government always had its way in such matters.

Nevertheless unknown to those women chemicals were frequently added to the water supply that would inhibit procreation on a near permanent basis. Their senior councillors and politicians had always followed orders from another source and could not diverge from their long-term program of survival, whatever it was. By so doing extramarital relationships were frowned upon while any other forms of sexual behaviour condemned. Those considered to be genetic deviants were simply altered during pregnancy or childhood. Others with serious and un-curable psychological problems were usually demoted and sent away to harvest the biological farms of Feltwol. Because of those disciplines and other sociological restrictions, young people lived extremely sheltered lives outside of their normal occupations.

Once the young had become of age, that type of life with its many restrictions became easier. At last the young could begin to socialize in order to find a suitable mate for life.

That significant change was usually initiated after their first visit to the regional psychologist on their twentieth year. At that time they would be selected for several further important interviews. During the final visit the respective young person would be issued their first credit card and a state bonus equivalent to hundreds of thousands of dollars. Those were their invisible state earnings that had accumulated since birth. From that moment they were no longer dependent on their families or state hand-outs. They were finally free to take a partner of the opposite sex with similar status. There were many clubs and places of entertainment that were specifically created for that purpose and many took advantage of their greater freedom once they were considered matured members of society.

Despite all those restrictions, the few surviving Caefonites were a highly responsible people. In general they would consider a creative career more important than one involving a family for the sake of having children, and the state fostered and reenforced those ideas. Nevertheless, despite those irregular fringes, the society cared much for its subjects, with its many state-financed facilities, including its many psychologists and doctors.

Coming from such a sheltered background Jon and his other associates were bewildered by the strange situation in which they found themselves. Albeit without their parent's permission, even when they had passed the age of consent. As always they needed answers, but also sensed a greater danger approaching and that danger was not to do with their present guardians, the Osmaronites.

JON

Jon was just over two metres tall, slenderly built and with a gentle toughness that had been acquired during his military training. His eyes were an inquiring brown. A colour that matched his long hair which was usually folded back and clipped into a neat ponytail. That style was quite fashionable and common among young Cantorian men. He excelled in physics and mathematics, which he used extensively in his position as Science Officer Grade Two. That was a supervisory position and made him responsible for one complete department with upwards of two hundred and fifty-six personnel. There were sixteen grade three officers beneath him. He was also a keen archaeologist and usually went fossil-hunting during his biannual vacations. That last item was his main hobby.

To Caefonites, professional hobbies were just as important as jobs and were chosen together at a young age.

One of his keener interests were of his planet's past history and in particular, the civilization of the Ancients before their extinction. Over the intervening years he had acquired much knowledge relating to the Ancients and their world. That period represented the way planet Caefon was over three thousand years before.

MEROL

Jon's friend Merol was a full five centimetres taller and the tallest of their group of six. He had a longer face, light brown eyes and dark brown hair. His hair was closely cropped as a precaution in his occupation as Senior Archaeologist, Grade Two.

His job had taken him to some of the most hostile places on his world, including the ancient cities of Nim, Mond and sandstorm driven Craile Desert. The Craile desert was part of the main continent of Akadia on which part of the original city of Cantor was built. However new Cantor was situated in the most fertile area of that continent near the Sea of Nem. Its new position was just south east of the original Cantor.

He was a professional archaeologist, linguist and historian of his world and all local inhabited stellar systems. He also collected ancient artifacts and items of art in general, which he displayed in his own small museum.

ECROL

Ecrol was eight centimetres shorter than Jon and stoutly built with broader features. He was fairer than both his male colleagues in every way, with reddish hair and a face full of freckles. He tended to be the most jovial of his companions.

Although spending most of his working years as a senior librarian, he was an historian, linguist and palaeontologist. He also had a profound interest in nutritional diets, with a view to longevity and good health. The latter were his main hobbies, but he was also a competent chef.

LIRA

Lira, the first of the three women, was just under one point eight-metres tall. She resembled a true brunette with beautiful large grey-brown eyes. Having a slender figure she would take great care of her looks and body. She was also a serious and pushy young woman with a fertile imagination.

She had spent many years at the medical branch of the Caefon Institute and considered a genius in human biology and genetics, having acquired all major qualifications during her teenage years. She was also experienced in the use of medicine and surgery. Her main hobbies were in rock climbing, recreation and outdoor activities.

When she was not pursuing her careers, she enjoyed cooking for friends and other fun pursuits.

PETRA

Petra was shorter and more stubbier than Lira with broader features, generally. She was quite proficient in astronomy and stellar navigation, and also quite knowledgeable in cosmology. She had until recently been employed at the local observatory on a stellar mapping project.

Her main hobbies were in sports, sailing and exploration in general.

JULIA

Julia towered twelve centimetres in height above Lira and was shaped and built like a Greek goddess. Her eyes match her light brown hair which was kept longer than the others as it dangled freely about her broad shoulders.

She was a wizard in telecommunications and robotics, but also played an active part in sports. She seemed to be the most athletic of her female companions and had taken part in many successful sporting competitions.

IN SUMMATION

They had been well chosen to complement each other. Being quite proficient in their respective fields, their combined knowledge appeared to be continuous when the group were taken as a whole and as astronauts.

Taking Lord Vektron's advice, the young group decided to retire early that day. After returning to their respective rooms they sorted their newly acquired belongings to their own personal liking, then showered. Finally they read through their training schedules on their personal pocket computers before retiring.

Those were issued to each before leaving the second building.

The following morning they awoke early. Jon was first to rise.

'Friends, I think we should learn as much as we can about this place. Therefore why don't we take a stroll before breakfast. The air might do us good,' he said and Lira and the others agreed.

He had observed some natural scenery during his previous travels and wondered where they led, so he asked them to join him for a stroll towards the elevated forest near the small lake. That area was barely two hundred metres from their living quarters. The trees and vegetation in that place were quite different to those on the surface due to their isolation.

Although delighted by his suggestion, breakfast was foremost on their minds. Following the local signs they entered the small adjacent self-service restaurant. It had at its centre four tables with sixteen chairs loosely positioned around its periphery. Jon and Merol selected two tables which they joined together and six chairs were moved around.

The wall was surrounded by an array of food and drink dispensers that were unlike anything they had ever seen. Standard meals of the non-Cantorian variety were served, following the input of simple coded instructions and there were many unknown variations.

'I think I have suddenly lost my appetite,' Lira commented with dismay, while observing the first slurry of concoction retrieved by Merol from the machine. However, Jon soon turned his gaze on Lira.

'What do you think all this is about?'

'Please call me Lira!' she insisted.

'So, what do you think, Lira?' he insisted.

'I think we are all prisoners, caught up in an ancient plan of sorts. As for the long-term repercussions, your guess is as good as mine,' an intuitive Lira replied, while gazing into his eyes.

'Do you think this place was built by the Ancients all those years ago,' Jon further inquired, realizing she knew more than she let on. Then Ecrol came forward with his more tastier concoction.

'I think Lira is correct. This place must be truly ancient. Anyway, how could such a place have been excavated recently without our knowledge?'

'All I can say is that I hope we are not their little play things in one of their sadistic experiments,' Julia interjected and the others cringed at that statement. Nevertheless having considered all the alternatives they thought they were there for some type of training program.

While at breakfast Ecrol soon got the knack of using the food dispensers. He chose for himself a greenish concoction which to the others appeared utterly repulsive. After checking the lists of proteins and vitamins, he considered the mixture to be his best choice and most nutritious while sampling several mouthfuls.

The computer listing said "Croyma sea weed and yaki". He realised its seaweed content was highly nutritious food, but had no idea what yaki was. When he asked Lira for an opinion and offered her some, she replied: 'keep your obnoxious yak to yourself!' and briskly walked away in disgust, leaving poor Ecrol to form his own conclusions. The others tended to use the other machine which seemed to dispense a more palatable pinkish mixture. Even so, before long they were all on Yaki. It was the most nutritious and filled them with lots of energy for the day, thanks to Ecrol.

A reputable Ecrol soon took his catering job more seriously. He began to serve them all his varying concoctions with specific nutritional values, once having gained enough experience by constant sampling. That process involved mixing and tasting from all machines. The special ones he would concoct by trial and error, tasting each new variation in turn until he was satisfied. Then he would give it a new name and log it's recipe in his portable computer. At the end of that program Ecrol had lost his appetite for all concoctions.

After having had their fill of the strange but nourishing meals, they decided to venture out on their first exploratory walk to the small lake. The food and drink although different, was quite substantial and made them feel in a mood for almost any challenge. In the misty distance they could observe many levels of vegetable growing under artificial light. They soon realized the underworld was fully self-sustaining.

THE MALAK

Merol halted his stride and called to Jon who was following several paces behind.

He was pointing in the direction of a narrow clearing in the small forest.

'Look, Jon, an animal! Look, it moves!

'It's eating the vegetation... How can it eat that raw stuff and be alive?' Merol couldn't contain his overwhelming excitement and disbelief, never having seen such a large animal before and of all things, a herbivore. The Javols had devoured all such animals from their planet's surface thousands of years before and they had only read about such life in the most ancient historical volumes.

Jon looked extremely surprise and followed in the direction of the animal.

'A special stomach, I suppose!' he replied and went closer to observe the very large and furry beast.

The other four followed some distance behind and were beyond view.

The animal seemed friendly enough. While they approached closer it casually glanced in their direction and continued to enjoy the young green shoots that were sprouting up everywhere.

They went closer, hesitantly at first and began to gently stroke the animal on the flat of its face. It responded by licking their hands with its abrasive tongue.

Both men were amused by the antics of the strange animal. The other four soon joined in amazement and began to do likewise.

Lira, soon out-staged the others by having a serious one way conversation with the animal who seemed to accept its present talkative company.

Then she turned to Jon to voice her opinion.

'It's a Malak! Many years ago its ancestors gave Calf-Milk to the Ancients!' She uttered those words with firm conviction.

John gazed at her with an expression of bewilderment.

'What is Calf-Milk?'

She immediately went to the rear of the animal and began squeezing one of its two udders.

'Look! This white substance. It's full of calcium and other valuable nutrients. It normally supplies this white substance to its young, after birth. You know, as food during the time they are unable to eat vegetation and for the forming of strong skeletal bones and build resistance against disease.'

'Really?' he replied in jest, wanting a full demonstration of the milking process.

'Like most primals called mammals, this one is a female like me,' and she wiggled her breast and other parts of her body to prove the point, while looking at Jon, as if wanting to elicit a particular type of reaction from him. Yet, Jon saw the funnier side of her naive demonstrations and continued to egg her on.

'What else?' he asked, with a keen romantic stare into her eyes. She soon realized he was playing her and began to blush. She turned away in shyness, but continued her lengthy and obvious conversation.

'Did you know, this substance used to be a delicacy in ancient times... a type of "Milk of the Gods", with supposedly great powers to heal?' she continued, with fervour and enthusiasm.

Jon, fully impressed by her manner, was deeply concentrating on her explanation, while trying to form logical conclusions by himself. Not having experienced the process before.

He also realized he was getting very attached to her. She was just his type of fighting woman. Then he began to focus more on the survival issues.

'But these animals are supposed to be extinct, if this one exists perhaps others survived?' he inquired.

With a keen motherly look, she responded.

'Don't look so worried, Jon, they can all be brought back genetically, if we really wanted them here at this time? It's a new process that is quite simple to initiate with the correct equipment. The Ancients were incredibly advanced and may have found ways, even thousands of years ago... to store all their relevant genes before their Great Disaster... to be recovered at an appropriate time. Perhaps there was no great disaster, just a master survival plan that was implemented while awaiting the arrival of an almost indestructible and most deadly foe.

'You know, all their genetic codes could have been stored away somewhere in this technological vault they call Lower Cantor, awaiting a suitable time when every extinct species on our world can be brought back.'

Jon glanced again at his female companion with even greater admiration, and the others were intrigued by her fertile imagination.

'What a brilliant and deeply organized mind. She must be one of the specials they talked about, to have formulated such a sensible hypothesis by pure observation and yet, she is so feminine and delightful in her expressions.'

It was getting rather late so a responsible Jon decided it was time they returned to their quarters and prepared for their daily duties, however gross they turned out to be. They could always visit the lake on another occasion, assuming they survived their first ordeal.

They soon arrived back at their hostel, enjoyed a second breakfast and were later escorted by two guards to a rectangular building about one hundred metres from the main square.

This time they were assembled in front of a different being. Although similar in appearance to Lord Vektron, it displayed a red-circled winged insignia and spoke to them in a very similar voice, as if eating its own words.

'I am Patron, Military and Security Coordinator to the Greater Purpose.

'I am to advise, counsel and prepare you as best I can for your Great Adventure. Although the training program may be stressful, it will transform you into better individuals for a greater purpose.

'Your training will take a period of three days.

'Although you are professionals in your own fields, your previous experiences will form a basic core on which your new knowledge will build and expand.

'During this first day period, you will be psychoanalysed. It is a painless process and quite necessary for your own safety, if we are to prevent brain damage while you are connected to the Psyro tron.

'You will soon be handed over to Shadite Plato. He is responsible for your future training and remaining time within this underground facility.

'Therefore, may I take this opportunity in wishing you success in all your future tests. May our Grand Lord Gerra always be with you.'

They had no idea of what he meant by those last words, and assumed the alien Grand Lord was probably a superior Osmaronite. Not even realizing for a moment that he was the god of their ancient ancestors, by the ancient name of Grand Lord Gerron and the one responsible for their present dilemma.

CHAPTER 26

Test 1 - linking of minds

Two uniformed guards entered and the six were escorted to a large room in the laboratory complex. That part of the building contained many advanced machines.

Semi-transparent blocks of glowing crystals were everywhere. Some included rows and columns of multicoloured blinking lights that constantly changed in rhythm, brilliance and hue. Several of the larger modules became more active when they approached and their living presence felt.

There were many human operators with three fingers and one large thumb on each hand. Their complexion were much fairer than Caefonites, even pinkish with golden hair. Their faces, although handsome in an authoritative manner, were long with a larger than normal nose. They were over two metres tall and carried themselves with poise and elegance. Dressed in their immaculate white gowns with shoulder insignia, they walked with an air of pride and dignity. But of all their peculiarities, their golden hair and penetrating sea blue eyes were the most notice-able.

One of the human figures came forward to greet the group. He wore a white tunic and displayed a blue-green winged insignia on his chest just below his left shoulder. He signalled them to follow him and they entered a small waiting room. While there he introduced himself to the group of six.

'I am Plato, Shadite. From henceforth you will be under my guardianship. Should you have any problems during your brief stay in this city, do not hesitate in contacting me or my personal assistant.'

Then he introduced them to his beautiful female colleague.

'This is Merian, my personal assistant!'

'I am very pleased to meet you!' she said, with a sensuous smile.

Merian and Plato had the same piercing sea-blue eyes and golden hair that glittered against the bright lights so the six youths were quite nervous at first. Never before had they seen humans with such complexion, hair, eyes and hands. To the six, they were completely alien in every possible way, although still human.

'Today you will be individually tested. It is not a painful or lengthy process, but necessary for your mission to Osmaron. Since you are the chosen ones it is imperative that each of you pay special attention to all your future tests. For the most benefit, you should have faith in us and the methods used.

'There will be three such tests. The inconvenience and trauma felt will be kept to a minimum. We have all been through those very same tests ourselves, so please do not worry unduly and take it bravely in your stride.

'You may wait here until your names are called. Please help yourselves to refreshments. Simply use the menu codes or ask the machine in a low and firm voice,' Plato said. Ideas of the most painful and gruesome torture soon left their minds.

The young six listened carefully to Plato's words and realized if he and his assistant had been through the same tests it couldn't be too extreme. Yet, they knew not what such tests were about so they were still nervous in anticipation. Nevertheless Plato was always calm and sincere in his attitude so they became calmer and began to trust him.

YOUNG MINDS ARE PREPARED

The female assistant soon appeared.
'Jon Tamil!'
Jon bravely leapt to his feet and they left the room together.
He was taken to another area and stationed near a large desk with three helmets pointing downwards from above. One of them was positioned directly above his chair and anchored to the low ceiling by a telescopic arm. Their appearance reminded him of a similar technology encountered on the strange spaceship and he couldn't help pondering his present dilemma.

'Could these people be the real descendants of the Ancients, with six fingers instead of my eight, excluding my thumbs? Their complexion is so fair... even pinkish with golden hair and they have such piercing sea blue eyes. How could they have existed down here all this time, without even our knowledge and who were they hiding from?' Jon was convinced something serious was amiss.

'How can my colleagues and I be descended, or even be remotely related to these people, if indeed we are? They are all so different... Yet, the Great Book says we are their descendants.'

Plato gazed directly through him with his piercing sea blue eyes and he remained calm.

'Please sit down and inhale a little of this harmless powder,' he insisted while pointing to a greyish substance in a small oblong container with a specially shaped nasal dispenser.

Jon put the small container tube to his nostrils and took a long sniff of the powdery substance. He felt like sneezing but held his nerve.

'You may now relax,' Plato comforted in a quieter voice, carefully observing Jon's features.

The helmet slowly descended from the ceiling towards Jon's head and contact was made.

His perception of reality slowly merged with another as he found himself in ancient times. It felt as if he was in the body of an ancient ancestor. He was a great leader called Meron.

Planet Caefon was then a truly beautiful world, with large cities, smaller citadels, clear blue waters and lush green and violet forests. Gardens were flowering with every perceptible colour. Fruit was in abundance and everywhere were life and animals. His attention was caught by a small four legged family pet that Meron loved. Several of the smaller furry animals lived and played with the children. There were human-like creatures called Gondrils that carried out domestic duties and escorted the children to and from school and for games in the parks. Those also displayed six fingers and two thumbs. Large creatures called Malaks and Pedris were grazing in the violet fields with many of their young.

'It was all so correct and beautiful and infinitely different to what it was today,' he thought.

No advanced technologies could be observed anywhere, except for the large pacifiers, humidifiers and other machines used for maintaining a perfect planetary environment. Since most of their manufacturing had been sited either on moons or on barren worlds, there was almost no pollution.

His and Meron's thoughts seemed to overlay each other in his mind. It was as if he was two people in one and yet the situation was pleasantly acceptable. Slowly he understood the technologies of the Ancients, or at least what was in the mind of Meron, the ancient scientist and military councillor.

The effect gradually wore off as he became aware of Plato observing a screen while making fine adjustments to a crystal panel. Plato immediately stopped what he was doing and glanced in his direction.

'How do you feel?' he asked, showing concern. 'Was it a long fifteen minutes?' Jon was surprised by his words, for although just fifteen minutes had expired since he inhaled the dust, to Jon it was more like a year had passed by.

Jon felt disorientated and held his reply, but Plato continued.

'You are perfect. You have a beautiful mind so use it well and do not abuse it.

'You have been passed to the next stage of your training.'

The helmet lifted and the assistant took Jon back to the waiting room, still slightly disturbed by his strange experience.

Jon was utterly puzzled by his observations of Caefon in ancient times and realized that out of a population of billions, its present population of over 11 million was all that remained, and they were so completely different to those ancient people.

'What disaster could have befell our world in ancient times to have destroyed all major life? Yet, there were no signs of a meteor strike. No such disaster had been mentioned in any of the holy books.' And so he reasoned while those questions constantly nagged and worried him.

Lira was next on their list and followed the assistant full of bravado and confidence, as if destined to fulfil some great mission.

She was placed under the most central helmet and Plato was amazed with the speed of her convergence. It was as if she anticipated every new memory implant and event well before they could take form. Her mind was almost identical to the donor's and she was able to correctly predict and interact with each overlay of information from one of her ancient ancestors called Lucia.

When she awoke Plato studied her with a nostalgic smile. She had reminded him of someone in the distant past. It was someone very dear to him and one that he truly loved. He held that smile and said nothing to her regarding those ancient experiences.

They passed the analysis test. Each with similar experiences of a past ancient ancestor.

In the case of Lira, it was the famous anthropologist and councillor called Lucia, who was also Meron's wife. Nevertheless most of the education and careers of their ancient counterparts were dissimilar, each being professionals in completely different fields.

By lunchtime they were escorted back to their hostel and again free until the following morning.

CHAPTER 27

Eight Fingered Freaks

That evening they decided to meet at the small club within the recreation facility. It was situated in an adjacent block and connected by an enclosed passage. The place was designed with comfort and relaxation in mind and included a human-like barman. He was not an ancient and neither did he look anything like a surface dweller. He was very efficient at his job of mixing drinks to order, despite the fact he never spoke a word.

Jon was the first to arrive and sat quietly at a corner table all by himself. He was considering events of the day and in particular those relating to the six fingers and corresponding thumbs of the Ancients. But that was not all, everything about them were so different to present day surface people. All those factors constantly nagged him.

Placing both hands on the table he began to carefully observe his fingers, finger nails and all.

Merol and the women had not yet arrived, but Ecrol was at the bar sampling some selected beverages. When they entered Lira excused herself and went directly to Jon's table.

'A credit for your thoughts?' Lira asked, as she sat down next to him in one of her playful moods. Observing his female companion in that frame of mind he greeted her in like manner and began to speak his worries.

'The six fingers of Plato and the others. They must be the Ancients or their direct descendants, but they are so different to us. We have been misled all this time in believing we are the true Caefonites when we are not. After all, most historical records and ancient symbols have always depicted them as a race of four or a multiple thereof, even our counting system is based on sixteen. And here we are, the chosen few, with eight fingers and two thumbs.'

'So?' she interrupted.

'Eight-fingered freaks, that's what we are!'

'Yep! Seems that way!' She began observing all her fingers in detail with a comical expression.

'Aren't you concerned?'

'Nope!'

'Then tell me one simple thing; why isn't our counting system based on ten, even twenty? Doesn't that fact bother you? Is everything about our past been incorrectly recorded. And when did we begin to have ten digits?'

She did not wish to accept his present moodiness and responded in a vigorous manner.

'Six or eight fingers, does it really matter? Why is this simple biological fact of such importance to you? I myself have always thought eight fingers to be much better than six, but that depends on how the individual uses them. The number of joints, size, length, and so on.

'Isn't that so?'

She shouted, trying to knock him out of his present state of melancholia.

He looked deeply into her brown eyes and shook his head as if to dislodge some negativity from his mind.

'I am sorry for my immature behaviour, Lira. It has been a long confusing day and I must be tired. Anyway, you will agree, it's an interesting topic for further discussion... Perhaps we can debate those matters another time when we are more settled,' Jon said, realizing he had made too much of his misplaced worries.

'I accept your misplaced apology,' she replied, jokingly.

'Shall we join Ecrol at the bar and attempt whatever he seems to be enjoying over there?' Jon asked, now in a more relaxed frame of mind.

Ecrol turned around to greet the couple as they approached.

'Why don't you try this pink stuff! It's a little strong but exquisite. I think it's because of a higher alcoholic content. You must sip slowly though, it has quite a kick. This one is much better than the others. I must have tried them all before settling for it,' he said, pointing an unsteady finger towards a pile of partly filled containers in the corner that the barman was about to clear away by automatic trolley.

She looked at the biological concoction he was drinking and asked the barman for one.

Every drink was prepared individually from an ancient recipe, but there were many combinations and every item had a specific colour. That way one could always tell if their drink was correctly mixed. The Ancients must have loved such variety in their lives with subtle colours and tastes.

She took a gentle sip of the liquid and smiled. Then she coughed.

'It's so strong!... But great! Also quite a pleasant aftertaste... I can get used to this! Please try one, Jon?' she pampered and he did likewise.

They sipped the strange substance together and when their legs began to lighten he asked her to join him at a nearby table. The others were by now at a distant table playing a game of general knowledge with a six faced dice.

'Are you from Cantor?' Jon asked.

'No. I am from Feltwol,' Lira replied.

'But that's virtually on the other side of our world. You live on the largest of our continents and remote.. and your parents...?' he inquired, humorously.

'They are all right, I suppose. They are farmers in the Great Feltlands. Our estate is just fifty kilometres from the city of Cad. We have a house there. I mean, close to the city. It's a great privilege you know.'

'Yes. I know!' he said.

'I was educated in Cantor at the Caefon Institute. Any more questions?' Lira added, in anticipation.

He stared at her in amazement but with deep affection.

'You went to the Institute on a full time basis?'

'Yes. I won a special scholarship at the age of twelve,' she replied.

'You must be a genius.'

'No! I don't think so,' she replied.

Then he told her about his parents.

'They were astronauts who went missing when I was about six

years old. My grand mother, that's on my mother's side, brought me up. So I have no real parents alive. My grand father died before I was born.'

'That's very sad! Do you remember them?'

'No! I have no real knowledge of any of them. From what I've been told they were always on some special mission for the government... so my grandma says. The government was always very generous to us though. Almost as if they thought they owed us a lot. Perhaps because of my adventurous parents.... They may have taken great risks for the bureau during those dangerous space projects,' he said with regret.

She was saddened by what she heard and took his hand in hers.

'I am very sorry, Jon, about your parents,' she replied sympathetically.

'No need, by now I've grown used to the idea. Anyway, we have quite an exciting mission ahead of us!'

'Whatever you decide, great adventurer,' she replied, humorously.

She suddenly changed the topic while gazing at him in a more sombre mood.

'I would like your opinion on an important matter when you have a little time to spare. It should be discussed in private. I don't wish to be overheard by any of the others and I am not quite in the mood for that topic at this time.'

'Ok! Whenever you are ready!'

He took her hand in his and they strolled unsteadily to the bar for another drink.

They were soon joined by the others at the bar with each having their own theory about the six-fingers dilemma.

CHAPTER 28

Test 2 - blueprints of minds and bodies

THE PSYROTRON AND MEGOTRON

The Psyrotron and Megotron scanners were housed in another part of that massive building. Those units were larger than most of the other equipment seen strewn about the main laboratory. The Psyrotron was placed in a circular room with a lowered ceiling and slightly raised floor. The floor of that area was made of a glowing substance, with thousands of concentric circles radiating outward from a most central point.

The Megotron appeared as a large hollow object resembling a giant robot. It was anchored firmly to the ceiling by large telescopic arms and chains. Three smaller supporting telescopic arms were used for greater flexibility, firmness and more precise alignment with its patients. Those powerful hydraulic arms also carried the heavy weight of the bizarre looking device.

That devilish looking unit was all black and radiated what appeared to be long tubular fingers of a variety of lengths and diameters along its visible outer surface. It was truly monstrous and could instil fear even in the most accomplished and well seasoned warrior.

A continuous bench ran along the inner circular wall. That bench contained an assortment of measuring instruments and several larger crystal cubes with more blinking lights. The main operators of those units, if indeed there were any, could have been in another room, since there were no seats available within the immediate area.

The six arrived the following morning at a different entrance and were shown into a much larger reception area. This time the laboratory appeared more expansive and the uniforms of the operators were different.

There they waited patiently for Plato, who greeted them on arrival.

'Hello, my most illustrious adventurers,' he saluted, with a broad smile.

'And how do we feel today? I trust you are now quite comfortable, after a long and refreshing sleep?'

They stared innocently at him completely lost for words. Little did he know of their previous evening's entertainment. Having only recently recovered from the after effects of those experimental drinks with significant alcoholic content. Since they were not used to such drinks the after effects lingered.

'Today, you are to be prepared for the Megotron and Psyrotron scanners. In order for us to complete such tests satisfactorily, you will be made naked, as on the day you were born. However, you will each take your turn in private. That process will alleviate any shyness on your part.'

They stared at him with more bewilderment.

'The Megotron will be used to accurately measure and map your individual bodies. It will plot all organic tissue in shape, size and composition. Thus looking for any physical defects and disorders. Which if found will be repaired immediately.

'It will create a specific chart of each of your beautiful bodies, down to the very last and minutest particle.

'The Psyrotron, in a similar manner, will plot your minds, recording even the smallest bit of data, including all positive and negative thoughts.

'When we are through, all such data may be stored to posterity. We shall then be able to completely rebuild you from scratch if necessary,' Plato said, with a somewhat sadistic attitude, although in jest. They shivered fearfully in anticipation.

They were utterly shocked by the idea of any civilization having the ability to create a complete human body from scratch, including all previous memories. They couldn't help wondering whether in such circumstances the spiritual being would remain the same and return to their new body, even after an accidental death. Nevertheless they were a very brave lot and had no one to assist them otherwise. The technologies of the Ancients were truly awesome and Plato appeared to know precisely what it entailed, so they followed like poor humble lambs to the slaughter.

The female assistant soon arrived and chose Merol. He, like the others, was by now quite nervous and imagined worst case scenarios. Anyway, he thought, despite Plato's sarcasm, he said there would be no pain involved, so he calmly went along like a frightened dog with its tail between its legs.

His head was completely shaved by another assistant. He was asked to undress and then handed a face-mask. The Operator thoroughly checked and scanned his body with special instruments, searching for metallic and none biological implants. Then she asked him whether he had received any medical operations or transplants and he replied negatively.

The operator may have known of the extensive use of implants on the surface, or so he thought.

He was asked to enter a large bubble bath where he was made to wash and scrub himself thoroughly. Then he was led towards a second similar container filled with a jelly-like substance. He was asked to rub the bluish material all over his naked body.

That process went on for several minutes until the substance began to grow a thick skin above his own. She subsequently removed his face-mask and carefully checked his body, ensuring a correct artificial skin growth of the right thickness. She checked to see whether sensitive areas on his face was left untouched by the substance. He was then led through a small corridor in the direction of the Megotron.

After entering the small circular room, the operator asked Merol to position himself above a small triangular mark on the floor. That mark was encountered just after he entered the sliding doorway and was close to a square translucent panel that was somewhat wider than a human's body.

His body was scanned by another smaller but movable device which she could slide along a vertical frame. The panel suddenly came alive and began to display both his skeletal and muscular tissue structures. By pressing buttons on a small portable device the operator could observe any layer of muscular tissue. The process appeared to be like placing layers of the body, one on top of the other in any direction. While in the reverse direction the images were like pealing thin layers off in order to get to a more precise level within an organ.

The operator carefully observed the screens with the aid of her small handheld computer. When she was satisfied with the image, she removed his face mask and gently nudged Merol towards the most central circle in the middle of the floor.

She pressed several more buttons and the Megotron descended from the ceiling towards his coated body. Suddenly he found himself standing in complete darkness. Nevertheless he could clearly hear the operator's voice. She asked him to position his nostrils and mouth in line with three projecting tubular extensions, which he did.

The Megotron began to vibrate about his body until it tightly fitted his form. The three tubes moved slowly into his nostrils and mouth. All he could feel was the warm sensation of being roasted alive slowly from the inside.

After what appeared to him to have been an eternity, the vibration slowly reduced in amplitude and the tubes gradually withdrew from wherever they had been. Once again the vibration increased in amplitude and the Megotron reduced its tight grip from about his body. Then it ascended towards its original position close to the high ceiling, leaving Merol slightly dazed and standing in a very bright room.

The light slowly dimmed as he regained his composure and his pupils gradually adjusted to ambient levels. At that moment the operator ran towards him to assist.

'Is everything all right?' she inquired, showing much concern.

'Do you feel like you normally do?'

He shook his head while resisting the tendency to collapse onto the floor, until he was able to regain his composure and speak.

'I think so. I feel fine, thank you!' he bravely replied, still feeling somewhat dazed.

'Would you like us to continue the other tests now?' she patiently asked.

This time he did not speak, but again nodded his head as to agree. He did not want to return to that place ever again.

She guided him to the psyrotron and positioned his body directly above the most central circle. A metallic belt was clamped about his waist, a crystal band around his neck and special goggles placed over his eyes. She tapped several buttons on her keypad. As if by magic, the belt and band adjusted to his physical dimensions. The belt lifted him into the air about a metre high and gently rotated his body until his head was facing downwards. Then it adjusted its level until his head gently touched the innermost circle on the floor. As the blood rushed towards his brain he felt even more bizarre, but held his nerves and sanity.

At that moment the numerous rings began to pulsate in brilliance until a strange rhythm was reached, further building up to a crescendo of multiple rhythms and reflections. Ever so often the rhythm would change into a different pattern and so it went on. The process continued for about three minutes until the brilliance dimmed.

The operator went up to him, checked his goggles and briefly observed his eyes with a small light. She replaced them and returned to her position in the far corner. He was subsequently rotated through one hundred and eighty degrees and the test repeated.

This time the rhythm started from the other direction and again continued for another three minutes. After the scanner had completed the process, his body was lifted, rotated in the air and was placed in an upright position on his feet.

By the end of that test he felt completely disorientated and drained of all his energies. Yet again, the operator went up to him, but this time she removed all attachments from his body and handed him a gown to wear. He was taken to a local room and asked to enter a tub containing blue liquid, where he thoroughly washed himself. As he entered the liquid his artificial skin began to dissolve like molten wax and was taken away by the circulating currents.

After the bath she inspected his body and handed him a greenish drink along with his neatly folded clothes. He was also given a tight fitting cap to wear as temporary headgear. Perhaps to conceal his now bald head.

The others followed a similar faith, with all jewellery and devices removed from their persons.

The girls were furious at the thought of having their heads shaved, but the operator insisted the loss was only temporary and that they had little choice in the matter.

Of all the tests the Megotron and Psyrotron were the worst they had so far encountered and they wondered whether those bizarre tests would get more severe.

After the events of that morning they appeared the most pathetic of souls. There they sat in the small waiting room begging for reassurance from anyone. By that time they had been re-clothed, but with little caps on their now bald heads.

Plato soon walked in with a confident grin. He was carrying several small containers and plastic gloves which he handed to each in turn.

'You may apply this substance to your bare scalps each morning and before bedtime. It will cause rapid regrowth within the necessary areas.

'Always replace your caps after each application, and never apply to other areas of your body. Also, keep well away from your eyes.

'How long before I can have my hair back?' Lira asked. She realized she had no options, but was furious all the same.

'About two weeks and perhaps one month to your previous length,' Plato replied. She was not amused and began to sulk.

'People, I know this test was a most intense operation, but you have all come through with flying colours. By so doing you have almost completed all your tests, but for the final, which is the psychological one. Therefore, please think of this hairless inconvenience as a minor setback in your important training.

'Now... your final test will be very similar to your first, but this time you will be given subliminal knowledge that will assist in answering many of your searching questions.

'You may retire for the rest of the day, and please have some fun,' Plato stressed with a cheerful smile.

Once again he strolled out with his assistant, looking even more confident, for the results of that day were all positive.

Plato had a way with the young group of six who trusted him implicitly and despite his sarcasm and negative humour, always tended to alleviate their worst fears.

Nevertheless the six young adventurers were still utterly confused and bewildered by all those tests and operations that was well beyond their imagination.

CHAPTER 29

Time to draw conclusions

That afternoon they had felt more insecure than ever before and decided to once again visit the small bar to unwind and discuss their problems with their comrades.

They had become good friends since their arrival and always tended to remain close together. That way they were able to cope with whatever strange and bizarre circumstances they were thrown up against by Plato and his eager assistants. Presently they felt like little insignificant puppets that constantly needed each others company for reassurance. Yet, they also had a great desire to unravel the complex jigsaw and discover the modus operandi of their future mission to Osmaron.

Lira had arranged to discuss her problem, whatever it was, with Jon in the local recreation room apart from the others. She didn't wish to be overheard. That room appeared to be always empty at that time of day.

'Jon, I am concerned for the safety of my family and friends on the surface. I am quite anxious, because while I am in this place I find myself unable to lift a finger to assist should anything go wrong. You know, they are up there with over ten million others and if something disastrous was to happen... I could never forgive myself for not being able to warn them in advance... they could all be killed by whatever was here before....' Lira said, filled with sadness.

She couldn't hold back her tears and begun to sob. Jon went closer to her and held her head close to his, almost cheek to cheek. Lira was highly intuitive and realized something was seriously amiss, although not quite what the danger was. They had also discussed aspects of their first test, in which Caefon was a fully populated planet with much beauty and filled with all kinds of animal life, while at their present time no large animals or herbivores existed. Their present world was void of all life and completely different from what they had observed during their first test. Those aspects worried them.

She continued to speak in a quiet and more loving manner.

'Do you think I am overreacting?'

'I haven't thought too deeply about it, but you have an important point... it is how to evacuate that many people quickly. This underground city is much too small to accommodate them all. Perhaps the Ancients have already prepared a way,' he replied, quietly.

Gently, she moved away from him to dry her eyes.

'For thousands of years no one knew of the Ancients' survival plan, if indeed they have one, except for the little that we have learnt since our arrival down here. You know, our surface people know absolutely nothing of what's happening down here or anywhere else for that matter. They are not even aware of this underworld place beneath their feet.

'If anything dire should happen they will all be caught by surprise. Completely by surprise!' she stressed with ever welling despair.

He nodded his head in his usual manner for uncertainty when he could not give a positive reply.

'Let's keep this information to ourselves for now and discuss it with the others after our final tests, just before we leave this place. After all, we don't want the others to be as worried as we are, do we? Anyway, I think the Osmaronites might be keeping a check on the local systems by their many sensitive observation probes.' He reassured her, knowing of the technologies used and she accepted his viewpoint.

They were soon attracted by the flickering lights of the game computers in the distant corner and decided to participate in a little folly. Jon went to one of the panels and grabbed a lever. The second one he pointed to Lira.

The game was a variant of Space Wars. They were commanders of thirty-two star-ships each, fighting an alien force called the Javols. The aliens were portrayed as small circular space ships. They were an intelligent life-form with the ability to duplicate themselves in the presence of high energy levels. They could also merge together and become a single unit in the absence of energy.

However they disliked merging and would go to any lengths to prevent their fusion together as one.

The object of the game was to keep the Javols away from animal populations which they could swiftly utilized for food. They were also to be kept well away from intense energy sources such as explosions and stars, particularly after feeding. However they were easily enticed away from such places with a brighter light. Using such methods they could be chased into dark zones by black ships called maulars and when they merged together due to loss of energy, could be destroyed with a special type of laser weapon. A hot plasmic beam could destroy more than one simultaneously.

The Javols were truly invincible and had the power to negate electromagnetic observation of themselves. After their disappearance they could usually be found again within a limited spectrum which they were able to change at will. All those aspects were easily adjusted on the large control panel.

'Wow! What a game! I hope we never meet these Javols in real life,' she said, jokingly.

'Even with two against one they still beat us mercilessly. And I bet they could repeat their success with even four against one. It's a great game, but much too biassed on the side of the Javols,' he replied.

'What if they were that good and we had to fight them for real?' she said.

'Then I think we wouldn't stand a chance without some real advanced technology,' he replied.

'I think I've had enough losses for today. Why don't we go and see what the others are doing?' she said and they joined them at the bar in the next room.

Merol was presently standing at the bar by himself. He collected his drink and decided to join the group. He enjoyed that particular mixture and tended to have too much of the partly alcoholic substance.

'Hi, Mere! Still on the pink stuff I see? Jon greeted and Merol steered at them while taking another sip of the pinkish substance.

'It sure moves the senses,' he replied and smiled.

'Make it two of the same for us, Rob,' Jon said to the barman. In a few seconds their drinks were ready.

'I've.. got to talk with you guys about some important matters...,' Merol said and they followed him to the main table. He had consumed more than his normal share of the pink substance and was staggering, so Jon thought it was time he sat down.

'I hope no one objects, but I would like our future journey to take us past planet Meron.... That planet was named after one of my ancient ancestors, you know... It was one of the first to be destroyed during the great disaster.'

'Really? Please, tell us more!' Lira said.

'You know... a recent exploration by one of our archeological teams, found equipment strewn all over certain areas of the surface. Many well-preserved skeletons were observed within the larger ruins. Some were headless and had been picked clean of all flesh. Many of the human bones were found to be dissolved as well... I presume a powerful acid was injected through their spacesuits. With very little oxygen on that world, they were very well preserved and dated close to three thousand years in our past. It was almost as if the aliens.. I mean the predators, were searching for certain specific items during their occupation.'

'Alien predators on Planet Meron? That's definitely one for the books!' Lira interrupted. They began to laugh again.

'All their machinery were disassembled and metals taken away. However, all plastic and wooden parts were left untouched.'

'Are you sure?' Jon inquired.

'They were most probably miners collecting metallic salvage!' Ecrol interjected.

'What? Predatory miners!' Lira said and they laughed again.

'It can be proved they were not miners or any others for that matter. All that happened close to 3000 years ago. What do you make of that, eh? Anyway, planet Meron is much smaller than our home world Caefon... and because of its greater distance from our star, Stelon, always remains frozen, even during its summers,' Merol said while taking another sip.

They giggled merrily for a while.

'Mere, what are you drinking?' Ecrol inquired.

'Only my usual,' he replied and pointed an unsteady finger to his glass. By now it was half filled with the pink substance. He continued his conversation and would not be deterred.

'It is said that, the Ancients used it as an industrial-scientific planet, where special and sometimes dangerous experiments were conducted. Did you know that during their time any form of polluting industry was banned from Caefon? Its atmosphere and biosphere were so pure... With correct dieting, genetic engineering and organ transplants, most of them lived for more than a thousand years.'

The others were by now in continuous laughter and thought the conversation quite hilarious, but he continued.

'Just you think... a mere child at one-hundred years. One could take another hundred years to complete a stellar mission and afterwards have over nine hundred years left... Isn't that something. We, on the other hand will be lucky to make one hundred and fifty... even with the latest synthetic organ transplants. The world...'

Jon butted in, remembering the strange objects that was recently sighted not far from planet Meron. They could have been hiding behind their own anti-probing devices.

'It might be too dangerous now. Five strange objects were sighted close to planet Meron only a week ago. I did not mention it to you before for security reasons. But because we are now all in the same boat, so to speak, I see no point in concealing such security matters from our group any more.'

Lira, gazed with surprise at Jon, contemplating her worst nightmares.

'Can we hear the complete story please, Jon? It could be important to our future survival.'

As always, Lira's mind started racing along. For a while she was ahead of the conversation.

Jon continued his strange story.

'I was stationed at Base-Central. You know, the large interstellar probing facility south of Cantor, close to the Museum. There must be around five hundred of us working there, assessing all kinds of data from local and deep space probes. Sometimes we even received specially coded information from very distant worlds, even galaxies, I think.'

'That's incredible!' Sintra yelled.

'I assumed all such collected data were to do with a search for intelligent life. Such intelligence could have been either a threat or useful for trading purposes. Anyway, all data is first relayed to the Headrons.'

He paused...

'They could be the spherical beings from Osmaron. Those that we met. Obviously they are not interested in the nitty-gritty, so that part is passed over to us for analysis.'

'Go on!' Lira insisted.

'They directly intercept all alien receptions and those we are not allowed to interpret. Most of the data we receive are usually found to be unimportant and dumped. That is, stored in long term memory for scheduled analysis. Eight days ago something very strange happened.' Taking a quiet sip, he went on to describe the observation in detail.

Petra soon interrupted the conversation. She appeared to be the youngest of the six.

'They just simply vanished from view?'

'Yes, and that's not all,' he replied and went on to tell the remainder of his strange story.

Once again, taking the initiative Petra continued.

'You think the Headrons know who they are and are covering up their true identity for security or some other reason?'

'Yes, I do. They must know, and I think it's the reason why we have been selected for this special mission or Great Adventure as they prefer to call it. We must all be part of some master plan, put into operation years ago,' Jon replied.

Petra, looking highly inquisitive, responded.

'But who or what are those objects. I mean, the ones that were sighted and why are even the Headrons so scared of them. The Ancients may have also known of them, hence the reason for this underground city. Kept in secrecy for such a very long time from us on the surface. Even our fingers are different in number.'

A naked clue dropped and Lira couldn't restrain her thoughts any longer, so she interrupted.

'Our fingers could be a security ploy. The objects sighted or their masters must know the Ancients as having six fingers and two thumbs. It is probable that if these aliens thought the Ancients were still alive they would consider them a great threat and perhaps destroy them, including this world. We, on the other hand, could be overlooked as a newer and different occupying race with basic technologies and having no connection with the more advanced Ancients. Even our technologies could have been deliberately changed and in some ways held back, to keep us at a more primitive level in order to mislead the enemy. What an incredible plan!' Lira said, full of excitement.

'I couldn't help observing the equipment of the Ancients. Although it's very advanced in comparison to ours, but for the Headrons who seem completely different, it could still be three thousand years old technology. If that stuff was extensively used all over the galaxy, as they may have traded extensively, they would have advanced a lot since. Wouldn't they? If that is the case, the outer and even the inner trading worlds would be regularly visiting us at this time, even from Osmaron. Wouldn't they?' Julia interjected.

Yes! You are correct!' Jon replied.

'Why are there no such visits and why is there no advanced technologies in our galaxy at this time? Was it all wiped out about the same time as the Ancients?' Julia added.

Lira almost choked on her drink.

'Great Lord Gerron! No wonder only primitive life with little threatening technology has ever been found; with the exception of Coln System, and they are so different from us, with flying wings and feathers. Yet their technologies are of our levels and they have recently fled from their previous home-world, perhaps to avoid those savage aliens. It is obvious that our surface technologies do not pose a threat to those aliens or whatever they are called,' Lira said.

She paused, taking another small sip, but continued.

'It seems then, that Osmaron is still safe. Although advanced in their own ways, these predatory aliens still do not possess the necessary technologies required for intergalactic travel and it may take them several thousand years to travel across intergalactic space to Osmaron. So the Osmaronites, led by their Lord Gerra, is now here to help their old friends with a technology that's another three thousand years more advanced, perhaps even advanced enough to kill the Aliens.'

She paused again for another sip.

'But why us? What are we chosen for and what is this Great Adventure?' Lira asked.

Julia, being a quiet listener for most of the time, entered into the conversation.

'One thing I have observed... the grey dust we inhaled... it's alive. It has a kind of inert life of its own and can be controlled externally. Perhaps they are even microscopic robots. I have a very sensitive system, even as a child. Whenever I inhaled that grey stuff, I am sure I felt them moving inside me... Thousands of them... even inside my head. Perhaps I am just imagining things, but small robots would answer a lot of questions. Sort of micro robots, but perhaps the size of a primal cell with some form of innate intelligence and suitably programmed to follow external commands.'

Lira butted in.

'But they would need numerous amounts of memory banks and control equipment to handle thousands of those things individually, wouldn't they?'

'Yes. I think those large crystal blocks must be their control media... some form of massive storage and control equipment. You know, that form of technology could be a lot more advanced than the Ancients'. For some odd reason the glittering and blinking blocks seem somehow out of place with the helmets and other more bulkier equipment of the Ancients. But I am just supposing,' Julia replied.

'If that's the case, then complete microid bodies could be made from that stuff, each individual following commands from a central nervous system. Better yet, through phased microwave communication or even a type of brain with its own synthetic neurons with synapses. But each of those micro robots would be required to store and use energy through some unknown metabolic sequence. What if all those micro robots were composed mainly of semi-solid metals and were able to store energy within some bonding chains with certain chemicals to initiate certain reactions or metabolic change?'

'Sounds like our worst nightmare!' Merol said.

'Think about it! A metal that can take the form and shape of anything... even to seemingly change its form into a liquid or gas,' Lira said, again excitedly.

Suddenly, she paused in deep thought.

'Great Lord Gerron! What a bloody nightmare!'

Jon suddenly remembered his encounter with the strange ship and glanced at Merol. Then he explained:

'We excavated just such a ship in the Craile Desert recently.'

They moved closer in anticipation and he continued his story.

'The ship had no doors or anything, just three insignias of the Ancients. So it could have been very old. Despite that fact, it looked brand spanking new as if made recently. Yet, age measurements taken on local soil samples placed it at around three thousand years in the past. Merol and I went to view the ship a few days ago... just before we arrived here,' and he continued his bizarre story until the end.

'A ship made of micro robots, over three thousand years ago and yet brand new today. Do you think it was placed in that part of the desert on purpose; to be discovered by someone... or could it have been just a coincidence?' Lira said.

'I think, although it's ancient in origin, it was placed there to be discovered. Perhaps it was dug out from another site and placed there to be found, but even that hypothesis does not hold out when all the facts are considered. You see, the different types of desert sand that were removed close to its body during the excavation displayed no traces of surface sand. So the only other conclusion is that it materialized there, which is an impossibility. Very soon after its discovery it was reported a hoax and no one bothered with that discovery any more, except Merol and myself out of personal archaeological curiosity,' Jon said.

Lira then commented, in an old and ancient tongue.

'And lo our great intergalactic adventure have begun.'

Jon looked at her in a curious manner.

'You think this ship is intergalactic in origin, with no jets or any other type of propellant?' Jon asked.

'The Ancients, with their Osmaron brothers may have solved the gravitation problem millennia ago. Perhaps it utilises some type of anti-gravity drive. Didn't you observe Lord Vektron and his other counterpart, floating in mid air without a sound?

'How do you think they did it, with jet propulsion and space drives?' she replied.

Jon remained silent for a moment.

'But if what we think is correct, then our enemies, the aliens, for want of a better name, may have a similarly advanced technology made solely and efficiently to destroy? If that is the case what chance do we have, even of getting to Osmaron?'

'Exactly! That is what the Ancients thought some three thousand years ago. That is why there is no advanced life left in our galaxy and finally the reason why the Ancients concealed themselves within this underground city until the time was right. And don't you forget, these aliens are now more than three thousand years more advanced.'

'My God! We are in such big trouble!' Ecrol exclaimed.

'These things, whatever they are, will not accept a threat of any kind. They appear to be anti normal-coexistence with life as we know it... even anti trade, and why trade if they can take whatever they desire by force, anyway. In fact, they appear to be anti everything concerning our kind of life, except towards their own and are perhaps completely rapacious and cruel by nature....' Lira replied.

Jon interrupted.

'But other worlds including ours must have been allowed to exist for a reason?'

'No more than you would allow Malaks to graze for their milk and not provide any green shoots for them to feed on,' she replied.

They continued the discussion until very late that evening. When they broke up, they were even more worried and confused than they had been before their first drink that evening.

They were now of the opinion that they were specially chosen since birth and realized their mission was of significant importance if they were to save the lives of family and friends in that part of Andromeda.

CHAPTER 30

Reflections of the past

The following morning they journeyed towards the small lake. That trek took them to the area where they had met the furry Malak on a previous occasion.

The route was again via the small clearing, but to their disappointment the Malak was no where to be seen, so they continued onwards to explore.

That underworld lake was situated on a small plateau at a slightly lower level than the forest and included a fountain on a green-moss area close to the path. Planet Caefon had not evolved grasses as on Earth. Instead thick purple and green moss would grow over the exposed land areas. There were many varieties that were suitable for all kinds of landscapes. Since there were no grazing animals presently on Caefon the moss was more numerous and grew to enormous size.

Ecrol in his excitement went directly to the fountain to take a sip of the seemingly clear water. He found it refreshing and took several mouthfuls by hand. It was the purest mineral water he had ever drank. The others were more interested in the other side of the small lake where they could faintly observe most beautiful water flowers floating close to its bank.

The lake was crystal-clear so they could observe small creatures swimming and flapping about underneath. Such variety did not exist within fresh water lakes or rivers, so they were surprised that such creatures could stay or even live under water.

Lira pointed towards one of the flapping creatures and explained:

'Fonides, these are the fresh water variety. Like some rear types in our deep oceans, they can breathe under water using an oxygen separating process. The seas and oceans used to be filled to capacity in ancient times with numerous variety of such life. They were then in great abundance everywhere.'

She was saddened by the thought of their disappearance from the surface, but realized there was still hope. Once they had existed, they could always be reintroduced. However that process could take a very long time and only be implemented after the surface dangers had been removed on a permanent basis.

'Today, only a few rear species exist in our deep oceans and seas and only the saline variety. Some say it was due to de-stabilization of the biosphere since the Ancients' demise, but I am not convinced,' she added.

'I never knew life could exist under water like this,' Jon replied. The others couldn't stop gazing at the beautifully coloured marine creatures that seldom came up to the surface for air.

They observed the wide variety of fresh water fish and other water creatures in their strange underworld. With its days and nights artificially mimicking those of the planet's surface above in almost every detail. They wondered, 'here is life in its abundance, beauty and variety. Caefon must have been a planet of great beauty in the days of the Ancients'. Once again Jon glanced at his small timepiece.

'Come on people! It's time for breakfast!' he yelled and they were once more on their way to the accommodation centre.

They had enjoyed that morning's trek, but a little disappointed for not having seen the Malak. Nevertheless they were now in a more confident mood for breakfast.

The guards always presented themselves in the mornings to accompany the six to the laboratory waiting room. Their presence at that time were to ensure the six were not delayed. Plato was always punctual and precise with his schedules and appeared to be always in a great hurry.

That morning they returned to the small waiting room through the laboratory. That was the one they attended during their first psychological tests. While there they awaited his arrival in a better mood than usual. They realized it was their last and final test before their trip to Osmaron, so they were more relaxed in anticipation.

Shadite Plato soon announced his presence. This time he was wearing a black hooded cloak. That cloak did not reflect any light and cast deep shadows. They became fearful of the form stood before them. Then he dropped the hood and his head popped out of darkness. The hood was folded back behind and above his neck, but he displayed the same insignia over his left breast. It included the two wings and blue-green inner circle. On his forehead was the imprint of what appeared to be the shape of a crucifix or sword to denote he was Senot.

'Ah... we have arrived at last to the final day of your assessment. I shall dearly miss this assignment when it's all over. I am to return to Osmaron shortly. Another assignment, you know. We shall meet again in the not too distant future under more mutually pleasant and favourable conditions. After your final tests, you should visit the lower city museum and learn more about our ancient customs and traditions before you depart on your Great Adventure. But now, we have work to do and an important operation to complete.'

He selected Jon, who quietly followed.

The final tests were in the same place as before, with the three helmets above and looking down unto three sitting positions next to his large desk. This time however there was an extra viewing screen to one side and also a larger array of crystal blinking blocks. One in particular was a multi-level unit with numerous multicoloured blinking lights. This device appeared to be very sensitive, for it gave a grand display when Jon was placed under the first helmet. He was made to sit and the helmet descended from the ceiling towards his head.

'Make yourself as comfortable as possible and relax,' Plato said.

He was then offered a bluish substance. Unlike the greyish type, it was kept in a small transparent container that was tinted blue.

'Now, inhale as much as you can and try not to sneeze,' Plato advised.

He did as asked and was told again to relax.

CHAPTER 31

Test 3 - Jon and Meron

The present soon faded into the Ancients' past about three thousand years before. Once again Jon found himself as the great scientist and politician called Meron. This time he was on a grand space ship of very advanced technology travelling towards a nearby planet. That same planet was later to be called by his own name, Meron. They docked at a large orbiting station to take on supplies before their interstellar journey.

The ship and its contents were of a military nature. Most of its crew wore uniforms, not too unlike the surface ones used at present times by the military. There were many operators wearing control helmets. Those stereo helmets made them at one with the ship's computer. They sat close to instrument panels in the control room where he stood.

A large circular viewing screen was apparent on a wall directly in front of their positions. He held on firmly to a circular rail while standing in an upright position in full command of proceedings.

Meron wore a long cream gown, with military stripes on his left shoulder and a metal head band that included a small crystal crucifix held firmly to his forehead. That symbol represented his religion which was Senot. The gown was largely creased with shoulders padded high.

A flexible metal belt held firmly to his waist. It was dotted throughout its length with beautiful gems. Dangling from the belt was a long scabbard, equally studded with precious gems. The scabbard contained a long sword. That ancient sword was Melor's own that had been handed down through the generations since Micol's time. In those days the Ancients used such swords to represent status and Meron was one of Micol's direct descendants. Only the most highest ranking wore such attire, usually worn on special occasions.

His golden hair was plumed like a tall fountain and contained by a second adjustable jewelled band.

He stood well over two metres tall and perhaps a head above the tallest local crew member. He signalled to the captain who sat at an angle to where he stood. The captain pressed several buttons and a code was entered into a panel on his chair. Some of the operators alongside the captain could be seen also wearing viewing helmets. Those facilities may have been used to prevent distraction from other crew members while on important missions. Since those Ancients had never accepted the idea of brain implants, helmets were the only alternative.

The captain responded to him by speaking directly.

'LPD's have been primed and tested, Sire, for commencement of our interstellar journey to Silo.'

Meron waved his hand to the captain and he pressed a large button on the panel. Nothing happened for a few seconds. Then a slight creeping sensation was felt. Slowly the position of the stars on the large screen changed. Then there was a blinding flash and within a fraction of a second, planet Meron simply vanished from the large viewer.

Lord Meron turned to the captain and in a powerful voice spoke.

'What is our estimated time of arrival?'

'About one sectron, 3 detons *(six point five hours)*, Sire, give or take half a deton *(five minutes)*,' he replied, in the language of the Ancients. Since Caefon's rotational period was similar to Earth's, those values were almost equivalent to Earth time.

Meron turned around and went directly to his cabin to catch up on lost sleep. His handmaiden assisted him to undress and he retired for a quick nap.

When they approached Silo he was suddenly awakened.

'A communication, Sire, from your brother Plato. He is now near Silo,' the officer said, through the communicator.

'Plato? What is he doing here? I thought he was in Osmaron!'

'He is an observer, Sire, on a remote station. He represents the Sword. By intergalactic license he has to observe, Sire,' the officer replied.

Plato was connected and soon spoke to his brother.

'Hello, Grand Brother, I had to visit this location in a hurry and

hadn't any time to announce my arrival through usual channels. My orders come from the highest level!'

'Oh!'

'I'm afraid our planet Silo and all its posts and installations have been lost. The things, for some unknown reason, have established themselves about the parent star. They are doubling in number every hour or so.

'Several attempts have been made to destroy them, but they appear to live on radiant energy as well. It is now quite difficult to get close to them. The most powerful beam weapons only make them replicate faster. Large quantities cannot be killed by this method. Only super-hot plasma can have any real effect and can only be used at close range.

'We are now analysing their behaviour for some weakness before they decide to leave this area... and the situation gets completely out of our hands. Our physicist and psychologists are observing their activity in case there is some small flaw in their design and methodology.

'Anyway, I shall see you soon.'

Then he broke off the communication and the screen went blank.

Meron was disturbed by what he saw. A complete inhabited world in ruins, including all artificial satellites and stations... Millions of settlers in that region were to be presumed dead.

He knew in past his race always won their battles and conquered all significant obstacles, but this one was an unknown. Its character was somehow different from the others. He thought of the great catastrophe before him and of a probable solution, but none came to mine. It was nothing like the days of his ancestors, when their world was almost destroyed by global warming.

'I wish you were here now, great Micol, to advise us of a way out of this mess,' he said to himself, before contemplating the almost unsurmountable problem.

'For any mass to reproduce itself in such a manner, it had to absorb another. Surely, energy by itself was not enough. These things must have some means whereby they collect and store raw material for synthesis during the high energy absorption phase within their metabolism. This meant they could only reproduce a limited number of times while the stored matter lasted. That was providing their secondary masses remained the same as their original mass. However, their size could remain the same in all cases, depending on molecular bonding, whether tightly or loosely bound.'

He pondered those thoughts while attempting to find a quick solution.

'But, the special ship I collected from the scientists on Silo was all right. I flew it myself to Cantor. What were these scientists trying to do, anyway? I was always unsure of those blocks of apparently solid matter, moving by themselves and changing shape at will. Each microid bit, with its own logic and partial intelligence. They may have tried to make them think and behave as a single entity. That's where the problem could lie.' He calmly took a small cup of water from a dispenser and drank.

'I heard about the experiments but didn't believe in the seriousness of those rumours. How could such a microid mass appreciate the importance of life with all its attitudes and attributes learnt and evolved over billions of years? It would only be interested in matter and energy for the sake of its own survival causation once it had an inkling of its own existence. The fear of its own demise may have driven it to those extremes.' He sipped.

'But why destroy all life? Could it be because of the abundance of rear metals stored within most living organisms. Their nourishment is perhaps easier to absorb in that manner?'

Suddenly he called one of his close assistants by name.

'Hamil, please prepare an operations room. We need to probe these things closer.'

Shortly thereafter engineers and scientists began to prepare a small area not too distant from the main control room. It was fitted with all types of monitors and computerized equipment hooked into the ship's main computer.

They decided to remain in a much closer, but fixed stellar orbit to observe the creatures. That new position would take them within twenty-million kilometres from the corona of the parent star. Although the heat and radiation would be intense, they could withstand it for a few hours with radiation shields set to maximum.

The objects still remained stationery, but replication had ceased as he had predicted. It was more than two hours since the last period of separation. His task was now a matter of calculating the relevant materials absorbed from the population consumed. That answer would give an indication of the total mass absorbed by the original parent things. He was not sure of all the chemicals used by the things in order to make accurate calculations. Nevertheless there were several reports of their original designs in Caefon's secured archives. Those he would view on his return.

Each thing was a little over a metre across and included a central bulge which may have represented its brain. They occupied a line of about one-point-six thousand kilometres. There were over one million of them and for some odd reason many were touching each other as if in some form of intense communication.

While being observed, they formed into several large spherical shapes, each containing about five hundred individuals. Then they departed in a direction towards the centre of the galaxy at incredible speed. That direction was towards the brightest points of light in the galaxy.

The disaster had been reported just over fifteen hours ago. During that time Meron and his crew had collected and analysed all relevant data until they were exhausted.

When Hamil was satisfied that there was no more data left to collect, they decided to turn their ship around and head for home. Everything was left as dead as they had become at that time in that part of the galaxy. Plato followed them home in a different ship.

Soon after the chief scientist Hamil went up to Meron and handed him a written note.

'Sire, their current route, if continued, will eventually take them to the centre of our galaxy.'

He took the paper and read it, glancing at Hamil with an expression of overwhelming defeat. This war he hadn't planned for and was unsure of its outcome.

'They appear to be extremely intelligent. They adapt and learn incredibly quickly. You and your assistants will calculate all relevant causal relationships as accurately as possible. We need to know when we are to expect the main group back within our system, given present populations within the inner galactic region. Here, we may assume they will return as a result of natural expansion away from the central galactic region for food and other essential resources. May glorious Seno in the Plains of Heron assist us in finding a quick solution out of this mess,' Meron replied, while touching the crucifix on his forehead.

Hamil went away while Meron observed the note. Then he crushed it within his angry fist and threw it away in disgust.

'NO PRESENT MEANS HAVE BEEN FOUND TO DE-STROY THESE OBJECTS, NOW NAMED JAVOL AFTER THE ANCIENT MYTHICAL GOD OF FIRE AND DE-STRUCTION.

ONLY AFTER CAREFUL OBSERVATION, DURING ACTUAL ENCOUNTERS, MAY WE DETECT A WEAK-NESS OR FLAW IN THEIR CONSTRUCTION OR REPRO-DUCTIVE CYCLES.

WE SHOULD FURTHER ADVICE CAUTION IN THE USE OF HIGH ENERGY BEAM WEAPONS AGAINST THEM AND RECOMMEND A REDUCTION OF ALL HIGHLY EXPLOSIVE DEVICES CURRENTLY HELD WITHIN POPULATED AREAS.

THIS IS NECESSARY TO AVOID OUR OWN DESTRUC-TION WHEN RANDOMLY ATTACKED BY THEIR FEW REMAINING WANDERING GROUPS. FURTHER, WE ARE TO SUGGEST THE SATURATION OF ALL POPU-LATED GALACTIC REGIONS, WHENEVER POSSIBLE, WITH UNMANNED DETECTION AND OBSERVATION PROBES FOR A PERIOD OF ASSESSMENT.

THIS PROJECT MAY HOWEVER TAKE SEVERAL YEARS, EVEN CENTURIES, AND WE ARE NOT SURE OF A SOLUTION EVEN AFTER THAT TIME.

DURING THE INTERVENING PERIOD SUITABLE CODED WARNINGS SHOULD BE BROADCASTED FROM RANDOM TRANSMITTING PROBES, TO FRIENDS, NEIGHBOURS AND OTHERS THROUGHOUT OUR GALAXY, WHILE SURVIVAL PREPARATIONS MADE AS BEST WE CAN AND AS SOON AS POSSIBLE.

THIS REPORT IS NEITHER ACCURATE NOR CONCLUSIVE IN ITS RECOMMENDATIONS, AS MORE PRECISE DATA ON JAVOLS HAVE NOT BEEN FORTHCOMING.

END OF NOTE'

The chief scientist Hamil again returned.

He saluted Meron and handed him a second note that he again read.

'MORE CAREFUL OBSERVATIONS AND CALCULATIONS HAVE INDICATED THE JAVOLS WILL GROW IN QUANTITY TO A MASS OF SEVERAL TIMES OUR SOLAR SYSTEM.

WHEN THEY RETURN OUTWARD FROM THE GALACTIC CENTRE, THEIR POPULATION WILL NOT EXPAND AS QUICKLY BECAUSE OF THE GREATER STELLAR DISTANCES INVOLVED BETWEEN FEEDS. THEY MAY EVEN BEGIN TO BE STARVED OF ESSENTIAL RESOURCES, LEADING TO DEATH. WE ARE UNSURE OF THAT ASPECT, AS THEY MAY ASSUME A STATE OF DORMANCY OR HIBERNATION FOR EXTREMELY LONG PERIODS.

EVEN WITH GREAT LOSSES TO THEIR NUMBERS, WE WOULD EXPECT ABOUT THREE BY TEN EX TWELVE WITHIN OUR SECTOR OF OUR HYPARON GALAXY. WHICH AS YOU CAN UNDERSTAND IS A NUMBER IMPOSSIBLE TO DEAL WITH, EVEN IF WE KNEW OF A SUITABLE WAY TO STOP THEM... AND WHAT IF THEY ARE STARVED AND EXTREMELY HUNGRY? WE MAY HOWEVER FIND A WEAKNESS DURING THIS PERIOD.

MAKING ALL DUE ALLOWANCES FOR MUTATIONAL CHANGES TOWARDS A MORE EFFICIENT ADAPTATION TO SURVIVE, THEIR MAIN GROUP MAY ONCE AGAIN VISIT US FROM THE CENTRAL REGION OF OUR GALAXY APPROXIMATELY THREE THOUSAND AND FIVE HUNDRED YEARS IN THE FUTURE.

WE SHOULD STRESS, HOWEVER, THAT SMALL GROUPS THAT LEFT IMMEDIATELY AFTER THE DESTRUCTION OF SILO, MAY INHABIT THE LOCAL INTERSTELLAR SPACE FOR A PERIOD OF TIME, BEFORE THEY IN TURN DECIDE TO REJOIN THE MAIN GROUP FOR MUTUAL SURVIVAL AND PROTECTION.

END OF NOTE'.

The second report was even less helpful. This time Meron saved the note.

On arrival to the ancient city of Cantor, Meron summoned his younger brother Plato, the Shadite, to his palatial dwellings. Plato was equally concerned and never too far behind. That evening they decided to discuss those matters in private. The two strolled towards the large balcony that overlooked a beautiful garden now in late spring bloom.

He gave orders not to be disturbed and security screens activated. He smiled at his younger brother.

'What's your opinion on this dreadful matter, Brother?'

Meron seldom ever called Plato, Brother, but at that moment every living thing took on a new meaning and his brother was now sacred in his eyes.

'I think we have a very serious problem on our hands... judging from the gestation period of these microid mutants, their abilities, lifespan, capacity to destroy... and their ferocious and rapacious nature. One cannot reason with such a life-form. They might even be provided with a crude but usable form of LPD propulsion. Something they would have been able to copy and reproduce from an original blueprint. Their motion suggests it and even that aspect can be improved with time.

'Really? Professor Andra have outdone himself this time!'

'Yes! And they are still evolving at an incredible rate.'

'What a bloody mess!'

'The ability to copy, assimilate and fabricate most technologies is one of their unique functions that was given them in the original blueprint. They will also have the ability to form wings and fly or glide within planetary environments, even without the use of LPDs. However, they may group together to use a single LPD and travel from place to place,' Plato advised

'Until they can fabricate them more efficiently?'

'Yes! Then they will be able to go anywhere and move in any direction. They also have powers and abilities to change into different forms of an equivalent mass, camouflage or become invisible.'

'A new and deadlier life-form than anything before, but conceived and engineered within our own laboratories and by our own scientists. Luckily, not closer to home, on planet Mohria for instance. But how could that have happened, Brother, and why?' Meron probed, utterly saddened by the fact with dismay and dread for the future of his world and its populations.

Plato continued to observe the sadness in his brother's eyes.

'Perhaps a simple error in a control instruction. Even a missing one during the conversion phase. Any omission or addition during a sequence of such instructions could have triggered a type of microid cancer. Then it could quickly have become established throughout the sample. With complex organic systems that are critically balanced, that situation seldom occurs and the life-form would eventually die. However, in this case there are no complex organs involved and the original blueprints was preserved.'

'A type of cancer that assisted in creating the worst monster in our universe!' Meron Replied.

'From what I learnt, the scientists were working on a new concept, to fuse mind and body as one. This would have solved the problem of the bulky external equipment needed to control each individual microid.'

'They have definitely solved that problem, with every living thing their enemy!'

'They also thought of further miniaturization of memory modules, but that was several years away and they had to satisfy your Ministry of Finance for more funding if the project was to continue. In order for it to have been more practical during use, they had to reduce memory banks by at least one thousandth, volumetrically. So they tried a different approach and you know the rest.'

'I suppose we can't really blame them for trying. By now we could all be celebrating if the method worked!' Meron said.

'That special ship, you know, was quite impractical. The main bulk of it was control and memory modules. Yet it worked practically enough to convince you and your council to pour more resources into Andra's project.'

'Yes! I also assisted them in congress! Our government could see unrest in a future of recession, so we needed a better army to quell revolts. Andra's methods seemed the only way forward for the perfect soldier.'

'They are perfect soldiers alright, but uncontrollable and are against all living things.'

'Where do we go from here, Brother? How can we evacuate a whole galaxy within a reasonable period and to where shall they go?' Meron asked, now completely lost for answers.

'It seems to me that we require some serious assistance from those who know best,' Plato replied.

'Who are they?' Meron enquired, while glancing at the Shadites cloak.

'Don't worry. Leave it with me for now,' Plato said.

Jon slowly awoke from his dreamlike state. Plato was still at the controls and Jon suddenly realised the close resemblance between the man Plato in his dream, over 3000 years ago. He couldn't help saying:

'Are you the real Plato?'

But Plato pointed to another vial, this time pinkish in colour and insisted.

'Please inhale once more. This is the final part.'
There was a period of silence and suddenly Jon found himself in what could only be described as a shimmering tunnel of light. Its walls contained all forms of data and images which blinked pass as he travelled at great speed. Ever so often a doorway would appear directly ahead with some specific detail, perhaps to stress an important point. It would slam open to let him through, and slam shut behind him as he passed, but the journey continued. The information was completely unrecognizable to him and yet acceptable to his subconscious mind.

The tunnel came to an abrupt end in complete darkness. He slowly regained normality and found Plato checking his eyes with a bright light.
'It is all done. You are now free to go.'
Jon soon regained his composure and was escorted to the nearby waiting room.

CHAPTER 32

Lira and Lucia

Lira was called next. This time she was more sombre, in expectation of something even worse than the loss of her hair and her previous gruesome encounters with the Megotron and Psyro tron.

Subconsciously she removed the small cap from her almost bald head and sat in the middle chair, then Plato observed her and smiled. The helmet descended and fitted over her clean shaven head. She was told to inhale the blue substance and relax, which she attempted, nervously.

A moment passed as the present gradually faded into the past.

She was now Lucia, patiently awaiting the return of her husband Meron who was with his brother Plato on the balcony. They were discussing some important and private matter from which she had been excluded.

'What was it all about?' She thought, 'What could be that important? After all, Plato was now a Shadite and Master of the Sword. His presence anywhere was never to be taken lightly.'

She was irritable and worried for the worst while mumbling to herself.

'They were usually present in an official capacity with that black hooded cloak... mourning gown... when there was an impending disaster or during one.'

The security screen was soon released and the inner balcony door opened as both brothers walked into the living room.

'Hi, Sis!' Plato greeted casually, and she nodded her head in a curious manner, but with slight annoyance. Being the youngest, she always considered Plato as one of her own brothers and treated him in like manner.

He greeted her again, this time in a more solemn manner and she gently bowed, showing him greater respect. Then Meron turned to her and pressed a bracelet on his left hand to seal the room. He spoke to her in a stun voice:

'Darling, we have serious problems ahead. A matter that will affect the future lives of all existing within our galaxy, now and very far into the future.'

Then he went on to describe all circumstances in detail.

'The things we call the Javols have left, but they will soon return to completely destroy our world as they have done to Silo.'

'Gracious Lord Gerron!' she exclaimed.

She was stunned by what she heard, but only listened, and when he was finished she spoke to them in an authoritative manner.

'From the holy words coming from the lips of our ancient profit and saint, Seno, we have had serious survival problems before and have survived. That last time our god came to our assistance. Although it's over 2000 years since, Grand Lord Gerron has not forgotten us. But we must try to find a way out of this mess by ourselves, since by universal law we are responsible.'

'It has been written in one of our holy books that a great disaster will one day befall us and make us flee to Osmaron. This is it!' Plato said in no uncertain terms and they stared at him.

'Really!' Meron replied, not wishing to probe his brother for his deeper secrets and knowledge.

'We must not tell the children, Darling. We must never let them know of the grave dangers facing us in the future!' she demanded and they agreed.

Although she was quite sad and worried for the future of her world and its people, as a senior councillor she was known to take the initiative as she had done on numerous occasions, so she continued to speak.

'We have to select a small group of trustworthy council members and others, to assist in formulating a survival plan. But it must all be done in the greatest secrecy. If word of impending doom or any of this information should leak out, there could be panic and pandemonium on an unprecedented scale. It could even trigger a mass exodus to Osmaron. Can you imagine the whole of our galaxy flooding Osmaron? Even if we had the resources, we couldn't build such large ships in time. Neither do we have resources in those quantities. And the creatures could follow us there with even greater problems.'

'I agree!' Meron replied.

'It must all be kept under wraps for now, until we can find a reasonable solution. All observers and scientists who have knowledge of this project and of those Javol things must go underground. Use them in our future groups or have them posted to some remote location on a new project. Words on this sensitive topic must only be mentioned to a chosen few.' She stressed.

Meron showing great concern, spoke again.

'The original information was relayed to my office security coded, with my own personal cypher. The information is stored in a dedicated twenty-four hour volatile memory bank. Only I can prevent erasure by entering a special retrievable code. So in two hours all the original information of the destruction of Silo will be lost for good.'

'That's good thinking!' she replied.

'As for the crew of my ship, they have all signed the oath of secrecy and will not divulge any of those experiences if they are to remain in their present senior positions.'

That's comforting!' Plato replied.

'However, a major problem still remain. How are we to prevent tourists and others from visiting Silo. Some people here on Caefon will expect communication from relatives and friends on that world. We shall have to mention about some form of pandemic disaster. Perhaps a most contagious and deadly bio-engineered virus, which is not too far beyond what had really occurred,' he said, and Lucia was pleased with that alternative.

Turning to Plato again, she spoke.

'Perhaps you will wear something more comfortable during your brief visit. One of my husband's latest tunics? They are very fashionable, you know, and you will look good and be more comfortable.' Plato had to agree. She could never get accustomed to the black Shadites cloak and thought it reminded her of death and destruction.

The two younger children soon arrived from their special classes with the Gondril named Moe.

The human-like creature had a crinkled face with pointed chin and had six fingers and two thumbs. He walked with a slight limp and was also slightly curved at the shoulders but always eager to run errands. She asked Moe to take the little four-legged creature called Sox for a walk in one of the local parks. Moe understood and soon disappeared with Sox wagging her bushy tail in her moment of enjoyment.

The animal was clipped to the Gondril's waist belt, being restrained by what appeared to be a thick elastic line. The innocent children soon departed to their section of the house for recreation and refreshments that had been prepared earlier by the domestic staff.

Subsequently Lucia made a list of all council members and others that she thought capable of responsible and honest action in the face of diversity and handed the list to Meron. He glanced down the list of names and selected some six members. She took the list and crossed out two names and added two more. Then she handed it back to Meron.

'Now we have also included Tomas,' she insisted. She remained silent for a moment, showing even greater concern for her eldest son. Wondering whether he was safe during his recent space trials for the Ministry of Defence, but continued to speak.

'Any more objections, anyone?' They nodded their heads as to agree.

'In that case we have our survival team! Now for a plan of action!'

The chosen members, were: Meron, Tomas, Plato, Hamil, Lucia, Sintra and Merian. They were experts in their respective fields and with the exception of the Shadite, Plato, were all senior members of the Governing Council.

Plato was flattered for having been chosen and explained that he could never be a full time member because of his other commitments and responsibilities as a Shadite, but would help as best he could on a part-time basis. They agreed to his answer, but nevertheless made him an honorary member. He was to assist in whatever way he could, whenever he could. Nevertheless Plato was their only link with The Greater Purpose, who turned out to be pivotal in their survival.

All members were now to be located and brought together in secrecy for their first meeting.

With the exception of Tomas, each were subsequently called and told it was about an important security matter and agreed to meet at a predetermined safe location.

It was decided to hold the first meeting in Central Cantor at Merian's home. It was situated in a very busy part of the city with good access to transport and communications.

The Cantor shown was a most delightful place. It was completely different to the one of present day, which had been resurrected from the southern ruins many centuries later.

Two massive thoroughfares cris-crossed the city, cutting it into four almost equal parts. At its centre was what appeared to be an ancient monument that held the statue of their once great leader, Micol. A large golden crucifix or sword perched on its topmost spire and in the central hall was a blue marble statue of their profit and saint Seno. That ancient building was also the last resting place of the Oracle, Mohria.

Pedestrians travelled throughout the city on moving walkways. Those formed two sets of three, moving in opposite directions. Each walkway forming a set of three that travelled at different speeds. The slowest was just a brisk walk, to the fastest which was equivalent to a high speed pedestrian race. Along each moving walkway were numerous vertical poles for passengers to hold. On the side of such sets of moving walkways were the usual side-walks. Walkways also crisscrossed each other for easy access to others or to fixed exit and entry points.

It was not possible to cross over from one moving walkway set to another without first completely stopping at one of the lay-byes, when moving along a diversion walkway. There were many such lay-byes. They were auspiciously decorated with small catering units and sitting areas about well lit sparkling fountains.

Destination signs were shown almost everywhere on-route in

ancient script and each route terminated with audiovisual messages. The whole scene, including all those bright and multicoloured displays were spectacular to watch

Most Ancients wore special identification cards clipped to their breast pockets. Those could easily be accessed by computers while in motion for security reasons and would further aid in their travel.

One could see numerous gaming and recreation facilities, video play houses, refreshment parlours, music centres, auditoriums and a lot more that couldn't even be described by Earth's broad variety. Anyone could always find a satisfying venue at anytime of day or night. Cantor was then the Empire's main trading city and seat of government. It dealt with a constant stream of visitors and dignitaries from that region of Galaxy Andromeda.

The city buildings tended to increase in size at greater distances from the centre while the local sky was filled with small specks of light that constantly moved to and fro within the great canopy. Perhaps they were space ships or even passenger liners. Despite its many features, there was almost complete silence within the city; except for the slight vibration and buffeting of the moving walkways.

The whole view, with the inclusion of advertising signs, portrayed a grand mosaic of colour and patterns.

The sky as usual, displayed two brilliant moons, Proteus and Simas, one much smaller than the other. Both showing a slight crescent. Proteus lay closer to the horizon.

Both moons contained well established mining colonies and production plants, having always been rich in relevant minerals.

Lucia felt excited by the great spectacle of a city alive and held Meron's hand tightly. Plato followed not too far behind, perhaps rediscovering youthful memories in his city of birth; for it was that kind of place.

As they approached their destination Lucia decided it was more prudent to exit at the next lay-by and walk the rest of the way to Merian's house. She had suddenly become more security-conscious and intended to minimize all risks on the day of their first meeting. So they ignored the busy underground tube-cars with their many faceless occupants in fear of being recognised, overheard or monitored.

They soon arrived at their intended location, Merian greeted and bowed to Meron. He was her senior and a very important and respected member of the grand council. She escorted them into a much larger room with many different forms of animals and insect carvings portrayed on walls. Two large crystal cabinets were positioned in corners. They displayed more carvings and artifacts.

Merian introduced them to Hamil and Sintra who had arrived earlier that evening. All apparently knew each other well from previous associations. They were sat comfortably around a small table in the middle of the room while Merian chatted about her family.

'My dear husband, Ranul, collected most of these artifacts during his interstellar travels. He has always worked for the government in one agricultural field or another. He used to be Chief Agriculturalist on Silo but has been recently made Governor.'

'This collection is most unique and fascinating!' Meron closely observed their natural forms and colour. Many in beautiful dark-blue lazulite.

'During past interstellar assignments he was able to satisfy this collecting hobby of his, but we have added many pieces to our collection since. He is quite busy since his recent appointment. Even with those new responsibilities he still continues his biological conversion project on Silo... even so, collecting has always been in his blood...' she said.

'Where is he now?' Lucia inquired.

'Last I heard he was still on Silo, performing his duties for the Empire. He has been away from us for two years, but I have my own interests. Our children are married and now live away independently,' Merian replied.

Lucia was saddened by that fact and sat her down for bad news.

She stared sympathetically at Merian not knowing quite how to break the news to her about her husband's demise, but soon took the initiative.

'For security reasons, which I shall explain to you later, no personal recorders will be allowed during this or any of our future meetings. Not even the usual notes may be taken. So please remove and disconnect all such equipment if used. This necessary precaution is for our own personal safety and that of the realm,' Lucia advised.

Plato pushed a hand underneath his tunic and retrieved a small black cube which he placed on the local table. The others wondered what it was and he explained.

'It will seal this room from other buildings by generating erroneous information to any would-be listener. All personal recorders and relays will be neutralized by its pulsating fields and you will be unaware of its presence.'

Lucia and the others were amazed by the technologies of the small black box, with no visible or audible signs of any activity or pulsations.

'Shall we continue?' Lucia insisted.

They listened quietly to the sad story about the destruction of Silo by the Javols. Merian broke down in tears when she heard of her husband's death. The others were equally saddened and very sympathetic. She was vehement on revenge for his death and swore to risk life and limb in the process. Doing whatever was necessary to curtail the progress of those alien monsters.

Lucia suggested they formed a special survival committee. They agreed and voted her as chairperson. Meron was selected as president and Plato as a chief advisor. The others would be assigned more specific duties at the next meeting, when it was hoped Tomas would be present after his aborted interstellar mission.

At that time Lucia became worried for the safety of her astronaut son, presently on a special mission for the government. Since that part of space was not too distant from Silo her worries were well founded.

Lira awoke from her dreamlike state and was surprised by Plato's resemblance to the one in her dream.

He looked into her eyes, observing something with a bright light.

'You know, you are so similar to my brother's wife,' Plato

remarked, but he did not wish to continue the conversation, as sadness filled his eyes. She gazed at him in amazement, having realized he was the same person that was there over 3000 years ago. She gave a half-baked smile but did not say a word.

'Your tests are now complete. You should visit the lower city museum and learn more about your ancestors. It's very important, you know,' he said. She nodded again in agreement and wiped her moist eyelids.

The assistant came and took Lira away to the waiting room to join the others.

CHAPTER 33

Julia and Merian

Julia was next to be tested. She quietly followed the assistant and sat in the middle chair. Plato put her through an identical procedure to Lira. She became Merian, the wife of Ranul. Despite her more simple appearance and stoutish build, she was one of the foremost biophysicists and historian of her time. She was also an eminent government advisor on matters of astrophysics and astronaut training.

After Meron and the others left Merian's home that evening she went directly to a crystal container. She removed a small symmetrical artifact that was made of a bluest material. It might have been a rear but natural stone that had been shaped that way by some volcanic process. She observed the object with sadness in her eyes and kissed it, remembering her husband Ranul.

'Darling, it was the first you sent me from Silo to commemorate our 125th wedding anniversary. Despite our differences we had some very good times together. I hope you are now much better off close to our Grand Lord in the ancient land of Goh, if such a place really exists. The children and I will have a celebration soon in memory of your passing,' she whispered, sorrowfully.

She gently placed the winged object back unto its little stool in the cabinet and focussed on their present dilemma, still with tears in her eyes.

'I knew of micro robotics. After all, I was one of the first to prepare a paper on the subject of microid transformations and cellular communications several decades ago; but why try to breathe innate intelligence into a mass without the necessary safety control modules. Such an independent mass would be extremely difficult to control, once its learning curve had changed from being microscopic with external processors, to macroscopic with internal processors in the form of a brain and neurons. Its mental processes would then be inaccessible to anyone other than the organism. Not to mention the correspondingly complex

macroscopic needs and desires of such an organism to maintain its own survival.

'The complete mass would tend to generate instruction pathways for the survival benefit of each cellular individual... Even a concept of pain or one of enjoyment could be created and felt. This would be necessary in order to establish a stronger survival bond between each microid and the remaining controlling mass for their optimum survival causation. This type of evolution would occur in a not too dissimilar manner as with primal organisms. However, the latter was gained through the interplay of numerous trial and error scenarios during a much longer period of primal evolution.

'Such a quickly evolving mass would tend to follow along its own learning, efficiency and population growth curves in order to establish itself and its progeny in different places over a large area. Thus having greater success in its survival against all natural enemies including forms of dangerous stellar radiation, climatic changes, harmful materials and predators.'

She sighed yet again, this time wiping her tearful eyes while talking to herself.

'We truly have an incredible monster on our hands. I am afraid we may not be able to do much before it is too late. Not being made of flesh and blood makes the whole process of finding a solution much more difficult.'

She went to a remote corner of the room, removed a cover and pressed a switch. A small computer came to life. She spoke to it in a different language, not of an Ancients' tongue, giving it specific details of a new concept. She typed more precise data via a small keypad. She did not use the helmet on this occasion.

After some time a form not too unlike a Javol appeared on the screen. She asked the computer to create the causal structures necessary for such a life-form to follow a specific survival curve. Those characteristics were based on the information received from Plato and others. With her high security grade she could also link directly with the original reports of Andra's experiments.

Then she went away from the terminal. She was still in deep

thought while trying her hardest to find a weakness in the structure displayed, but none could be found. The creature so formed was a perfect alien survivor and war machine. It had the necessary means to mutate into almost any form and could create tools of virtually any shape or size for hunting or manufacture, and most importantly to reproduce. It could even become invisible at certain wavelengths by modifying its structure. She pondered over numerous questions.

'Poor Andra, why were you so thorough during your design of this monster's parent? Why so perfect in every detail? Why didn't your Destructor Template destroy the sample? But it has to have a weakness. Everything must have some form of weakness, in relative terms.'

She asked the computer to display reproductive parameters in mass and energy requirements and the single Javol that was displayed vibrated into two separate individuals, one above the other. Their individual masses were now 50 percent of the original parent's and yet because of molecular bonding their individual size was only 30 percent less than the parent. Even so, it required more than 50 percent above its original stable mass in order to reproduce. Any lesser mass increase would only allow a concentration of its molecules and increase its size only slightly. Therefore separation was associated with molecular saturation and high energy. Further, each microid had the ability to store certain chemicals for later use. Energy in the form of intense radiation was the catalyst that triggered their metabolism and reproductive cycles.

Its size was obviously limited to a minimum at birth and a maximum at separation, but energy had to be absorbed in order to trigger that cycle and lots of it. This form never died in the normal sense while dividing. Both birth and death represented almost a single point in time as each new twin was born with all its parents knowledge and intelligence.

She made the computer function in reverse mode and saw the two individuals merge back into a single unit, but this time there were a significant energy drain of about 50 percent due to molecular bonding. This new energy level was above the amount required during the separation phase. They had a negative reaction to reforming, almost as if they hated it and preferred to be separate individuals. She pondered that new observation.

'Perhaps there is a flaw in the infidel's armour after all... What happens if they are prevented from joining at that crucial moment, by... an external energy of enough....'

She talked to the computer and a ray of intense heat equivalent to their separation energy was targeted between the rejoining Javols. They literally shattered into bits and did not reform.

She became very excited and asked the computer to calculate target geometries, optimum energy requirements with a range of other relevant parameters. Then she asked for a printout.

'So any trauma at that critical moment is too much for you to take,' she mumbled to herself. Then she read the information from the screen.

'**THE FORM DESCRIBED IS SUSCEPTIBLE TO MASS DESTRUCTION DURING THE REJOINING PHASE, GIVEN THE FOLLOWING CONDITIONS...**
AN ENERGY LEVEL OF THIRTY-FOUR POINT SEVEN PERCENT OR MORE....
THE MOST SENSITIVE TARGET AREA BEING AT THE POINT OF MERGING, ANYTIME DURING PHASURE... AT THE CENTRAL BULGE, WHICH IS THE MAIN CONTROLLING AREA OF THIS LIFE-FORM....
OTHER FORMS OF ABSORBED ENERGY OR MASS BELOW THE ADDED FIFTY PERCENT REQUIRED FOR SEPARATION, IS EITHER USED FOR STORAGE OR FOR ITS METABOLISM....
IT IS ESTIMATED THAT A PERIOD OF FOURTEEN DAYS WITHOUT ENERGY, IMMEDIATELY AFTER SEPARATION, WILL LEAD TO RE-EMERGING, GIVEN PRESENT CRITERIA....
HIGHER ENERGY LEVELS WILL LEAD TO A SHORT-ER GESTATION PERIOD UNTIL A LIMIT IS REACHED-....'

And so the report read.

She was by now over excited and thought she was well on the way to finding a method of the Javols' destruction. Then a new and not well favoured idea slowly crept into her mind.

'With all the numerous quantities of life and energy within our galaxy, how are we ever going to keep these things away from energy and food long enough for the merging phase to begin... in order for us to kill them by this method. Perhaps Plato or Meron may have an idea on that topic.'

She quickly pressed several buttons on the Vidicom. Lucia answered and called Meron. Merian tried to keep the conversation as vague as possible for security reasons.

'Hello Meron. I would like us to meet as soon as possible; something I found out about our nasty little friends, a weakness I think.' She was excited. Once more she went to her computer, double checked all her results and calculations, making sure she was correct in her theory before printing seven separate reports.

Even then she realized things seldom worked out as in theory. As they evolved, the Javols would learn better ways of survival and adopt better social habits and devices to cope. Those devices being physical and psychological, including cultural models, to prevent things they didn't like happening to them. Therefore her latest methods for their destruction could be a double-edged sword that would only work in her favour for a relatively short period, until they had evolved methods to circumvent them.

Julia suddenly awoke from her dream. Once again Plato checked her eyes in his usual manner, telling her she had passed the test and was required to visit the lower city.

Soon after his female assistant escorted her to the waiting room to rejoin the others.

CHAPTER 34

Merol and Tomas

Merol was next. He was asked to sit in the first chair. The helmet descended as he inhaled the bluish dust. Shortly thereafter he fell into the dreamlike state.

He was Meron's son who was an astronaut called Tomas. At that time he was practising deep-space manoeuvres and certain tests on board a specially fitted frigate. While on his way to the Ryle Nebula he received a distress call. It was very faint and distorted at first, but after filtering and reconstruction, clear and alarming.

'OUR PLANET SILO IS UNDER SIEGE BY AN ALIEN LIFE... MANY PEOPLE HAVE BEEN KILLED.... AND CONSUMED!

SOME FORM OF POISONOUS SPRAY MAKE THEM HELPLESS... WE THINK IT IS GENERATED BY THE ALIENS...

AN EARLIER ANNOUNCEMENT SAID THE THINGS WERE CREATED BY A MICROID EXPERIMENT THAT WENT WRONG....

PEOPLE AND ANIMALS ARE BEING CONSUMED EVERY-WHERE...

THEIR BODY PARTS ARE DISSECTED AND SUCKED-UP BY THE MONSTERS... ONLY FATTY TISSUE AND WATER IS LEFT BEHIND!

THEY CAN ENTER EVEN THE SMALLEST CRACKS.... AND TRAVEL THROUGH ANY SPACE AT WILL, EVEN OUTER-SPACE...

WHEREVER THERE IS LIGHT AND LIFE THEY WILL FOLLOW....

THEY CANNOT BE KILLED BY OUR MILITARY WEAP-ONS!

I AM AFRAID OUR WORLD SILO IS LOST... TOO MANY OF THEM.... TOO MANY BRILLIANT EXPLOSIONS, EVERYWHERE.... PLEASE KEEP WELL AWAY FROM THIS WORLD SILO! YOU MUST FOR THE SAKE OF YOUR PEOPLE!

THEY ARE CONSTANTLY INCREASING IN NUMBER... YOU MUST KEEP WELL AWAY FROM OUR WORLD SILO AND WARN CAEFON AND OTHERS OF OUR PLIGHT....YOU MUST WARN CAEFON!

IT'S OF PARAMOUNT IMPORTANCE THAT YOU WARN CAEFON IMMEDIATELY OF OUR PLIGHT....'

The communication ended and the carrier wave ceased.

'Wow! What's all that about?' Thomas exclaimed turning to his communicator, who had placed the recorded information a second time through their headsets.

'Sir! It contains all the necessary secure codes and its carrier is identifiable. So we must follow procedure in this matter and warn Caefon immediately.'

'I hope you are right for your sake, because if it happens to be a hoax heads will role, and mine will be the first on the chopping block,' Tomas advised while the communications officer double checked the information.

The first thing Tomas did was to call his father, Meron, on a specially coded frequency channel.

'Dad, I think we have a serious problem on Silo. Here is some distressing information we recently received from that world.' He relayed the transmission on a secured channel.

Meron could not believe the story at first but knew his son well. He was a trained astronaut. One trained to observe and not prone to exaggerate in any way. Once again Tomas replayed the distress call to his father in coded form.

Meron immediately called his trusted friend and chief scientist, Hamil, explaining the situation as best he could. The chief scientist was in dismay.

He knew of the special project. He had visited the site several years before and had observed the preliminary experiments which were successful. Even so, he had pondering doubts about their methods. As far as Hamil was concerned the distress call was genuine.

'We must keep the lid on this thing for now!

'I, with your permission, Sire, shall place all future data on this tragedy through a private channel, within a specially timed volatile storage unit with a retrievable code option for a period of twenty-four hours. The security number, I shall despatch to you shortly. That will give us enough time to plan our moves and make decisions. I shall call Tomas on a secured channel and advise him not to communicate further with us and to immediately return home,' Hamil advised.

'I must go and see for myself. Can you arrange that trip for me? Find a fast ship and include all necessary scientific equipment, in case we have to observe them. Schedule that journey as one of my diplomatic visits to a distant colony. If such was the case, as councillor I could always make a quick call to Silo on-route to meet someone of importance. Find something in my journey's log to validate such a trip.'

'It will be arranged, my lord.'

'I might have to hold the baby on this one if things go topsy-turvy, but that's my position and responsibility, isn't it? This is very important, so make it your best effort ever.'

'Yes, Sire,' Hamil said.

'Call me when things are ready, and I want you to come along as my personal advisor. Also, take along some of your trusted scientists and engineers. This is just in case we need them. Please arrange it urgently!' Meron ordered. Then Meron walked out of the building to prepare himself for his supposed diplomatic mission.

A class two frigate was hurriedly made ready and within the hour they were on their way. Meron was by then dressed in full diplomatic attire.

Tomas had by now received new instructions from his senior, Hamil. He was to return home in the quickest time possible. He immediately made a one hundred and eighty degree change in direction and was on his way back to Caefon. He gave instructions to his loyal crew and everything was placed on red alert with screens, guns, beam projectors and missiles in full readiness.

Silo, although not in a direct line with their homeward path, was only fifteen light-years to starboard. Even so, he least expected to be attacked by aliens or whatever they were called in such a short time.

As they passed the crucial point on their navigation charts, they found their ship being chased by about fifty of the objects. The Javols remained on their screens for a few minutes and suddenly vanished while approaching. Then he changed to visuals and they were found within a narrow spectrum.

'Clever! They detected our scanning frequencies and responded immediately!'

'Yes, Commander!'

'Go to Red Alert and train weapons!' he ordered.

'Weapons trained and set to auto-fire!' the female gunner acknowledged.

'Let's see how good they are at evading our missiles?' Thomas said. Thinking his future engagement a good test for his prototype frigate, but he was sadly disappointed.

When they became in range orders were given to fire. Everything were unleashed against their foe. The space was brilliantly lit by the massive fire power of his scout-frigate. It had been specially designed and prepared for almost any form of attack and fitted with the most advanced weapons of destruction at their current levels of technology.

The one-sided battle continued for about two hours, with the creatures darting hither and thither to avoid and minimise the full force of the weapons. Then to his utter surprise the aliens formed into a large spherical shape that began to grow in size as each member interlinked with its neighbour. Then the sphere began to slowly rotate.

All weapons now targeted the alien's sphere which concentrated all its individuals into an almost single point in space. When the sphere had absorbed enough energy it began to pulsate, then grew in size and suddenly moved towards them at great speed. It uncoiled itself and like a giant can opener ringed the ship, rotating their sharp edges together until the ship was cut in two halves and emptied like a can of beans.

One part dangled off into distant space, while the other still being randomly propelled by its drive system. Both exploding parts being chased by several of the aliens, perhaps for their rich human cargo.

Tomas, being a highly trained and experienced astronaut was always prepared for any eventuality. When he analysed what was happening, he immediately transmitted the usual distress call to Caefon, also giving them his position. Just in the nick of time he donned his special recovery spacesuit which also had neutral screen generators with a homing device. At the precise moment of the ship's separation he assumed the shape of a dead lump of inert matter which naturally floated out at the correct moment with other debris.

He remained motionless and in that position for the best part of sixteen hours. There were debris all around him and he could hear the things rampaging about as if searching for something of great importance. Even so, they were not very thorough and had just missed his position. The searching attitude of the Javols were an inbuilt part of their design. They were always desperate in finding anything specific to their survival, and in the process would collect and analyse most materials. Suitable metals they could consume by a process akin to osmosis. During the intervening period every bit of the ship was either taken apart for food or disregarded.

Most of the metals were absorbed, although not all. Nonmetals and items of a none biological nature were discarded.

He wondered what had happened to his loyal crew, if indeed any had survived the explosions during the ship's destruction.

After the Javols had fully satisfied their requirements they formed themselves into a much larger spherical shape and departed at enormous speed.

He was left by himself in deep space, awed by the incredible ferocious, rapacious and destructive nature of his foe. An alien life that had cleverly used his own destructive energies against his crew and himself, to have even reproduced more of their own kind in the process.

He had undergone sixteen hours of dormancy before his body was recovered from deep space and saved just before his oxygen supplies ran out. The delay was caused by a general alert within Caefon and the local systems. During that time all interstellar ships from Caefon and local stations in his vicinity had been temporarily grounded. Only a few important military vessels had been allowed special clearance. No one knew who issued those orders, but it was carried out under the pretence of important atmospheric tests.

On arrival he was taken directly to Meron's house, where Meron, Lucia and Plato awaited his report. They were extremely happy when they realized he was still in one piece, so they sat him down, had lunch and brought him up to date on current developments.

All four members, including Tomas, took a slightly different route to Merian's home that evening. She didn't mind their friendly company in a period of uncertainty, further accentuated by the loss of her husband. She relayed the painful news of Ranul's death to her children, and they mourned his passing. However nothing about the Javols and the destruction of Silo was said and no hints were given. Everyone thought it was due to a most deadly planetary virus.

Merian preferred the use of her place for their meetings for several important reasons; most of all she had direct access from that central position to the main system computers and the most powerful communications array. Also, having a grade one clearance she could search through virtually any type of secured information. It also gave her the ability to carry out calculations during the course of their meetings with her small and powerful research computer.

Their group were always security-conscious and preferred Merian's location in the centre of the great city, with all its movement and excitement. Such could also distract any wood-be snoopers from gaining knowledge of their true intentions. They had become good friends, which was a natural progression, having so much in common and lots to accomplish in a short time.

Despite everything, including the loss of Silo, Meron and the others were surprised that no one, not even seniors at council level had asked a single question about the grounding of spaceships on the day of his despatch to observe the Javols. It didn't take long to realise how inept the whole security structure had become in a period of peaceful complacency. But thank goodness it was working in their favour and not in some would-be invader's.

They soon had a folder put together and set certain wheels in motion before leaking the tragic information to the press. Although many mourned the passing of their relatives and friends on Silo, the supposed virus was exceptionally contagious so all bodies had to be cremated to prevent its spread to other worlds. From that time all ships were banned from visiting the infected world that had been placed under permanent quarantine. Since that information came from ministerial levels no one questioned those orders.

It was a known fact that most of the other systems bought their advanced weapons and technologies from the Ancients. Because of their dependancy and inabilities, they dreaded the empire's fire power and war machinery. But the empire and its federation had taken far too much for granted over the years. Their complacent attitude had begun at the start of the so-called Great Empire after Micol's death and later, the Greater Federation of Worlds, now in its third century of power.

Since the start of the Great Empire, they had learnt an important lesson in giving freedom to the masses. Such freedom could only be enacted through their brand of democracy with real power always at the centre.

During that long period of the empire, Caefon only interfered in the internal affairs of federation members when it was for the mutual benefit and safety of the whole. Anyway, in such situations they could always gain the major share of the votes. Nevertheless they were always in a superior position and could blackmail offenders by not supplying them with arms or other essential technological resources. Therefore its complacency had become a measure of its military might.

Since the union, the Great Empire with its Federation of Worlds now had the cake all to itself in the form of its advanced technologies. They would constantly use such power as a lever on which to expand. In time, other poorer systems would join out of necessity, thus increasing even more the strength of the new imperial federation with its centre at planet Caefon, whose main city was Cantor.

When they arrived Hamil and Sintra were already seated comfortable in the living room. Merian immediately went to her computer table to collect a pile of reports. Then she handed a folder to each member in turn and took one for herself.

'Please read it carefully. You may ignore the calculations for now. They are not essential at this stage.'

They carefully read their documents for a while and were intrigued by its concepts and preparation. Meron was the first to speak.

'Beautifully done, Madam. Now we know a lot more about the metabolism and behaviour of these monsters.'

'And a weakness!' Julia exclaimed.

'I think we are finally getting somewhere. Perhaps a tiny light at the tunnel's end, but still a light, nonetheless. As indicated, we still have a major problem however, and a much more difficult one than killing them. That is in keeping them away from large quantities of energy for just long enough... in order to weaken them into merging.' Meron said.

They freely expressed their views and finally Tomas told them about the speedy and efficient destruction of his space cruiser and loyal crew.

This time Plato interrupted.

'Within Osmaron will exist the necessary technologies to destroy the Javols.'

The whole group, with the exception of Meron and Lucia were

surprised of his knowledge of such matters. He stood up and removed his outer coat thus revealing the black Shadite's Cloak.

They were even more astonished and Merian smiled with curiosity.

'Great Lord of the Sword, a Shadite. I always thought you were sons of myth, but you really do exist, even in my own home!' she exclaimed. She remembered reading one of Seno's holy books as a child. A Shadite by the name of Siit had assisted them when their world was in danger. Therefore he gave her hope.

Her excitement busted into tears that she tried her utmost to hold back as long as she could and then she smiled in sadness at her recent loss.

'Perhaps even Goh and Grand Lord Gerron exists?' She wiped her tearful eyes.

'We have large radiation proof ships called Maulers. They can use anti-gravity fields of great intensity. Originally they were designed and used to assist in rescuing worlds from collisions, novas or other destructive occurrences, by deflecting colliding bodies and dense clouds of hot ionized gaseous matter. Those can also be used for funnelling superheated matter and radiation streams away from populated areas of inhabited worlds. They can sometimes rescue other vessels in distress. By using such technologies we can destroy the Javols. But the problem is in getting those ships here in time. They were not designed for speedy intergalactic travel,' he said.

He pressed a button on his large buckle within the metal belt. It was the one with the winged insignia about his waist and there was a distinct change in the room. A large area was suddenly filled with a greenish glow. The glow appeared just ahead of them and a spherical object or thing appeared as if from nowhere.

The sphere spoke to them as if eating its own words.

'You need me that urgently, Plato. What is the matter?'
Plato quickly explained the problem to him.
'See what you can do, please, Lord Vektron!' he pleaded.
'Your present dilemma has been predicted, so do not be alarmed nor should you worry unduly about the future.

Plans have already been made; for the nature of the beast is well known to us and so is its demise. However, this galaxy is lost and so is your world. Its destruction will occur within a relatively short time from now.

You will each be given a duty to perform. Do it well, for several plans must be enacted before their final return to consume your future generations some three thousand years hence. Although your galaxy is lost, many will survive, including this present company, and one day you will return to set things right.

'I myself shall assist you then.

'Please take this,' Lord Vektron said.

Hands of light suddenly emerged from the sphere and faded into the figure of a human being in glowing light. He carried a large golden book and handed it to Plato, but explained.

'This is the book of your survival. Follow its instructions well.'

The figure resumed the shape of the sphere and faded out of their perception.

The book was subsequently called The Book of Final Light or to the Ancients, the Anachromagnon. This book held all types of - information, some of which were beyond anything they could have dreamt. There were many pages written in an unknown language that they could not understand or interpret. Perhaps those instructions were meant for another civilization or a different time.

Sintra was made chief interpreter and given the Great Book for translation. She was to be aided by Merian for scientific support during her interpretations. They were both required to rewrite relevant pages for use in their immediate survival strategies.

By now their special survival committee was more closely linked and got together quite frequently, mostly at Merian's home. The solution, although simple, would take several centuries to set in motion and they thought, would be completed within their natural lifetimes. But as always with life, things were never that simple.

They realized it was most unlikely they would not be alive in three thousand years time and had to include those factors into their long term plans.

Merol suddenly awoke from his dreamlike state and found Plato observing his eyes with a bright light.

Plato spoke to him, knowing him to be a close descendant of Tomas.

'One large family, eh?' he said.

Merol knew exactly what he meant by those words and also knew the same Plato was alive in the past, around three thousand years ago. Like the brand new ship over three thousand years old, he was also brand new himself, perhaps even immortal. Merol, although not fully recovered from the circumstances of his dream, asked a question not knowing exactly why.

'Uncle Plato, are you truly immortal?'

Plato was taken back by that question, but judged well the situation.

'All Masters of the Sword are immortal and I am Shadite,' he replied.

Merol did not get the full significance of his reply, but left with the notion that he was his ancient uncle and also immortal.

He was soon taken to rejoin his group in the adjacent room.

CHAPTER 35

Petra and Sintra

Petra was next, and sat in the middle chair under the special helmet. She inhaled the blueish dust and slowly became her ancestor, Sintra. The historian and linguist who had existed over three thousand years before.

The point at which her dream began was at the moment of receiving the strange golden book from chairwoman Lucia.

Sintra subsequently had a special stand made for it. The stand included a transparent crystal hood with a secured latch. The latch lifted whenever she wanted to gain access and consult its pages, which she thought would be frequent. Mistakenly she assumed it was just a normal book used by Osmaronites. That was until she began to observe certain strange occurrences that she could not explain by the natural laws of physics.

Sintra was primarily an historian, but also functioned as senior librarian and interpreter. Her main subject being ancient history. She was not a superstitious person by nature and had always thought that seemingly strange occurrences could always be explained or attributed to a physical cause. Even the appearance of Lord Vektron the Osmaronite could be so explained. For although this Osmaronite was quite strange in his appearance and actions, he could have been the byproduct of a superior technology and intelligence.

She reasoned that even her people several centuries from now could have attained those levels of advancement. That was, assuming there were no great disasters or wars in the intervening period to slow their progress. If there were no great obstacles to circumvent, they could eventually attain virtually any levels of technologies. That was providing it was technologically possible. Some things however, she thought, was just not possible.

Her list was quite simple and included the following: neutral objects could not move on their own accord; one could not be in two places at once; spirits either bad or good did not exist; no one could live forever, for all living things had to eventually wear out, grow old and die. There was no afterlife in the great sky city of Gohenna or Goh, as the Senots and natives called it, not even within its valleys... and so her list went on, but before long she had to amend her list. What she considered to be her real world had begun to drift and merge with a completely different and stranger one.

It was one that had begun to contradict her firmly held concepts and beliefs. Soon, that opaque veil that separated those concepts began to tear and release a stranger light unto her own. It shown so brightly that the veil itself became transparent and invisible to all actions and thoughts, thus merging both worlds together as one.

The Book was placed on its stand and she attempted to open its covers by undoing both of its two golden buckles, but as hard as she tried nothing happened.

She searched for a lock and thought perhaps there would be a hidden key in a concealed pocket, but the book was completely smooth in those areas and there were little indication of anything, not even a hidden slot.

She was utterly confused and left for a while.

She decided to call Merian for some advice on her present dilemma, but Merian was not available, so she went back to try again. As she approached its stand, she found to her utter surprise it had opened in half and at a page that read:

When technology improves to infinity,
And chaos is no more a certainty.
Within the Greater Mind we grow,
Until even matter exists no more.

She was amazed by what she saw and read the verse several times trying to make sense of it. When she stopped reading, the book suddenly shut its covers all by itself and began to glow. This sudden activity made her retreat from the stand. However she plucked more courage and went closer to observe.

She stared at its cover in awe, while to her further amazement a small square within the centre of the cover began to glow. An image of her face appeared on its cover with her name engraved beneath.

Then the mirror image of herself began to speak to her in her own voice.

'I am the Final Word;
The one who guides the Sword.'

'Say after me!'

'May the Sword of Truth, guided by the Hand of Wisdom and
Decision,
Restrain the Horned Serpents of Treachery and Deception.'

'Say after me!'

'So may it be forever,
Till they are both torn asunder.'

She said as it commanded and held on bravely to courage, for her main urge was to bolt like a petrified Pedris. Those were the larger mammals sometimes used for carrying and racing in distant lands. However there was too much at stake and she decided, come what may, she would stay and learn.

She nervously plucked the courage to ask her first question.

'I wish to know... how to survive a great disaster that will affect our galaxy.... Can you assist me?'

The Book suddenly opened its pages again,

'You have initiated the survival race,
So you may see my truest face.'

The Book closed its pages, revealing a beautiful cover with an engraving in gold of the Sword of Truth held in balance by the two Horned Serpents of Treachery and Deception. Both serpents forming the figure of eight.

This form she thought depicted the eternal struggle between good and evil. Good represented by the sword and evil by the two horned vipers. She was now convinced that the struggle had begun.

The Book continued to speak in her own voice,

'From what I see, your course is clear,
So be decisive and don't you fear;
When there is no quick decision,
Certain plans are set in motion.

To live a surface life in fear and danger?
Why not build a city way down under.
Which in time can grow in size,
All un-necessaries you could minimize.

But never on the surface dwell,
For very soon the Javols swell.
They will destroy most surface life to feed,
For their long reunion voyage and to breed.'

Although precise data was always given in written form, which she copied down enthusiastically, she was soon to learn the Book spoke mainly in poetry and verse.

The Book was a living entity in its own right. It could prevent anyone it didn't like from reading its pages, either by using its own method of strange language or by total concealment.

It was necessary for both interpreter and book to be as one. Both minds had to be perfectly synchronised during the process of conversion and assimilation. Further, it could acquire the powers to visit any world for information and sometimes be in several places at once. Being truly indestructible, it had an almost infinite range of knowledge. Each page was of the mind and tuned directly into the innermost nature of its one and only authorised reader. To all others, it was just a large book with funny and strange pages and even then, the readable pages were not always the real story but just a clever ploy.

The Book gave Sintra information as and when she requested, but only what was relevant to their survival plans. Whenever she interpreted its pages, she entered the information unto storage discs which she later transcribed into three great books called the Anachromecrons.

There were weekly reports which she supplied to each of the other five chosen members for their own assessment and inspiration. She soon learnt that the Book was truly inexhaustible in its content.

Sintra had by now become quite an expert at interpreting the Book's ideas and concepts. She thought it was not a highly logical entity and yet, she found that a sometimes simple or meaningless word could trigger a string of ideas on very relevant topics. At other times its information was equally vague and did not lead to anywhere.

She thought its mind functioned on a different level to humans and attributed the translation problem to errors during conversion from a much higher level of thinking down to her levels. She compared the situation with human thought restricted in just two dimensions, while the Book's mind functioned in a much higher and more conceptual three-dimensional manner. The problem, she thought, was equivalent to translating three-dimensional information down to the two dimensional level while using different concepts in the process to transpose those thoughts. This might have been a great problem for the Book and hence the sometimes indirect manner in which it supplied the information.

Very soon details of a large underworld was retrieved from its pages. All such data were handed to Meron and Hamil, who had put together a team of experts to decipher the information for their own use. Those sincere workers had no idea of the Javols' future invasion and assumed they were normal government projects. Further, Meron could wield much political power. Being from an ancient dynasty he was well respected by all.

It was during that time that many probes were designed and sent out towards the centre of the galaxy. They were made to repair themselves and could last for many centuries in the cold vacuum of space. However it was doubtful that they would last beyond the specified time of 3000 years. Nevertheless they would remain on their respective routes long enough to inform them of the Javols progress within a period of 500 years or so.

Once the majority of those probes had become operational, they acquired knowledge of the whereabouts of the local wandering clusters of Javols. Those were the few renegades that had decided to remain behind and harvest what little life remained in that part of the galaxy. They had so far missed Caefon and had moved in the opposite direction to a few more distant worlds. However Javols were not morons and would have had plans for all stellar systems within that galactic region, including Caefon and its inhabitants.

During all this time the Ancient six were storing materials and foodstuffs for their many survival projects. The Great Book was instrumental in their progress.

For several weeks The Book had not spoken a word to Sintra. Every bit of information being retrieved in text form, and she wondered why.

'Perhaps it was due to my recent intensive and nagging attitude. That was during the period when I was placed under constant pressure by Meron and Hamil. After all, I am not a biophysicist or geneticist. I was also partly to blame for the vague answers I received, since I didn't fully understand the questions myself. What was genetic splicing anyway? ' she murmured.

'The Book was never very clear on that subject. Perhaps it had too many life-forms to choose from and also, six fingered humans were extremely rear to find. Thank goodness Hamil settled for the eight fingered type, although with Meron's disapproval. Those types of humans were apparently more plentiful and a lot more successful than the six fingered variety.'

She thought it was time she and the Book had a break from each other.

That day as she lifted its hood covering she began to speak directly at the beautiful golden object resting on the special stand.

'Dear, Book, would you like a period of time to yourself? A period in which you can do as you wish? Perhaps a fortnight will be enough? This is because I am to visit my father in the country. He is recovering from a recent organ transplant and we have not seen each other for a while.'

The Book fully understood her every thought and knew that she was exhausted and needed the rest. Even so, it remained silent in its neutral condition. There was not a single spoken word from its facing cover. She was worried and knew not what to do to improve her relations with the book.

The following day, as usual, she lifted its hood covering, but decided to ask it a more personal question instead.

'Perhaps it will see the funnier side of my question and decide to talk with me,' she thought. Anyway, she needed to know the truth on that particular topic one way or another, so she asked the Book her question.

'Dear Book, is there a Great and Wonderful City called Gohenna or Goh, even better than our city Cantor and is Goh where you are from, with your vast knowledge of the past, present and future?'

There was a period of complete inactivity while she waited for an answer. Perhaps the information was not appropriate for comment, or the Book was deciding whether she deserved an answer. She realized that if she became her most stubborn self and tried different methods, the book would have to respond sooner or later, so she persevered.

Finally the Book opened its middle pages and Sintra began to read its contents.

CHAPTER 36

The Book speaks

PRESENT and FUTURE

'Knowledge of the past perhaps, for the present, even while we speak, is neither past nor future. The relative future is made by the present, which in turn was created by past events and amplified by their degree of separation. So does it really exist? Further, every entity can only exist within its own local time, since the relative past will move away in all direction from every observer. For instance, the distant star we now observe can never exist within that same space in our time and would have moved elsewhere since. So in this respect, time is our fourth dimension and is inseparable from space.

'I can visualise events in great depth, but do not predict the future. The future is due to the accumulative effects of an almost infinite array of causal events. Every event like a wave leads into another and yet another while altering others. The future will exist because the probability of a reoccurrence of past events are infinitely more certain than those that have not yet existed.

That is the reason why our universe is so stable within its space-time boundaries, otherwise what we perceive as solid things would suddenly begin to dissolve into nothing and little black holes would begin to appear everywhere randomly. Although we take such stability for granted, it is truly an enormous feat.

'An ability to predict the future presupposes a knowledge of everything in existence. Every particle, wave, molecule, cell, individual, and so on, ad infinitum, including every causal event. It could also be a repetitive program where our destinies are already known or predetermined. Such a unique system would have had to have been designed by a superior intelligence. However this latter concept is less likely.

Only the Greater Purpose can accomplish the great feat of predicting our futures to great accuracy.

THE PAST

'No one can visit the past in material terms within their given time-line. Since your very body atoms could have belonged to a whole variety of animals, plants, minerals and so on, at any particular time period.

'How could anyone duplicate matter or life, even specific atoms that form part of the Causal Matrix, when they by themselves have also acquired a causal history relative to us in space-time? They formed part of events leading to this one. Further, all changes in a temporal world of any given space-time continuum will depend on certain orderly changes within the Sea of Chaos and of All Possibilities. Anyway one could not destroy or duplicate energy in any space-time continuum.

'Could you return to the past with a specific atom in your body and on arrival tell its former self, that it never really existed in that location or time because it can now only be found within your own body?

'How can identical units both occupy the very same Space-time? Therefore the past in any given time-line will be a blank slate, since all its contents are constantly kicked into the future.

'Historical events cannot be precisely duplicated, for every atom is different to all others by virtue of their causal histories. All such personal experiences are continuous in time.

'This now is where the concept of Plane or Plenum may be related.'

Sintra realised that she was not going to get a simple answer, but found the subject an exciting one and decided to read each page that followed. Any way, her beloved book was now speaking to her and she would not distract and disturb its current flow.

DIMENSIONAL PLANES

'Just as you are separated from another, in the same way are planets, galaxies and universes. Yet those that share a common

plane are each causally related.

'Life within a given plane cannot causally interact or affect those of another, since their primal and geometric structures are inherently different; for even an atom in one plane may be the size of a planet in another.

'Any entity entering a given plane has to somehow acquire the primal substance of that plane for its own survival causation.

'For instance, within this universe the primal substance is electromagnetic type energy in the form of matter, with its necessary laws to govern causal continuity for the evolution of primal life. In another plane it may be something else. We are born into this plane and are given a suitable material body, as a baby, clone, siliconic brain or even a Javol perhaps. Each of these living vessels being made from recycled atoms, perhaps billions of years old. Yet, they together, in that mind and body form will project a special symmetry that can be felt by certain Identities.

'At first the joining process at conception was very strange for the Identity, but it soon learnt the ways of its new plane in much the same way as you would learn your way about a new house.

'A type of rebirth from some previous state. Hence, because of the 'one plane cannot affect another causal' relationship or perhaps the lack of one, the young life-form cannot remember from whence it came originally. However it is constantly aware of its own existence by a strong desire to survive and fulfil its own desires and ambitions, partly driven by social and biological needs within its newly found environment.

'When your material body - the part that attaches you to this plane - becomes unsuitable as a special container, due to death or a misalignment of the original symmetrical order. The bond is once again broken and the Identity once more released; freed from this plane, to return to wherever it originally came from or perhaps a different one. One that is more sympathetic to that Identity, due to more permanent changes within its higher ordered symmetries. A change in essence, if you like, most of which will be due to permanent changes within its psyche. In this way, we are constantly changing and developing in line with certain goals, depending on our psyche and our place in the Cosmos. However,

at the cessation of life our Identity will adopt a different state to the one we were during our previous corporeal existence. A state of existence within the Cosmos can also be referred to as a singular continuum within another.

'This could have been the Primal Identity Matrix, sometimes called the Nexos, which is in a sense a different dimension but interlinked to all planes by virtue of mutual coexistence. Although invisible to Primal Life, the Nexos is all around us and permeates everywhere throughout the Cosmos within a higher dimension. It is the source of all Identities and also the source of order and chaos. If this was its final place of call, the identity would "await its turn" once again through eternity before beginning another corporeal existence. But even here, the words "await its turn" presupposes that time and causation exists continuously within that realm. What is a billion years to us here and now, might pass them by in the blinking of an eye. Since time and space does not exist at that level to our perception, time becomes irrelevant.

'There are specially chosen Identities, however, that are collected by the Greater Mind and placed into the Created Plane called Gohenna or Goh, which is not of the primal type.

'To all intents and purpose, you may assume all primal life may traverse and transcend every plane to eternity. This is necessary for the Cosmos during the recycling process. Every form or entity is constantly recycled for its long-term survival, and the Book began suddenly to speak to her in her own voice,

‘For a name is but a name,
And a form is but a frame.’

She was overjoyed, but the pages continued to be written, so she continued to read.

'They take nothing when they leave and give nothing when they enter. That way, the primal system remains always in perfect balance.

'Each plane has its own unique causation or causal history and every Player initiates or activates in whatever form, shape or

physical law.

'Each individual, great or small, playing its part for the Greater Survival Causation or Greater Purpose. Obviously, Historical Causation in any given plane presupposes a temporal relationship within its modus operandi. What you call past, present and future along a given time-line. Hence, all planes are related in that way or else they simply could not exist.

'I am inter-planner and inter-dimensional, not made of primal substance. I am also from where you call, the Great and Wonderful City of Goh. But now I find myself among lovely mortals in the plane of Seth.'

The voice continued to speak in its poetic fashion.

'We occupy organisms, to live and breathe as one,
To observe light in all its colours and enjoy sounds of music alone.
We sense feelings and emotions with conviction and conscience,
To think, create and invent, in art and in science.

All this from an aggregate of microcosmic cells to form a macrocosmic being?
Because of an urge to survive from some strange primordial beginning?
A union of conscious spirit, mind and cell,
And in death, where will my Identity Spirit dwell?

Within a Cosmos of infinite proportions,
For how long will I remain devoid of senses and emotions?
Will I be once again conceived to another race?
Into a different land of time and space?

What is reality or even solid mass.
Is a ghost within its own universe as real as shining glass?
Perhaps within a Greater Computer Mind,
We are all just players of a different kind.

Appearances can be deceptive, for mass reduces to nothing,
And only when matter with matter touch we think there is
something.
A form of Causal Order imposed upon a sea of chaos prime,
A self sustaining battle till the very end of time.

For time itself, whether forward or backwards be, is just
another player,
And our laws of science here may not relate within another
Cosmic Layer,
But I am sure that any death to me will not be long,
For within a Cosmos of infinity, a space time traveller I be-
long.'

Victor E. Roche

She listened and was astounded and amused by what she heard. She was once again very happy when she realised the City of Goh really existed, and that somehow the Greatest Mind had found a way to create its own Plenum of perfection called Gohenna or Goh.

She thought again with admiration.

'That must be some Mind and some Place.'

Suddenly her old negative ideas had been completely eroded away by the Great Book of Goh. Finally the Book added:

'In summation, every atom, molecule or individual has its own unique history, that unlike a recording or footprints, can never be erased from the Sands of Time.

'Its absolute development, either to its advantage or detriment, determines the actions of others within the causal interplay of events.

'Is the body for the sake of the mind, or perhaps the mind for the sake of the body? If something was to go wrong with either mind or body would it not also affect the other and therefore the complete person?

'This is the way of the Cosmos. The little affects the large and

vice versa. They are all players in the eternal struggle. For that reason, every player however insignificant, is important to the system. For the more the players, within reason, the greater is the game.'

The voice again took over.

'Against the Sands of Time the Causal Sea must beat.
Unimpeded in its progress, yet resistant in retreat;
And waves will beat until the sea runs dry, till every causal
thing is unified.
As if a wheel, its speed reducing to defy, constraint and yet a
whirling sea within a tide.

Yet, all its losses will be entirely covered,
A form of compensation for services rendered.
As when the old gives birth to die, the Mother of All must try,
And give her best before all things run dry.

And yet, those losses themselves will form,
A Sea? No! An Ocean within a storm!
A new beginning, a Plenum, a Universe unfold,
A beauty as yet unimagined. Magnificence
untold.'

The book then added.

'All preconceptions out the door,
Or do you wish a lesson more?'

Showing an affectionate smile, she responded.
'Yes! And what will you do while I am away?'

The Book replied.

'Perhaps a simple rotation to Osmaron;

For a brief visit to advise a Chosen Son.
But don't you worry beautiful daughter,
Enjoy your well earned vacation with your father.'

The Book suddenly closed its covers, its buckles clicked into place and it radiantly vanished from its stand. She thought for a second, then pulled the crystal hood in place and walked out of the room with grace and dignity in her stride.

With all her misconceptions gone, Sintra's mind was now free and able to absorb all kinds of information relating to dimensional physics and other more complex mathematical subjects which were beyond their current technologies. Those she would enter in the third book for their future requirements. From that moment on her translations were more precise.

Her father became well again from his organ transplant and back to normal duties and Sintra returned from her vacation a happier person to continue their program of survival.

With a smile of satisfaction Petra suddenly awoke from her dreamlike state, but with the strange Book and experiences of the past still imprinted on her mind.

A bright light was in her eyes and as the light receded she could clearly see Plato.

'Did you have a good dream?' he asked.

'Yes Plato. I saw the serpents and the sword!' Petra replied with a broad smile.

He knew what she meant, but would not pursue the conversation. She was then escorted towards the waiting room to be with her other friends.

CHAPTER 37

Ecrol and Hamil

Finally, it was Ecrol's turn. He was taken and placed under the third position.

The helmet descended and he inhaled the bluish dust to become the Chief Scientist, Hamil.

The dream began at a point in time with Hamil at his desk with a worried Meron standing in his office close to the door. Both were soon joined by Sintra who delivered a secured report. Hamil snatched it from her, quickly scanned its pages and turned his head to complement her.

'Success at long last. It is not one hundred percent, but it will have to do. I am sorry, Sintra, for the recent pressures, but we could not find an easy way ourselves and time was pressing. Perhaps it was because we considered our own biological form more superior to those of the other types. We soon realised, however, that for survival reasons we were not the most suited in a harsh planetary environment, having been technologically assisted for so many centuries.

'Our immune systems have degenerated as a result and will now be prone to even the least virulent strains in a more contaminated environment. We have also learnt that the Javols will carry all types of disease and parasites that they may have collected during their wanderings. Although they will not affect the Javols, all natural organic life like us will be infected sooner or later. Therefore, during that time of turmoil and destruction our biological systems will not be able to sustain such viral attacks without the necessary advanced medication. Further, we shall not be able to produce any such medication in quantity as the situation worsens.

'Lord Meron and I have discussed this problem at length and have decided, although with much regret, on a specification very similar to this one. Which is also the one that you have proposed for the optimum survival of our species within an unprotected

planetary environment.' Hamil continued his apology while regretting an irrefutable course of action.

Looking closely at a particular page, he commented.

'This is very good. Your Great Book have excelled this time. We can now splice all our relevant genetic substructures unto this much stronger helix. The only major difference to our future kind will be the extra fingers, hair, eye and basic skin colouration, but that may be an asset in misleading our enemies. Nevertheless, we have to discuss our findings with the committee before we can make any positive commitment on this project.'

During all this time Meron listened to his friend Hamil but did not utter a single word.

Not very long after, the six discussed the problem at length and agreed unanimously to accept the cloned eight fingered genetic versions of themselves. There were virtually no drawbacks that could be attributed to the extra two fingers and other basic colouration changes.

THEIR SURVIVAL PLANS

Hamil, Meron and others of the special six, with the aid of Sintra and the Book, had formulated worst case scenarios for all aspects of their survival plan. The six had achieved much with the aid of their master computers and other statistical methods of deduction. They had finally optimised all critical aspects of the Master Survival Plan for their race, but this was based mainly on suitable genetics. According to worst-case scenarios, after the Javols departure, survival within a somewhat degraded planetary environment would have been very difficult. With little or no animal life remaining. Assisted only by basic technologies, the few newly introduced genetically engineered human couples would have found survival extremely hard.

Given those almost insurmountable problems, it was still necessary to aid in some form of partial planetary recovery after the local Javols had departed from that part of the galaxy. Any such assistance from the underworld would have been required for a period of approximately three thousand years, until the Javol's next and final return to harvest the local stellar systems.

They predicted that almost all surface life would have disappeared during the first two hundred years or so, with the exception of plants, microbes, insects and other smaller creatures. All the larger life-forms would have been consumed by the Javols during their final onslaught. Finally, they had to find some way to store all relevant genetic material before the Javol's first attack. That program was essential if they were to bring their planet and other parts of the galaxy back to normality after the destruction of the Javols.

The program of collecting, recording and storage of such materials had to be accomplished very urgently before the Javols' first visit, which was expected anytime. Suddenly the group was in a great hurry to find answers to those particular questions. They were also required to find safe refrigerated storage for the millions of genetic capsules that had been collected from local and distant worlds. After all, many of those inhabited worlds hadn't any facilities or technologies of their own. Even so, only a very small percentage could be saved.

Such collections would also include historical, sociological, cultural and other forms of important information, including artifacts of different species and races. Then there were drugs, clothes and foodstuffs. The task was truly enormous and the lists almost endless.

As a pilot scheme, it was decided to build a small sealed underground town utilising the latest engineering techniques of tunnelling. They were at that time unsure of the long-term psychological effects on humans in such a confined and sealed environment over long periods. Not with a large and mixed multiracial and multicultural population. Such an environment could also include none humans and aliens, working and living side by side.

That scheme, if successful, could eventually lead the way to a much grander project. It was not intended to evacuate every surface individual. Such an underground town could only accommodate about five thousand individuals initially for any sustained period of time. Given the availability of energy and food resources, it was thought the survivors would consist of specialists in important fields. They would be assisted by automatons and other systems that could aide in the survival of all important species concerned.

Because of the secrecy of their survival project, it was not possible to warn the surface population or the military. The Military also held large reserves of high explosives in the form of missiles and other weapons of mass destruction which did not help. Meron realized that many of those weapons would be used against the Javols to further boost the Javols own energy requirements and population gains to the detriment of the human population. This latter aspect significantly worsened the surface people chances of survival at the present time.

It was therefore imperative that their future race survived to assist in the final destruction of the Javols, for after all, they by intergalactic law, not to mention laws of conscience, were responsible for causing the existence of those Javols in the first place.

They had to be the major players in their destruction and be there to see things right afterwards. Therefore they would continue their work on the surface until the very last moment. Further, it was not feasible to re-site the large computers and power systems underground, initially. If they did, the curiosity of many on the surface could be aroused and suspicious officials begin asking questions, particularly when important equipment went missing.

Nevertheless most of their efforts on the surface came under the banner of charitable works for the poor and needy throughout the local stellar systems and their supposed charitable organization grew in leaps and bounds.

Three teams were subsequently formed to enable positive implementation of their plans.

Team-A would include all construction engineers and builders. That group included many scientists and was placed directly under

Meron. He was assisted by Plato who was always up-to-date on advanced Osmaron technologies.

Team B were in charge of collecting, recording and general storage of all relevant information and artifacts. This group came under Merian. Her team of field workers were the most active. They frequently visited local stellar systems for samples and such like.

Team C were responsible for work on all biological, genetic structures and storage of relevant information. That responsibility included the storage of genes, embryos and cells of all relevant life, including food and drugs. This group was led by Hamil, with Sintra as his second in command. The others would assist in relevant areas as and when required.

They soon acquired an old building close to the museum at Southern Cantor and from there began the drilling of the first pilot hole. All debris from the digging could easily be explained as renovation to the building's foundation. Then a tunnel was drilled underneath and connected to the nearby sea. Soon after, automatic locks and pumps were fitted to allow despatch of all further debris unto the local sea bed.

CHAPTER 38

Lower Cantor is constructed

Lucia, now leader, was currently responsible for the complete program and their respective groups. The other members of the six would assist those appointed whenever possible and in whatever ways necessary to fulfill their requirements in completing the project.

A random set of scientists and their families were to be selected as the first underground dwellers. Those it was hoped would supply all necessary feedback to the other relevant scientists and construction engineers. That information would aid in the creation of a more habitable underworld environment. To many it was just a scientific project in underworld survival and no one queried their true intentions.

Those few chosen, but unknown families, were informed of the project's importance, although not of the Javols' invasion or of the loss of their surface world in the foreseeable future. They would be briefed accordingly and only on a need-to-know basis. Further, most professionals were considered very responsible people and seldom the type to break agreements.

That first experiment would only last a period of five years. After that time they would be released from their contracts and once again freed to visit the surface as and when required, providing the Javols did not visit first.

It was assumed the underground town would become fully functional within the first five-year period of its habitation.

They had to go underground for survival reasons and yet remain close to the main city of Cantor because of its many advanced facilities. The tunnelling experts soon came up with a simple yet novel idea. They were to excavate the first underground city by initially drilling an array of tunnels leading outwards from a central elevator shaft that ran vertically to the maximum depth. After the shaft was drilled, a secondary tunnel was bored from that main shaft to the local sea. Unknown to the local surface people, part of that shaft extended to the museum in lower Cantor and was connected to its internal systems. New wings were constantly added to the museum and its zoological additions during that time. It was mainly to mask their operations.

Soon after, all waste from digging could be dumped through specially constructed locks unto the nearby sea bed. That part of the sea was just five kilometres away and to the south of Cantor. Its canyon was very deep in places and could easily absorb large quantities of the tunnelled debris without any significant rise in sea level. Their tunnel drilling machines were specifically built for that purpose. The Large central elevator would be used to move machines, workers and debris from place to place as and when required.

Although the volume of matter increased substantially over the years, with the addition of undersea conveyance, the sea level remained virtually unchanged. Any observed topographical changes could always be attributed to subsidence or earth-movement. Anyway, some of the senior councillors were members of the six and could always play down the situation or supply more favourable reports before any political situation got out of hand.

After the first experimental area had been completed and tested, the underground city constantly expanded as and when more space was needed.

Anti-gravity and other advanced technologies necessary in its construction were imported from Osmaron. Many such modules were located in relevant positions on the large reflective canopy, with its many powerful light sources and natural image projectors. Those projectors could create a similar visual skyline to the one observed from Caefon's own surface, including its moons and clouds, making the place less claustrophobic.

The main lamp with its other smaller light sources supplied more than enough radiant energy over the relevant spectra. Its intensity and wavelengths compared favourably with Caefon's sun. The other powerful lamps were under computer control and assisted by projecting moving clouds and different colourful horizons. So controlled, it would make the whole underworld environment almost indistinguishable from the surface world. Nevertheless there were many naturally created clouds, evaporated from small lakes and circulating ground water. The underground world soon formed its own ecosystem, with its many newly introduced animals and plants originally brought from the surface. Food growing crops were specially selected and some genetically engineered for high yields. Those would grow on prepared steps.

  The near spherical canopy was supported by four stout reinforced pillars, excluding the central elevator shaft that led directly to the surface museum in Southern Cantor. The bulk of the underworld lay beneath the southern part of the Craile Desert towards the northwest of Southern Cantor.

NO SURVIVORS

Hamil and others realised all major surface life and technologies, including his race of humans, would be nonexistent within 200 years. After the first of the Javols' visits, the few remaining pockets of human survivors would soon have become savages. By that time many would be infected by the predominant bacteria, viruses and other detrimental organisms brought by the Javols, now free to multiply. With no medical help available those few would spread the contagious diseases and die. Detrimental conditions would further reduce the remaining human lifespan by about forty-five years.

  Such smaller surviving groups with virtually no agriculture, medicine or basic technologies to assist their survival, could not hope to sustain their kind for very long. Thus leading to the final extinction of all major species within perhaps another hundred years. Well before then the Javols would have realised the diminished populations not worthwhile for harvesting and departed elsewhere to feed and breed. By then most of their food supplies in those outermost galactic regions would have diminished to almost zero. The Javols could not travel across space to the neighbouring galaxies and would journey towards the galactic centre, attracted by the brighter lights almost like moths to a candle. This was probably because they could naturally assume a larger primal population density where the stellar density was higher.

By that time the Javols would have calculated a recovery period of about three thousand years for most life within the outermost regions, with the exception of the many extinctions. After this time they would return for another harvest.

This period of a few thousand years, Hamil thought, would give his people a breathing space in which to introduce the stronger genetically engineered human life to the planet's surface.

They could then rebuild some of the old surface cities and with the occasional underground assistance from Lower Cantor, which the underground city was then called, tactfully introduce some basic technologies and knowledge to give them a new start. Assistance to their bio-engineered children could only have been carried out anonymously and in the greatest secrecy. It was not possible for those temporary surface dwellers to learn of the lower underground city or of the Javol's existence for obvious security reasons. At least, not until the appointed time, several thousands of years hence.

Because of the future evacuation of all human life from Caefon some 3000 years in the future, the surface population could not be allowed to grow too quickly without population control. Food supplies would be restricted to certain remote areas on land. All sea and ocean foods would be kept well below worthwhile fishing limits by the introduction of bio-engineered marine bacteria. Religious and historical indoctrination would also be implemented in a negative way, and achievement goals correspondingly made high to compensate. For all those reason, their ancient religions based on the Senots for the procurement of all life was discouraged in favour of a more practical model in the absence of planetary life.

The development of a truly techno-altruistic society was to be created, where each member utilized his talents for the benefit of the common-good. But with the freedom to change careers or choose any desirable hobbies for their own personal benefit. All this Hamil thought was necessary in order to avoid boredom within the small stable society and most importantly, to avoid problems associated with mass evacuation of too great a population when the Javols returned in the distant future. But even then some people would be consumed.

They had by now completed all the relevant plans. The underground upper town had been completed and made ready for the first few surface scientists and their families.

However, one major problem remained and that was how the six could live through it all and remain alive for over 3000 years, if they were to assist in the Javols' destruction.

The six held a meeting in Plato's absence. It was convened during one of his frequent missions to Osmaron. During that meeting they discussed the possibility of freezing their bodies in cryogenic chambers and whatever ideas appeared feasible. Even clones grown from their frozen cells were considered and accepted as a secondary choice.

With all their ideas and advanced technologies, there was yet one remaining problem they could not circumvent or solve. That problem was how to bring back their original conscious selves including their original Identities at the appropriate time. They could only have lived another five hundred years at most and those details worried them. Getting nowhere, Lucia arranged another meeting for the following week. It was to coincide with Plato's next visit from Osmaron.

While considering their dilemma, Lucia turned to Sintra for assistance.

'Can your book help us in this matter? Please try to find a solution as soon as possible, if you can?'

Sintra nodded her head positively, looking equally concerned and they left feeling utterly despondent. It was the first time in his life when Meron considered the limitations of his race and realised that not everything could be solved by science.

After all, how could his exact identity be resurrected several thousands of years in the future, even after death from old age. They argued: if ten identical clones were made from an individual, in which of the bodies would the identity of the original individual find itself since each clone would be a different individual with different memories. And what if the original person was still alive? Surely, not in all ten bodies at once, including the original. Therefore an Identity was unique to that individual, non-transferable and isolated from all others.

As far as they were concerned, the cloned bodies, although seemingly identical, were completely different people and could not have contained the original being or identity. That original identity would always remain in its original body and after death would be somewhere else beyond reach of any of their technologies. Nevertheless could the technology of transplanting Identities have really existed? Only God might have that power, and so they reasoned.

Meron turned to Hamil, who was at that time by his side and looking equally lost for words.

'Perhaps the good Book or even the Osmaronites might shed some light. Have faith, my friend,' Meron said, sadly.

Lucia, now walking by his side overheard the conversation and tried to calm her colleagues.

'So far we have always found a solution, even without the aid of the Osmaronites, so we should not worry unduly. I am sure we are making too much of this issue,' she advised in her usual matter-of-fact manner.

As expected, Plato arrived the following week to lend his help in whatever way possible, but when he was told of the problem he smiled and said it was not his field. Sintra was also not aided in anyway by the Book, who said it could in no way interfere with the process of transcendence, whatever that meant.

Although they prayed for guidance in the solution of that particular problem, no answers could be found through their brand of science and they decided to wait until their next meeting.

CHAPTER 39

The Megotron and Psyrotron

This time the meeting was held at Lucia's home. They were seated comfortably reviewing their agendas while awaiting good news from Osmaron.

They were always extremely happy to see Plato, who was always cheerful and brought a ray of light and hope in the midst of their darkest hour. He tended to tell them of his journeys and they gossiped extensively about the beautiful worlds of Osmaron. It was apparent that he had the powers to travel anywhere with the aid of the Greater Mind and that aspect gave them hope.

On his return he introduced himself in his usual manner with a broad smile and did not comment on anything, but just nodded his head when they greeted. When they had all finished their agendas for the following week, Plato stood up and pressed the button on the winged buckle in his large metallic belt.

A strange greenish glow began to expand in the centre of the room, about one and a half metres above the floor just in front of where they were seated.

Lord Vektron the Ploran appeared in much the same way as he did previously and began to speak to them in his usual manner.

'I know it is a great problem, but one that can be surmounted with the permission of our Grand Lord. So all your worries are unnecessary.

'The special spaceship is to be refitted at the appropriate time with a new form of technology of which you will soon learn. It will be used to bring you back when the time is right.

'The Great Book has been updated with all necessary information relevant to the reforming of your bodies.

'I myself shall return at the appropriate time to assist in its implementation.

'You must not be too concerned, because we have the technologies necessary to reform your bodies and bring you back, even

after death. However, you are required to build these machines.'

Suddenly Lord Vektron grew hands to offer them a small computer disc. Then he disappeared in his usual manner.

They couldn't help being amazed by what they saw and heard.

Meron could never accept the incredible powers of the Osmaronite beings and began to think that perhaps Lord Vektron was a type of god. After all, who could wield such powers, to even resurrect the dead after several thousand years. Something that he always thought impossible. If he, the Osmaronite, could accomplish that feat so mildly and be there three thousand years in the future to assist in the program, what other great achievements could they have accomplished. How long could he have existed. Was he truly immortal and perhaps even indestructible?

He pondered those thoughts until he accepted the concept of all things being possible, eventually. That was, given very advanced technologies and perhaps Lord Vektron's race was an extremely ancient one.

Merian was given the special disc to translate, aided by her computers. After translation she passed the information over to Hamil and his team of scientists who were instructed to build the two large devices. The Psyrotron and the Megotron.

Those units would together scan and record every particle and neuron data from any living thing. There were different attachments for different life-forms, including a wide range of adjustments to accommodate virtually any type. All acquired data could be stored in mass storage units indefinitely for their re-creation at some later date. The only thing these machines could not achieve was to supply a new or even the original Identity.

That function was of a much higher dimensional order and better left to the gods of the Universe. The Great Builders of Goh and of similar dimensional planes, not of the primal type.

THE MEGOTRON

After its construction, that unit was like a gigantic hollowed robot. At least, that was the way it appeared with the human attachments fitted. It was usually placed around the living body to be scanned and automatically adjusted itself to firmly fit the shape of its patients.

Using micro robotics and many cleverly focussed fields, even the minutest cell structures could be scanned in any direction. It also utilized many mini portal devices and others unknown to our sciences. Most of the basic changes to the normal body could be implemented with a simple serum made from the subject's own blood. In most cases the body was simply scanned to memory and none of the special serums or its special devices necessary. Those were only used to implement changes.

It could also mend bodies by introducing micro robots and biologically grown tissue that could quickly change into specific organs, once given an initial genetic plan through specially synthesized footprint drugs. Even severed limbs could be completely regrown within minutes by such methods.

At the other extreme, a biological form could be changed to another of an equivalent mass. However, more subtler changes had to be done to the minds of the different life-forms so they could merge together as one. For that purpose a different device was used instead of the basic Megotron.

There were many tubes and telescopic arms connected to this device, giving it a most hideous appearance. It's patients were always fearful of its unknown processes.

THE PSYROTRON

The Psyrotron was fitted below the surface of the floor. The highly raised upper level comprised of many scanning rings.

The patient's brain was placed as close as possible to the central ring in the middle of the floor. There were literally thousands of those rings that radiated outwards from a most central point.

Several metallic recording rings and transmitters were usually placed at suitable positions around the patients body to collect and relay the numerous amounts of information for storage within small and completely sealed memory blocks.

That device automatically aligned itself to measure the position and strength of all electromagnetic fields within the brain and other relevant areas dynamically and in many dimensions.

Both of those devices, when used together, recorded all information relevant to the re-creation of any living organism, in form, memory and intelligence. However, the only drawback being, any newly created individual always lacked their experiences and memories since the original recording. Therefore some education was necessary to update their more recent experiences.

If the patient was dead, then all that was finally required after the bio-forming process was the original motivating life-force or the Identity. That which identified the individual from all others and gave the created being a purpose for its own continued survival and self-awareness. In most cases the Identity or Consciousness was linked to the person's memories.

Both devices were assembled in permanent locations in one of the main laboratory buildings within the small underground town. Several of those highly-secured buildings were constructed at that level, situated almost a mile below the planets surface and another mile above the main town of Lower Cantor.

CHAPTER 40

The underground city of Lower Cantor

That city expanded outward in all directions from the central elevator shaft which connected both environments together. The Lower City was about two miles below the planet's surface at the museum. At that time the main Cantorian museum on the surface was its main entry for workers and equipment. It was also the place where the main elevator terminated.

Plato assisted in its construction by introducing anti-gravity devices and other special materials from Osmaron. They were used for supporting the heavier weights above until properly reenforced by certain metallic supporting structures. The whole place was cleverly engineered with the elevator shaft forming a main supporting member. All areas under stress were reenforced by super-strong alloys, the knowledge of which came from Osmaron. To further assist structural stability, the pressure within the lower city was kept approximately four times above what it was at the surface. This was done with automatic locks between the different pressurized areas where the elevators travelled.

Its atmosphere was also different to that at the surface and maintained that way by several desalination plants and air purifiers. Many such machines were linked to the surface seas via concealed ventilation shafts.

Oxygen and other nutrients and chemicals were extracted from the nearby sea, so there were no visible links to the surface world, other than the concealed elevator. However few of its citizens could have noticed any difference after the initial acclimatization period.

The upper town was kept in an isolated bubble at only twice surface pressure. This engineering feature was used for the pressurization of travellers while moving in either direction.

Although the main elevator on the surface had a ground level that could be used normally by its many visitors, the entry of special codes could interlink both elevators via a concealed door. That feature prevented unwanted intruders entering mistakenly from the surface. However it was intended to extend the main underworld elevator within the museum itself. Those changes were later added after its temporary closure for refurbishment.

They commenced their official organisation under the auspices of a charity. Its sole purpose to promote health and survival assistance to under developed worlds within the federation, and they lived up to their charter in every detail.

Their organisation were however mostly used to warn recruited members within other worlds of impending dangers before it was too late. Many trustworthy officials of the newly introduced worlds were made members of their rescue organisation. Those were given special kits of equipment and asked to collect genetic materials, survival information and whatever was required for their world's re-creation after the Javols destruction. A few selected members of those worlds were subsequently chosen to be scanned for reconstruction and senior officials evacuated to Lower Cantor before the first Javols' attack.

Due to their growing popularity, their organisation was soon backed by every member of the Governing Council and allowed generous financial and other assistance as and when required. Yet, the government of that day, with the exception of the six, had not the slightest hint of the true nature of their organisation, not even when the Javols arrived. They saw the usefulness of a unique genetic databank and assisted.

The underground city of Lower Cantor, as it was then called, continuously expanded. As it grew so did all forms of entertainment and other types of activity common on the surface. It soon became fully self-sufficient, with its farms, lakes and forests. Agriculture was soon made very efficient, with the introduction of new genetically engineered plants with extreme high yields.

Those within Lower Cantor who wished to visit their surface relatives and friends were either deterred or released on a temporary pass. They were under strict contract and allowed limited short periods of holiday on the surface. No one was allowed to speak of the lower city or were to invite friends and relatives to visit. Despite those restrictions, the specially chosen earned very generously from their new occupations. Salaries and credits were over double what they could earn on the surface.

The underground city, although more confining, soon became almost as pleasant, if not more prestigious, than some of the better places on the surface. Therefore they never uttered a word about their underworld existence and neither did many have a serious desire to visit the surface. They would say their job was for a secret government organization and left it at that.

During all this time Meron and Hamil were constantly experimenting with every type of technology to improve the general welfare and health of its inhabitants. There was a code to be followed in case of fires and viral infection. In such an enclosed environment such dangers could run rampant. Many types of vaccines were created for every conceivable ailment and stored in special cryo-refrigerators for use as and when required.

After the Javols had left that area of the galaxy, it was hoped soldiers could once again visit the surface in special suits to observe the damaged world and collect materials and samples for a full assessment.

CHAPTER 41

Javols attack Caefon
(About 2000 years after Seno initiated the
repairs to their dying world Caefon)

Fifteen years had passed since the underworld foundation of Lower Cantor was laid and suddenly a few Javols were sighted by a military star-ship within their system. At first they thought they were small space probes, as part of an unscheduled experiment. They soon learnt that there were no such experiments scheduled or otherwise. Then they assumed they were probes sent by an unknown civilization from outside their system.

It was not long before their quantities began to increase dramatically, from just the initial five Javols to several hundred thousand. By that time they realised those things were not of a benign origin or nature, but instead an unknown alien life-form that could not be destroyed by simple means.

All initial attempts at communicating with the Javols had no effect. When they suddenly disappeared from their viewing screens only to be found later in a narrow spectrum, warning bells sounded and all stations placed on red alert.

Meron, being their senior war councillor, was in charge of all military operations and knew well his foe's methods and intentions. He also realized he could do little for his people, so he briefed his seniors on the type of creatures they were dealing with while they brought out their largest weapons. After that meeting they decided to fight to the last person to save their race. Nevertheless to avoid wide panic only the military was told.

Meron had fitted a secret escape tunnel that led by rail-craft directly from the main control centre of his war room to the elevator shaft under the science museum. That tunnel also led to areas underneath the city via the drainage network system towards the main concealed elevator. One of the concealed doorways that led into that secret tunnel was part of the wall in his private office. That secret exit could only be used by him either in an emergency or at the time of his evacuation.

At the first sign of the Javols' invasion all essential personnel within the society were evacuated to the underground city of Lower Cantor. More than ten billion people still remained on the planet's surface within all its major cities, towns and villages. All those would be sacrificed.

Before long the skies were swarming with the alien monsters, each slightly over a metre across. Their noises were fearful. They could mimic other life-forms and take their form. Many adapted forms of the most efficient predator types with weapons to match. They used a microid spray which when inhaled by animals would poison their victims into a slow and painful death, literally tearing their bodies apart from the inside. Others would combine together to form gigantic monsters for levelling large buildings and structures to get at the occupants.

Since they bore a natural hatred for all biological life, they took pleasure in agonizing their victims in the most hideous and painful manner. When they were finished in a given area they would simply grow wings and fly off to somewhere else. Such were the potential and flexibility of the unknown foe, the poor Caefonites had little chance of survival.

Despite the Javols callous attitude towards primal life, they were well structured and organized within their own communities. I suppose primals to them were more like gutter rats to us, for that was how they considered such life. Nevertheless within their methods were the crudest of sadistic predators.

The military tried exhaustively, but failed utterly and the Javols, as expected, enjoyed every bit of the hot beams and explosive power unleashed against them. To them, it was probably equivalent in human terms to taking a relaxing sunbath after an enjoyable meal. The viciousness of their quarry and the weapons used against them were an essential part of their feeding frenzy which led to an increase in their numbers.

As far as Meron and his associates were concerned, better a quick death with pride and dignity while facing the enemy, than a slow and painful one as entertainment fodder in some slave pit before being used as cattle for slaughter. After all, his race was a proud one and nothing could be done to save them. He realized their faith was truly sealed.

Meron had wanted to plant poisonous devices throughout the planet to silently and peacefully put his people to their final sleep. That method, although the most humane was not accepted by the others for many reasons. Further, it was necessary to find a weakness in the Javols' methods, but not to arouse suspicions, either with Javols or the human population. Therefore the complete event of the destruction of Caefon was to be recorded and held to posterity. It would be used as a warning to other civilizations and for future analysis, so that a weakness could be found in the Javols armour.

Meron saw the first of his people swiftly decapitated and absorbed. He said a quiet prayer for them to his Great Lord Gerron of Goh. Then he swore on the name of all his great ancestors like Seno and Micol, and on his ancient sword. He grabbed the sword by its blade so firmly as he prayed that his hands bled profusely. He did not wipe the blade but returned it to its scabbard in that way, still dripping with blood.

They unleashed every weapon against their foe, but within days all the cities and towns had been completely destroyed. Only small pockets of human life remained.

After the first wave of Javols more than 90 percent of the population had been absorbed or killed. During all this time Meron and Hamil recorded every bit of data on the Javols for later analysis.

Soon after the world's destruction, video recordings were relayed to all within the underground city of Lower Cantor. It was then that they were told of the master survival plan and given their long-term duties. During that time remote monitors constantly scanned the planet to observe the Javols' progress. All such information being directed to the survivors within the underworld.

After about fourteen days of onslaught all military structures had been completely destroyed. The few human survivors, now reduced to below 500 million throughout the planet and its satellites, took shelter wherever they could. Some took to the hills and caves while others hid in old underground mines, gutters or under collapsed buildings.

The Javols now many times more numerous than before left as briefly as they had appeared.

Slowly at first the human survivors began to rebuild their decimated societies, farms and cities, but with somewhat lesser resources and little will to survive. After all, they knew little about the true nature of their indestructible fore or when they would return to reap more havoc a second time.

At that time the great technological devices and machines that once maintained an almost perfect environment were no more.

Over fifty years had passed. By that time all human life had stabilised within comparative tribal societies. They would fashion tools and basic machines from metals and building materials left after the previous Javols' onslaught. At that time they were still able to find most raw materials in abundance, despite the constant spread of infectious diseases.

Once again the Javols returned. There was another major onslaught and about 90 percent of the remaining populations des-troyed. During that time most life-stocks had perished, being easy prey. Only about fifty million humans remained throughout the planet.

Most of the remnants became renegade, moving about in large gangs while others had become cannibals. The remnants quickly became degenerates and as predicted, had a much reduced lifespan of around forty-five years.

The third and final attack came after another fifty years or so. At that time although the renegade Javols were much fewer, they wrecked irreparable damage on all major planetary life. Almost everything was eaten with the exception of plants, insects, small animals and sea creatures. After that onslaught over ninety percent of all human life was destroyed.

Just over one million humans survived throughout the planet. Those soon perished due to the new diseases introduced by the Javols and other detrimental factors within their somewhat harsher environment. With little or no proper protection from the now unregulated climate and the lack of proper food and medicine, the race and all other major life-forms, to all intents and purpose, ceased to exist.

During those periods of Javols' attacks, Lower Cantor had completely sealed itself from the surface. The only method of observation from the now sealed underground city was via shielded space satellites and stations. Any other type of observation may have led the Javols to their underground facilities with disastrous consequences.

After the Javols left, close surface observation had revealed virtually no large animals remained. They knew the Javols would not return until the appointed time. This would be about 3000 years in the future. They also realised it was almost time to introduce their own brand of human life unto the planet's surface. Their newly cloned and genetically stronger relatives and descendants were soon prepared and introduced unto the new and almost sterile planetary environment. Within a short time the most virulent contagious diseases had disappeared; not having a proper animal host in which to propagate their kind.

Soon after, the surface museum was rebuilt and the foundation laid for the new surface city of Cantor. The old ruined city of Cantor, to the north, would be left as a temporary reminder, until the new surface humans had increased in number and the new city expanded within those areas. Yet, there was much knowledge to be acquired about Micol's Ancients within its old and broken buildings to serve the new community.

Meron, Hamil and other scientists would sometimes visit the surface in sealed protective suits. At that time all ecological controls were virtually zero. Hardy strains of bacteria multiplied wildly. The eco-balance had been tilted as every living thing tried to seek a higher level within the survival matrix of the planet. Even the trees were affected by their multitudes.

The planet's surface had become a strange place indeed to visit. With the exception of trees, one could see no life in its skies or fields.

Hamil beheld the sight of desolation and thought that even the worst type of existence within the underworld of Lower Cantor was paradise compared to anywhere on the surface. But he hoped in time and with the introduction of the new and genetically improved humans, the planet would once again establish a more stable order. All of that however was only a temporary measure. Just a small part of a greater plan.

It was not intended to reintroduce all primal life back unto the planet's environment until the Javols were gone for good. Any introduced life would be purely makeshift. Its sole purpose to repair the planet's surface and maintain a better survival order until its rightful masters returned in the distant future to establish normality.

So far, the Master Plan had worked. Even the prediction of the Javols' arrival and the complete destruction of their race within the two-hundred years limit had been on target and Hamil was convinced their plan was fool proof.

He nodded his head to himself and thought of the greatness and technological achievements of the Osmaronites, considering what he and his colleagues would have accomplished without the help of those great friends. It was through them that they had received the Great Book of Goh from which they were able to design all that was necessary for their survival.

He pondered his visit to Osmaron in the distant future, some 3000 years hence.

'After all, Lord Vektron had said so, but how could it be done after my death, either prematurely or of old age? Perhaps I might end up in the great city of Goh if such a place really exists.' He soon realised the planet's surface was too distressing to watch.

Once again he began to imagine the faces of his friends and relatives being consumed alive by Javols and quickly returned to the safety of the hidden elevator. It would take him downward into the bowels of his mother-planet to his new subterranean home. Never again would he return to this graveyard of over 6 billion deaths. Not until his greatest enemy had ceased to exist.

When they had done all that was needed of them, they had a final meeting together and Lucia took the stand.

'Family and friends, we have done all that was required of us. By now, we should all have realized that we cannot exist in this way for another three thousand years. I would rather retire while I am ahead of the race. Also, by so doing more resources will be made available to those responsible for the maintenance of this under-world while we are gone.

'The fusion generators and associated matter convertors have been designed by the Octans to last, with the ability to self-repair themselves over the required duration. The master computer and its many self-repairing robots have all the necessary information for their activities over the require time period. The supervisors and other life-forms know their places if they are to survive, so they will follow our instructions to the letter. All that remains, is a suitable method of despatch from this world to the next, until the time is right for our resurrection or re-creation,' she said.

'You think we should all die together?' Meron inquired.

'Yes, my loving husband. I think we should all have an enjoyable last supper together. During which time we should take a painless drug to send us on our way. Then our bodies may be preserved to posterity. But all the same, I think we should take a vote on the time and method used,' she replied, calmly.

After careful consideration and with great sadness they voted for death in the most pleasant manner.

Ecrol suddenly awoke from his dreamlike state. The helmet lifted off his head and returned to the ceiling. He realized he was dreaming of ancient times but very confused. He could see Plato with his strange sea-blue eyes closely observing his own with a bright light and for a brief moment found himself misplaced in time.

'It's all finished... I mean your tests, so you may return to your friends,' Plato smiled, relieved that his training program was now at an end, but Ecrol remain stunned for a while as if in a daze.

Plato nodded to his female assistant who took Ecrol away to join the others in the waiting room.

CHAPTER 42

The Javols' empire

The nano-bot Javols had been designed by their creators to be the ultimate warrior. They could exist within virtually any planetary environment using whatever materials that were available for food and fabrication. They also possessed unique abilities like stealth and camouflage. With LPDs they could move at high velocity in any direction in space. They were able to change their form at will with one of an equivalent mass. This was because they could only use their original mass during such transformations. Their only limitations being their stench, due to decaying biological organisms that remained with them. That problem was mainly because of their unclean eating habits.

Their unique abilities extended to transformations into rocks, dead trees, giant griffin-like bats, and other dormant and colourless objects to mislead or trick their quarry. Nevertheless with additional technology they could become close approximations to humans and most animals of a similar size.

They did not utilize artificial intelligence and had evolved their own type of intelligence during their creation. Therefore they were conscious living entities in their own right. Because of their unique differences, high intelligence, greater efficiency and superior abilities, they viewed all Primals (naturally evolving biological life) as inferior and only necessary for food.

Since they had the ability to copy virtually any structure, including the most intricate technological designs, they could always use and improve them for their own purpose.

The Javols learned the survival game well. Their rulers and super-intelligent computer called MasterMind communicated from the near galactic centre to all groups throughout the galaxy.

Despite their need for unification among all Javols, there were still renegade groups operating without direct connection to their MasterMind. Those they intended to collect and realign with the greater whole for mutual survival.

Several such renegade groups remained in the outer regions of the galaxy and did as they pleased regarding food and other necessities. Those were crude and opportunistic survivors with little desire for any type of technology or respect for superiors, least of all population control. It was one of those renegade groups that destroyed planet Caefon and the local systems. Once their resources had diminished to unsustainable levels, they would naturally seek new alliances and in the process join with Master-Mind for their mutual survival.

In a sense, outsiders were not christened into the order of Javols and as a result had not been given their own unique identification codes. Such Javols were on their own without any communication or assistance from others linked to MasterMind and could not benefit from their extensive knowledge. Those few renegade groups remained for a while within the periphery of the galaxy. They took whatever they needed from those still populated worlds, with little consideration given to their own population growth or their future survival needs after their food resources had been exhausted in those areas. Even so, they were able to communicate with other more distant clusters and soon learnt of a better and more productive way to survive. As their resources grew scarce they found it more advantageous to join with the most successful body even when under their control.

Finally all such renegade groups would commit and visit local centres to become as one with their MasterMind and its Master Plan. Then they would once again be released under Master Control for the greater good and benefit of all Javols.

MasterMind could communicate almost instantaneously throughout the whole galaxy. She used the H-wave, a form of imposed causal symmetry, that travelled at a much greater speed than light. It could traverse the whole galaxy within a fraction of a second.

Javols that were linked to their MasterMind behaved like individual parts of a greater whole. More like bees in a hive controlled by a single queen. They were inseparable from their MasterMind and followed all orders implicitly. Nevertheless, they were also guided by their insatiable instincts and desires. Those had been embedded deep within their blueprint and guided their survival. Their two main instincts were predation on primals and copying other technologies. Their long term goals were elicited by MasterMind and everything they did were confirmable to those plans.

Not being highly creative or inventive, they soon realized it was not to their advantage to destroy all primal life within the galaxy. It would have taken them too long to gain the necessary technologies, particularly those needed to visit the local galaxies. Further, all food supplies within Andromeda could very soon be exhausted and as a consequence, severe drawbacks to their kind.

When resources were scarce they had two options; death by a form of lengthy hibernation or joining together as one to share resources. Joining or chemical bonding with other members of their kind was less than intolerable. Although an option when food and energy resources became scarce it was not an acceptable one. During that process two Javols could coalesce into a single Javol with both their previous knowledge and experiences intact, but shared by a common mind and body. They would split apart after absorbing enough energy and nutrients. That process was not the same as linking together to form a giant destructive monster.

Renegade groups were not assisting the process of unification, since it was decided to multiply only where there was a surplus of food and whenever they were severely threatened by advanced technologies. Despite those problems they were a very successful species and a balance in numbers was at last being maintained.

Once organized, their greatest urge was not to destroy wantonly, but instead to conquer and control in their corrupt and vile manner, using the easily learned technologies they had acquired from their victims.

Although they were extremely clever at duplication and copying, they were not patient thinkers and could not invent new technologies by themselves. Because of those limitations, they dominated several advanced species who had little choice in accepting them as their masters.

Some of those clever races had been conquered before and didn't mind being dominated again, providing they were able to lead their own existence in peace. The Javols never allowed them that peace. They considered them a constant threat and poisoned their worlds, destroying all life. Those were considered too small and un-worthwhile for harvesting. Nevertheless, all their most important scientist were considered special and taken away. Two typical races were recruited initially.

THE THORAXI

The Thoraxi were a small insect-like form, very advanced in microminiaturization and efficient energy generators and converters.

Their world was indeed a hash and extremely inhospitable environment and did not allow for the evolution of reptiles or other types of animals like mammals. Their oceans and seas were almost nonexistent, having evaporated several billions of years before due to their impetuous binary stars.

They had to be clever and hard in order to survive within their planet's environment, even when they dwelt in deep caves within its surface.

THE PRAILLE

The Praille were completely different and resembled a small octopus with five tentacles which could be used for legs or hands while on dry land. Each tentacle had an array of suckers and hairy hooks tipped with poisonous stings.

Their world was mainly oceans, but they were also land dwellers that lived on their planet's two small continents close to its shores.

They were conceptual thinkers and would occupy their time between wars playing complex games of strategy while experimenting and solving mathematical and scientific problems for its own sake.

The Praille were hideous to observe. That was because they had five large eyes that were spaced equidistantly around their large almost spherical heads. Their gaping mouths were positioned at its very top.

They were not fond of the Javols. This was because Javols had little to offer them by way of knowledge. They simply regarded the Javols with contempt and considered them another juvenile species bent on domination, not knowing their true beginnings or rapacious nature.

The Javols plagued those races for knowledge of advanced technologies, but they knew very little of inter-dimensional travel. Nevertheless Javols considered both life-forms too small to be worthwhile for food. In any case, their mental powers outweighed any physical energy potentials, so they took the clever ones and allowed them and others to design equipment whenever necessary. The Javols supplied them with all their requirements for that purpose, including equipment captured from other civilizations. Many of those they would copy and in most cases improve on original designs.

In time the Javols had become quite organised and found ways to synthetically manufacture the materials for their own energy requirements, including an improved version of their microid LPD systems used for interstellar travel.

Initially those propulsion systems were very scarce. Only a few of their leaders were allowed them. It was then necessary for them to travel in large spheres. However since the commencement of production, every Javol could avail itself with a full set of six. Those units gave them full mobility at incredible speed.

Javols were so constructed to be regarded as a living spaceship. Being microid in design they could easily transform parts of their bodies into wings for flight. Unlike most primals like us that could only moved freely on flat surfaces of planets, they were truly 3D in motion and could move equally well in any direction.

Their buildings never contained stairs or such forms of access. Only large stairwells were available for vertical flight and access to different levels.

LPDs were readily distributed among themselves, even during reproduction and could be considered part of their microid body, like a spare replaceable organ. However, there was seniority even among Javols and their most senior members tended to have more of the technologies and pleasures, if one could consider such alien qualities in human terms.

Javols did not require clothes or any form of protection against the environments. Their semi-metallic construction made them fully self-contained. They were probably the most robust and successful species in the universe, not being of a primal type. They could survive under extreme temperatures, from near absolute zero, to close to the surface of a star, and at extreme pressures, including the vacuum of space or deepest oceans, without any technological assistance.

They did not require the larger primal life-forms any more and considered them a mere natural source of energy, but they allowed plants and minor life-forms to exist since they did not pose a threat.

All highly intelligent primal life now posed a threat and could create problems for them during their future conquest of the universe, so their MasterMind decided that all such life be conquered and made subservient to their empire. Those that resisted would be harvested for food at the appropriate time.

Their food supplies were stored on chosen planets and moons, or in large mobile vessels for use on long intergalactic voyages. Some stores were used for rations in dead stellar zones and unpopulated worlds. All Primal food would be stored and used appropriately until they found a speedier way to visit the neighbouring galaxies and harvest more resources. Nevertheless, Javols also used intelligent primals to farm the larger animals for food.

Because of such little opposition from Primals, combined with their soaring victories, they now considered their kind to be the most superior in the universe. Any new technologies could always be learnt from those they conquered before they in turn were harvested.

They would dominate and spread their own form and influence

throughout the universe, until they were masters of it all and so they reasoned. But reasoning was one thing and conquest quite another.

THE PLASMA PIT

Despite their unique organization, not all Javols were obedient slaves that followed orders implicitly. Some were highly ambitious and broke rules less favourable for their promotion. Others just took advantage and rode roughshod over others. All such anti-social behaviour were contemptible to MasterMind. Those few disobedient ones were held in special prisons until their day of execution in the arena.

Javols were like ancient Romans in this respect. They made their prisoners fight each other to the death in their many arenas with an array of weapons for their entertainment. Then their remains would be disposed in super hot plasma pits. However those pits were also used for executing all those notable primals who had directly fought against them in wars and suchlike. It was a gesture of respect on their part and much better than the alternative.

In the case of primals, it was indeed a great honour bestowed by Javols, instead of the alternative of being flayed while slowly eaten alive. Depending on how well they fought, their forms and other attributes would be copied and used by senior Javols in the future.

During those periods of entertainment Javols had real fun; for they would place bets on the unfortunate Gladiators, who consisted of Javols and Primals alike. They would gamble during such contests on how long they would last or how many screams they enemies would make while subjected to the intense temperatures of the searing plasma pit.

IN THE FINAL ANALYSIS

Javols had sadly underestimated the thinking potential of their

Osmaronite foe, for they were babies by comparison.

While great minds planned their final destruction, large maulars and destructive fortresses were already on their way to Andromeda. Those robot-driven machines, which had taken several millennia to cross the great distances between the two galaxies, were arriving at strategic points within Andromeda, ready for their slow and unrelenting progress towards its centre.

Those ships were designed to mislead the Javols and seed the galaxy with shielded observation probes so that the Javols' progress could always be monitored. They would continue their unrelenting task until they approached their Great Intelligent Mind close to the largest black hole within that galaxy. By then the first intergalactic wave of Javols would be arriving in the Osmaron galaxy. At that time all necessary devices and weapons had to be put in place and made ready for the defence of Osmaron.

In that future the technologies within Osmaron would be advanced by another three thousand years and perhaps even advanced enough to allow the Osmaronites to travel across intergalactic space within days instead of millennia, to assist in the final battle for Andromeda against the unrelenting Javols.

The Osmaronites had a lot more in their bag of tricks that would keep for later. Those would be released at an appropriate time.

Some demigods like Jull, the former Patriarch, and a range of other most deadly and indestructible Supreme Lords could destroy Javols by just glancing at them. That was when the New Titans would reign.

CHAPTER 43

The lower underground city

Now.... about 3000 years after Meron and the others.

With Ecrol's final test, the young six had passed with flying colours and realized all their unwarranted fears and worries were almost over. However they still knew nothing about the dangers they would face during their journey to Osmaron.

It was their final day in the underground city of Lower Cantor. Led by Jon they were escorted by the guards towards the first laboratory building. It was the one used by Plato for their psychological tests. That building gave direct access to the central multiple elevator station. From there the elevators went to all levels from H-Control to Lower Cantor proper. They were escorted to a lower level within the upper town of the underground city and directed to one of the main elevator stations.

Waiting at one of its entrances was Plato's female assistant. She was beautifully dressed and almost unrecognisable in her elegantly applied makeup. She walked towards the six and greeted them.

'Please follow! I have been assigned to you for the day. Plato's orders, I'm afraid. I am to show you around the lower city and explain everything to you as best I can. This visit is not official. The trip will make a pleasant break for me as well.' Merian was cheerful.

She led them towards one of the secondary elevators and entered a security code by pressing several round buttons on a small panel, then she entered her security card in one of the slots. The door opened and they followed her into the padded cubicle. At that time there were no other passengers on-route to the lower city. They felt their weight change significantly as the cubicle accelerated then decelerated and held firmly to the hand rails. Their ears almost popped on route with the changing pressure.

After about two minutes they arrived at what appeared to be the main station of Lower Cantor. That part was about a mile below the upper town where they had only recently taken their tests.

From that moment on all similarities with the upper town, its colleges, science buildings and laboratories ended. They entered an extremely busy city with every form of activity and entertainment imaginable.

Life was bustling everywhere. Many strange aliens could be observed partaking in its numerous activities. Robots could be observed everywhere carrying out the most simple tasks of maintenance.

Although the atmospheric pressure at that level was over twice that at the upper underground town, they felt little discomfort and soon acclimatised to its more intense environment.

The strange bird-like people from the Coln System were everywhere assisting in its administration. The city's occupants were quite a genetic mix, with all its varied life coexisting peaceably together for a common cause. The bird people were obviously one of the first species taken in by the Ancients over three thousand years ago. Their descendants on planet Coln had somehow survived or evaded the initial onslaught of the Javols at that time while on their original home world.

Jon pondered the incredible determination and planning by so many different and diverse species, who had little choice other than cooperate to fight a common foe. He wondered where all those aliens had come from and how they had journeyed to the underground city unobserved. Perhaps they had been there for centuries, even millennia. Merian guided them to a block of buildings away from the main street. After they had passed several blocks she halted their progress.

'This is the Museum of Ancient History. It contains most of the exhibits from the original city of Cantor. That was the one destroyed by the Javols several thousand years ago. Did you know our original city of Cantor was built by Micol the Great? He was just a little boy at the time of its construction. This beautiful monument was brought here from the ancient surface museum about the same time.'

Showing her credentials to the security guards, they entered the hallway. Then carefully observed the statues of Seno, the ancient profit, then Melor, Micol and Sefran. Merian keyed in the necessary security code on the door panel which slid apart to reveal a large maze of crystal containment units. They displayed all forms of ancient artifacts. The six were surprised by the numerous exhibits on display. As collectors and archaeologists, Merol and Jon were overjoyed by the unavailable treasure and made comparisons with similar types in the relatively new public museum in Cantor, but of all things they were enthralled to be in the presence of their past. Some of the clothes and weapons displayed could have been worn by ancient warriors in the days of the great clans and tribes, including the original Ancients before the planetary wars. Those were over nine thousand years old.

They browsed for a while, asked Merian an occasional question, to which she always gave a precise and positive answer. After they had viewed most of the important artifacts she took them towards a rear section of the building into a more secured area.

She entered another code on the large vault door before it clicked open and allowed them into the chamber. Turning to Jon, she continued to speak.

'Over three thousand years ago some of the Ancients consulted a great book for answers during their troubled times. Here is the main volume. It was given to them by the Osmaronite, Lord Vektron.'

'Not our Lord Vektron!' a startled Jon exclaimed.

'Yes! He is a Ploran, you know, and they are immortal!' They were amazed by that discovery but she continued to explain.

As they approached, Merol couldn't contain his excitement.

'Look! The original book. Great Lord Gerron, it's absolutely brand spanking new... after so many generations!'

Merian pushed several buttons on a local panel and the crystal frame lifted, revealing the great golden book in all its glory.

'You are to return this book to Osmaron along with the sword,' she said to Jon with disappointment.

They closely observed the book, but it was held in a smaller, more ancient crystal container and all they could observe was its front cover. It now displayed the two horned serpents with the sword engraved and embossed on its golden front cover.

'This book is called the Anachromagnon or "the Book of Final Light". The three abridged versions shown over there are called the Anachromecron or "a book of light". They were used for copying the translations.

'A copy was lent to the surface dwellers over two thousand years ago, to aid in the planet's recovery. During that time it has been your bible of survival. Only your surface leaders could gain access to its pages.

'They have since been returned to this place for safe keeping, being sometimes required by us for reference and translation purposes.

'Despite the common use of advanced computers and other modern means of storage and retrieval, the Ancients preferred the use of books. Perhaps that method of learning aided concentration and memory. It was also a hobby to some and a safe method of storage for others.'

'Really? It could have been mainly cultural.' Lira was amazed.

'Yes! After all, life might have been extremely unexciting, with all the technological assistance of that time, leading to boredom. So they turned to many different types of diversion, like sports, music, poetry and more basic forms of adventure and recreation. However, most of the Ancients simply preferred to write books and compose songs and poems on synthesized paper which they added to their own personal libraries or shared with their friends and colleagues. The paper itself was a byproduct, previously discarded as waste from certain chemical processes.'

'That's fantastic!' Merol exclaimed, realizing how novel the idea was, but Marian continued.

'It is thought that trees were used several thousand years before to produce the materials required. After a few decades of so doing, most of the great forests had been destroyed, while large areas of our world almost became deserts like the Craile. Since then that practice was banned. I suppose the use of paper and book writing can be compared to your different hobbies like archaeology and painting on the surface. But they also used those professions as well.'

She uttered those last words while glancing at Merol and Jon, but continued the historical conversation.

'It was a type of diversion from the great technological advances of that age, which subsequently became fashionable. I suppose, it's because information recorded in computers can be so impersonal. We humans prefer to attach ourselves to things on a more personal level.'

She pointed to another case a few metres away. The Book's outer case was replaced and they went across to observe Meron's sword. It was held within a studded scabbard and fastened to an equally studded flexible metallic belt. It was the type a great warrior would wield and obviously handed down to him by one of his distinguished ancestors.

'We don't know where it originally came from. Some say it was given to our ancestor Melor by the Oracle, Mohria, who in turn received it from Grand Lord Gerron. It was subsequently handed down to our great ancestor Micol by his father, Melor. Since then it has been passed on to his descendants. Lord Meron was the last.'

They admired the sword's scabbard, with its glittering jewels and intrinsic beauty for a while, then they were taken to a more modern building another block away. This time the place was swarming with more security officers. They had to enter three security levels which included Merian's grade-one clearance.

The third and final area housed a strangely glowing object. The light energies from it did not move away in straight lines, but was instead curved and absorbed back within the object after travelling about a metre away. Different colours were curved differently, giving a beautiful rainbow effect with ultraviolet blue furthest away.

They stood in that position for a while as if transfixed by its emanations, admiring the large globe and being completely absorbed by its beautiful scintillating colours. The colours would visibly change when they moved either closer or further from its fields. It was almost as if the device felt their presence.

That perfectly spherical object floated in mid air and did not physically touch anything. It was held in place as if by magic. There were several small pulsating black units positioned at a fixed distance from the object, apparently holding it in place by an invisible force within its specially designed chamber.

Merian soon explained:

'This is the main part of the Omegron Portal. It consists of two identical units, like identical twins. Yet completely opposite in polarity... like a positron is to an electron when taken from the same original parent particle, but even more so.

'Both symmetries are equal and yet opposite, like left and right as in a mirror.

''They are so similar, that they are always kept a great distance away from each other. Less they interfere with the intervening space, causing temporal and spacial distortion.

'These devices oscillate within the H-Dimension, where space and time, within this plane, are merely vector points.

'This technology was recently learnt from Osmaron through the Great Book. It has opened up the way for a new level of technology in space-time travel within the Cosmos.

'Anyway, when these portals are switched on, the sympathy or wanting for each other becomes so great that they will together even shrink space and alter time, in any manner, to assist their bonding together as one.

'I suppose a form of symbiosis on a cosmic scale. People sometimes say that in a not too dissimilar manner very close twins can on occasion sense each others' feelings and emotions.

'They were both moulded from regenerated matter of a new and specific variety, not like primal matter.

'They cannot be destroyed while apart by any known means, because each one constantly imprints on the other through the H-Dimension. This can occur at any distance within our plenum and will, by virtue of the "matter cannot be created nor destroyed" modus-operandi, be recreated in much the same way as a piece of matter leaving or entering our space-time continuum.

'Such objects would either be re-created, where there was a loss

or destroyed where a surplus occurred, thus leaving the system in its original stable causal mode within its space-time boundaries of what we call stasis or continuity.

'Both parts made the whole. Each containing just one half of something which was not quite the whole and yet, when brought together they became normally vectored matter with the release of a great amount of energy.

'As far as the primal system is concerned, both parts are the whole and in one place, despite the fact that they are not. For we, the observers know differently, don't we?' she said, with enthusiasm.

She smiled with fervour and commitment, while streamers of light continued to pour from the object and they wondered where the other one was situated.

Then Mcrian took them to an old building. She asked them to remove their sandals as they entered and spoke to them calmly.

'This is another ancient surface building. It used to be in Central Cantor but was reassembled here in ancient times. It is one of the oldest of our historic buildings and existed well before even Cantor itself was built. It formed the main gateway to a citadel that then existed. During that period our world faced serious climatic change and our history was very volatile, with many warring clans and tribes. This monument also house our ancient Oracle called Mohria, which was created by another race of Ancients over 5000 years before for their survival.

'Lord Joel Meron was descended from the great Micol, who was from one of the greatest clans called the Safa. They say his ancestors, including the great Micol, met and communed with the Grand Lord of Gohenna... the one we call Gerron. But that could be just myth, because the ancient tribes seldom recorded every aspect of their history and all we have to rely on are relics of that bygone age. This magnificent building has a tall spire which includes a golden crucifix at its very top,' she said, with sad reflection.

Merian took them further into the building.

'This monument is now used as the last and final resting place for the Ancient Six, whose places you are to assume during your Great Adventure.'

They became curious and continued to follow her towards a specially sealed chamber.

The bodies of the six, although worn by time from natural aging when they were alive, were retained fresh and almost lifelike. They were sealed in blocks of transparent crystal.

'Here is the Great Prince Meron and on his side, Lucia his wife.' She uttered those words with a tone of sincere gratitude in her voice but with sadness in her eyes.

She went on even to name their pets and family members which were in a separate but much larger chamber. The Ancients were serenely laid out in their beautiful family tunics and robes, with different markings that represented their families and status. Each had identical winged insignias pinned to their garments above their chests, and looked so real and peaceful, as if in a deep sleep. The only Ancient missing was Plato, Meron's brother.

The last body they visited was also called Merian. She was Merian's direct descendant. As Merian approached her ancestor, lying so peacefully in the large crypt, she sighed and smiled with both affection and sadness for that great lady. Although determined to maintain a responsible stance, she could not hold back the tears that streamed down her cheeks.

'I am sorry. I always get like this when I visit this place,' she apologised while wiping the tears from her face.

Jon and the others were saddened by her sudden change in mood, but not saying a single word, followed her out of the building towards a small square in the direction of the main station.

They soon approached a large modular structure. Using her grade one security clearance, they entered. The place was dimly lit with a bluish light.

She uttered an unknown voice command and the light gradually brightened, revealing the special spaceship. The young women and Ecrol were surprised by the bizarre shape of the large object, but realised it was the one mentioned by Jon and Merol.

'It has been refitted with all the latest technologies acquired from Osmaron.' She was happier than a moment before.

She uttered another strange command and a shimmering staircase suddenly grew out of the ship and left an entrance for them to follow.

This time the voice spoke in a precise manner.

'*You are welcome!*'

Her companions froze where they stood and did not wish to move a step further, but she beckoned them forward.

Hesitantly at first, they followed her up the glittering stairway into the bowels of the spaceship. Jon was surprised by the new changes. He found himself in a spacious and beautifully decorated environment. The pilot's cabin now contained six carefully positioned sleeping units, each with its own movable canopy.

The central floor area could ascend vertically to become a large table with just enough room to sit all its six exclusive passengers simultaneously. Everything within that room was pleasant and comfortable. Jon thought it was so different to that first time when he and Merol climbed its strange glittering steps. That was soon after its excavation.

There was not a single trace of the three helmets or their surroundings. A larger part towards the rear had also been removed to make space for its human passengers. In their estimation only about one half of its internal structure was taken up for that purpose and they wondered what was contained within the other half towards the rear.

Merian admired the beauty of her handiwork and addressed them all.

'Do you like your new surroundings? I personally designed it for you... It's meant to be as comfortable as possible on your relatively short trip. I think it's acceptable, don't you?'

They nodded their heads in agreement, but she continued.

'I wish I was accompanying you on your great adventure, but my work here is not yet at an end. Anyway, I have been told by Plato that I am to visit you in Osmaron at a later date. I am to assist with a new project there. You should not worry about anything because you are all in very safe hands.' She tapped the body of the ship as if it were a person, but there was no reply.

When they left the spaceship she uttered another strange word to which the ship replied.

'Thank you! Great Daughter of Goh!'

To their further amazement the stairs melted into the ship and the entrance sealed itself in a reddish glow.
They were then led out of the building.

By this time the group was extremely hungry so she decided to take them across the main street to one of the larger restaurants. As she entered the human manager bowed his head gently, giving due respect as if she was royalty. It could have been because of the winged insignia on her left lapel. Then he escorted all seven to two tables at the rear. She patiently explained the Ancients' menus to them and ordered for each in turn.

The manager was always close at hand to give advice when asked and began to take their menus down with pen and pad. Not by hand-held computer as on the surface. Then he asked her for her autograph before taking the information to the kitchen.

They enjoyed their first real meal since their arrival at the underworld. Those meals closely resembled the types from their own surface restaurants and not the sloppy mush from the machines of the upper town.

Merol observed closely the methods used for writing, and questioned why there were no hand-held computers for that purpose as on the surface. Then he realized that method was most efficient and did not rely on batteries, an external power source or machine failure.

Despite their relief from hunger, they felt extremely tired. Thus far they had a most extraordinary day, filled with more than the usual physical and mental effort. They also realized that almost all travel within that city was by foot.

While they sat in the almost transparent restaurant, they could observe a few small robot driven street cars transporting important individuals to and fro. There were no elevators or moving walkways at that level within the underground city and they realized their omission was for safety and energy efficiency.

When they finished their meals she asked them if they wished to say a prayer for their ancient ancestors and families in order to be blessed on their journey. At first they were not quite sure what she meant, as surface people lived in a completely different society and were not familiar with ancient religious customs and beliefs. Nevertheless they agreed to go along with her and take advantage of this new cultural experience.

She explained the basic concepts and symbols of the ancient Senots religion and mentioned the significance of the Great City of Goh or Gohenna as it was sometimes called. It was the place where all good beings journeyed after death. During that process of enlightenment even seemingly impossible dreams could be fulfilled.

After she had explained the basics of her religion to them, she got up and went over to the small desk where the manager was sometimes stationed. He glanced at her special insignia. Then she handed him a small card which he inserted into a machine. He retrieved the card and handed it back to her, thanking her and bowed his head in the process.

They assumed some form of payment or reward was given for the meals. They used computers and metallic tokens on the surface for smaller purchases. Here, there was obviously a different currency method used between its citizens.

This time they followed her in the direction of the old ancient monument.

While they travelled very little technology could be observed. Almost every effort was manual or by specially designed robots. Despite the lack of a more efficient transport systems, the passages and streets were well laid out to optimize travel. Every-thing they could observe had been specifically designed to minimize the use of electrical energy. Buildings were distributed in local groups for entertainment, recreation, supplies and others. An array of streets and passages assisted in point to point access with travel at different levels throughout the city. That underworld city presently boasted a population of around one million. A population that contained many different races including aliens from afar.

On arrival at the monument they removed their sandals once again before entering.

She guided them to a large alter with many candles burning. The place had a sweet but unnatural smell about it.

She positioned herself directly in front of the altar while the others passed on either side. Then she knelt with both her palms clasped and began to pray quietly and solemnly. The others followed her every move. After they had finished, she went to take a last look at the Ancients bodies in the crypts. With tears in her eyes she turned to Jon, now in charge of his six colleagues.

'Our destiny is in your hands. So you must try your utmost best and follow that destiny with our Grand Lord and the Osmaronites. You must be brave and have faith in our technologies and The Ship; for it knows best and can accomplish all its programmed tasks to perfection.'

'You should never worry for us. We shall do our utmost best to save our people, even unto death,' Jon promised, while the others nodded in agreement, and she was satisfied by their determination.

She opened a small purse and retrieved a small metallic crucifix which she handed to Jon.

'Take this ancient symbol of our faith and keep it always with you to remind you of us here on Caefon and for good luck.'

'Thank you, Merian!' he said. 'I shall always cherish it!'

They were soon on their way back to the upper town, after what was to them a most revealing and eventful day. They realised why Plato was so insistent on their making that journey to the lower city. It had opened their minds to many new concepts, but seeing those great Ancients in their crypts did stress the importance of their mission.

They were fully decompressed on-route and subsequently taken back to their quarters within the recreation facility.

'Great Lord Gerron, what an experience!' Lira exclaimed.

'I feel like I have been drained of all my fluids! I didn't realize Merian could walk such great distances!' Jon complained.

'I saw an awful lot today and the images of those poor people in their crypts will never leave me. My God, they sacrificed so much for us!' Petra said, almost in tears. Then suddenly the experiences of that day overcame them. They burst into tears and began to sob while holding on to each other for comfort. It was then that they realized the importance of their mission to Osmaron.

They were given the following day to relax and make preparations. Their space journey was to commence on the day that followed.

CHAPTER 44

To be or not to be an Ancient

By now the young six had begun to put the great survival puzzle of the Ancients together. For some reason they had to unravel the complex web of events enacted over the past several thousand years. That was necessary if they were to find reasons for the grand deception and secrecy of the Ancients, including the real purpose of their mission to Osmaron. That part of the complex jigsaw had not yet been revealed to them by anyone.

They had learnt much about the past regarding their world's problems from Merian, even about the time when the great Melor fought field battles for his tribes' survival. They also realized their world almost died about 5000 years before because of Global Warming. That was during the time of king Melor and Micol. Of all those Ancients the great prophet Seno was the most regarded. It was his books on poetry and history that gave the most insight into their past.

Merian also told them that the original ancestors before Micol's time were more like them, with brown eyes, brown hair and, a tanned complexion, but with six fingers plus two thumbs. During that ancient time their world was filled with numerous cities that got covered by the rising waters as the planet warmed.

The more recent Ancients, with sea-blue eyes, golden hair and a pinkish complexion were Micol's and Sefran's direct descendants. They had been the only survivors since the time of Global Warming and severe climate change, and the unfortunate ones to be destroyed by the Javols.

Copies of Seno's books had been kept well away from the surface dwellers, who had no real knowledge of their ancient past before 3000 BE, while the original more advanced civilization with their large cities existed before about 5000 BE. That was before the present era (BE) corresponded to the precise time of arrival of the Osmaronites to their world. Lord Vektron and his people had arrived about two decades ago, just before the birth of the young six.

Merian had made copies of Seno's historical records, including the Senot's bible and handed them to each of the six. They held them to be most sacred.

Despite the additional knowledge gained from their visit to the lower underground city, there still remained many unanswered questions so their worries were many, including the following:

If Merian's Ancients were the only true survivors and so different to them, in what manner could they be related? Were they in some bizarre manner their real children, grown from their 3000-years-old frozen embryos? Those embryos could have been implanted into surrogate parents at the appropriate time.

Such chosen parents could be any infertile women desperate enough to acquire offspring by that method when they were chosen. If it was so planned then those parents could have been inseminated at a time that coincided with their planned conception.

That parent might not have been aware of the substitute embryo during the artificial insemination process and would naturally have assumed the child to be their own offspring.

Further, questions would not have been asked by such parents, since all present day surface dwellers were of similar genes, with almost identical features, including brown hair, brown eyes and a slightly tanned appearance. It was always a great honour to be chosen to bear offspring within the 10 year period.

The Ancients had golden hair, sea-blue eyes, pinkish skin and were on average about one third of a metre taller. They were almost giants by comparison. The physical features of the young six were not similar to average surface people by such comparisons. They were well above average height and build, and fairer than most with grey to brown eyes.

Were they also over three thousand years old? Despite those anomalies, the hands of all surface dwellers including those of the young six were so completely different to Merian and Plato's. The Ancients like Plato and Merian had three fingers on each hand compared to their four, excluding their thumbs.

Each member of the young group of six could have the answer to one or more of those questions. Perhaps it was time the group shared their induced dreams in an attempt to unravel the complex survival jigsaw and find links to their ancient ancestors.

They discussed some of those questions while on-route to the recreation centre and as usual Lira was concerned; so many questions had been left unanswered.

'Jon, I think most of the answers to our questions are in the dreams they gave us during our final test. We should form a group, perhaps at the small bar and have a free discussion on those topics. Any answers might help to alleviate some of our main fears before our trip to Osmaron.' Jon nodded his head in agreement. He immediately called the others together.

'Guys, I think we should meet at the little bar after we freshen up. It's imperative that we hold some type of discussion in an attempt to resolve any questions that may still worry us during our long journey. Shall we make it after dinner?' he stressed while glancing at his watch.

They agreed as he and Lira walked away together.

'They always treat you with such respect and admiration,' Lira commented and held on firmly to his hand.

'We are in this thing together and they know I'll sacrifice everything and always give my best to get us through,' was his reply.

The young six were sitting in their usual corner. This time they joined two tables together so they could be closer.

Merol and Ecrol had acquired some of the synthetic paper used by the lower Cantorians and with pens in hand pretended to take notes of their present discussion. Merian had included such stationery items in packs she gave them after their trip to the lower city. They liked the novelty of it and considered the process more fashionable than handheld computers. Not being practised in the art of writing, they had trouble holding their special pens properly. They even considered pens suitable only for three fingered people, but after further consideration and having observed the objects to be symmetrical, were convinced they were not biassed one way or the other. Further, when they observed Merian with it, she always used two fingers and thumb. Therefore those three digits seemed adequate enough to correctly hold the object while forming the Ancient's characters.

Although the practice seemed strange and difficult at first, they were determined and encouraged by their quick progress. They knew a little of the Ancients' language and out of respect considered writing to be a hobby worth reviving and preserving to posterity. They had also taken well to the Senots' religion and realized there were very advanced beings involved, including Grand Lord Gerron. After all, they had met Lord Vektron. Although they knew the name from ancient writings, they thought it was just religious folklore.

'Look people!' Ecrol shouted, while displaying a note on paper he had just composed. They observed his writing and realized it was a very economical method for conveying information without a computer.

'Writing is so cool!' Petra said.

While they sat, Lira was the first to speak.

'You should all know that several questions remain unanswered and still give worry, even on the eve of our urgent trip to Osmaron. So if you don't mind, I intend to pose my questions for discussion. The first of which being... are we the real children of the ancients? I mean, their true embryonic offspring. Secondly; how do we take their places in person or vice versa and finally, what happens to the ten million people now living on the surface, including our families and friends after we leave for Osmaron?'

'Nice choice of questions!' Jon said.

'Perhaps we should each compile a list of such questions and attempt to answer them tonight. If answers are forthcoming, we may depart on our trip to Osmaron with greater peace of mind. Otherwise, I am afraid we are not going to give our best if we are still concerned about such matters. We must therefore resolve them, even if I have to consult Lord Vektron myself in the morning!' Lira said, forcibly.

Jon knew Lira well and realised she was determined and very

proper in her reasoning, so he replied in his usually calm manner.

'Guys, I think we were each given all the necessary information during our final test. You know, those long dreams we had during that last test... It's possible that we were each given a different dream for security or some other reason, known only to the Ancients. May I suggest when a question is asked by anyone, we try to answer that question as best we can; just in case one of us has that part of the answer in their subconscious.'

'Good idea!' Merol said.

'Perhaps the pink drink might help us remember. The last time I had some... I felt on top of the world and remembered much of the past without even trying... and other things besides. Anyway, we need a little relaxation and break after a most tiring day, so perhaps we can combine both,' Jon replied, enthusiastically.

Ecrol was quite keen on the idea. He enjoyed the chemistry and concept behind the social habit of drinking. Although such habits were not allowed on the surface, he saw no problem, providing the process was not taken to excess. Anyway, as far as they were concerned, it was not poisonous or in any way addictive to the human body. Like writing, that habit was fast becoming a social habit by all members of the young group.

Ecrol and Merol downed their pens and pads, and eagerly darted off to the small bar to collect the pink drinks for their comrades. They would acquire them from the quiet bartender they called Rob, who they later realised was a type of android.

Most of their installed dreams had been forgotten or so it seemed to them, except for a few strong and painful areas that still lingered.

Jon thought perhaps they could use those dominant impressions to restore most of the original stories.

Lira was quite correct in her reasoning. It was much better to depart on their trip with a clean breast of things, so to speak, than have lingering doubts in the midst of serious and life threatening decisions.

When the drinks arrived Lira stood up and popped the first question.

'My first is, are we the real children of the Ancients?' Then she abruptly sat down.

This time Ecrol answered, looking very pleased with himself, having already drank two mouthfuls of the pink liquid.

'I think, yes! In my dream I saw Hamil... my supposed father... I think each of us had a dream specific to their parent's experiences.... Anyway, he was discussing genetic splicing with Meron... They were having problems... He couldn't find an easy way to do it with six fingered humans... their human type... something to do with regressive genes.'

'Go on!' Lira beckoned.

'His type... I mean the Ancients. They could no longer live on the surface for that reason... Could have been some genetic weakness in their immune system to the new and more deadlier forms of bacteria and germs found on the surface at that time. Most of the disease had been brought to our world and left behind by the filthy aliens. Anyway, I think that's also the reason why those Ancients left on the surface... that is, after the aliens attacked, did not survive for long. They had to use their original genes, but slightly modified to remove the regressive strains. They further had to strengthen them against new viral strains,' he said, jovially. While smiling he flexed his muscles.

'You are now looking at one of the most advanced humans in existence.' Then he took another sip of the pink substance. The others were not amused, so he stiffened up and continued.

'There was also some talk about storage of family genes. Certain humans and animals were to be brought back on the surface when the time was right. But there was no specific information regarding whom or when,' he added and sat down.

'Great Lord Gerron of Goh! That explains everything. We are the new Ancients.... Their race could not survive anymore on the surface of Caefon, so they gave us their brains and physique... made us stronger, genetically... to survive where they failed. But they could only have achieved that great deed with eight fingers. That also answers your question, Jon.'

'Partly!'

'Good Gohenna! I can't imagine Lord Meron ever agreeing to

such a decision... It would have been against all his principles. They might have had a critical time schedule and little or no choice in the matter,' Lira continued.

Jon then entered the conversation.

'Yes! He had very little choice. He even cried tears for his children and people, but Hamil, being a good friend convinced him... that it was the best choice for all concerned. That is why there were always heated arguments between them. Like always, when Meron had his back up against a wall and all other avenues failed, he would say a prayer and ask for guidance, but he could find no answers. At that time survival of their race was the most important thing, so he had to agree. The Great Book, with Sintra's interpretation also helped as best it could, but they discovered... from the Book... that eight fingered humans were the most common in the universe. That was because they were better survivors than other human types, for some yet unknown genetic reason. That is possibly one of the reasons why they never visited the surface again in all that time... condemned to this underworld for the remainder of their lives,' Jon said.

'That is so very, very, very sad!' Petra exclaimed.

Then Lira interrupted them with another question.

'From Merian's words... when we were in the temple... there was some mention of the Ancients taking our places or vice-versa. I would like someone to throw some light on that topic, please?' she asked, with woeful foreboding in her manner.

This time Petra entered the conversation.

'I think what she meant was, that perhaps we were being prepared to take their places some time in the distant future, when things were once again back to normality in our galaxy. Some form of linking with Osmaron is indicated during this recovery period. Even if they were brought back, they could not return to Caefon to live normally on the surface, even after the aliens were destroyed. So I think we were chosen genetically for that purpose. Perhaps in most essential aspects, we are almost identical to the Ancients. Did you not observe their faces in the crypt... did you not imagine which one you would resemble at their age, even with all that makeup? I did! I imagined I would look exactly like

Sintra... can't you see a likeness? But for my light brown eyes, brown hair, eight fingers.... our heights are so similar. You know, we are a lot taller than most surface people and I don't think we are our parents' children. No, I think we have been specifically engineered from their genes and are identical to them in all important characteristics. Therefore, to all intents and purpose, we are they,' Petra said, dismayed by her own utterance.

The others were astonished by that answer and did not fully believe what she said, so Jon interrupted.

'Great Lord Gerron! So during those special dreams we were subconsciously implanted with parts of their real history, as when seen through their own eyes. A method to link us even closer to them,' he said, astonished.

Then Lira spoke. This time she remained seated.

'The dreams might not have been all. We could have been given a lot more, even delayed subliminals, to be released at the appropriate time when they are required. The incredible powers and cunning of those Ancients, with their superior technologies. But why in such a manner?' she said and had another drink.

They couldn't help but admire their ancestors for the extreme lengths they had taken in order to ensure the survival of their race and galaxy, even to the point of their own rebirth.

The creation of the six was probably a safety measure in case other plans failed and they were unable to be there, in the future themselves to set things right.

Then Julia began to speak. By this time Jon and Merol had just returned from the bar with a tray of more drinks which they handed around.

'They had to return some three thousand years in the future, but could not find a suitable way to do it. After all, they could only have lived about one thousand years at most from birth and most of the Ancient Six were already middle-aged when the aliens arrived. By intergalactic law they or their race had to be around to assist in the destruction of the monsters they had created, even though in error. They felt responsible for not only the... the aliens destruction, but for the creation of a newer and perhaps an even better galactic order. So I suppose our creation was another guarantee, to ensure their program was continued even after death with the help of the Osmaronites.'

'How clever of them! They must have given us all the necessary information in case we are to replace them,' Jon did not appreciate being part of anyone's long-term plans.

'Yes! I think so,' Merol said.

'You see. One of their main problems was how to bring their entities back after death in order to take over where their original selves had left. They thought that even if they reformed their bodies and minds in the distant future, there was no guarantee they would find themselves in those new bodies. Nevertheless, Lord Vektron gave them his word that they would all be present to see the demise of their enemies, the nasty aliens. Well, you know Lord Vektron. He is immortal and the type to keep his word even to eternity,' Julia said, awed by her last utterance.

Then Jon spoke.

'Yes, the monstrous aliens are called "Javols" and as we thought, they are made from micro robots, like we are made from biological cells and Lord Vektron must be a supreme being from Osmaron to live... eternally...' he said, regurgitating the unimpeded flow of information.

Then Lira interrupted, but she was on a different wavelength.

'Do you mean our entities may be killed and their entities take over our bodies?' she asked and Julia replied: 'No. I don't think so. Lord Vektron or Plato, even Merian would have mentioned something if that was the case. Anyway, I don't think it's possible to do it that way. After all, they couldn't accomplish that feat even with their own identically cloned bodies and we are much different, even in age.'

'I think I understand!'

'Roc's Principle states, that even with identical bodies, certain other dimensional conditions must be met before Identity Convergence can be initiated from any given source for a new corporeal existence. Which happens to include an historical time period for the player or causator within a given space-time continuum, and that single factor alone makes the whole process almost impossible. Only a supreme Being with relevant knowledge can bypass the natural order for this process.' Julia had a sip, but continued.

'Girl, you are so darn clever!' Jon commented in jest.

'I think the Ancient Six will be re-created in some manner at the appropriate time. After they leave our world for their own missions, we'll be experienced enough to take their places here, on the surface of Caefon in the way that we are and in our own minds and bodies. Because I trust their honesty, despite their strange ways of doing things,' Julia said.

'Yes. I agree with Julia. After all, the reason why we are here in the first place is due to the fact that they cannot replant their entities, even within a duplicate body and we are not exact, are we? Anyway, from what I was told, they could completely regrow their own bodies with the aid of the Megotron and Psyrotron... including every bit of memory... Even their original intelligence in youthful form with genetic changes. So why use us for that purpose?' Jon replied.

Lira and the others were by now convinced that their bodies would not be eventually taken over by the Ancients and she decided to ask her third question.

'What happens to our relatives and friends on the surface after we are gone? Because they will not all fit within this underworld.' She held a worried expression.

'I think the Javol things will return in large numbers within the period of one year. This is because of the initial sightings and their modus operandi from past historical records. That is the reason why our mission is so important. I also think the Osmaronites and our people will use the Omegron Portal to rescue everyone, including the surface people, but it will all depend on us. We have to take the device with us to Osmaron to complete the link and if we fail... everything will be lost, because there won't be anything left of Caefon or of our galaxy Hyparon (Andromeda) to return to any time in the future.'

'Go on!' John said.

'And to where will the surface people go; even the lower underground city is almost full to capacity. We can't really do anything to save them by remaining here, so we have to concentrate on the success of our mission and focus all our abilities in that direction if we are to succeed,' Merol said, in a most decisive manner.

Jon knew Merol, but he had never seen such decisiveness in his character before. Despite his sometimes naive attitude, even verging towards eccentricity. He had suddenly become a natural born leader. He also realized Merol was most likely the embryo of Tomas, Meron and Julia's own son. Jon admired him for his more recent leadership qualities and realised there was a great change in him since his arrival in the underworld, or was it the after effects of those subliminals. Perhaps that part of him was always there, in his mind, awaiting a moment of arousal. He wondered whether they would all change into more responsible adults during their Great Adventure.

Jon wondered whether he represented Meron, genetically. Then if that was the case, which of the ladies represented Lucia, Meron's wife? Would he learn to love the female as Meron did? Little did he realise that his fiery friend Lira was none other than that very same person. Although he observed a slight resemblance, he was not yet absolutely sure. She always applied more than her fair share of makeup and jewellery, and appeared much younger than her predecessor. Anyway, they were quite young and in their early twenties. Their embryos having been inseminated at about the same time.

The Ancients had considered every detail within their complex survival plan and that great survival plan was still being implemented, even while the young six discussed such matters.

The deep space probes had enabled the Osmaronites to learn of the exact time of arrival of the Javols, thus giving them enough warning and time to initiate the birth of the six. Subsequently, to complete their schooling and training just at the precise moment when their enemies, the Javols, were due to return. Luckily for them, every one of their bio-engineered offspring had survived several thousand years in screened cryogenic storage.

Each one lived to partake in their master plan now three-thousand years after the Javols' destruction of Caefon. In all this, Lord

Vektron was the main instigator and initiator of every part of their plan. For he had given his word to them and Plorans always kept their agreements, even to eternity

CHAPTER 45

Their first space voyage

On the day that followed Merian escorted them to a small building in the upper town to be further briefed for their journey. Then they were dressed in highly reflective space suits. Each suit carried the winged insignia as worn by the Ancients. In their case the central circle of the insignia was a radiant purple. They were taken to Lord Vektron's building and stationed in front of his large circular desk. As usual he appeared very pleased to see them and bobbed up and down in the air in front of them making his presence felt. He began to speak to them in his usual excitable manner.

'I must say... you do resemble your ancient parents; even you Jon... the way you stand and carry yourself. I personally knew your ancestral parents well and have always admired their spirit and achievements in the face of such dire dangers and extreme difficulties.

'I trust you will all follow proudly in their footsteps during your great adventure; for it is a truly important service you render to us all and I am sure you will aspire and accomplish all your aims and ambitions, to eventually become noble children of The Sword.

'Neither should you be unduly concerned about our situation here, even on the surface; for your parents and friends will be resettled to the lower city shortly.

'However, your mission is of the utmost importance and to that end you have my heartfelt blessings... may the Grand Lord assist you on your important journey,' Lord Vektron showed pride and satisfaction in his manner. His stay on Caefon had finally come to an end, as one of his important promises to their ancestors had been fulfilled.

He returned to his exalted perch while Merian escorted them out of the building and towards the main elevator shaft. They entered a secondary elevator which was programmed for the surface.

Although the young six had only been away from their surface homes and families for just six and one half days, to them it was like a lifetime. They remembered and loved the surface for all its familiar noises and multitudes, despite its sometimes harsh weather conditions which was not under any techno controls, and wanted to be back.

Surface life was unlike the underground city, with its more limited spaces and hence a much too restrictive environment for young explorers like themselves. On the raw surface of Caefon they felt much more at home, despite its greater exposure to changes and the unexpected dangers.

Even with everything that had been done to reassure them, they were still worried for their families and friends on the surface above, while unknowingly exposed to potential dangers. The young six also wanted to say a proper goodbye to those they loved before their departure and those unknowns worried them.

Merian, being of direct Ancient descent, did not wish to expose herself to the dangerous surface environment for fear of becoming infected. So she arrived well prepared, having previously taken her special doses of anti-virus medicine. She entered the ship's enclosure while wearing a specially prepared suit with nasal filters fitted. Anyway, she had decided much earlier to follow them on board to say her personal farewell.

The ship was kept in a concealed surface hanger not too far from the main elevator shaft. A large shutter kept it covered. The shutter opened unto a courtyard from where they would depart. That area was shielded from any would-be surface observer.

The old museum, now H-Control Building, was surrounded by a high wall which further restricted access to probing eyes, assuming they existed in the first place.

After their arrival to the surface they were guided through a long corridor and taken to a waiting room not too far from the elevator shaft. After entering the large waiting room their eyes were suddenly filled with ecstasy. Just ahead of their group were several others standing in queue and their parents were among them. By some unexplained coincidence their parents were taking the opposite route towards the place they had just left and with many of their personal belongings tagged and awaiting collection by trolley robots.

The young six were overwhelmed by the sight of family and friends standing ahead of them. They could not control their emotions and ran to embrace them. After they had finished, they formally introduced families and friends to each other.

They explained the reasons for their absence and the nature of their space mission to Osmaron as best they could, but did not mention anything about the Javols or impending dangers. After all, Lord Vektron had kept his word and had arranged for them to say farewell to the ones they loved before commencing their long intergalactic journey.

At the time of their departure Merian slid into her special environmental suit once more. With nasal filter tightly fitted she guided them towards a secured entrance that led into the hanger. By that time they had already said farewell to their families and friends who were not allowed to observe the ship's departure.

Merian uttered the usual voice command and the ship formed its staircase and entrance which they mounted with her in the lead.

'My dearest friends, this moment brings tears to my eyes. The Ship is programmed with all the necessary maps of our galaxy and Osmaron, and is always precise in his undertakings, so you must let him make the difficult decisions for you,' she said.

'Do we have any important tasks to perform during our Journey?' Jon inquired.

'No, not until you get to Osmaron and don't worry! Every eventuality has been considered for your short trip, so just follow the ship's advice!'

'How long do you think our journey will take?' Lira inquired.

'Less than a day. It uses a special drive that can take it outside our space-time,' Merian replied and they were surprised.

'What about these nasty Javols. Will we meet any of them on route?' Merol inquired and they remained silent in anticipation of the worst things happening to them. She remained silent for a while.

'They are not local to your path during transit. Anyway, our ship is faster than any of their transport, so don't you worry.'

'So, my beloved friends, may I wish you a most pleasant journey. I shall dearly look forward to joining you in the not too distant future,' she said. Each embraced her in turn and thanked her for all the help she had given them. They had grown to love her and considered her and Plato part of their family.

'Please give our thanks to Plato!' Lira said. Plato had already left for Osmaron via the Greater Mind.

It was a sad moment for the six, but they were determined and knew they would be back some day, come what may.

After a short while Merian left the ship. It automatically absorbed its stairway and sealed its entrance. The hanger shutters lifted and before they could sit down the ship was on its way.

Its route would take them away from planet Caefon towards a spiral vertex close to a local star, but within an unpopulated region of space. That worm-hole link was about sixty light years away. Luckily, they were not on-route towards the galactic centre; for the density of Javols increased significantly within those regions. The galactic nucleus was presently the realm of the Javols' empire.

They journeyed to the vertex with neutral shields fully extended to avoid detection.

The Ship contained two main areas. The cabin, which could be adjusted for almost any requirement and the rear storage area. That part held the Omegron Portal, the Book, the Sword and whatever other special items that were required on their trip. It also included energy reserves for the ship's own operations.

The cabin area included a large viewing screen on the wall just ahead of their bunks. To one side was a helmet with integral stereoscopic viewing, not too unlike those commonly used by the Ancients, but of a more modern design.

The larger screen was directly linked to the ship's master computer but could be controlled manually by an operator while using the helmet. There were several buttons and levers close by for more basic control. However its main function was for use as a telescope to relieve boredom or control onboard entertainment for its crew by the use of special discs. The large screen remained under The Ship's control during emergencies and special announcements. At other times it relayed images of planets and stellar systems on route. By so doing images could be simultaneously displayed to all members of The Ship's crew at once.

The rear part of The Ship was completely sealed from them, so they were confined to that single large cabin for the duration of their journey.

They had no idea how long the trip would take. From what Merian had indicated it would be a short time. Further, from what little they could observe about their cabin, given the lack of essential facilities like cooking, bathing and recreation, it could not be a very long journey.

Just a few small drink and snack machines were inconspicuously fitted towards the right of the bunk area and here again choice was limited.

Jon decided it was not practical for everyone to remain awake during their supposed long trip and suggested each took an active part in a learning program or game with their personal computers when not at sleep. It was not essential that any such program be relevant to their trip, but it could be used as a means of occupational therapy. They subsequently formed a double shift, with three being on active duty while the others slept or pursued their learning program.

The three on duty were assigned to the viewers and general maintenance in much the same way as a normal ship's crew. That situation was a lot more acceptable in a cramped environment. Not that it mattered, since The Ship new all about their trip. It was linked to the Greater Mind and followed the Grand Lord's instructions.

Merian had allowed them ten kilograms each for their own personal effects so they had taken advantage of that privilege to carry some of their possessions like hand-held computers, pens, notepads and books on board.

Jon, Merol and Ecrol decided to take the first watch while the women rested. They would keep them informed of any life-threatening developments on-route. The spectre of the Javols still haunted them so they wanted to be forewarned well before they could take action.

After they had organised themselves for the trip, Jon went over to the corner and placed the helmet over his head. He soon found he could think directly into the master computer. When he thought into the helmet, certain specific bits of data were displayed in stereo vision on the small visor within the helmet. He assumed it was perhaps some kind of manual control device that directly linked the mind of the human operator to The Ship's computer. After some practice he felt a strange feeling of oneness with The Ship whenever the helmet was placed on his head.

They were now approaching the vertex while the screen displayed an acute scarcity of stars within that region of space.

CHAPTER 46

The small nova

They approached the small spiralling vertex and became deeply alarmed by what they observed on the large screen. The small black hole (wormhole) was spewing out columns of superheated matter and intense radiation along its primary axis. The material being ejected by its internal eruptions soon fell back into its intense gravitational centre and disappeared into its blackness.

When they approached the area several Javols could be visibly seen guiding large meteors while setting them on a collision course with the vertex. They kept well away from its strong gravitational fields and were obviously trying to neutralise or destroy it. They were unable to make use of its facilities themselves and considered it a threat. Neither could they get close to its powerful generators and dismantle them before being disrupted and killed by the intense gravitational waves. It was of Ploran and Octan design, and well beyond their current levels of technology.

'What in the deepest inferno is this?' an innocent Jon exclaimed.

'It's a...' Merol said but couldn't figure it out.

'I know what it is. It's a black hole, but much smaller gravitationally than what would be expected from a collapsing star over 10 times the size of our solar system... and what is it doing in this place, so close to home,' Petra interjected.

__It's an engineered vertex, created by the Plorans and their Octan friends to get us out of this galaxy,__ The Ship said in his matter of fact manner.

'Wow! Some design?' Ecrol exclaimed.

One of the Javols' massive inter-stellar craft soon arrived on the scene and was detected by The Ship's acute sensors. It was more like a base-station and contained many powerful beams that had been specially constructed for the purpose of moving and guiding large objects like meteors precisely to a target.

'Mi co na to ko! No lo ina Kat!' shouted their commander.

Which meant "Keep them rolling in! We must quickly remove the Clots abomination!"

That Javol was in the form of a black Tauren with cloven hooves. On his forehead were shiny metallic horns. Javols could acquire the form of almost any creature of an equivalent mass, but preferred to adopt the form of a most horrible primal with its most basic attributes and desires. That aspect gave them a personality and made them different to others. Usually they adopted the form of their first hard kill. However that was not always the case. Their seniors always chose a superior form that instilled fear and trepidation in their underlings.

The powerful black Tauren form soon changed his orders when they detected the small ship.

'Nana co-o nana? Ohi ga! Ohi Kat!'

("What's this... What! A ship... It is trying to escape through the abomination!"). One of his captains yelled.

'Ita! Ita! Ita Clots kud! No Kat ni kud O Kat!'

("Kill! Kill! Kill the Clots at all costs! Their ship must not escape!"). He commanded them and the chase began. They always called Primals, Clots, because those animals always bled profusely during their feed and blood congealed with the resulting bacteria and other forms of disease that it harboured. Because of those reasons Javols always smelled like the decaying dead. Primal bacteria and disease were not dangerous to Javols, but they preferred a less messier way to get their food.

Although originally designed with the necessary systems for absorbing the bulk of food minerals directly for their needs, they required special mining technology to recover some rear chemicals which in some cases were difficult to find by such methods.

Anyway, why bother with such a drab method of recovering food when primals were a ready meal. There still remained so many primals left for harvesting. They also took pleasure from the kill and in seeing their underlings wallow in the mire, not to mention all the fun sacrifices. Therefore although they preferred solid food which was less messy, they followed their current savage trends embedded in their culture for the power and satisfaction gained. Despite their convenient choices in such matters, they relished the frenzy of the kill and a ravenous feed before multiplying. Those were uncontrollable urges within their design.

That inter-galactic wormhole link had been constructed by the Osmaronites for a specific purpose and they had taken the necessary precautions against Javols. Nevertheless those Javols were determined and fully intended to prevent any would-be intergalactic traveller from leaving that part of the galaxy to warn other civilizations of their existence.

Very soon the small ship was detected. Once the Javols realized it was not constructed from normal technologies they decided to capture it and its crew at all cost. However their large craft was not in the correct position to aim their tractor beams, so the massive carrier had to be manoeuvred and turned around. That procedure took time. They wanted desperately to find out whatever information they could gather from its occupants before taking the ship apart to learn its secrets.

The young six Andromedans were quite alarmed by what they saw. They stood close to the main screen and observed every detail with dread and dismay.

'I think they are trying to prevent us from leaving!' and intuitive Merol exclaimed.

'And why do you think that?' Jon replied sarcastically and in jest, realizing he had stated the most obvious.

'I just hope we are not too late?' Jon added.

'Go and wake the girls! We have to make some quick decisions!'

Very soon the women joined the men and were equally disturbed by what they observed on the viewer. Soon the large black outline of the massive Javols' craft could be observed as it approached their position in space. John cringed by its enormity, but was never the type to surrender to anyone, least of all Javols.

He tried to find a way to stop them from doing further damage to the vertex, while Lira held on to him, petrified with fear. By then they had stopped dumping matter into the vertex and were instead focussing their attention on the small ship. At that time The Ship was being chased by individual Javols. Those were much faster than their large craft, and didn't wish to lose their valuable prize.

Suddenly Lira had an idea which she nervously aired to the others.

'We could make them follow us... if we had a very bright light... release our screens so they could follow us and lead them to a cold, black, lonely spot in space... somewhere far enough away from the vertex. Then they couldn't return without first merging to save energy... With some luck, we might even be able to destroy a few in the process, just as they began to merge. It would be very similar to the game we played in the underworld. However we must act quickly if we are to prevent complete negation of the vertex. Because if that happens, we won't be able to make the trip to Osmaron in the required time,' she stressed, nervously. This time the fear had gone from her voice and she was in control.

Jon reflected on those games and realized they lost each time they fought the Javols, but real life was no game, so he changed his attitude and was prepared and eager to face his awesome foe.

He thought into the computer via the helmet, trying to find answers to that particular problem, but instead the computer began to communicate with the whole crew verbally and on the large screen.

'We are not equipped with a bright light... nor are we with weapons of any description, except... the Plasma Conversion Module?'

The Ship paused for a while and began to explain.

'That device can convert all normally vectored matter into its raw state and back again. Each small part of myself is fully accountable, having been recorded and stored, and the same principle applies to you. Obviously because of the high radiation and other component energy levels met during the explosive phase, some areas of myself will have to be kept under intense gravitational screening. When that happens, the powerful fields and forces will vaporize any biological systems in the vicinity, including Javols.

'However, the small operational part of myself that survives

will have to be programmed before other parts of myself becomes a small nova. Timing is critical if we are to destroy them all in one single blast. During the initial phase we must also be well away from the vertex to avoid its destruction and yet, not be too far away if we are to return at the appropriate time... when it becomes normal again... while making due allowances for the time required during its re-stabilization.

We must destroy them all at once if we intend to return to this galaxy in the not too distant future via the same route.'

The Ship paused for a moment, but continued.

'But... regrettably, you will all die... for a while.
Only for as long as I am able to get close enough to a hot star to re-vector your bodies and the missing parts of myself.
'This is because I shall require matter in its plasmic form in order to recreate all lost elements during the remoulding process.
'However, I can assure you that everything will be back to normal in due course, and you will not, in any way, be conscious of the dying process, either before or after.'

The young crew was amazed by The Ship's casual suggestion of temporary suicide on their behalf and was not highly appreciative of the concept of death, even for a fraction of a second. After all, what if something was to go seriously wrong with that part of the ship's computer or the matter conversion unit during that enormous explosion.

The Ship observed their concerns and displayed the sequence of detonation and reformation on the large screen and again spoke to them, sympathetically.

'You will be re-created again, as soon as possible. I cannot fail this mission!'

They pondered the depressing thought of being nothings in deep space for thousands of years while awaiting recovery by the Osmaronites or even Javols. Then Lira replied to The Ship in no uncertain terms; for that was the name they called it among themselves.

'You will have to find another way, you know. Because, no way am I going to be blown up into cosmic dust. Not by you or anyone!' she stressed, while twitching her fingers nervously. To Lira, their present situation was more than 10 times worse than losing her hair.

It thought for a short period, but came up with the same answers.

'Do not worry. Your bodies and minds have been recorded and placed within the Greater Mind.'

It replied in a compassionate voice.

'This method is well tried and proven. It will not fail. Even Shadites like Plato have used it on occasion.'

She did not realize death to Shadites were like changing clothes.

Once again they discussed it among themselves but Lira just couldn't accept the idea of dying, even for a short while.

'We can't just be blown up like this. If that happens, we might never get to Osmaron in time to save our world. Please find another way, if possible, dear Ship,' she pleaded. Yet, The Ship's reply was still negative. There was no other way out of their current dilemma.

Jon remembered what Merian said about letting the ship make those difficult choices and soon discussed his ideas with his friends. But even then, choices had to be made.

They had to make a quick decision and had just two choices: whether to return home and risk the complete destruction of their world and galaxy in the not too distant future or take a risk and forfeit their lives temporarily. They realized they had less than a 50 percent chance of saving everything if things went to plan and were brought back in time, but no chance whatsoever if they went home.

All sat comfortably down to discuss this dilemma, but found themselves at an impasse that could only be resolved by a majority vote.

There was so much of the Osmaronite's technology they knew so little about. The Ship was obviously rebuilt to those very advanced specifications and perhaps Lord Vektron and his seniors had their own reasons for their temporary demise as part of their greater plan, as Merian had indicated.

Time was not in their favour and too much was at stake, so they took the vote and decided unanimously to go along with The Ship's decision, which it was hoped would be a much more pleasant death than being slowly taken apart and eaten alive by sadistic Javols.

The Ship took a little while to program the new parameters into its central core. All its external screens were suddenly released and gravitrons energised. It caused a small plasmic glow to appear at its rear which pointed in the direction of the Javols in chase.

The massive explosion had been initiated and the fuse lit. That plasmic glow would progress to engulf the whole ship, slowly at first, while the Javols followed, thus giving them enough time to regroup. When the glow touched a particular point on its front, the nova would be initiated. As predicted, once they had been detected, all Javols dropped everything and went in pursuit.

The ship was now travelling at extreme speed away from the vertex. It progressed just a little faster than the fastest Javol and would at the appropriate time reverse its direction into the flock of Javols and whatever else was in its way while moving towards the vertex. The explosion was timed to occur once The Ship was on a precise course with the vertex's centre.

After the explosion the ship would have lost most of its mass with the exception of a small spherical core. The remainder was barely five metres across and would contain all the necessary ingredients, including the Omegron Portal, Book and Sword.

'Hurry Ship! Hurry before they catch up!' Merol Yelled.

'Hurry! Hurry!' Lira egged on, but the process of plasma conversion could not be speeded, even while the ghastly Javols drew closer.

'They cannot hold onto my super hot plasma and my strong

fields will neutralize their tractor beams, ' the Ship replied.

The massive Javols craft had gained speed and was bearing down on them with its forward port bay open to accept its quarry. Their captain did not bank on the small ship changing direction so abruptly towards him. He tried to change course, but could not make the change in time.

'Ka ho! Ka ho!' ("Change left! Change left!") he shouted to his controllers, but his commands were to no avail. The little ship crashed through the central part of the Javols craft as if it wasn't there and progressed onwards amidst many a massive explosion. Exposed to hot plasma over tens of millions of degrees centigrade, large areas of the massive Javols' carrier soon vaporised into cosmic dust.

When anti-matter and matter came together there was always an enormous reaction, which converted almost all vectored matter into intense energies. The sequence was triggered by a unique self-destruct mechanism that was designed to take everything within planetary distances.

During the massive explosion that followed, The Ship's central core was ejected towards the vertex and held together by strong negative gravitational forces that were more than enough to counter the forces of the explosion. The intensely hot plasma was kept away from the insulated core by super-strong magnetic and other generated fields. Therefore, to all intents and purpose the core could well have been at home within the centre of a small star during a supernova, because that was the level of technologies used in its construction by the Octan engineers.

All forces were maintained just long enough for the hot gases, the Javols and their craft to be atomised and dispersed far enough away. Soon thereafter, whatever debris remained within the vicinity of the core quickly cooled to almost absolute zero. The complete blast had taken just under fifteen seconds to its completion.

The explosion was short but quite effective. As The Ship went into self destruct, so also did hundreds of thousands of Javols. Many of the local asteroids were also vaporised in the process, including their massive craft, its crew, captains and commander.

Within a short period of time the vertex had stabilised and was quickly recovering from what appeared to be clogged inlets due to excessive matter intake. However the vertex was designed with those self-repairing features.

The Javols were taken by surprise and had no time to communicate with their central mind in order to rethink and plan a new strategy. By that time the central core of The Ship was already entering the now stable vertex and finally on its way to Osmaron.

No one could guess how long it would have taken that part of The Ship to get close enough to a hot star and re-vector their bodies from the raw atoms of space. However, being inter-dimensional in design, time was not a relevant parameter while outside of normal space-time.

During this period the young six firmly held hands with eyes closed and said a prayer to the Senots' god, Grand Lord Gerron, for success during a time of extreme danger. While they prayed all the alarms went and the screen changed to the new commands.

'You must now put on your special suits and return to your bunks in order to be transposed,' The Ship said and they did as advised.

Just as suddenly they found themselves in radiant brilliance and swimming in an ocean of energy. It was an incredible feeling of oneness with the Cosmos. During that brief moment they became pure individuals, divorced from all things including The Ship and their friends.

CHAPTER 47

Within the planes of Goh

While they swam in the sea of energy they were at perfect oneness with the Cosmos. Like wandering souls they followed the brightest place like moths to a candle. It was not long before they came upon a solid surface and began to walk out of that strange place into what appeared to be a dense bright fog.

Gradually the fog lifted and they beheld a most beautiful scene. Yet, since the ship had transposed them in that manner, they had no sensation of the explosion or their demise. Neither were they conscious of the loss of their original bodies. Anyway, it was not always possible to know whether an instantaneous death anywhere in space and time would have been any different to the soul or identity involved. The Cosmos obeyed its own natural laws of transcendence and recycling which were universal. Therefore all systems within had to follow those laws and Gohenna was no different.

Gohenna, called Goh by many, was not a city in the truest sense of the word. Perhaps a better description would be a different plane of existence where everything imaginable could be made possible.

Within its realms every level of achievement was attainable and any enjoyment or pain felt. All entities came from outside the Plane, more like visitors in transit. New entities could not be created within its boundaries. Nevertheless anything could be experienced within that universe of the mind, even dragons and dungeons or indeed any concepts of heaven or hell.

Any of those individual experiences could be made to change at will or be retained to eternity and if that was not enough, one could always become mortal again if one really desired the experience.

Although its environment appeared solid enough to its inhabitants, its space was curved wherein all surfaces carried on to infinity.

Seen with human eyes, its clouds, when they existed, were silver with multicoloured fringes and never rained. The surfaces and air all around exuded a brilliance of their own; for there was no sun or stars within its radiant skies.

By a simple thought one could cause its structure to change, slowly at first, but precisely to their new desires. It was truly a world of the mind and yet, solids and liquids could be experienced and felt in whatever manner that was expected. If not, it would gradually fade away and become transparent to the observer.

It was a new experience that anyone could quickly get used to, but any two people could very soon be lost from each other, because no two individuals ever desired the same things in exactly the same way.

Jon and the others found themselves walking along a very wide and paved avenue about five miles across. Ahead of them in the distance they could just observe the hazy outline of a large golden gate suspended by two great towers.

To their rear, the broad avenue disappeared into swirling currents of mist. Their local sky was cloudless, but displayed a beautiful blue with no sun or satellites.

There were many souls including aliens and lower life-forms moving in the same direction. They followed their own paths towards the great gate several miles in the distance. The young six walked together, side by side towards the great gate and their suits shown like radiant silver.

No trees or vegetation could be seen on-route. Nevertheless, distant hills and mountains, even silvery lakes could be faintly observed on either side of the great avenue of souls.

It had taken them several hours to reach the main gate, while walking at a brisk pace and in silence.

As they approached one of its three great domes, they were greeted by a glowing figure dressed in white. He attended to them, saying:

'As predicted, you are on time. I represent the Greater Mind. My task is to collect, screen and store identities within this Matrix

Sector of Goh. That function also includes you my children. However, you have been selected by the Grand Master for a special purpose and because of that reason you will be kept in storage for a while... not to be released until the appointed time... when your mortal bodies are once again reformed. Then you will be placed back into the plenum from whence you came.
  'But first, I must ask for your toll of entry!'

They were not sure what he meant, but he continued,

  'Anything will do, even jewellery or a small part of your clothing.'

Jon searched his pockets but couldn't find anything, so he offered him the ancient crucifix that Merian had given him. The others gave whatever they could find.

Anything of substance was accepted by the guardian. When he was finished, he pointed them in the direction of another distant gate, saying:

  'Please make yourselves at home at the gate-house. Everything is available there. You need only think for what you wish. This world is as real as any other, you know!'

They continued their walk towards the citadel for perhaps another three miles. This time they greeted each other and were chatting like newly met strangers. Their past existence including their names had been forgotten and only specific ideas were in their minds.

They entered through magnificent ancient gates and were greeted by six figures wearing a mix of beautiful costumes. Because of some unknown reason, Jon immediately recognised the tallest figure wearing an official costume, but without the sword and scabbard. He was leading the others.

Jon greeted him, not quite knowing why he knew the human figure or what to say, but bowed his head respectfully.

'Hello, Sire! It's nice to see you again!'

Jon suddenly remembered his name and those of his group and continued to introduce them by name. Then Meron turned towards his group and introduced each in turn, starting with his wife. Suddenly, the six young adventurers realised who they were but not where they were or from whence they had come.

Meron was expecting them and had been briefed by one of the great books for that occasion. In order to avoid further delays, the Grand Lord had obviously made a way for them through that complex dimension of the Greater Mind.

'Destiny has made our greatest wish come true and have brought us all together in one place and time.'

'So it seems?' Jon replied.

'All of what you see here, Son, is a mirage, engineered for you and your friends to find correct passage through and not allow entry to outsiders. It's a plane of the mind that only attracts those of the Greater Purpose.'

'I think I understand?'

'In order that anyone may leave this dimension, or become mortal again, one has to have a place prepared for them within that new plane by the Greater Purpose. A physical body or embryo must first be prepared, before an entity can be dispatched from here to any of the lower levels.... in our case, within the third-temporal dimension.'

'This is all so incredible! Am I really alive!' Lira exclaimed, but could not remember her past existence.

'We are all alive, but in a different way to corporeal existence. There are many kinds of existence within the Cosmos,' Lucia replied while Meron continued with his explanation.

'The gates towards the centre contain higher dimensional beings that are mostly in transit. Any request for corporeal existence can always be arranged by the Greater Purpose, for any time period within infinity and towards eternity.'

'I see!' Ecrol replied, unconcerned.

'We shall not travel any further beyond this gate, but remain here at the lay building, since our time here is of a temporary nature.

However, you can still visit places within the outer city with an escort. Since we know our way around, we can be your guardians. Each one of us for one of you in the appropriate order, that is if you wish to visit the city proper?' Meron advised, enthusiastically.

They agreed with Meron's suggestion of visiting the city of Goh to see for themselves. Then Meron guided them into the Gatehouse and showed them around their temporary dwelling.

'This will be your home for the duration. So make yourselves comfortable. If you have any questions, please ask.'

The place was bland and almost like a blank slate. Lira thought of the way she would like the room to look and it began to transform to that new structure in front of their eyes. Since they always accepted her choices, it remained that way for the duration.

'Strange place! It's nice to know I can wear anything I like by looking in a mirror,' Petra commented.

Meron waved his hand and suddenly a large table appeared with bowls of food and fruit for a feast.

'Now, lets eat!' he said.

'So we are really in Gohenna? I never thought it was a real place,' Merol said.

'Real...I don't know much about that! This is indeed a most bizarre place, but I can get used to it,' Jon replied.

'We must be all dead to be here!' Lucia replied, but in a happy disposition.

'Why the nine gates?' Lira asked while pulling a chair.

'They are because of the different levels of Identities throughout the Cosmos.

'As far as I have been told, the Greater Purpose has permeated all things and all dimensions since the beginning and will to the end of time. It collects many stray identity cells at all levels that are considered suitable and realigns them in a more positive and constructive manner for further corporeal existence. A form of cleansing if you wish.

'Most primal cells float about the H-Dimension in their primordial state within a place called The Nexos. There they remain while awaiting a period of material existence by tuning into a suitable DNA symmetry during the conception cycle of each new

life-form. This is because all things in existence are mutually dependant on each other... a form of symbiosis if you will, between spirit, matter and energy... with correctly linked symmetries within the higher and lower dimensional orders.

'This process of Identity recycling and inter-planar causation has existed since the beginning of time. It helps to promote a stronger cosmic order. In other words, through this process of renewal all things are recycled. This method is also used by the Cosmos to recycle life. Life creates a special order necessary for cosmic survival.

'Corporeal existence to any entity is much the same as putting on a new suit of clothes for going on a short vacation. In our case, the clothes will be a human body. This process, although quite strange to us, enhances causal continuity within the planes to thus promote the plane's survival causation, much like cells do in a healthy body.

'Goh itself is mainly composed of Identity Cells like ourselves. All such Identity Cells are collected at the moment of death and many are channelled into this dimension from all levels of cosmic existence,' Meron advised, enthusiastically.

Meron had made a serious study of Gohenna and read many of its mind books within the Great Library. He had also acquired answers to many searching questions from several of the Seven Great Books of Goh. To him it was the most fascinating place in the entire Cosmos and could not reduce his enthusiasm for this newly found way of life. Jon and the young six were also keen to learn about Goh and listened to what he had to say in case it was important to their future existence.

From what the Ancient Six had learnt, Gohenna was composed of seven innermost gates. Those were beyond the gatehouse and towards the city centre. There were also two outermost gates which included the Citadel Gate and the Toll Gate.

The total made nine all together, but the real dimensions with all their strangeness began beyond the second inner gate.

It was thought each layer or level represented the relative powers of the identities contained within them and that the higher powers existed closer to the central core of Goh, if in reality such a place really existed. It was assumed the Universal Mind for the Greater Purpose utilised the Central Core which was beyond the Final Gate. That one was number seven from within the Citadel's Gatehouse.

It was not known whether lower identities could ever visit within the two innermost gates without special permission.

Those higher levels were each individual dimensions in their own right and may have observed different causal and symmetrical laws from the other more unified realms that were adopted to more basic primal identities.

No primal life could ever fully appreciate delicate and real beauty in its truest sense and no two individuals could ever see or visualize in the same manner. Even much less could any two individuals admire beauty to the same extent, and beauty was not all. The place exuded a living energy of its own. One that could fill the blank aspects of any personal defect, wish or dream. It became part of the entity as much as the entity became part of it. Because of its unique ability to change its environment to the wishes of the entity, anyone could be forever lost within the constantly changing panorama of events.

Jon and his companions could therefore understand why guides were needed for first-timers and why it was safer for them to always remain together, since any new desire or wish could have taken an individual away to another place of their hearts desire. Further, that new place could have been in a different space-time from the others.

They were given special wristbands and asked to hold each others hand. That way they travelled through the Sixth Gate and into the sixth city of Goh.

The first building they visited was the city library. It was the largest structure on that block. Its many tall columns radiated a light of their own. It was the only place where they could gain knowledge of their time of departure or release from Goh.

'I am Alcon, chief librarian. How can I assist you?' the brilliant white angel-like figure said.

'We would like to see the great books,' Meron replied and Alcon knew what he meant.

The chief librarian ushered them to an area that was occupied by the seven great books of the seven universes and major planes. To their amazement the seventh book was none other than the Anachromagnon. On its cover was displayed the sword and serpents.

'That cannot be possible,' Sintra muttered to herself. As if somehow remembering her previous existence on Caefon some 3000 years before and she became attracted to the book.

The Book was glowing more than the others as if charging itself, but when Sintra got closer it opened its pages to her and the others.

The seven great books had power over mere three-dimensional mortals. They could visit any place in time and space, including other planes. However the seventh book could only record data for the benefit of the seventh part of all seven planes within the seventh parts of all seven universes. Those were its responsibility. The seventh part of the seventh plane was even a greater responsibility. It so happened that both galaxies Andromeda and Osmaron were within the seventh part of our universe.

It was indeed a strange way of collecting information, but the other books did likewise. The first great book collected its information in the first part of all planes and the first sector of our universe.

They were themselves entities of a much higher order so form meant very little to their existence. The book form was just a symbolic representation of knowledge.

When Sintra was ready, she read its pages.

'Your trip is sure,
And ship's secure,
So don't be scared,
Your journey's prepared.'

It did not say when and she assumed time on that plane meant very little to anyone. Their circumstances could not have related temporally to any other plane. Causation did not exist in the normal sense and neither did our days and nights. Here, an experience of weeks could in all probability have taken several seconds or even a thousand years.

 From the library windows they viewed the beauty of the swirling central city, but did not wish to enter into its realms, in case they became permanently lost from each other. So they returned to the more solid way-gate building close to the Citadel's main gate and there awaited their time of release.

 When it came it was quite sudden. The way-building began to fade. Then they were in complete darkness. Gradually the lights became brighter. They found themselves in small sealed units looking up at what appeared to be the most beautifully painted ceilings, but everywhere else appeared white.

 Suddenly the translucent covers lifted from their bunks to reveal a completely different environment. From that moment on they had no knowledge of their brief stay within the city of Gohenna, only of their previous existence on Caefon, but with a slight loss of memory regarding previous whereabouts on-route. Even so, the purpose of their present mission was still very clear to them.

 To Jon and his young company, The Ship, despite its original identification, was now quite different and a lot more spacious. In their estimation it now appeared to be over twice as wide and similarly disposed in the other direction. There were now twelve separate bunks on two levels and they were much larger than the original six. Their covers could now be darkened for more privacy.

 There was a larger toilet cubicle, with filtration units and atomizers. Larger food and drink machines were situated at the rear close to a small sitting area. It also included a library placed at a higher level that contained several books of the Ancients and a wide range of information disks.

 All of their personal effects, including those given to the guardians at Goh's gate, could be found in their bunk cupboards within their canopies.

 The Ship responded to their sudden movements.

'Ah, you are awake at last. Does your new body feel in good condition?' he inquired.

'New body? I feel fine, thank you. Where are we off to, now?' the Ancient, Meron, replied, with curiosity.

'To Osmaron, by way of Terminus,' the ship replied.

In a short time they knew what their special mission were about and became conscious of its urgency. They were to save their world and the galaxy. Everything about their mission now fell into place for their Great Adventure in Osmaron.

The young six began to prepare for the rest of their supposed long journey. Even then they were still in the dark regarding their destination or true nature of their mission. They had left all such decisions in the capable hands of The Ship, who was usually quite vague in his replies to their questions.

CHAPTER 48

Their second voyage

Jon being the next to rise, was surprised when he observed the figure of the Ancient Meron talking to the computer in his original dialect. Jon viewed his strange surroundings and realized he was not in the original ship. For some unexplained reason the new ship was completely different to what he expected. He considered the possibility of being 3000 years in the past during Meron's time. Finally he accepted the likelihood of strange occurrences during their special trip to Osmaron. "in time and in space" as Lord Vektron had put it,' he mumbled those words to himself. Without further ado hc walked towards Meron to ask about progress.

'Sire, I seem to recognize you from somewhere. But I am not sure where. Anyway, to where are we headed?' At that time Meron was in a most joyous and tolerant mood and replied with sarcasm.

'I am Meron your ancestral father and according to this incredible feat of engineering known to us as a clever space ship, we are apparently on route to Osmaron by way of Terminus. However I am not sure where this Terminus place happens to be, if indeed it is a place,' Meron replied. It was then that he realized he was presently on board the original ship that had changed to its present form for some reason or another.'

'Ok, Father!' he replied unconcerned.

Jon accepted the lengthy reply in Ancient dialect, which he knew well for some reason but couldn't fathom why, so he bowed his head and walked away. Then he went off to freshen up before the others. Lira soon followed and was surprised to observe the six Ancients preparing breakfast. She remembered observing their dead bodies in stasis within Lower Cantor and of all miracles, here they were as real in the flesh and talking with each other. She felt fearless and decided to face them head on.

'Oh my God! I thought you guys left for Gohenna over 3000 years ago, but here you are now... as lively as any living person.

How can that be?' Aghast by it all, the young six continued to stare at the ancient six as if they were ghosts.

'I know, Lira. As was promised, we have been re-created by the technologies of the Osmaronites. Their technologies are truly awesome. Don't you think?' Meron replied casually. Then the women of different ages viewed each other for a while. Then they embraced.

'How beautiful our children have become,' Julia said. Then the young six realized they were with their embryonic parents on their trip to Osmaron.

Having been through the process themselves, they soon accepted the strangers for what they were and settled down to a haughty breakfast.

Although the young six were extremely surprised to meet their Ancient parents, they apparently knew a lot about each other; almost as if they had began the voyage together.

After breakfast Meron being the most senior called the crew together for a general discussion and delegation of duties.

The new ship had a much larger curved main screen, with a smaller one positioned towards a corner to the right. There was also a communications helmet. That ship was a lot more modern than the original and appeared to be almost human in its attitude and response.

It was not long before The Ship began to vibrate. Merol began to shout, excitedly.

'Great Lord Gerron! What is that large imposing object on the screen?' Jon and the others' senses froze while they watched the intense bluish radiation emanating from around the vertex. It reminded them of a previous incident with Javols and they hope there was no repeat. However the details of that ghastly encounter was still hazy in their confused minds.

'It's the mother of all black holes. I think... a truly enormous one. It appears to be completely devoid of anything at its very centre... with swirling clouds of matter falling within several cones of activity causing intense gamma radiation along its axis of rotation. Now we know why there are no stars in this volume of space. A complete galaxy could have been devoured by that... mother... like one gigantic inter-spacial tornado. But this is not the centre of our galaxy. The stellar density out here is almost zero in comparison to the galaxies. It must be a loner... out here all on its own... but so massive and with such awesome power.' Jon replied.

'Because of its angle of radiation I doubt if it's visible from any of the local galaxies,' Petra replied, absorbed by its immensity.

'It's obviously an ancient galaxy that has since been consumed and recycled for the greater good,' Meron interjected.

They continued to watch, almost hypnotised by the massive swirling object, until The Ship spoke to them:

'This is Terminus. Here, primal matter and debris, which was formed during one of the initial phases of creation, is collected and transposed to certain areas of this universe within our Plane of Seth. It contains its own sibling universe.

'This great vertex or Cycler may be considered a gigantic cleaning machine, because it removes unwanted matter from between the galaxies and transposes them elsewhere to form new stellar nurseries. Eventually all our present galaxies will follow the same path, as our universe is constantly renewed and replenished. All such Cyclers are themselves the seeds of new sibling universes that remain within their own space-times and universal planes.

'We must keep well away from its swirling mouth to avoid intense radiation and speeding asteroids, while approaching the departure terminal just beyond one of its main spirals.

'You may return to your bunks in order to be transposed to the Osmaron Galaxy.

'All causal matter must now be transposed!'

The Ship's sirens sounded and the screens indicated their new mode of travel. They quickly returned to their bunks and the canopies descended, sealing them in. They did not understand the implications, but always did as The Ship requested.

It was not long before the whole ship vibrated as if shaking itself apart. Then came the brilliance. Everything, even their bodies glowed. Suddenly they had memories of the plenum of Goh, but this time they found themselves swimming in liquid energy as if between dimensions or within the centre of a star. Nevertheless they were able to control their movements to a degree and physically felt their new environment or so it appeared to them.

The inter-dimensional ship was now crossing the boundaries of two dimensions, unhindered by any material objects from meteorites to stars as it progressed towards its programmed destination.

Once again the brilliance turned into darkness and they found themselves in their bunks looking up at their enclosure covers. The hoods lifted, and The Ship spoke while displaying images of Osmaron on the large screen:

'We shall enter the Osmaron galaxy at a point towards its rim away from any stellar clusters. So I shall now set a more precise course.'

Suddenly there was another flash and The Ship began to speak again.

'We have arrived close to our programmed destination.'

Meron was amazed by the incredible speed of travel. All around their present position were numerous constellations. He muttered quietly to himself in disbelief.

'Almost a million light years in under ten metrons. Is that really possible?'

The smaller screen had always displayed time in equivalent metrons, sectons and other arbitrary interstellar units at its bottom left-hand corner. A metron was about 0.625 seconds and sectons, about 16 times larger. That last value was almost 10 seconds. The timepiece had only progressed a few seconds during that hyper-spacial jump from the moment they had appeared close to Terminus.

Once again The Ship replied as if reading Meron's thoughts.

'Yes! It could not have been accomplished with the original

model of myself that self-destructed to destroy over two hundred thousand Javols, including their large craft.

'I, like you, have been remodelled and recreated from a new matrix plan and now use an Infinite Probability Drive system, IPD for short. This method of travel is much quicker than all other types, assuming one is preprogrammed with intergalactic maps and special inter-dimensional routes. But it is not as accurate as Linear Progressive or other similar methods. Therefore, only small jumps are allowed within densely populated regions of space.

'Since we are moving in a direction perpendicular to the galactic rim while at the outside, great accuracy is not essential and a 1 percent error on target is quite acceptable.'

Meron and the others were not too sure of the ship's comments about the Javols, but they had an inkling something of consequence had occurred during their voyage. If that something also involved the destruction of that many Javols then it was fantastic news. They were overjoyed about the demise of their enemies and thankful they were still alive and in one piece. Therefore, everyone cheered together: "death to all Javols!" and hoped none would be encountered on-route.

The massive Osmaron Galaxy was now displayed on both screens. Merol couldn't help commenting on the array of red spots shown around and within its three main spiral arms. They extended outwards into deep space. He turned to Jon and the others for an explanation, but no one had any ideas on the subject.

The Ship however explained:

'These crimson specks indicate the location of special observation and defensive areas within the Osmaron Sphere of Influence. They have been designed by an intelligent race called Octans, under the guidance of their Ploran masters.

'As a matter of fact, the system itself is so sensitive that despite our great distance away, we have already been scanned and analysed for entry within its inner perimeter.'

Then Meron remembered the famous name, Octans. They had once represented the arm of his Grand Lord Gerron. Their great deeds had been written down by the profit Seno in one of their ancient bibles which he could observe on one of the shelves. He wondered whether that civilization still existed, but the ship had just confirmed their present existence and he was pleased. They had saved his people once before so he and his owed them a great debt. One of his greatest desires was to visit their home world called Orban on a pilgrimage. It had always been the main spiritual home of his religious people, the Senots.

It was then that he realized the fulfilment of an Ancient Prophecy relating to Micol's descendants making Osmaron their permanent home.

They had now passed the outermost stars within that part of the galactic rim and slowly entered one of its larger arms. That one was dotted everywhere with red points amidst its numerous stars. They were now within the Osmaron galaxy proper and suddenly felt a lot happier and safer than they had been for a very long time. Yet, from their present position they could observe a small galaxy colliding with Osmaron. That image was the most spectacular one they had ever seen.

'The colliding galaxy is called Balion or Hydra to others. It's the ancient home of the Plorans and Octans. Both galaxies now form Osmaron proper,' the ship said.

Although they had never been to Osmaron before, like lost children they felt they had returned to the safety of their second home after an incredible survival struggle against enormous odds. They hadn't observed any Javols on-route and neither did The Ship, so they assumed their enemies hadn't yet arrived in Osmaron. But The Ship travelled very quickly and had most probably missed them on route, and so they reasoned. For a while they pondered the expansive stellar canopy and beauty of Osmaron.

So much has been said about Osmaron by their great poets. To ancient space voyagers and mariners, it was the brightest jewel in their skies, although barely visible from Caefon, and here they were, after all they had suffered. What a miracle of miracles.

Meron was even more excited than the others and had hijacked the smaller screen all to himself. He couldn't stop relaying his excitement to his companions via that screen. With the aid of the helmet he found he could control the images simply by issuing thought instructions. The device could become a very powerful telescope, among other things and images could be relayed to others via the larger screen.

However that screen was mostly under The Ship's control. Both screens now displayed the stellar environment while they cruised close to binary and individual stars of all ages and stages of stellar evolution.

Many stellar systems boasted some form of planetary structure, from orbiting asteroids to a very large planetary system with numerous moons. There was primal life everywhere and in every variety within that galactic arm.

The Ship had now switched to sensitive wide-band detection, which included radio wavelengths. Since the more advanced species used a type of H-Wave, those more simple types of transmission were best for detecting basic technological species. By now Meron had left his new toy and settled down with the others to view the information relayed by The Ship's computer on the main screen.

For sometime no indication of advanced primal life was apparent, until The Ship made another small jump to enter another galactic arm. Then suddenly it zoomed into a large planetary system and they were amazed by its incredible size and number of differing worlds; each so uniquely positioned about its parent star. Many planets being accompanied by several moons of their own.

'Oh what beautiful rings,' an excited Lira exclaimed as the ship took a curved path and manoeuvred around a massive gas giant. Then gently slowed and made an announcement to its crew:

'This part of the third spiral arm of Osmaron is not as densely populated as the others. However, this is the Torian System. It is the largest in this area. We sometimes use it as a stellar-mark. The habitable planet is Pleron, but the natives call it Earth. Would you like to observe some of its inhabitants?'

Meron and the others shouted a definite yes.

The larger screen focussed unto the planet's bluish globe and zoomed in on specific surface areas. There were massive oceans, continents, seas, islands, mountains, lakes, cities and towns. By this time Meron seemed to be completely absorbed by what he saw, in anticipation of some miracle to occur.

He closed his eyes and looked again, as if doubting his own senses, but this time they were filled with tears of happiness. He could no longer withhold his emotions and suddenly bursted out aloud with an uncontrollable stutter.

'Hu... hu... humans!... Lucia!... humans and animals!... like us darling!... just like us, but more like our young ones... our offspring, with eight fingers!' He was overwhelmed by emotion while tears of joy rolled down his cheeks.

He lifted his wife, Lucia, from her seat and both began to dance around the floor. Sintra, Lira and the others joined the couple and couldn't stop until they were exhausted and fell back into the long soft bench.

The Ship did not want to visit the planet, because such an intrusive move could have contravened interstellar laws. At that time higher technological species and cultures that were directly within The Greater Purpose were not allowed to land or trade with planets of much lower classifications. Such disturbance could have prevented the natural evolution and growth of lower civilizations so disturbed. Therefore all ships authorised by The Greater Purpose were required special clearance from the Grand Council to land on planets like Earth, then considered a Class 1 system. Only a Shadite could have allowed them to land, and The Ship was not aware of the presence of any Shadites on Earth.

Suddenly The Ship spoke to its crew:

'We can only land on Earth if a Shadite is in control and I am not aware of such a presence on Earth. However, the Book would know, providing it is on board and still has a strong rapport with its special reader.'

Sintra was the only one the Book would have accepted for that purpose. She made herself comfortable near the small screen and through meditation decided to ask the Book her questions. She was not sure whether her method would work, but knew its personality well, so perhaps if she tuned into that part of its psyche it would communicate.

She did not have to meditate long. While she concentrated the large viewer became alive. A likeness of her face appeared on the screen and began to speak. The words were displayed on the smaller screen in original Ancients' script.

> ***'Lumak, the Shadite, is on Earth,***
> ***You may use his help to follow your path.'***

She knew it was the Book and translated the words to others of the crew. The Book gave The Ship Lumak's special identification code. They waited for a while. Suddenly Lumak's adopted human form appeared on both screens simultaneously.

'Greetings to you, my dear friends. I have prepared a place on the surface for your ship. You may transpose directly on my beacon. Living quarters have been arranged. We have been expecting you.'

Meron was amazed by the subtlety of those clever Osmaron minds at play. Jon and Lira found it difficult to grasp the intricacies and fulfilment of those complex plans. Even the accuracy of events during their long and dangerous journey was predicted well before The Ship had left their planet in Andromeda.

All those operations scanned a period of over three thousand years, and yet the Javols were none-the-wiser. As far as they were concerned, the ship model they chased had a defect in its design which caused it to explode during the chase, taking many of their own in the process. Yet, because of that explosion The Ship and its crew had become untraceable.

Although its crew had not yet realised the full implications of their journey, their destinies were implacably linked. The Shadite Lumak would become one of the major players in their survival.

All future operations regarding Earth had been transferred over to him; a transparent genius and subtle player in the sands of time.

For he was another anointed Son of Destiny and Master of the Sword.

Lumak was a super genius and knew well the plight of those on planet Caefon in Andromeda. He was to become a major part of their survival plans and held a clear picture of their future. Further, he knew Plato well and had been kept up to date on the progress of the Javols towards their home world.

Their arrival on Earth was in the year 2043 CE. At that time the whole planet was undergoing political and technological change. Not to mention the effects of Global Warming. They were the first primal aliens to have visited that world from a distant galaxy during its complete history.

CHAPTER 49

I am Lumak, Shadite

Earth-Time... 2043 CE

Lumak, The Shadite... Doctor Jeffery Longhurst

During his previous existence, Lumak, the Shadite, was a Semonite (a giant bee-like creature). He had arrived on Earth just two years ago. During that most important of all his missions for his Grand Lord Gerra, he was transformed through the Greater Mind into a human male.

He had acquired the false identity of one Doctor Jeffery Longhurst for that most important of all missions. Despite his clandestine existence in southern Turkey, it was not long before the whole world knew of his name because of his general cure for cancer. That great feat was accomplished by using a unique type of anti-cancer serum that could be created from the patients blood. That cure also made his patients about ten years younger and extended their lifespan by over 10 years.

Doctor Longhurst also had plans for biologically growing new limbs, eyes and internal organs. The list was endless and those were not even his main fields. With his future designs in micro-robotics(nanites) and stellar drives, mankind was on their way to a new and better existence. However his main purpose on Earth was to improve our levels of technology from Class 1 (current levels) to Class 5 (about 100,000 years more advanced). That level was necessary for us to survive the Javols.

That incredible mind was of a Grade One Shadite and although Lumak gave the impression of a simple doctor, he was a servant of Grand Lord Gerra, Supreme Lord of our part of the seventh universe. He was the one known to the Ancient Andromedans as Grand Lord Gerron. Despite the urgency of Lumak's mission he could never knowingly risk the lives of others in any of his projects. Within his code of Shadites, all life was precious.

Lumak had indeed opened up the virtual pandora's box. For the first time in Earth's existence mankind was beginning to realise longevity and other benefits. Those new technologies would significantly improve the quality of life of every individual, with the not too distant possibility of eternal life. Finally the blind could see, the deaf could hear and the cripple could walk, and that was not all.

With the use of his brand of Brain Implants the need for schools and other such institutions would soon become outmoded. A tiny implant could be inserted in the brain of an individual and in the process extend the powers and memory of that mind by over ten times.

But that was not all, every implant contained several pre-programmed doctors, embedded invisibly into the user's mind. So instead of spending many years in schools and universities, all that was required by the user, was a knowledge of the use of the menus within their implants. Since those implants linked directly to core elements of the mind, it placed the user into Virtual Worlds that could interleave directly with the real one and other Virtual Worlds of a similar type.

His genius could irreversibly have changed the future course of mankind; to make them see things in a more cosmic sense as apposed to their then "little fish swimming in the proverbial little fish-bowl" with the resultant wars and conflicts from such petty narrow-mindedness, with disastrous consequences.

Lumak had tripped the fuse which had initiated the great explosion of awareness and had begun a new epoch in the history of mankind. After his first achievement he had gained the Nobel Prize. Although continuing his lectures on biology, he gradually introduced his main field of Micro Robotics, an important branch of Nano-technology, along with many other very advanced topics on inter-spacial travel.

As usual, he had his fair share of insults and abuse from the scientific fraternity, in particular from those jealous senior members. Even Isaac Newton and Einstein shared those platitudes, but with little patience for ignorance. He realised that any incredible and sudden change was usually difficult to accept, even with the highest elements of proof. That was because people always needed time to adapt to change. Nevertheless most of his concepts still baffled the topmost scientists on Earth. It was a time of Global Warming where many became unsure of their future and wanted change that would improve their lives and mend their dying world.

Many in the middle-eastern countries considered him a profit, while those he cured called him Lord or Messiah. Others like extremists wanted him dead because of his popularity and influence on their followers.

After he and his wife Sarah left their place, situated in the hills of Turkey close to the river Tigris, he was invited to the USA to live on a permanent basis. After escaping an explosive attempt on his life and considering Sarah's safety, he soon left that country for the USA.

Lumak was always in great demand internationally. During this time he had acquired an army of secretaries and experts, mostly based in North America.

He was soon unable to cope with the ever increasing demands and requests from ecologists and naturalists regarding the frequent extinction of rear species. While at the other end, the planet's human population was still increasing in leaps and bounds with - resulting pollution to the global environment and subsequent increases in global temperature.

There were numerous problems associated with global warming due mainly to human over-population, and the resultant extreme changes in weather patterns and ocean spread made everyone more insecure. Lumak soon realized all those problems were increasing together. Therefore even with his large staff he would be unable to stem their course significantly in the allotted time.

He was a Shadite whose main purpose was in preserving life, which included preventing extinctions, so he was obliged to stem those almost insurmountable problems. It was not long before he recruited his lovely wife Sarah and her father Khan to assist in some of those areas.

He was an excellent teacher while Sarah and her father were patient and retentive students with the aide of advanced technologies. Both soon became doctors and geniuses in their own fields.

During the following months Sarah was made in charge of all finances in the form of Solarian Banking, their main financial organization. She travelled widely throughout the globe to assist endangered species and starving humans and soon began the building of many great domes globally. Her intention to isolate all endangered species from the hands of man was a brilliant idea. By so doing many endangered species could be saved from extinction. During all this time Sarah and her many charities under the name of BioLive had grown in significance. She soon became well-known and was respected by many.

Presently she ran the largest and wealthiest charitable organizations on Earth, with branches in almost every country. Her global empire, included Solarian Banking, dealt with the financing and distribution of all their special products.

Lumak (Doctor Jeffery Longhurst) was to concentrate on the delicate experiments presently conducted in North America with the aid of a few large international organisations and governments.

Sarah's charitable organisation, BioLive, was presently the most well known charity on the planet.

CHAPTER 50

Their visit to Earth

The Ship could not visibly enter Earth's atmosphere. Any knowledge of such a visit would have been dangerous to the ship's crew. Firstly, their bodies were not used to our environment with its millions of different strains of bacteria and viruses. They would be required to slowly acclimatize while being administered certain drugs. However those were not the only reasons.

If there was any knowledge of their arrival, at the very least they would have been quarantined by the authorities for long periods, while being checked by scientists for dangerous extraterrestrial microbes and bacteria. Those actions were necessary to prevent the contamination of our planet's environment. There were always lengthy protocols for dealing with all extraterrestrial visits. Because of those reasons all such delays were to be avoided during their urgent mission. Therefore they were to transpose their ship invisibly to a hidden surface enclosure.

During that type of transposition a special beacon was used to accurately guide the almost massless ship to a predetermined landing sight on the surface. This process was not the same as inter-dimensional transposition. During this operation all radiation would either be absorbed, screened or redirected by the outer shielding to camouflage the ship during its descent towards the planet's surface. It was then impossible for anyone to observe its path using any form of electromagnetic detectors such as radar. This was a relatively lengthy process, since local air turbulence could be created if they descended too quickly. All such atmospheric effects were to be avoided.

This method of travel was only necessary in highly populated and confined areas. After its first precise landing the process could be automated without the need for further aligning beams. Then the ship could use its inter-dimensional drives.

The landing area was newly built and sited just in front of the helicopter pad situated at the rear of Lumak's large country manor.

That part of the house was enclosed by a high security wall which allowed limited access to the rear of the building. For further concealment a small entrance led along the side of the house while bordering a tall fence. That way the ship and its crew, once landed, could not be observed by anyone outside of that area. Anyway, Lumak always used that landing pad for his frequent foreign visitors. Due to previous problems at the Manor security was second to none.

Lumak's sudden appearance on the viewer reminded Meron of his younger brother Plato and realized he would still be alive after those many millennia. Plato was almost the same height as Lumak, with similar features, except for Lumak's skin complexion which was slightly darker. Lumak had the complexion of the young six.

Meron wondered whether Lumak knew his brother Plato and thought he should inquire about his whereabouts after The Ship had landed. He hadn't seen his biologically younger brother for over 3000 years. In real life terms it was only a few days since he left them in the underground city of Lower Cantor.

It was early on Sunday morning when they arrived at the location prepared for The Ship. Lumak was standing close to the hanger with a small laser beam generator mounted on a large tripod. When The Ship landed and became visible, he went forward and uttered the special words. The Ship melted into its stairs and entrance.

'You are welcome! Great Son of Goh!'

A confident Lumak strode up the shimmering stairway into the bowels of the ship. Its twelve passengers were overwhelmed with joy when they realised they were finally on terra-firma and safe from ravenous Javols.

The moment he entered they bowed respectfully, and were so pleased to see him. All twelve touched his black Shadite's cloak and held on to him as if to gain reassurance from the reality of his existence and presence, but also to confirm the fact they were not having another dream.

As a keen geneticist, he closely observed the differences between the two groups, one young with a brown complexion and the other a lot more mature in years, with Plato's features. He soon concluded that although they were obviously from the same gene-pool, certain characteristics were way off the mark. Among other things were the strange ancient dress worn by the six elders. He soon realised they were from different time periods. He was also familiar with certain types of clothes worn by merchants and politicians in ancient times. There was the matter of the six fingers displayed by the elders in contrast to the eight of the young six, who were almost identical to certain types of Earth's humans.

He considered the whole situation to be quite strange and yet, some of their features were otherwise so similar, genetically.

After their initial excitement had calmed, he began to introduce himself to them.

'I am Lumak, Shadite. Known to the natives of this planet as Doctor Jeffery Longhurst. I am currently assigned to this world to assist in its conversion to Class 5.' He spoke with confidence. Then Meron began to introduce his family and crew, both young and old.

Meron and his older companions were overjoyed by his presence, but surprised by the figure dressed in black speaking to them in their own ancient tongue. The young six also understood what he said because their minds contained the ancient language, previously unknown to most of them.

Merian couldn't hold back her emotions and began shedding a tear of joy.

'Great Lord Gerron's glorious Shadite. Again for our deliverance!'

'May I take this opportunity, on behalf of my people and myself, to sincerely thank you and your superiors for a most pleasant, and may I emphasize, most unique journey?' Meron said, again bowing to Lumak in a most noble fashion.'

'That's no problem. I shall endeavour to make your stay on Earth a most pleasant one. Please follow me into the house. Your belongings can be brought in later,' Lumak replied, equally nobly.

They entered the house through its rarest entrance that took them along its main hallway and into a most spacious sitting-room.

The large room included a small bar, television viewing area and pool table, with large settees, chairs and padded stools that were distributed equidistantly close to the bar.

The wooden mosaic floor was well polished with several thick rugs covering communal areas. That room was further highlighted by a very large crystal chandelier that hung almost at its centre. Its walls were adorned with several beautiful paintings, portraying land and seascapes in sunrise and sunsets, with wood carvings and statues mounted on strategically placed pedestals and shelves.

The large house was designed for comfort and relaxation by all ages, and there were always the outdoors, with its ranch, horses and local wildlife for those of a more adventurous nature.

The young six observed the small bar and wall cabinet with many crystal containers called glasses for the purpose of drinking. They realized Earth's people were freer in many ways than their more controlled societies on Caefon. It also brought back memories of the time spent at a similar small bar in the upper town within the underground city of Lower Cantor. They wondered whether the vegetarian food and drink on their new adopted world would be any different to those served at their surface homes or even the more automatically produced meals in Lower Cantor.

They were soon commenting about the comfortable rooms and their intricate decoration, with mention of the artistic manner in which it was all put together. Lucia couldn't contain her feelings any longer. She knelt down to kiss the very thick rug and they did likewise.

'Osmaron! Oh beautiful Osmaron!' she cried. They had suffered greatly for so many years, the release and freedom had suddenly come home to roost.

Once again Lumak spoke to them in one of their ancient tongues.

'Take your time and familiarize yourselves with your surroundings in your own way. I must however state a few salient points before you get started. You should all realize that this world has many invisible microbes that can infect the unaccustomed. So please wear the facial filters provided and take your daily dose of medicine until your bodies adapt and become immune,' he advised.

In the absence of his wife, Sarah, who was responsible for all financial and household affairs, he explained those domestic matters as best he could. He had also arranged a set of educational videos to assist them in attaining local knowledge and other relevant skills pertaining to their new world and its people. There was also the Television with its many channels and the World-Wide-Web.

Finally he called Madeline McCririck, who was responsible for running the manor during Sarah's absence. She appeared to be in her early thirties and Lumak introduced them to her. Like her children, grand children and great grand children, he also called her Mad. She was just over 95 years old and the first woman on Earth to have received Lumak's age-reducing serum. After she had gained her youthfulness of about 30 years, he decided to changed her nickname from Ma to Mad, short for Madeline..

'Mad! These are some good friends of mine, so please take good care of them for me when I am not around.' She closely observed their strange attire.

'Will they be staying long, Doc?'

'Yes, Mad! They are assisting me on a special project and will be with us for while.' She always called him Doc.

'In that case, I shall brief my girls and make them as comfortable as possible during their stay.'

Then she left for her local home on urgent business.

'You should now relax after your long and eventful trip. Feel free to do as you like, even to visit the farm with its animals and wild life. There are horses in the stables, ask Joseph or one of his children to teach you to ride.'

They kept staring at him while listening patiently to every word.

'This part of the planet is free of any dangerous virulent strains... only basic varieties exist and they can be controlled by simple drugs and diet. Perhaps sometime tomorrow we can have a friendly chat on topics that interest you. Whatever thoughts still worry you may be aired at that time. In the mean while, let me take you around and familiarise you with the other rooms and utilities.'

After Lumak had finished showing them the house, they returned to the large living room. He handed each a personal kit which included several pairs of silk gloves, tablets, nasal filters and inhalers. They took the items and added them to their other meagre possessions that were brought from The Ship.

CHAPTER 51

The visitors embrace Earth

They spent a little while familiarizing themselves with the house and its appliances. Many of which were alien in design, yet they soon deduced their modus operandi. Then they observed the strange variation of attire used by young and old alike. They soon realized Earth's humans preferred lots of variation in all things, even when some changes were less comfortable than others. However, their food was never colour coded and here lay a significant difference.

The elder group of Ancients were wearing special gloves they had modified to show eight fingers by stuffing the smallest with soft foam packing. Lumak had provided several closets filled with clothes of different sizes for both young and old. Each item clearly labelled in size and function. Those they modelled with the help of Madeline's grandchildren until satisfied with fitting and fashion. Their original robes and spacesuits being packed away with their other belongings. Jon and his young companions had donned Jeans and tea-shirts. They found them relatively comfortable and wanted to blend in with the locals as best they could.

The McCririck kids were always at hand to assist, although not realizing they were aliens from another galaxy. They assumed they had come over from a middle-eastern country, with different dress and customs.

The table-bell rang so they ran downstairs to investigate and were shown into the dining room by a well dressed Madeline. They were surprised by the sight of so much food. It was laid out in such plenty and variety on the large circular table that they knew not where to begin. Lumak and Sarah were strict vegetarians and so were Madeline's family.

They nervously smiled and bowed to Madeline and her helper and she bowed her head in return. They could not yet understand any of the local languages. The waitress accepted them as foreigners on vacation and pointed to the small brass bell, meaning for them to ring if they needed anything else.

Madeline was the first to start eating while the others followed her every move. Lumak had obviously briefed her and her family on the strangers unfamiliarity with western ways. Therefore she prepared a suitable vegetarian menu for that day. As usual, Ecrol was the first to take the plunge with knife and fork and was completely stumped. Then he was followed by Jon and Lira who was more dexterous, having carefully watched Madeline. Nevertheless, they had decided to assist the young helper and serve their elders.

As it happened, the Andromedans fully enjoyed the two courses, to be followed by ice-cream, which Meron thought was delightfully exquisite. He commented on the once similar food product made from Malak's milk.

Then he turned his attention to Jon and the younger six, speaking to them in the Ancient's tongue:

'Delicious! Most Delicious! Try this and tell me what you think!'

Jon and the others took a spoonful each and enjoyed the sweet creamy substance.

'We used to have a very similar delicacy in ancient times made from Malak's milk. This one must be produced from a similar herbivore on this world. As you can see, our worlds are not too dissimilar. I think, with little effort, we can be very happy in this place, despite the urgency of our mission.'

Jon realised he was referring to his ancient world several thousand years before the arrival of the Javols who destroyed it all. That was over 3000 years ago before he and his young group had even been considered for life.

Jon immediately placed his fingers across his lips to silence Meron. In case they were overheard by Madeline. Then they realized she could not understand their strange language, so Meron burst into laughter and so did everyone else, leaving poor Madeline somewhat bewildered and none the wiser. Jon soon dismissed spoiling thoughts of the Javols destruction and continued enjoying his ice-cream. Then he nodded his head in agreement with Meron. The Ancients were usually precise in their diets and could tell the ingredients in a soup or drink by its subtle blend of colours. That way they could always maintain a precise diet. It was not the same on Earth, but very delicious all the same.

That day they were out and about in the local fields and meadows, completely overwhelmed by the numerous variety and abundance of life. There were large animals and insects everywhere. They inhaled and filled their lungs with the precious clean air. They worshipped the plants and were fascinated by the green grass which they compared to a type of violet moss on their world that covered large surface areas. Here also were numerous birds, butterflies and bees, all partaking in its abundant bounty of flowers and fruit. They were now in their paradise. The way things should have been on their home world.

Despite those feelings of joy and safety, the spectre of the Javols were still rooted in their minds. Somehow, the beauty brought back memories of their own desolate world.

When they had taken enough of their new paradise to almost bursting point, they collected a few small flowers and returned indoors to entertain themselves. Then they would view the many learning tapes and disks that Lumak had supplied.

Despite the beauty of their newly found paradise, the Andromedans felt a sense of uneasiness with all that open space. They realised they had lots of ground to cover by way of learning a new language and in getting to know each of their own groups better.

When they returned indoors, it was in the general direction of the bar and television. They also learnt Earth's humans, like Ancients, had a great desire for books and pen-writing, despite the use of a less sophisticated computer technology. They could observe many parallels within both societies, even with a time difference of several thousand years between technologies.

Pens and note paper could be seen on the bar and were generously distributed about the house for taking messages, but there still remained the communication problem to surmount. They were not yet acquainted with any of the spoken languages on Earth. Such knowledge was of paramount importance if they were to communicate with its people and utilise local assistance for their evacuation program, or so they thought.

They socialised, while drinking the strange concoction of beverages held at the bar. Inadvertently some of the drinks were of high alcoholic content and improperly mixed. That was until the beautiful domestic maids came to their rescue. When dinner was ready they staggered into the dining room barely able to remain standing on their own two feet.

Lumak arrived later that day to join them for dinner. Afterwards he decided to answer any questions their wanderings had aroused so he took them into an adjacent room.

Jon was the first to speak and stood up to ask his questions, always showing respect for his elders.

'Sire, I have two questions to ask, if I may?'

'Yes, Jon?'

'We do not understand any of the languages of this world and are not sure what type of education is needed to establish the necessary skills. Secondly: we would like to proceed with our main mission as soon as possible. Although we appreciate your kind hospitality and love this world and all within it, we are also aware of the plight of our people in another distant galaxy,' Jon stressed, with concern.

'Can you shed some light, please?' Lire said.

Lumak stood up to answer those questions.

'Jon, your points have been well noted, but there is absolutely no need to worry about your present situation here nor of your people on Caefon. All relevant aspects have been designed within your learning program. Gaining basic knowledge of local animals, plants and the native human culture, will contribute significantly to your learning. How can you know the word for grass if you have little knowledge of its structure, composition and colour. You are required to study and learn about every object within this local farming environment in Sunolingua, the ancient trading tongue. This was the main language of the intergalactic and interplanetary traders. Through this implanted language you will find interpretation of local tongues greatly simplified. To your surprise, you will shortly find that you are quite fluent in that language, despite the fact you have no implants installed within your brain. You were given certain subliminals to assist the process.'

'Really, Sir?'

'Yes! Within this world are numerous languages and dialects. The local one is a dialect of the language called English which varies internationally. The historical video tapes will explain its derivations and emergence on this globe as one of the main languages, if not the main one. Now, do you clearly understand my Sunolingua?'

The twelve suddenly realised he was speaking to them in a language they knew little about and yet, they understood every word he uttered as clearly as if it was in their own native tongue.

'I brought some more study discs and tapes from my city library, so please exert a concerted effort to learn as much as you can, for tomorrow you speak fluent English.'

Once again Lumak turned his attention to Jon.

'Does our program meet with your kind approval, Sire?' He was being sarcastic.

'Yes, Sire! I am very impressed and apologise for being so naive and over anxious,' Jon replied, and in Sunolingua.

'Should you require any additional items for your own pleasures or convenience, please feel free to ask. Passports and other important documents will soon be arranged for you. Thereafter, I shall begin to integrate you into the native human society. And soon you will become my employees at one of the development laboratories situated locally.'

Then Lumak said his farewell for the day. He tended to spend most of his free hours in the laboratory on special projects. At that time he was trying to complete several projects at once but was also involved in the evacuation program.

They were excited by the promise of assisting Lumak in his work for the benefit of their distant families and friends, and looked forward to their involvement. In their opinion, everything regarding their special mission was moving at a much quicker pace than they had initially anticipated and they were once again in a lively mood.

While they drank the splendid mixtures that evening, they could find faint traces of English in their speech which when expressed slowly was understood by the staff, who sometimes giggled at their pronunciation. They also realised why Lumak wanted them to learn, through their senses, the intricacies of life, colour and form within their new environment.

To the young six it was like being in another underground city learning new technologies and concepts as they did on those previous occasions within Lower Cantor. Even so, Earth was no underground city, with comparatively limited resources. Of all things, the young six found its music, art and varying fashions more exciting than anything they had previously experienced.

Very soon Jon and his young group of six were dancing to the music and appreciating the videos like any other young Earth human. Meron's Ancients were more reserved and acted like parents to the others. Nevertheless they missed their other children, who were not resurrected with them and on another spiritual path. The young six missed their surrogate parents.

CHAPTER 52

A Twinning of worlds

The following day Lumak called them together. He was to make an important announcement, after which they were to have another general discussion. Once again they were gathered in the dining room when he entered. He was wearing his cream suit with winged insignia emboldened on his left lapel.

'People, within the larger picture we have an enormous challenge ahead of us.

'We are on a very important mission to save our worlds and in the process contribute towards the future survival of several galaxies and numerous worlds, including Earth. Therefore within the Greater Plan this world has been selected by Grand Lord Gerra, who is also your Grand Lord, known to your ancestors by the name of Grand Lord Gerron, to be an important part of this program. With that in mind, Earth is to be included as one of the main forwarding bases within this galaxy, Osmaron. This is because of its remote position from the Javols' forward troupes and its closeness to the rim of the Osmaron galaxy. Also there are not many advanced civilizations within this galactic arm due to predation of past. Because of those and other important reasons, the Grand Lord has decided to include this ... among other worlds, as the hub of initial operations... even to the extent of twinning your planet, Caefon, with Earth. Thus linking both galaxies together as one.

'From henceforth, this will be considered your world as much as it is ours and by similar decree your world becomes our world. Furthermore, the Omegron Portal will be sited within this system, on a stable planet yet to be designated for the purpose of mass evacuation.

'Shall I remind you of the significance of what I have just said?' Lumak asked.

'Both races adopts each other's technologies and important cultural norms that are beneficial to their separate species. But they must also agree to the process and it's obvious that we do not have much of a world left to offer anyone. Perhaps we could make them a promise... to be fulfilled after the Javols have been destroyed and we have rebuilt Caefon. But that might be a very long time in coming,' Meron's wife, Lucia, replied.

'Yes, Lucia. But you have a lot to offer by way of science, technology and culture. Such subjective concepts like beauty are little appreciated by those within the survival equation, with war and destruction looming large on the horizon. Further, as you have seen, they are not yet ready technologically and have not learnt to appreciate the gains and values of peaceful and harmonious coexistence. To achieve our mutual goals, we must assist each in many ways, if we are to succeed at all levels of the master plan. Those on this world are good listeners, quick learners, and with a modicum of knowledge may become quite capable. Therefore we are to work closely together if we are to survive the Javols onslaught.

'The brand of Class 5 technologies soon to be introduced will make this world one of the most advanced in this galaxy, and you have been chosen to assist me in that greatest of all missions.

'Your world has barely six months before the Javols' final strike and this world just under two hundred years. Even as we speak our enemies approach this galaxy at enormous speed. Therefore, each one of us has a difficult and urgent task to accomplish. Further, you have all been chosen for that glorious task and are each special in the eyes of our Grand Lord.'

'Must we return to Caefon in due course after the Javol's defeat,' Lira asked.

'Since Earth and Caefon is now as one, both surfaces may be considered same, therefore to all intents and purpose, you are now on the surface of Caefon,' he replied and she was pleased with that answer.

Suddenly there was a misty presence in the room that slowly took on a human form. Lumak went up to the hooded figure and both men placed their fist on their chest in Shadite salutation, but the other also bowed his head gently, showing even greater respect for

Lumak as his senior. Then they embraced each other as close friends. The form removed his hood to reveal the smiling features of Plato.

Meron was so utterly surprised. This person was no other than his younger brother. He realised both Shadites knew each other well. Plato couldn't restrain his excitement in seeing his family and close friends standing with his older brother Meron after more than 3000 years. He embraced each in turn with tears flowing. Then he greeted the young six in like manner.

'I shall remain here with my family and friends for a while, if they will tolerate my presence,' he said in jest.

They went up to him and insisted he stayed.

The following morning they went out into the fields and farms to observe the variety of life in greater detail. It was now part of their daily routine and they had grown to love the larger animals with their frolicking young.

Lucia closely observed the animals, insects and birds on this beautiful world called Earth and pondered their similarity with those on Caefon before the Javols arrived. For some cosmic reason, life within certain planetary types were so similar but appeared to follow a standard blueprint. That aspect depended on certain environmental conditions, resources, predation and catastrophes, which could alter their genetic pattern in an almost predictable manner to enhance their survival causation. This strange symmetry was probably because the original forms that began reproducible organic life were of a limited variety. Perhaps only three was meant to survive giving rise to crustaceans, insects, squids, reptiles and suchlike.

She thought, 'the Malaks were a little more bushy-haired than the cows. Perhaps more similar to the ones called bison, but with hair of golden brown. The only basic difference between both worlds were the number of fingers and toes. The shape of paws and hooves here tended to reflect that aspect in their structure. All other differences could easily be attributed to basic changes due to natural selection.

'Perhaps in the remotest primordial past evolution with mammals on my world Caefon diverted slightly towards three or six. It is possible that the original primordial sea creatures or primal reptiles had a lesser number of fins or flippers. Those very same questions had baffled scientists for generations, with little conclusive evidence to prove the matter either way.'

She plucked a lily, closely observed its form and sampled its fragrance.

'Despite those minor variations, we are well used to six fingers and two thumbs. Perhaps in some ways we are more dexterous than eight fingered humans. After all, each finger has four joints, giving greater latitude to swivel. They are a lot more flexible, with stronger tendons for a firmer grip and greater speed of movement. Even the nervous system could be considered more efficient at handling just six fingers. It was just a matter of learned manipulation from childbirth.'

She remembered how she enjoyed playing the Litra.

It was a six-stringed instrument and wondered whether such musical instruments existed on Earth. Yet she continued to ponder their differences.

'Planet Earth was so similar to the old world of my youth, several thousand years before the Javols arrived on the seen to spoil it all.

'Perhaps a comparative time would be the period of the great tribes and clans... before the brilliant clansman-scientist Micol... one of our elders... came on the seen. Very soon thereafter he conquered the whole planet and began to turn his attention outwards, into the great void of space. Albeit with the help of Octan technology.

'This planet Earth is still in the throws of tribalism and nationalism, not too unlike that very same period on Caefon. Further, planet Earth does not have the necessary technologies for interstellar travel. That expansion came with the invention of the first Linear Progressive Drive System or LPD modules, as they were usually called. When that happened Caefon could trade with neighbouring worlds and learn of even more advanced technologies from older civilizations, thus taken her even further along the

technological advancement curve.

'Many years of inter-continental wars had made us superior as a people, not only in the use of weapons, but also in special medical drugs and transplants. But even during those turbulent periods we never succumbed to the use of nuclear or other weapons of mass destruction. Wars were always fought with great dignity, pride and honour. Anyway, those nuclear devices were banned under treaty for the sake of the mother planet and its other life-forms and eco-systems. Who are we to take it upon ourselves to include other evolving species into our pathetic disputes and wars, but the Javols came and destroyed it all anyway.

'The technologies for generating power by nuclear fusion was discovered well before the last great intercontinental wars. With the onset of other superior technologies, risky and environmentally dangerous products and devices were soon banned from Caefon. Those that were still required sited on sterile moons and outer planets.

'Large plasma generators and installations were then built at great depth within the planet's surface to recycle its core elements and supply all our energy requirements. Those were sited well away from Caefon's beautiful biosphere which by that time was under many forms of satellite and techno-controls.

'During that period of growth everything became so efficient that very soon the use of physical money became too cumbersome for day to day trading. The only means of identification being a simple card that could be automatically scanned by security computers even while in transit. Even so, each individual had to complete a yearly quota of work. The time spent was equivalent to only three months of normal effort on Earth in a single year. After that short period of service anyone could pursue whatever professions or hobbies they desired, being free to change any such careers or hobbies on an annual basis. Even with those greater freedoms most scientists, professionals and other creative individuals enjoyed their occupations far too much to take leave on long vacations. During life, food, clothing and shelter were freely available to every citizen but with the added option of certain incentives and promotions. Then there were extra credits

given. Those corresponded to financial bonuses on Earth..

'Many preferred to continue their relevant professions on a more permanent basis, but always with the option to change if so desired. They would still have completed the longer hours worked if their extra remunerations were withdrawn. Earth was very distant from that type of altruistic and technocratic society. She was a capitalistic society still in the throws of international wars and conflicts, due in most cases to greed and self-indulgence.

'All such self-indulgent behaviour and their outlets created for the sole purpose of appeasing one's primitive emotional needs and responses has always been wasteful on planetary resources and always led to disaster,' Lucia thought. Then she considered the present time.

'There was always the urgent matter of rapacious Javols and the positioning of the Omegron Portal to save my people.'

She suddenly felt chilly from the cool morning breeze and decided to return to the warm comfort of the house. By now the others were seated in the living room playing a variety of Earth games, while Jon and Merol were at the snooker table practising shots.

Plato had gone on a special mission for Lumak.

An excited Plato soon returned. He was still wearing his black Shadite's cloak, and went directly to see Lumak in his private study.

'Finally I have made contact with the President of the USA! Do you know what that means? We can now become part of a greater whole!' Plato exclaimed. Lumak was intrigued by that knowledge.

'Seems we have made a very important breakthrough. If we have the current President as a good friend and ally most of our worries will be over,' Lumak replied with a smile. Then Plato went on to explain the circumstances to Lumak.

After a short while Lumak and Plato called the group together.

'Guys, we are to visit a different part of this continent today. We have received invitation from the President of the United States of America. This invitation is for dinner at his country residence and includes every one of us.'

While glancing at Jon and the younger six, he continued:

'Our journey will be a lot quicker if we take The Ship.'
The Ship could be quite useful in case they had to make a speedy retreat from capture or so they thought.

The meeting of two separate galactic races was no trivial matter. They were ambassadors of their respected home worlds and galaxies. It was therefore necessary that certain formalities and protocols were observed during such meetings. Meron, being a senior member of the Ancient Council was well versed in such affairs of state and decided to advice everyone on etiquette, attire and posture as was practised by the Imperial Federation in ancient times.

Despite the excitement of the moment, they wanted to make a memorable impression on one of Earth's most important leaders. The ladies, young and old alike, soon departed to advise each other on attire. A practical and well-travelled Madeline was always there to add her advice.

Lumak, Plato and Meron disappeared for another discussion, while Jon, Merol and Ecrol went their own separate ways.

Each wardrobe was stocked with every garment imaginable, so they followed the advice of Lucia and other members of the Ancients who had a much better dress sense than the young six. When everything failed, they turned to Madeline.

The men felt quite awkward in their Earth-type suits and neck ties. The concept of buttons and zips were quite unknown to them, having been accustomed to small clips concealed within seams in their garments. Luckily, the bow-ties were the clip-on variety. Nevertheless, Jon soon learned the relevant techniques from Lumak and assisted his comrades.

Although awkwardly, the young six were formally dressed in acceptable evening attire that matched their age.

The Elders, excluding Lumak and Plato, were officially dressed and appeared more like ancient Greeks in their chosen garments, but as usual, the Shadites always wore their black cloaks invisibly underneath their clothes and carried something extra within its bottomless pockets.

Meron was wearing the Ancient Sword which had been recovered by Lumak from The Ship.

The Ship was subsequently called, they entered its cabin and were soon in the stratosphere on their way to the private country residence of the president of the USA.

CHAPTER 53

Plato meets the President

President Gerald Fraser of the USA had only recently recovered from a severe bout of pneumonia. His Democrat party was not yet three years in office when the pressures of his administration, combined with an intestinal virus, compelled him to take another short break. He was presently recuperating at his preferred country residence in Wisconsin.

That place used to be a small border ranch, but after its acquisition he decided to convert it for general farming and golf. The large private green straddled his stately mansion. He would spend many hours on the golfing green planning strategies with his close senators during a competitive round.

Within the ranch he bred several thoroughbred horses, cattle and pigs. Among the horses were his favourite. A beautiful mustang called Shiloh. The large ranch was serenely placed and could inspire even the most weary and unimaginative.

Despite his constant battles with the opposition in Congress and elsewhere, due mainly to the continuing hard and unrelenting recession, he managed to maintain a dignified and positive posture. However that attitude was not enough, since many farmers and small manufacturers were almost up in arms due to high debts and bankruptcies. During that period of recession interest rates were high and many severely taxed; how else could the government pay its many debts and keep its other global commitments during a period of extremely bad weather.

To compound his problems were the current high level of national debt. There was little money left in the kitty for other important and necessary projects. Further, promises of financial assistance made to friendly allies by previous governments in a more favourable past had to be honoured.

Although he relished his new position as president, he had not realised the dire financial mess in which his country floundered, mainly due to a previous incompetent and spendthrift opposition.

Then there was the predicted reduction in fossil fuels globally due to eastern demands and subsequent high prices which did not help. The process of Fracking was almost at an end.

He knew he would be partly forgiven and tolerated during his almost three year period of office, but it was just a matter of time before a scapegoat would be found and he was obviously the prime target.

During the present crisis he had observed his party's popularity dwindle and he wondered whether he could find a way out for himself and his government. Something to keep the people in place and his main opposition less arrogant and at bay, until he and his advisors could find short and long term solutions to the present financial crises.

As one very determined person, he was not used to passing the buck or using the word "can't" when he could see a genuine cause that needed his help. And his missions were not always for political gains. Further, he had always thought any problem to be surmountable if tackled in a correct and honest way.

That morning he felt much better than the previous day and decided to ride his horse Shiloh to the northern side of the ranch to check on his pigs. He found that particular outlet soothing and took pleasure feeding them.

He was riding through a wooded area when for no apparent reason Shiloh stopped dead in his tracks. Try as he did, the animal remained transfixed and did not budge. Being close to his destination, he decided to dismount and attempt to walk the remainder of the way leading Shiloh by hand. The horse took a few steps forward and again stopped. The President lifted Shiloh's hooves individually, observing each one in turn for glass splinters, stones or any foreign object that might have lodged within and cause the animal distress, but nothing was apparent.

The moment he turned to look in the forward direction he could hardly believe his eyes, for just twenty metres ahead of him stood a strange figure dressed in black.

He was sure the person was not there when he glanced a second ago, but there he now stood as sure as daylight. He felt a cold sweat come over him as fear engulfed him and he became worried for his own safety.

Although he employed several security personnel throughout the area, they were mainly stationed in and around the house and golf course in what was considered strategically sensitive areas.

Only two junior security officers were stationed at the pig shelter and they were not in a position to observe that wooded area. Anyway, any access to that part of the ranch was over an electric fence and it was constantly scanned by close-circuit cameras.

He did not like his security to follow him everywhere he went and preferably never on his own ranch. During those private moments he preferred his own company.

This character, he thought, is dressed in a black hooded cloak for no other reason than hide his features and therefore could only be an assassin. While he stared at the aberration, slightly shivering from fear of death at the hands of blackness, the strange figure walked towards him. The blackness progressed in his direction and as he did, Jerry could hear his heart thump even louder.

There was nothing he could do. Even Shiloh had been frozen in his stride by the strange spectre. He could have taken along a small firearm, but he was always against the use of guns and had to set an example, being the current leader of the anti-ballistics committee.

As the figure came up to him his hood fell back to reveal a human likeness, but with golden hair and piercing sea-blue eyes.

He stretched out his hand in greetings and the president bravely did likewise, for he could do little else. The handshake was not what he expected, as the stranger grabbed his wrist firmly. It was more like the type of handshake used in ancient times by Greeks and Persians.

The man displayed three fingers and one thumb on each hand and began to speak in clear and polished English.

'I am Plato, Shadite, Son of Goh,' he said showing a glint in his eye.

The president nervously, but proudly, stood his ground.

'I am President... Gerald E. Fraser, some call me Jerry... others

Gerald... I am pleased to meet you.' Jerry stuttered.

The president was still worried, but thought, if this strange fellow wanted to kill him he would have done so by now. He must be one of those sadistic people that take pleasure from pain. The Shadite Plato then moved a few paces away.

'Mister President, please observe me carefully!' he said, politely.

The president held his gaze and became even more distraught by what he saw. In front of his own eyes the hooded figure faded like a shadow into absolutely nothing and faded back into himself. Plato continued in his usual positive and to the point manner.

'Mister President, I am not of this world. In fact, I am not even of this galaxy. I am from the one you call Andromeda, your sister galaxy.'

'You are?'

'Yes! I am! Your world has been made sister with my world by intergalactic degree and with the blessings of our Grand Lord, Gerra, who is Lord of this part of the known universe.'

'Is he, really?'

'Yes! He is!'

The President was stunned and still could not believe the most sincere words uttered by the strange three fingered human.

'He is so much like a normal person, but for the fingers, golden hair and incredible piercing sea blue eyes. His hair could have been dyed and contact lens worn to give that impression. Yet, how could any normal person disappear like that?' he thought.

Despite what had occurred, Jerry could not come to terms with it all and decided to continue the conversation, if only to humour and keep his would-be assassin occupied. He prayed for a chance in conversation to gently talk him around; for he was still quite nervous of his present circumstance. If those plans failed, he hoped the guards would become suspicious of his late arrival and begin a search. He would therefore try his utmost to humour this strange spectre or whatever it was as long as he could.

'What does twinning entail.... I mean ... mean being sister to your world?' Jerry, the president, asked, still stuttering.

'Your world becomes like ours and ours like yours, we both gain enormous benefits from the union... you may come and go as you please... learn new technologies... have freedom of choice in all things within our mutual laws and democratic rules.'

The president could not hold back a sarcastic grin while continuing to speak.

'You mean, travel all the way to Andromeda and back. That trip could takeover a million lifetimes and I can only live another forty years or so, if I am lucky.' Jerry felt more relaxed.

'Do not worry, Sire. With our brand of technology that trip can be made in a single day,' Plato replied.

The president closely observed Plato and realised a sense of authority in the way he carried himself. It was something to do with his precise mode of speech. He also realised the sincerity in his words.

He thought for a moment, 'this is indeed a strange situation to be in. What if this person was really who he said he was: a visitor from another galaxy.'

He and humanity would have so much to gain from such a union, even from the technology of being able to fade into nothing. Think of the security implications, given the ability to fade away even into another place, and the powers, not to mention the freedom of movement. Even he, the president, would be able to visit anywhere without the constant horde of security men and reporters that were always annoyingly present. The list was endless and despite his still nervous disposition and diminishing fear, he was beginning to like this Plato character, whoever or whatever he was. He also remembered the tale of the previous president who describe meeting a supreme being about two years ago. Was this strange guy something to do with him, and there was the enigmatic Doctor Jeffery Longhurst. So he turned to Plato and spoke to him equally positively but bravely.

'You have no intentions of harming me?'

'Why should I, a Shadite, wish to harm anyone?' Plato replied, with certainty.

'I think I can trust you and believe in most of what you say, but perhaps we can continue this conversation at my home in a more private and comfortable environment. So, may I formally invite you and your associates, if any, for dinner this evening at my house?'

'That will be most acceptable, Mr President!' Plato replied with a broad grin.

'Shall we say at eight o'clock this evening?' Jerry said, cheerfully and grinning nervously, but still with appreciable apprehension.

Plato was very pleased with himself for having made such an enormous breakthrough and again shook Jerry's hand in the ancient manner. Then he placed his fist above his chest in Shadite salutation, slightly bowing in the process and then dissolved into thin air in front of Jerry.

'Oh! Oh! Oh! Oh! Oh!' Jerry panicked quietly, while trying desperately to get back into Shiloh's saddle. Try as he may he couldn't climb the stirrup. It was due to a combination of extreme nervousness and fear. It was as if a primordial fear had surfaced from deep within his being to prevent any of his intended motions. There he remained for a while and rested, with his heart still thumping hard against his chest, until his overwhelming fears had dissipated and he regained control of his legs..

'Patience Shiloh, Patience, my boy,' he said in a quiet whisper while trying to calm the horse so that he could mount the saddle.

After that encounter Jerry was in no mood to continue towards the pig farm so he remounted Shiloh and turned him about for home.

CHAPTER 54

A Presidential dinner

Lumak had fitted in well with his new human identity as Doctor Jeffery Longhurst and wanted his present lifestyle to remain precisely that way. Therefore as far as he was concerned, the Andromedans were the only aliens on Earth. They had to make their political moves on their own, albeit with a little help from him and his organization.

That evening the extremely active and nervous president gave new orders to all staff, including security, that under no circumstances should he be disturbed. He dismissed most of his external security people for the remainder of that day. It was on the pretext that he had fully recovered and would remain indoors, during which time he would entertain friends until the following day. Anyway, they were pleased with his recovery and desired a little time off themselves. Even so, he insisted a small contingency remained in the most sensitive areas.

He had retained his most trusted and loyal officers, whom he hoped would be more than adequate in deterring any unexpected intruders during the course of that evening. He soon brought them together in the dining room.

'Guys, we are going to have some people over for dinner and a little entertainment this evening, so don't worry if the dress is a bit fancy. They have come to cheer me up, and you know the sort of games my acting friends like to play on me to get their own back. And don't bother to search anyone for weapons, the door detectors will be good enough.'

Once he had organized the staff for that evening he became aware of security matters regarding himself and his wife, if something should inadvertently go wrong.

Emergency communication was always available via telephone or radio on several of his private channels. There was also a direct line to the Pentagon and other relevant places during any serious emergency. Pressing a simple button could bring down protective shutters, screening the main rooms from outside intervention, causing the might of the army and air-force to bear down on any would-be assassin. All that recent security was at close range and handy remote button, so he left the rest in the hands of destiny.

Jerry did not want any surprises that evening. He knew not what to expect from his Andromedan visitors, so he had to maintain a low profile and restrict knowledge of their presence to as little numbers as possible, and yet be prepared for an emergency if things didn't turn out as expected.

He thought, 'after all, what if they came by space-ship... Perhaps I should arrange some lights on the helicopter landing pad.... On second thoughts... such a display could attract attention.'

He subsequently gave orders for a row of lights be placed on the lawn for his late visitors and it was done.

He asked his resident chef to prepare dinner for a full complement of important guests, not knowing how many would arrive. Anyway, nothing ever went to waste with hungry security officers and guards about.

The large family dining table was prepared to sit sixteen guests including himself and his wife. At the last minute he arranged two small tables placed on either side with extra chairs. The smaller tables could quickly be joined unto the main one with additional table cloths. When added, they increased sitting capacity by another twelve.

Although he made sure everything was prepared and made as welcoming as possible, he was still doubtful as to whether his special guests would turn up. That was until he heard a slight vibration that caused the chandelier in the dining room to ring and rattle and the lights to flicker. What materialized on their front lawn gave the appearance of a strange but large silvery oblong tank.

He and his wife glanced out of the window and were stunned by the sight of a large object suddenly appearing in front of their eyes to blot out all distant lights. To their further amazement, the side of the strange spaceship melted into a stairway and entrance, revealing in queue their dinner guests, chatting and laughing while making their way unperturbed down its glimmering stairway. As they approached the front door, Jerry nervously grabbed his wife's hand, holding it firmly in his as he pulled her along to greet his guests.

'Darling, it's a surprise. Some friends I would like you to meet. They are part of a very secret project. So please make them feel at home for my sake.' Both were extremely nervous.

She knew he was up to something because of all the last minute preparations; not to mention his erratic behaviour since he returned from the farm that afternoon. She attributed it to his recent illness and medication. Nevertheless what she presently observed was quite a different matter and extraordinarily strange, to say the least.

Being the responsible first-lady, and despite all her nervousness, she composed herself to deal with her strange guests. She trusted her husband implicitly in all matters of state security and accepted his explanation; that they were part of a special project. But even so, how could a ship appear out of nowhere and melt like that? It put the very willies into her bones.

The visitors introduced themselves, uttering their names in clear and concise English and followed the couple into the house.

On their way in Plato gave a hand command to the metallic object and to their further surprise The Ship replied in a most resounding and powerful voice:

'Yes! Great Son of Goh!'

The stairway then melted into the body of The Ship and the entrance sealed itself in a reddish glow, thus revealing a perfectly smooth surface, not unlike a strangely shaped submarine or large submersible standing on three firm telescopic feet.

Jerry was a profound politician as he was a skilful actor and fully intended to see his plans through for the evening, so once again a very nervous president held his wife's hand and whispered in her ears.

'It's incredible! Isn't it, Darling?' He held on to her in an attempt to contain his foreboding and relieve their nervousness.

'Is it one of those fancy dressed parties, Darling?' she replied excitedly. He nodded positively while forcing a nervous smile and they followed her to dinner. She could not recognize anyone she knew in the group and realized they were not local.

It was purely coincidental that the table accommodated the full party, with Jerry and his wife seated at either end. Two security guards stood outside the door, but could not view the front where the ship had landed. They were not allowed to enter the dining room and neither could security cameras view the front lawn. They had been previously adjusted away from that area by orders of Jerry.

Meron introduced each in turn then Jerry took them into the dining room.

They silently enjoyed the meal. Meron, who was seated not too far from the president, remarked on the enjoyable and delicate flavours which reminded him of certain menus from home.

'This is really delicious. Your food is very similar to what we have at home.'

'Yes, one of my favourite vegetarian dishes.'

'What a beautiful place, Mr President!' Lucia commented.

'It's been recently decorated! My wife's choices.'

Jerry liked the man, Meron, who was dressed in an almost ancient Greek costume and considered him to be an old traditional eccentric not too unlike a few of his English friends from the Embassy.

Jon was next to speak in his not yet fully acquired English tongue.

'Sire, do the other Osmaronites also... I mean... live on this world with you?' He showed a slight stutter.

Jerry was not sure what he meant by that question, and had no knowledge of a place called Osmaron, even of its peoples and turned to Meron who looked the most senior for an answer. Instead Meron nodded to Lumak and he in turn stared at Plato.

Plato immediately stood up to answer the question.

'Mr President, First Lady, fellow Shadites and friends. We are all on a very important mission to stop the progress of a deadly fore. One that will detrimentally affect all our lives from now and well into the foreseeable future. Even while I speak to you they move closer to this world...' Plato continued in his matter of fact manner.

The president and most of all, his wife, gazed at Plato in utter bewilderment.

'What are you saying?' The first lady inquired.

'I am saying that we have a serious problem in the future and will be in grave danger! Let me show you what I mean!'

CHAPTER 55

The silent video of death

Plato removed a small black box from under his cloak and placed it on the table. It immediately began to project a cinematic image on the nearby wall.

Jerry, being short sighted, put on a pair of thin-framed metal-rimmed glasses retrieved from his jacket pocket. The displayed images were of a high quality, but without any associated sound. The scenes began with the destruction of the Ancient's capital city called Cantor. The time was over three thousand years ago.

Strange monsters of many hideous forms could be clearly observed swarming in large numbers throughout the city. They were destroying and absorbing their human prey and other large animals at an incredible rate. The missiles and other weapons of mass destruction released against them had no effect. They appeared to absorb radiant energy as part of their metabolic functions. It aided the reproductive cycles of those whose appetites had been previously satisfied. Those divided into two separate individuals even hungrier than their original. Since Javols divided into two separate individuals, with all the knowledge of their previous original, there were no parents. Also, death from aging seldom occurred in such a nano-bot microid life-form. Some would even join with others temporarily to form giant monsters to crush buildings and large structures. They were truly a formidable foe.

Jerry watched intently and couldn't believe his own eyes. At first his wife thought it was some new horror movie that her guests had brought to shock them, but its realism soon dawned on her and she almost choked on her pudding. After those first few horrific scenes she couldn't stop sobbing and had to leave the room, followed by several of the other women. They were completely sickened by the ordeal. It was then that the women told his wife Sharon that they were from another galaxy, including the episode of her husband with Plato earlier that day.

'You can't be! That is truly incredible!' she commented, still not fully believing their story. Then the Ancient, Merian, removed one of her gloves to reveal her 3 fingers and single thumb, then Sharon was convinced.

Jerry couldn't keep his feelings to himself any longer and turned to Meron for an explanation.

'This is what happened to our world three thousand years ago. At that time everything was destroyed with the exception of a few of us who took shelter in an underground city. We have come here to assist, because they are also on route to this galaxy, known to us as Osmaron. You call it, The Milky Way,' he said with sadness.

'A beautiful society and culture, yet such utter and complete destruction. I have watched the worst types of horror movies, but never in my wildest nightmares have I ever seen such brutal slaughter.

'Our classic movies like "the wars of the worlds" and "the day of the triffids" have portrayed invading monsters from outer-space, but all those invaders were child's play when compared with these ones... and you say these... Javol things, are on their way to Earth?' Jerry was somewhat troubled by Meron's words and disposition.

Meron nodded his head meaning, yes, but was himself very solemn and not in any mood to answer lengthy questions. Even small teardrops could be observed rolling down his cheeks. Plato explained the nature of the Javols to Jerry, but he could not fully believe what he heard and began to speak to all and sundry.

'What do you mean? Even those film monsters had an Achilles heel and could be killed eventually... and you say these Javols are not even carbon based... metal based, and flexible metals at that!' he cried with nervous anxiety.

By now he was a most perplexed president, being hit by the realization that this most deadly problem was almost insurmountable and the gross and evil monsters were on they way to Earth. He realized if that was the case, all of Earth's governments and its people would have to organized to face the enormous threat.

Jerry observed all those faces sat in the room; the sadness and tears, and became overwhelmed by emotions. Suddenly he stood up and walked to a private cupboard where he entered a personal code by pressing several buttons on a small panel.

It was not a national security code, but instead one used to summon his most trusted advisors in times of crisis. Through the communicator he could be linked internationally from his country residence. He knew his chosen advisors would be there within the hour, in helicopters, jump jets or whatever it took. So he ordered drinks for all and awaited their arrival.

It was not long before the first five helicopters came hovering within sight. An air-force helicopter escorted the others and landed on the main pad. Apparently the two middle helicopters contained advisors and special personnel. They were escorted at front and rear by two more air-force helicopters filled with military personnel. They landed and the officers jumped out to station themselves around the house and within the golf-course.

The group leader, one Captain Mallory Colman, called out to two of his junior lieutenants.

'Take them in! I want no problems!'

They immediately went forward to assist the advisors and other personnel off the helicopters.

The doors opened and they dismounted, one by one, to be escorted by more senior guards towards the front of the house.

On their way towards the front door they observed the strange object parked on the lawn and knew not what it really was. It could equally have been a new type of submersible. Jerry had several strange experimental hobbies and was also keen on certain types of underwater pursuits.

They were escorted to the dining room. Many more chairs were brought from an adjacent conference room and placed on either side of the large dining table, but many were standing.

Jerry went towards the senior officer.

'What's your name?'

'Captain Mallory Colman, Sir,' he replied, while saluting the president with precision.

'Well, Mallory, you run a tight ship. Do me a favour... please keep your men away from the front lawn and get them some food and drink from the kitchen. This is mainly an informal meeting so take your time and give them a break. Anyway, if we have any trespassers we are more than enough to take them on ourselves,' he said.

Once again the captain saluted his president and shouted an order to one of his lieutenants.

'Let's get fed! Pass the word!'

They departed in the general direction of the large kitchen, leaving behind twenty-two worried delegates.

It was not long before Jerry began to speak in a stun but sincere voice.

'First of all, I want your solemn oath that whatever transpires in this room this evening will never be repeated elsewhere. Not under threat of death or even on your death-beds. Believe me when I say this is absolutely necessary for our long term survival.'

'What's all this about, Jerry?' One of his senators inquired. Jerry ignored the question.

'Please swear!' As a church-going Protestant, Jerry insisted.

He took a copy of the bible and handed it for each to kiss in turn.

'This measure is necessary if we are to protect ourselves and others,' he added, but gave no further explanation.

Then he turned to Plato, who once again retrieved the small object from under his cloak. He placed it on the table and the same images projected on the nearby wall. Members of the Ancients, the younger six and Jerry's wife, did not wish to watch those distressing images a second time, so they excused themselves. Jerry's wife, Sharon, asked some of the other Andromedans to tour the house with her and they agreed to go along.

Jon and his young friends had observed the horses playing in the fields during their arrival and decided to view the stables in the bright moonlight, so they journeyed in that direction.

'Ah, Lira, a horse herbivore! How I love this world with all its beautiful creatures. Because of twinning, perhaps one day we can introduce most of them to our own world,' Jon remarked.

'Yes, I saw its kind in one of the magazines. They ride them and also use them for racing. Pity we have no such animals left on our world. Not even a single Pedris remains,' she replied, sadly. He had no idea what a Pedris was, and stared at her, while the others of their group caught up with them.

'You archeologist are quite lacking in your basic knowledge of our past. Even Merol must know what a Pedris was!' she said.

'Pedris! What Pedris,' Merol exclaimed, equally bewildered.

'For your education in the topic of ancient history... they were used like horses in ancient times for riding, racing and carrying.' she said.

CHAPTER 56

The visitors are introduced

After Plato's recording was shown everyone in that room was utterly repulsed and shocked. They assumed it was to do with a new movie project in which the president was involved. Perhaps he wanted them to review it and give their opinions. Then Jerry took his chief technical advisor, the one he called Mickey, away from the others for a quiet word.

'I only wish our Doctor Longhurst was here with you guys to take notes. Lets wait and see what transpires. Anyway, let me introduce you to some special friends.'

'Ok!' and intrigued Mickey replied.

'This is Meron... Lumak... Plato... and the young ones over there. They are all from Andromeda.' He pointed to each in turn with conviction in his voice.

'Oh? Really?' Mickey replied, uncandidly.

Mickey, whose real name was Michael Cockburn was by now completely confused by the proceedings and shook his head in an uncertain manner to those sitting, as they were introduced, but the president insisted.

'You know, the bloody galaxy, way up there in the sky!'

Mickey was by this time even more confused, having watched the dinner guests with their fancy dress and now a film he considered to be a very realistic horror video. He knew his President had taken leave for a rest, but didn't realize he had also taken leave of his senses. Then he thought perhaps he was either kidding him, high on drinks and drugs, or even perhaps completely out of his sad mind. But why would he make such an important call that time of night just to callously invite them to a fancy dress party and offer him and his mob a drink. Didn't he understand the seriousness of that call, not to mention the wasted time and effort by The Pentagon. Such wolf-crying might not be tolerated so lightly in future.

Jerry again turned to Plato for a sign, something to profoundly stun his audience into the more painful reality and Plato obliged.

Plato stood on a chair and swiftly removed his outer garment to reveal the black Shadite's cloak.

'Behold, friends, a Son of Goh!' he shouted.

He faded like a shadow into nothing and slowly formed back into his original self in front of their petrified eyes. Mickey was astonished by the sight. They went up to Plato and touched his garment to ensure he was not a generated holographic image, and soon backed away. Then he followed after the President.

'Jerry, is all this for real? I mean the film, Andromeda and these guys here?' he asked with profound disbelief.

'Yes, my friend. It is for real and we are in danger like the people in that film. That could be our now beautiful planet in less than two hundred years if we do nothing to stop them.'

'Is it really as ghastly as that?'

'Yes my friend. So I would like you to create a brand new project. Make it as secret as the plasma weapon experiments. Tag it as space research. Yes, why not call it Intergalactic Research or some new fanciful name. You boffins are good at that sort of thing. Get professor Jeffery Longhurst involved. His is the most brilliant mind on the planet. He will find quick answers.'

'Ok! Ok! Mister President!'

'I want you personally to head this project. It's a pity Lennox is no longer with the committee.... Anyway, try and get Professor Longhurst involved as soon as you can. Use the latest technologies available for security screening. I want no leaks to the press or the military. Not to anyone except those well chosen few. Professor John Laroche and Senator Nicholas Wilson are good men and trustworthy, so use them when I'm not available. They are also here with the others.'

'Yes, Sir!'

'You get my drift?' Jerry stressed in no uncertain terms.

'Yes, Mister President,' Mickey replied, still recovering from the initial shock of the visiting aliens. A moment later Jerry went over to the large window, pressed an electrical switch and the security curtains lifted. It revealed the glittering space ship in the bright moonlight. There it stood majestically on its three firm metallic feet.

He called them all to the window.

'You see this thing out there, guys. Well, it might not look too fancy, but it's an intergalactic ship. It can make the trip from here to the galaxy of Andromeda in a single day.'

'What? You must be kidding?' Nicholas Wilson, the Vice President shouted.

'No! I'm Not! What do you think of that?' Jerry replied, excitedly.

They were amazed and thought it not possible, but Lumak made a sign from inside the house and The Ship melted into the stairway and entrance. He withdrew the signal and the ship melted back into its original form.

Mickey and his other companions were transfixed and almost frozen from its strangeness. It was all too much to accept in such a short time.

'Good God! What a bloody technology!' Nicholas commented.

'I knew it was possible. You know, micro robotics... but never to this level of perfection. I visited several of Doctor Longhurst's lectures on the subject... but this here is brilliant.' Mickey interjected.

'Yea, what a technology. They are virtually thousands, if not hundreds of thousands of years ahead of us in everything,' Jerry said.

'What a set of bloody geniuses!' A nervous Mickey drank the almost half filled glass of whisky in a single gulp.

Then Mickey went towards Lumak and Plato to personally shake their hands, but his feet underneath him was not as firm as he would have liked, so he staggered and it was not all due to drink.

'You guys are so damn human. You are almost exactly like us. You must be a great bunch of people. We shall try and help you as best we can.' He was sympathetic, realizing they faced the same threat and would need each other in the future.

By now the waiter had arrived with more drinks for Jerry and his close associates. The discussion went on for several hours, until both groups became better acquainted.

During all this time, Jon, Merol, Ecrol and Lira were on a stroll in the bright moonlight.

The single full moon reminded them that they were on a distant world within a distant galaxy and not on Caefon, their home world, with its two more distinct satellite moons. Nevertheless they still worried about their families and friends. Thank goodness they were no longer on the surface while exposed to unforseen dangers. They wondered how far the Javols were away from Caefon and whether they had enough time to save the remaining surface population.

Shiloh, Jerry's horse, was still standing by himself. He was not yet asleep and still chewing at some oats. He appeared king of kings in the shadowy moonlight and welcomed the visitors. As they approached a second time he gave a short neigh, snorted and went back eating his oats.

At first they were afraid to touch him, but Lira plucked the courage and began to chat to him while stroking his upper front thighs as she did. They recalled their encounter with the Malak in the underground city of Lower Cantor, with an element of nostalgia for distant families and friends. Shiloh completely ignored her and continued eating his oat meal.

They returned to the house and were greeted by Jerry at the door.

'Ah, the young ones have returned. Would you like another drink?' He hailed the barman who briskly went over to take their orders.

'Do you like my favourite home? These days most of it runs surplus to requirement, but it's a great retreat. You guys are invited to come and see the place whenever you like. However, you should learn to play golf, then we can have a game together.'

'What is golf?' Jon asked, and Jerry took them to the hallway. He removed a club and ball from a tall cupboard and began to demonstrate. Lira soon had a go and hit the spot precisely.

'Wow! I like this game!' she said and handed the club to Jon. Then Jerry explained some of the more subtler stances and rules of his favourite game. Then he took them back to the dining room for another drink.

'My two daughters are now married and have moved to the big cities. My son, Donald, the youngest, is in the air-force. I only see them on special occasions. You know, these days it can be too risky for a president to go visiting anywhere without a full complement of security men and publicity agents.'

'I understand, Sir!' Lira replied.

'Since I became president, I find myself based in Washington DC and that is when I am not visiting some foreign country or the other. It gives me little time to be with my children and grand children. I suppose it's the crucifix every president must bear,' he said, sadly.

Jon now spoke in almost perfect English.

'Sire, do you also believe in the Crucifix?'

'Yes, Son, most of our Christian religions are represented by the Cross or Crucifix. The Saviour died on one it is said, but that symbol was also used by many ancient peoples, even before Christianity came into existence. It could have represented the form of an ancient sword,' Jerry replied.

'Sire, we also have a sacred Crucifix on our world that is very similar to yours, which has been used by our ancient religion, the Senots, since the beginning of our civilization.'

Jerry realized that although both civilizations were far apart in distance and science and technology, many of their traditions were in some ways parallel. That aspect eased and benefited their associations. It also reminded him about what Plato said earlier that day about the twinning of both worlds.

Lucia soon came along and pulled Jon away from the president who was now standing close to her and her husband, Meron.

Meron looked decidedly grand in his costume, with dangling jewelled scabbard, headband and normal hairstyle. Jerry liked the man for his sincerity in feelings and thoughts. They were both so similar. He could talk to Meron without expecting some vague or imprecise answer. If he didn't know, he would simply say so. He was obviously royalty on his home world. However it took him a while to get used to their penetrating sea blue eyes.

The older ones, unlike the young, had a delicate poise; something that could only come with experience in certain higher circles. The man, Meron, was also a good six inches above him in height and they wore gloves, with the exception of the one called Plato who had six fingers. Could his elder companions also have six fingers? But Lumak and the younger ones could be considered Caucasian humans although more like Italians or Greeks, all having eight fingers and two thumbs like normal people.

Meron was not as advanced as the other two, Lumak and Plato. He still hadn't fully recovered from his afternoon's encounter with Plato in the outer farm on the road to feed his pigs. Those two guys gave him the willies. They had so much power within themselves; almost as if they were from a completely different race to their other twelve companions. And what formidable technologies they possessed.

He thought it all to be quite incredible, but decided not to ask any delicate or personal questions in case he offended his guests.

Plato soon called Lumak to one side for a private word. Having attained the president's audience, he had achieved more than was expected of him. He and his people had since been invited to dinner and that in itself was a great honour.

Plato had done what was necessary and had made first contact, but was not sure about the next step in their master survival plan.

THE EPISODE CONTINUES

Chronicles of
Galaxy Osmaron - **The Solarian empire**

Epilogue

With the Javols' future invasion of Osmaron and the local galaxies, it was imperative that Lumak altered mankind's attitudes and technologies in line with the Master Plan. It entailed changing Earth's technologies from Class 1 (its present levels) to Class 5 (100,000 years more advanced). However he could not inform the human population of the Javols invasion nor of their unrelenting progress to decimate all major life on the planet. Neither could he tell them of his long term plans towards Earth. Earth was just a simple cog on a wheel within a much larger machinery.

With the arrival of the twelve Andromedans and their knowledge of advanced technologies, Earth would soon be able to take a new direction. However its humans were still children, emotionally and were not ready for such cosmic insights and progression. One of the greatest problems faced was that of overpopulation, leading to Global Warming, deforestation and other planetary ills.

Since Earth had not a single global government to implement such changes for the common good, its people continued along their original path. Unperturbed by those detrimental changes. They were like an addictive cigarette smoker that knew the possible consequences of their actions but did the dastardly deed all the same to appease their most basic emotional needs.

Lumak realized the complexities of humanity and Earth's unsuitability as the hub of operations within Osmaron, so another local world was chosen. It was within 50 light years from the Solar System. That most beautiful and perfect world would be called Eden.

www.ingramcontent.com/pod-product-compliance
Lightning Source LLC
Chambersburg PA
CBHW050111120726
47904CB00004B/1309